M000206917

A THRONE OF RUIN

Also by K.F. Breene

A Throne of Ruin

Ruin

By K.F. Breene

Copyright © 2021 by K.F. Breene

All rights reserved. The people, places, situations and craziness contained in this book are figments of the author's imagination and in no way reflect real or true events.

Contact info:
www.kfbreene.com
books@kfbreene.com

CHAPTER 1

MY HEART THUDDED in my chest as I searched the Forbidden Wood for the beast, the same ground-bound dragon I'd once run from in terror. My animal roiled inside me, stalking him with me. I'd left home hours ago, in late morning, and there was still no sign of Nyfain. Granted, he had a substantial head start, since he'd left my family cottage last night after feeding us sleeping herbs to keep me from following, but I couldn't shake the fear that I'd stumble upon his broken and bloodied form.

His duty might be to guard the wood, to protect our kingdom's villages from the creatures the demon king unleashed on us each night, but he was in no shape to play Mr. Hero. It didn't matter that he was our prince, our only hope of escaping the curse. The tracks I was following only proved he needed time to recover, curse the goddess. They zigzagged on the trail, bumping into a tree here, stomping through thorn bushes over there.

Everlass made for a potent cure, and I'd learned that the leaves of a crowded plant, which could be lethal if used incorrectly, were capable of reversing the effects of poison. Still, it was obvious the elixir I'd given him hadn't fully restored him. The effects had worn off, and he was in pain.

But he'd refused my request—my *order*—for him to rest.

The dappled light highlighted a huge splotch of deep red on the ground. My gut twisted as I slowed, panning my gaze over the area. I spotted the extra set of tracks mingled with those of the dragon. These were slender and long, with three toes and an imprint in the dirt that suggested claws. The creature, whatever it was, walked on four feet. It must've lunged out from the trees, because its tracks seemed to come from nowhere.

The bark of the closest tree had been abraded by a tough hide. Branches lay on the ground, ripped from the trunk.

This was the third battle scene I'd come across since leaving home. Evidence suggested Nyfain had won the others, but panic still skittered through me as I followed it away right. A large hole had been chopped through dense bushes, Nyfain's huge dragon form forcing the foliage to make room. Blood smeared the green and streaked the ground. On the other side, I heaved a shuddering sigh.

A strange creature with oily, grayish scales lay twisted, its back broken and its head torn off. Nyfain's tracks led away, heavy and clumsy. Blood splattered the ground. He'd taken damage.

I could feel my animal holding her breath. Pain and sadness radiated from her, the effect of Nyfain's dragon ripping away our connection to them. Nyfain hadn't said why, other than that he wished to grant us freedom. She was just as terrified to find a broken dragon at the end of this trail as I was.

Nyfain's mouth-watering smell of pine and lilac tinged with honeysuckle dusted some bushes. His tracks led left now, not going toward the castle. Stubborn man that he was, he'd been looking for more creatures to dispatch.

After another hour and more blood splatter, I saw that he'd found one. A large biped with small arms and a large jaw. It had its stomach ripped out. Even more blood led away from this battle.

I don't like this, my animal said as we took in the scents and followed the tracks. *He lost too much blood.*

As a man, yes. But his dragon is big. Maybe if he just stays in beast form until he heals it'll be okay?

She didn't answer. She probably didn't know, since I'd never shifted. The same curse that haunted these woods had sickened the villagers throughout the kingdom, paused time at the royal castle, and, perhaps worst of all, prevented our people from shifting as nature intended. As far as I knew, only one person still could—Nyfain—although it had cost him dearly. His dragon's wings had been shorn off.

I could hear my animal's thoughts, feel her emotions, and use her primal senses, but that was where it stopped.

We wound deep into the wood, the gnarled trees bent and twisted, much like the dead bodies of the demon creatures that had been set loose last night. Scraggly bushes reached across the path, some of them stomped and broken from Nyfain coming through. I didn't even need to follow his tracks now, just had to watch for the crimson droplets that announced his passage.

A bird chittered in the treetops, answered by another. A small rodent scrabbled out of the way. My connection with my animal had also increased my sense of hearing. Not much farther and I heard voices, a man and a woman talking.

I hefted the dagger I held, content to keep the pocketknife stowed, and crept closer, staying behind a wall of browning and crackled greenery. My animal plucked smells out of the air, analyzing them as we made our way. Clean smells, like laundry and lavender soap, layered over the more pungent scents of sweat and blood.

I stopped behind the large trunk of a hollowed-out tree and peered around. Two people stood in a clearing beside what looked like a station for field dressings—a table stacked with gauze, a box with a red plus sign, and various instruments I hadn't seen before. A stretcher sat at their feet, the white material stretched between the two poles stained crimson.

The middle-aged woman stood with perfect posture, her shoulders thrown back and head held high. A blue dress made of fine fabric hugged her trim frame, and a white apron was cinched around her middle. Her bearing suggested someone highborn, and the delicate way she gestured when speaking screamed of cultivation. The man opposite her was a bit younger, with smooth gray trousers, a white button-up shirt, and hair with a perfect part down the side. Like her, he had an air of refinement.

I remembered hearing that Nyfain met with villagers within the wood. The butler, Hadriel, had thought they were all men, but Hadriel openly admitted he was terrible at his job.

The bloody stretcher was empty, its occupant gone, and although Nyfain's scent lingered, it wasn't fresh.

Taking a deep breath, hands tight around the hilt of the dagger, I stepped out from my hiding place and into clear view.

The couple didn't notice me at first, their voices low and still indistinguishable. It was like they expected creatures with expert hearing to be passing by. I made it halfway to them before the woman finally glanced over.

She startled, her mouth forming an O and her fingertips dusting across her chest. The man snapped his head toward me, very slow on the uptake. A demonic creature would've made short work of this pair.

I stopped where I was as the woman recovered from her surprise. Her gaze slipped down my front, taking in my pants, my dirty top, and finally the dagger in my hand.

"My goodness," she murmured, glancing at her companion. "She looks positively wild."

The man did the same sweep, but his conclusions were clearly different. His eyes lit up, and a little grin played on his lips. He stepped forward, his gaze dipping to my chest before roaming my face.

"You must be Finley," the man said. "Quite the beauty. He said you would come."

My heart lurched. "Nyfain?" I asked. "Is he okay?"

The woman's brows knitted in disapproval. "You are to address him as—"

"Not now, Claryssa." The man waved her away, continuing to close the space between him and me. "Yes. He followed a warbler to the edge of our village. Just…" He turned and pointed west. "Just beyond those trees and down a ways. We rushed out to help, but he'd downed the creature by the time we made it to him. He was in bad shape. We brought him here, away from demon eyes, to patch him up."

"And you did?" I asked. "He's okay?"

"What village are you from, girl?" Claryssa asked, walking closer. Her pinched expression said she expected me to smell.

I ignored her, my gaze rooted to the man.

"As best we could," he said. "We carried him to the edge of the Royal Wood nearest the castle." He turned and glanced down at the stretcher. "He'll make it. He's made of sturdy stuff. You have no need to worry." He paused for a moment. "But you are, though, right? You *are* worried about him?"

I frowned at the eagerness in his question. This meeting was starting to get weird.

"Did you tell him to stay in tonight?" I took a step away. "He needs rest."

"How presumptuous," the woman scoffed. "He is

the prince. You will remember his station and address him as such, girl."

The man shot a look of annoyance at Claryssa. A placating smile took its place as his attention returned to me. "He has a duty to this wood. To his people. He'll insist on clearing the wood again tonight. No one can make him do something he doesn't want to. But have no fear—the first couple of nights after a full moon are the worst. The number of demon creatures loosed in the wood will diminish until after the next full moon."

"You're sure you got him safely to the castle?"

"Yes. He'll be quite safe. I have seen him worse, and yet he trudges on. Ever our courageous protector."

I blew out a breath and stepped farther away. The man continued to watch me, a strange gleam to his eyes, like a starving man looking at a plate of dinner. The woman analyzed me as well, disapproval in every line on her face.

"Great, thanks." I attempted a half-smile, didn't even remotely pull it off, and about-faced. They wouldn't be pointing me toward Nyfain, it seemed. At least they'd seen to his wounds. Granted, if he could just take a night or two off, he wouldn't need to be patched up in the first place.

I slipped through the bushes and behind the trees, out of sight. Once I knew I was alone, I paused for a moment.

Could I trust those people? They could've been any-one. They didn't smell like demons, but that didn't mean they weren't working for them. Who knew what the demon king was capable of? He could easily have the villagers on his payroll. If my village was any indication, the people in our kingdom were hungry and scared—they'd take a helping hand wherever they could get it.

However, Nyfain had clearly allowed himself to be doctored. He must've trusted them somewhat.

Still…

I started jogging in the direction of the castle, cut-ting over a bit after passing the location of those people. It didn't take me long to hook up with his scent, leading through the trees. Three sets of boot prints lined the way, two people carrying a stretcher, and someone moving alongside them to tend the patient. And then, exactly where I'd expect based on their information, I found a little bloody patch next to a few tracks of bare feet in the earth, followed by dragon tracks leading toward the castle.

They hadn't been lying after all.

I sagged and leaned against a tree while looking up at that majestic castle. What must it have been like in its heyday, when the grounds were alive and tended, nobles walked around in their finery, and dragons glided through the air? That must've been a real sight.

Go to him, my animal pleaded, relishing in his scent. Desperate to keep following it. *He'll be happy to see us. You heard that man. He expected us to follow.*

He'll be mad as hell. He wanted to cut ties, or what *do you think it means when someone drugs you to sleep, severs your connection, and leaves the equivalent of a breakup note?*

He'll be in a rage at first, sure, but it'll turn to passion, just you watch.

Sure, passion immediately followed by regret and gruff barks not to touch him again. We'd been down that road. There was nothing for us there. Nyfain and his animal might want us, but they didn't want to want us.

Time to go home.

This was for the best.

As I turned, my animal fought for control. Fire blistered through my body, boiling my blood, and a shock wave of power blasted out of her, out of *me.* It was her cry for him. Her misery at them severing the connection.

This is not the way to act in a pseudo-breakup, I said, wrestling her. *This is the way crazy girls act. Ask me how I know!*

How do you know?

Because I've taken this road before, and it just makes a person look like a fool. Let it go! It's for the best.

It doesn't feel like it's for the best, she cried.

It was never going to work. Now it's over. We move on. We have things to do.

She kept grumbling, but once I regained control, I pushed her away. I needed to maintain a hard grip on logic. Because yes, I did want to flail and cry and run to him. I wanted us to fight and argue and fuck. I wanted to bask in his strength and power, and quake in fear and excitement from his imposing presence. The prince was like a crowded everlass plant, lethal and potent and unbearable in almost all situations...except for the one that would save your life.

But it wasn't my life that needed saving—it was *his.* It was this kingdom's. He needed to focus on that, not on this strange push-pull he felt with a foul-mouthed commoner.

A hollow feeling permeated my middle, but I ignored that, too.

I walked home, thinking about Nyfain and crowded everlass plants. Thinking of ways to cure the villages of the plague, thus giving Nyfain more time to break the curse. We didn't have to be together to work together. Just like we didn't have to get along to feel the rush of each other's kiss...which I probably shouldn't be thinking about either.

Letting go of him might be a little trickier than I'd thought...

CHAPTER 2

L ATER THAT DAY, I stood beside Father's bed, feeling more hopeful than I had in years.

"This is going to work, Hannon, I know it."

I combined the ingredients of my new nulling elixir, which I'd dubbed the crowded nulling elixir to set it apart from the less powerful version, and added hot water. Father lay beside me, his mouth open and his cheeks sunken. How he'd held on so long I wasn't sure, but I was grateful. This would do it; I felt it in my bones.

"But he's not poisoned like Nyfain was," Hannon said, as anxious as I'd ever seen him.

"The sickness *is* a kind of poison. It's just not as potent as the venom that almost killed Nyfain. So the elixir's not as strong, either. And given Father is about as bad as you can get, and the normal everlass elixir won't work…"

"We've got nothing to lose."

"Sadly, no." I reached out and took his hand. "It's going to work, though, Hannon. I can *feel* it."

"Did you sing to the leaves?"

"Sable did. I think she was saying gibberish words, but that probably doesn't matter."

His brow knitted with a thoughtful look. "That plant is like a child."

"Yeah, it is." I mixed the brew, took a deep breath, and handed it over to my brother.

I dropped my hand to Father's forehead, his skin clammy and too hot. I could very well kill him with this new elixir. His early death would be on my hands. But if I didn't take a chance, he'd only have a few days to a week left anyway. The kids had said their goodbyes already, and now it was my turn. Hannon had said he'd be the one to administer the medicine, because I couldn't bear to see Father die if I was the one who'd killed him. There was no antidote I could offer. There was no way out. If this elixir was too potent, there was nothing I could do to fix my error.

I took a moment to think back on the good times, when he'd been happy. We'd never truly gotten along, Father and I, always quarreling about something, but we loved each other as a family ought to. This house needed its leader. Its parent.

"It's going to work," I told Hannon again, feeling it in every fiber of my being. "That plant is of the dragons, and a cornered dragon is more powerful than a demon, any day. It will save the day, just you wait."

I straightened up and ran my fingers through my hair. I *hoped* it worked, at any rate. I was running out of answers.

"I'll be in the living room," I said softly.

I closed the door behind me and gathered what I'd need to do the shopping. After that, I might go set some traps, anything to stay busy. I couldn't let my mind wander. If it didn't drift toward the aching hollow of Nyfain's absence, it dwelled on my father and the others who were dying of the sickness.

Sable and Dash sat on the couch, their faces long, not speaking.

"It'll be okay," I said, tears stinging my eyes. "It's going to work."

The more I said it, the less I believed it.

Guilt tore at me. Maybe I shouldn't have tried this. Maybe I should have chased Nyfain into the castle and demanded more information on the crowded everlass before attempting such a rash experiment.

Regardless, it was done now.

Hannon came out of the room with a drawn face. He held out the empty tin mug, showing us. He'd gotten

Father to drink all of it, so there was nothing left to do but wait.

I nodded and slipped out the front door. I wouldn't be waiting at home.

The afternoon sun was bright and warm, winter's chill starting to recede. Villagers traveled the lane, one laden with a sack of bread and another pushing a small cart of grain for her goats. I smiled in hello and received confused frowns in return.

At the market, I looked over my shopping list before deciding which stall to visit first. In front of the stand of lettuce, I caught sight of a familiar face. His orange-red hair glowed brilliantly in the sun, like a firestorm around his freckled face. James, my first boyfriend. My first love.

Or so I'd thought.

He glanced my way, and his pale blue eyes widened. He turned, and it was the first I'd noticed his lanky frame and lack of grace. His black T-shirt hung off his narrow, bony shoulders, a brown belt cinched his trousers around his waist, and his skinny arms swung at his sides. He kind of flopped his feet out when he walked.

"Hey, James," I said when he neared, expecting the punch to the gut that I usually felt in his presence. This guy had torn my heart out and thrown it in my face, right before asking for a goodbye bang. I was still pissed I'd given it to him, crying the whole time. Begging him to please reconsider.

But now...nothing.

Is this your doing? I asked my animal, having opened myself to her—just a crack—upon returning home. She hadn't communicated with me at all. I got the feeling she was giving me the cold shoulder.

Leaving the dragon so we can carry on with this hollow, meaningless life? she replied. *No, it is not. That was your doing, you goat-faced cumsplat. Just wait until you can shift.* Then *we'll see who wears the pants in this relationship.*

She was clearly still quite angry...and colorful.

I don't feel anything for James anymore. Is that because of you?

James who? That red-headed git stopping in front of us? Why would you feel anything for him? I can't even feel his animal. He's subpar, at best. He couldn't protect us if his life depended on it.

There are more important considerations than whether a man can protect us. Besides, when we work together, we don't need anyone's protection.

She huffed. *When we are with child, or protecting our young, or attacked by demonic creatures in the wood—like you were* two days ago—*we need a strong mate to protect us. We need a defender. There is none stronger than that alpha dragon. None. Everyone else is a waste of time. End of story. There is no one else we can mate who will make us happy. Now stop being a wench and* go back to him!

Except he was the one who left us, not the other way around...

They're males. They get confused which head is for thinking and do stupid shit. As females, we need to set them right.

I rolled my eyes.

Okay then, nice talking to you, I thought, and pushed her out of my head. She needed some time to cool down, clearly. Maybe a lot of time.

"Hi, Finley." James gave me a toothy smile. That smile used to make my heart pitter-patter. But now I felt...absolutely nothing. Literally zero. "I haven't seen you in a while. Pulson and Mary across the street from you said you'd left for a couple days. Is everything okay?"

"I've been busy hunting and working on a new elixir for the sickness."

He nodded, taking in my clothing. "Still dressing like a man, huh?"

"Have you ever tried hunting in a bushy dress?"

He snickered and rolled his eyes. "Always the rule breaker. You think you can get away with anything because you're pretty. Someday you'll finally settle down, though. You'll have to give up your pants and craziness then."

"Or maybe I'll just stay single forever and fuck demons in the pub, hmm?"

His jaw dropped in surprise. His face turned red.

I grinned and pushed past him. Apparently the trip to the castle, however brief, had made me just that little bit sexually coarser. The good news was that his put-down didn't hurt in the slightest. Nyfain's sweet words about liking me down to my soul had soaked under my skin. They'd changed me. They'd made me feel like it was okay to be myself, even if I was an outcast.

Ignoring the people staring, I walked to the next stall and picked out my items. That done, I worked my way through the market, grabbing what Hannon had said he needed, and then stopped by the booth with the furs and skins, seeing what sort of quality was in vogue right now.

"See anything you like?"

A cold trickle ran down my spine. *Here we go.*

I straightened and turned, finding Jedrek just behind me. I used to think him tall and broad, but now...he looked almost petite for a man. I was used to

Nyfain's size and girth. His imposing presence. Jedrek standing there was just…anticlimactic.

"No, actually. I can do better." I walked around him, to the daggers in the next stand over. One of them caught my eye—a new weapon with a red jewel in the hilt and silver lining. It was an absolute treasure. I picked it up and hefted it, enjoying the balance and fit within my hand.

"That would suit you perfectly," Phyl said from behind the stand, shifting his girth with his thumbs tucked in his belt loops. He was the only guy in the village who'd retained his size after the curse. It was a staple of pride that he could keep his family well fed even when everything was falling down around us. "You'd get many a kill with that one, Miss Finley."

"Nonsense—she doesn't need a blade." Jedrek stopped beside me again, reaching for the dagger.

I pulled up my animal, who was happy to lend power to my fighting words. Especially since I was sending away a man who was not Nyfain.

"Back off," I said.

Jedrek jerked ramrod straight. He staggered backward as though someone had shoved him. Phyl's eyes widened, and he reached for his chest. When his fingers touched down, he clutched and closed his eyes.

Taking my time, I touched the blade with my

thumb, testing its edge. I held it a little higher, analyzing the dagger. "This is a work of art, Phyl. You've really outdone yourself."

His eyes fluttered open, and he looked at me like he'd never seen me before. He put one of those big hands on the tabletop in his stall and braced himself.

I probably shouldn't use my animal's power around the other villagers. Hadriel had warned me about giving off too much sparkle. I didn't need people talking, or word would get around to the demons.

With a grimace, I set the dagger back down. Jedrek stood a few paces away, staring at me with shock and unease written clearly on his face. My animal glowed with pride.

"I...uh..." Phyl shook himself and cleared his throat. "Yes, I...uhm..." He ran his fingers through his hair. "I made a sword like that once. Let me see..." He ducked down and started rummaging through the bowels of his stall.

A firm hand gripped my arm and swung me around. Jedrek leaned into me, his face a mask of rage.

"What do you think you're playing at?" he seethed, spittle flying from his mouth. "You dare command me?"

I'd commanded him plenty of times in the past. He'd always ignored it or assumed I was joking.

It looked like I'd learned more than crassness at the castle.

My animal seeped fire into me.

"Get your hand off me," I said in a low, calm voice.

His eyes flicked back and forth, looking at each of my eyes in turn. My mind jumped to something my sister, Sable, had told me this morning. She'd said my eyes were glowing. Nyfain's glowed, too, when his animal was pumping power into him. His dragon's eyes glowed all the time.

"You've been gone a few days, haven't you?" Jedrek said softly, peeling his fingers from around my arm. "You've found him, then."

I furrowed my brow, not daring to say anything. Could he know about Nyfain?

"What did you ask for?" he asked. "To get out? No, you're a slave to your family—you wouldn't have forsaken them. You asked to save your dad, I'll bet, right?"

"What are you talking about?" I finally spat.

He smirked. "Just remember, anyone can barter with the demon king. Even me. But I won't ask him to save a waste of a parent. I told you I would be marrying you. I'm a man of my word. You will strip off those ridiculous pants, and you'll put away your silly little weapons, and you will serve your man with a smile and open legs, do I make myself clear?"

My animal thrashed, trying to take control and attack, but I held her back. I needed only words to handle this ape.

"You would enter into a bargain with the demon king, the slyest, most cunning bastard in all the world, in order to make me marry you? Of all the things you could ask for—freedom, riches, two coherent thoughts to rub together—you would choose instead to force someone to pretend to love you? How fucking sad are you, Jedrek? How small, insignificant, and...desperate are you?"

He gave me a smug grin. "You won't be pretending anything. The demon king is all-powerful. He can make you love me. He can make you salivate for me."

"What a change from your normal nightly routine, then, huh? Make sure you ask him—if you can find him, because last I checked, he was in charge of his own kingdom—to make me believe you satisfied me when we both know you never could. That would be a *real* shock for you. A happy woman after your terrible excuse for a lay."

Jedrek gritted his teeth and pointed at my face. "I'll make you pay for those comments." He turned and strutted away.

I clenched my hands into fists before releasing them

again. "I hate that guy."

You should've let me at him, my animal said. *I would've rocked his world.*

Then he would've cried foul. He's a small, little man with a fragility issue, and he can't stand anyone to make him look the fool.

There's that thesaurus again. Why not a small, little, tiny man?

Oh, shut up.

I turned back toward the weapons in a rush, wrestling with my animal's desire to run after Jedrek and attack him. How did Nyfain deal with this all the time? Why did anyone miss it? When this beast didn't get her way—which was always, lately—she was fucking exhausting.

Phyl was staring at me with wide eyes.

"Sorry," I said automatically, shaking my head. "He's the second dickface that has accosted me today, and my patience is wearing thin."

Phyl licked his lips and leaned over the stall some. "You're an odd duck around these parts, Finley, but don't you take that as a bad thing. You weren't meant to fit in here. The day your mother asked me to make you your very own hunting knife—remember that?—I knew then that you were different. This village used to be a haven for the lesser-powered shifters in the kingdom.

Them, and the ones that didn't want to fight for the king and kingdom. But just because you were born in a place, doesn't mean you belong there. Your mother didn't have much power, but she was fierce. She came from a long line of fighters. The power gene must've just skipped a generation. It didn't skip you, though, did it? She let you be tough and wild for a reason."

He held out a sword, the color a little dull from age. A deeper red stone shone in the hilt of this one, and the silver design swirling around it was much more intricate. The leather was supple and soft against my palm, the edge of the blade sharp.

"This is gorgeous," I said on a release of breath.

"Yes, I made that before the curse, when traveling merchants used to come through. I spared no expense. I thought maybe a noble would end up with it, or the prince himself! Could you imagine?" He smiled sheepishly. "It was always fun to dream big back then. No matter how fine I made them, those merchants always bought from me. There was always someone they could sell to. So I just made them better and better."

"This one would've gone for a pretty price, Phyl. A real pretty price."

"Yes, I had hoped so. It was the finest I'd made. But now…I don't think I'll get to sell another piece like that."

I handed it back. "You will. We'll beat this curse, and then we'll have merchants again, just you wait. Maybe the prince will wield it yet. Or…well…walk around with it, since he'd probably fight in his dragon form. Hang it on the wall, maybe…"

"Well." He shrugged his meaty shoulders and put the sword back under the stall. "I think the sickness is starting to take root. I figured it was bound to happen sooner or later."

Pain struck my heart. "Does Margie know how to make the nulling elixir?"

"She does, yes. She's made some already. It's just that…well, she's not so good at gardening. I'm no good at it either. I tried to trade for some leaves, but everyone is running low because of the lingering winter season."

I put my hand flat on the table. "Don't worry about that. I'll get some for you. And I'm working on a stronger elixir. I'm still trying to find a cure. You're not going anywhere, Phyl. You won't lose any of your size, I promise."

He laughed and patted his belly. "Well, now, we'll see about that. Here." He pulled the jeweled dagger from the display and held it out. "You don't have any more plants than anyone else. I know where you aim to get them, and I don't think I'll be able to stop you. Take this. You'll need it."

"I'm hoping I won't, actually. And no, I—"

He leaned forward and pushed it into my hands. "I'd give you the sword, but I sure would like to see the prince wear it someday. All we have left are our big dreams, you know? But this dagger was made as a companion piece. It's solid, if not quite so fine. I couldn't really afford any better. You'll be great one day, Finley, and when you are, I want you to hold my dagger."

I shook my head but let him put it into my hands. He was as nice as they came, but he had a stubborn streak. We all did.

I held it up. "Thank you. It's too much."

"Nah. Now I know that you'll keep me alive as long as you can. That's good enough for me."

"I would've done that anyway."

He winked. "I know."

With a stupid grin, I held the dagger to my chest as I carted all the supplies back to the house. It wasn't until I got to the front door that my smile thinned and then vanished. A crowded everlass plant took a bit to get working, but it didn't take much time at all to kill.

The moment of truth was upon me. Had I just killed my father?

My heart sank at the sight of the empty living room. Fear lodged in the pit of my stomach.

I set everything down on the table and steeled myself. With slow, determined steps, I made my way to Father's room. The door stood ajar, and voices murmured from inside. I didn't hear crying, though.

Barely daring to hope, I edged into the room. Hannon leaned over the bed, blotting Father's forehead with a towel. Dash and Sable sat in the chairs at his side, looking on.

Dash glanced my way, and a huge smile lit up his face. Sable gave me a relieved sag.

"You did it," Hannon said softly, continuing his ministrations.

"Did what?" Father asked, his voice scratchy.

My stomach lurched and then fell out of my body. I grabbed the doorframe for support, my legs wobbling. He'd spoken! He'd said coherent words! He hadn't done that in a while, and even then, the effort had been fraught with coughing and hacking.

"Finley created an elixir to bring you back from the brink of death." Hannon looked up at me, his eyes shining with tears. "You always said you'd make a cure, and you did it."

"Whoa, whoa. Let's not..." I put out my hand to stop him.

"My Finley was always good with plants," Father said, smiling at me with bleary eyes. "She has the divine gift from the goddess, she does. Everyone always said so. She was wild, yes, but she could work miracles if you gave her an everlass plant and some time. She would've stood before the queen one day if the world hadn't ended. I was always hard on her, but I had to be! If she was going to stand before royalty, she needed to know how to act. You can't be a foolish, silly girl when speaking to the queen. She was going to be our hope for a better life."

Tears flooded my eyes. I'd never heard him say anything like that. I'd never heard anyone suggest that I might have a bright future. Then the queen died, and the curse had descended on us. Father had kept up the pretense of trying to calm me down, but when Nana got sick, and then Mom…

His hopes had been dashed.

"We'll have a better life." I went to his other side and took his hand. "We will, someday."

I felt his forehead. Cool. The fever was down. His eyes were a bit bloodshot, but they were clearing.

He smiled at me before his lids drooped. "Yes, we will at that, Finley."

"Can I speak to you in the living room?" Hannon asked softly.

"Yeah, of course." I followed him out, barely able to breathe through my shock. "How can we be sure it is a cure, though?"

"Honestly…I shouldn't have said that. It's too early to know. But even if it's not, it's a huge step in the right direction. A *huge* step, Finley. We'll wait to see how much of the sickness is cleared, and then we'll have a better idea."

"If it isn't cured, then it gets dicey," I said, my mind racing. I wiped the tears rolling down my cheeks. "It would mean that the first batch probably wasn't strong enough. But I can't just top him up. That's not how the crowded plant works, I don't think. Damn Nyfain for leaving so soon. I need more information."

Hannon squeezed my shoulder. "He might've left sooner than you wanted, but he was ultimately responsible for your discovery. By saving his life, you were able to save Father. And eventually the other villagers."

"And you're suddenly A-okay with him now? Your grudge over being drugged has been dropped?"

"Forgiven, not forgotten. I don't hold grudges quite like you do…"

I scowled at him. "Fine, whatever. Anyway, I got your stuff—"

"Our stuff. You're not doing errands just for me—"

"Yeah, yeah, you know what I mean. Anyway, Phyl is coming down with the sickness, and they don't have any everlass. I need to get him some and also harvest more of the crowded plant. I have to go to the Forbidden Wood again."

"When?"

I glanced out the window. "I could either hurry now and try to get back by dark, or go later when the wood is…possibly being cleared by a limping dragon."

"Go now. If Nyfain was as bad off as you said, I doubt he'll be much good at clearing the wood tonight. Make him some salve and healing ointments. Leave them at the field if you don't see him. He's bound to stop by."

I stood there like an idiot. "Why would he stop by?"

Hannon shrugged. "He seemed to enjoy playing games with you. I doubt he'll give them up because of duty and honor. Men claim to be that noble, but when it comes to a woman…they rarely are."

"Oh really, mister guru? And when did you become such an expert?"

"You're not the only one who reads. If you see him, tell him we'd love to have him around for dinner if his schedule permits. Or a midnight snack."

There was no way I'd see him.

Oh goddess, would I see him?

If I did, I'd have a helluva time keeping my animal off him.

CHAPTER 3

SHADOWS DRAPED ACROSS the path as I made it to the birch next to the everlass field in the Forbidden Wood. With the sun holding any demonic creatures at bay, I approached it with a scowl. As soon as I got close, out came the jig. Snitch.

"One day I'm going to bring my axe, and then how cheerful and zippy will you be, huh?"

Stop talking to a tree. It's enchanted, not alive, my animal grumbled.

You could do with a little zip. How long do you plan on moping?

Until you pull your head out of your ass, screw it back on, and go get that alpha.

Would you stop bringing that up? It's getting old.

Do you know what's getting old? Your eggs. Best get that big alpha dick up in your cumquat so you won't prove that red-headed wankstain right by dying old and alone.

I won't be alone, I thought cheerfully. *I have you. And what a delight you are.*

As I passed the shaking birch, the most delicious smell caught my attention. All my senses snapped taut as it slithered across my skin and soaked into my body. I groaned, recognizing it immediately. *Intimately.* Pine and lilac and a hint of honeysuckle. It spoke of lazy afternoons with sex hair and oversized T-shirts. Of fingertips gently grazing bare skin. Of hard bites while soaked in exquisite pleasure.

I turned toward it slowly, attuned to the feeling it evoked in me. Melting even as I breathed it in.

Nyfain had been here. Recently.

Within a thick bush at the base of the birch, I could just make out a rectangular package wrapped tightly in waxy material. Bright yellow. With my animal's power, I could largely see in the dark using a white, black, and yellow color spectrum. This would stand out, even at night, especially if I were also using my animal's increased sense of smell. The covering would prevent any sort of weather getting at whatever was inside, and coarse brown string kept it closed.

My animal pushed not so patiently for me to get inside the package.

I unslung my knapsack from my shoulder before reaching into the bush and hooking two fingers through the string. I pulled it to me, sliding it across the ground.

Hurry, my animal whispered.

I pulled an end of the string and watched the bow fall away. Pushing the rest of the string off, I then peeled back the material, one side at a time. A folded piece of parchment waited atop a leather-bound book.

My heart surged. Excitement shot through me, and I grinned like an idiot.

What is it, a book? my animal asked in confusion.

It's something magical.

I unfolded the parchment first. To maximize anticipation, you should always read the card before opening the present.

Dear Finley,

I apologize for how I left. I knew if I'd given you the choice, you would've made me stay for a few more days. My duty forbids it, but I wouldn't have been able to resist you. As it was, I could barely control my dragon. That was why I put you to sleep. The struggle with him would've woken the whole house. Then I would've been at your mercy.

You have become my greatest weakness.

After this correspondence, we can sever all non-urgent ties, communicating only about creating and distributing the elixir that nulls the effects of the demon-spawned sickness. Before that, however, there are some promises I must keep.

1) On the next sheet, I have created a table indicating when it will be safe for you to travel to this field. As long as I breathe, I will clear the way for you. Certain parts of the moon cycle are too dangerous, but most nights after a certain hour you will be safe. Please pass by the birch so that I know you are in residence, and if I suspect danger is near, I will come to your aid. It is my duty as your prince (don't sass me about it).

2) I will continue to tend this field for your use (I have always tended it for your use). Please see that your village is fully supplied with whatever they need.

3) Please send me any questions you may have about the everlass plants, and I will supply whatever information I may. Soon you will have no more need of me in that regard, but until then, I am at your service. My mother would've insisted.

4) A peace offering is enclosed. Take it for as long as you need. Forever, if you'd like. It's my favorite story of late, about escaping prison and exacting vengeance. I'm sure you can relate. If you'd like more books, fiction and nonfiction alike, just let me know and I will bring them. I will be your personal library until you are settled elsewhere.

Yours truly,
N

I let out a long, slow breath.

I didn't quite know how to feel. He was still taking care of me, just doing it in a way that didn't require direct communication. How the hell was I going to forget him if I knew I would alert him every time I came to this field? Every time I asked for a type of book (because I was going to use the hell out of that library)? Every time my way was clear at night? Whenever I walked through the everlass, I'd be able to smell him. I'd imagine him walking through the tidy rows, singing to them and touching their leaves. How was this going to work?

It won't. Go to him.

"Oh goddess, please shut this fucking animal up," I bit out, feeling the heavy volume and holding it to my chest. "A new book," I whispered, half forgetting why I was here in the first place.

But seriously, a new book I hadn't read yet? That hadn't happened in…a very long time. I couldn't wait to open it.

"Maybe just a peek," I murmured, pulling open the cover. I gritted my teeth and pushed it back down. "No. Mustn't. Must do work…"

I pulled the healing supplies for Nyfain out of my knapsack, wrapped them into the yellow cover, and stashed it back into the bush. His note went into the knapsack. The book should've gone with it, but I couldn't bear to part with it yet. He'd said it was his favorite of late. That meant he wasn't just protective of his library because it belonged to him—he enjoyed reading, too.

As if the man needed to be any sexier.

"What was up with the formal-sounding letter?" I murmured, clutching the book to my chest as I headed into the everlass field. "His handwriting is super elegant, too."

He's a prince, my animal thought, and it was a sobering reminder that his education and childhood had been different than mine.

Finally, grudgingly, I put the book in my knapsack, pulled out my crossbody tweed bag that I used to carry the everlass leaves, and got to work in the everlass field, harvesting leaves and checking his pruning work. That done, I took the leaves I needed and went on my way. I had a book to read.

THE NEXT DAY, I could barely keep my eyes open as I worked the leaves. I'd just intended to read a couple chapters. Then just until the exciting bit slowed down. Then…

Before I knew it, the sun was peeking through the window and the book was finished. It had been a wild ride, filled with treachery, sword fights, escape, and vengeance. The happy ending had been fantastic, and I couldn't wait to read it again. Nyfain had chosen well.

"Finley…" Hannon popped out of the back door before looking down at the metal tins and buckets arrayed around me. "What are you doing?"

"Nyfain is making good on his promises, so I need to make good on mine. I'm making elixirs." I pointed at a metal canister with a red stripe. "I have the demon sex magic-be-gone draught for the people in the palace." Although they hadn't been beset by the sickness, time had stilled for them. They didn't age, they couldn't have children, and they lived at the mercy of demons who'd sexually twisted them. I pointed at the metal canister with the blue stripe. "Nulling elixir for the other villages. The potency will wear off because of the travel time, but that can't be helped. Plus, there's more salve and healing stuff for him…"

"How are you going to transport all of that? How is *he* going to?"

"I'll stow everything in a big bag for his dragon's mouth. Might take a few trips, but it'll be fine."

He gave me a flat stare. "I told you so."

"He's not playing games. He really is making good on his promises."

"Whatever happened to you hating him?"

I scowled. "Don't worry. Give me five minutes in his presence, and I'm sure I will go right back to hating him. His personality is hard to take."

"Uh-huh. Well, you should check on Dad. He's plateauing. He's weak as a kitten and groggy, but that's to be expected, given how long he was on the brink."

"I checked on him earlier. There are no visible signs of the sickness, but that doesn't mean they aren't there in small amounts. It's impossible to tell if he's been cured without more time. I'm going to work on a weaker elixir tomorrow for Old Man Fortety down the street. He's not nearly as far along as Dad, and he's been asking all his neighbors to just kill him off before he starts wetting the bed. I figure he'll let me try out a new concoction on him if I promise it might finally end his suffering. I just won't tell him which type of suffering I mean."

Hannon cracked a smile. "Wise. What time are you headed to the field tonight?"

My pulse fluttered. "Not sure. I need to check Nyfain's chart. Late, though. I'll go to bed early."

A night bird cried out a warning as I worked my way through the Forbidden Wood. Gnarled trees lurked in the darkness, shadowy shapes hunkering by the small trail. Stars crowded the sky, but a slice of pale moon only gave weak light. My animal was right near the surface, helping me discern any dangers that might be hiding nearby. So far, Nyfain had stayed true to his word. The way was clear.

The enchanted birch rose in front of me, and everything in me said to go around it. It had been drilled into my head from an early age that to set foot in this wood was death. To get out was lucky. The tree's habit of shaking like some clown on drugs was not great for my comfort level. But Nyfain had said he'd run to help if he thought I was in danger. Plus, I had a shiny new dagger, thirsty for demon creature blood. Or maybe that was just my animal.

The tree started up like a dancing girl trying to

shake her boobs out of her dress as I ducked around it and darted to the bush. Nyfain's smell zinged through me, heavy in the area. It wasn't as fresh as it had been yesterday, but it was more plentiful. He'd lingered.

I reached into the bush and then yanked my hand back. The yellow package had been filled again.

Biting my lip, suppressing a smile, I hooked my fingers through the brown string and carefully dragged it out. I pulled at the end and then disentangled it off the package. Another parchment lay folded up inside, over an additional leather-bound book. My stomach fluttered.

His writing was not nearly so delicate this time. A bit of a mess, really, as though he'd brought the supplies and written it here, crouched down next to the bush.

Dear Finley,

I remembered seeing a romance novel in your house, grouped with the book on our people's history and ~~poison~~ trees, and wondered if maybe action/adventure wasn't within your interests. I therefore brought you a book from my mother's section of the library.

Such stories were not allowed by my father, so it was essential they be kept in a secret room accessed by a hidden door. They were snuck in from travelers, sold to her by merchants in whispered deals, sent by her sisters, and pulled from libraries in the villages. She now has quite the collection.

I have not read any of them. Should you wish to provide some guidance, I'd be happy to explore them with you. I'll choose something for you, and you can choose something for me. Attached is a sampling of titles. If you recognize any good ones, I'll start there. We can compare notes, if you'd like. Scholar to scholar, as it were.

If I may be so bold, I'd like to inquire after your father.

Yours truly,

-N

I pulled out this volume and noticed there was extra parchment and a fountain pen stashed beneath it. I smiled to myself and pulled it out, sitting back against the birch, whose antics had simmered down, and spread a piece of parchment over the smooth surface of the book.

Dear ~~Dickhead~~ *N,*

Lovely to hear from you. My father is doing well, actually. Really well! I took what I learned from you and applied it to what ails him. He's weak and a little muddled, but speaking well, not coughing, and awake. If not a cure, it is at least a huge advancement. We'll keep watching him to see. So I may have a way to slow the progress of the sickness and bring people back from the brink of death. Only time will tell whether there is a cure in the mix. I'm about to try the crowded nulling elixir on my neighbor, so we'll see if I'm a healer or a murderer.

In my other letter, I detailed the purpose of the enclosed elixirs and how to make them. These are samples of each. I have more, but they were too heavy to bring all at once.

Now, on to important matters. I've already finished the book you lent but intend to do a re-read. It's very exciting!!! (I nearly put four exclamation points, but there wasn't even a little romance, so that diminished my excitement just a smidge.) I like all books, so if you have any about ~~poison~~ mushrooms or anything, those are great, too. I just don't get through them as quickly as fiction.

Anyway, more info about the stuff I brought (my letters clearly aren't so organized as yours—I didn't have princely training). I do better when I can do at least ~~eight~~ one rough draft. I hope you will bare with me.

Some very dense people in my village have worked off the directions, so I have high hopes that the healers in the other villages can work it out. This is the safer nulling elixir. It won't kill anyone. For the other, I would prefer to be present, since there are still so many unknowns. I'm not sure whether I can just travel to other villages? I know in the past people would die for trying, but in the past you couldn't cross the magical boundary, either. It seems ridiculous that no one does if they can. Or maybe they just never come to our village, and no one from the other villages wants us? That certainly seems likely, given the frosty reception I received after I followed you the other morning.

My animal is not amused by whatever you did to the connection, by the way, which I didn't realize was a thing. She has been a surly cunt ever since, and if I told her that, she'd thank me for the kind words. That's how mad she is. It's probably a good thing I can't shift, or she would surely take over and do something crazy, like find you and fuck your brains out, or burn down the castle. It's really hard to know with her. I think she's crazy.

I took a moment to glance at his list of books, twenty in all, and only eight I recognized.

I've placed numbers beside the books that I know. It's a riddle. Choose the one that you think I want you to read first, and read that one. Give me your favorite scene. I'll then know if you chose the right book.

As the other note says, I've left some stuff for your very many wounds. I saw how much blood you lost. I've put something in the bag for that as well. Take care of yourself. You can't let your duty kill you. I think that's my animal's job after the stunt you pulled. Stay healthy so she can claim a little vengeance, will you?

I sat with the pen in my hand, thinking about what else I could say. What else I might want to tell him, or get him to tell me. I didn't want this to be the end of the conversation—I also didn't want to use up all of our topics in one go.

With that in mind, I took a chance.

Since you are fulfilling all your duties, I find myself remiss (is that the right word? I'm second-guessing myself) in taking care of your mother's garden. So, if you aren't too busy, maybe wade through there and cut out all the plants that don't belong. The vines, for a start. What the hell are they doing in there? The blackberry bushes are out of control. Those need to go. Weeds, obviously. You know, help out a little. Hadriel can assist you. He'll hate it, but he needs something to do in my absence besides shame-fuck. He'll thank me eventually.

Warmest regards,
Finley

The birch shook when I left, and I had a smile on my face all the way home.

The next day I went back in the afternoon, carrying more canisters. I knew it was probably too early to hope for a return note, but I figured I could add at least more canisters to the bag. A dragon could carry much more than I could. Besides, I wanted a few more crowded plant leaves so I could start experimenting. I'd also written out a bunch of questions about everlass for Nyfain.

At the birch, his smell caught me again, snapping

my focus taut and sending a zip of fire through my body. It was recent and potent, deliciously curling through my senses and wetting my panties. My animal purred in delight, and I wondered just what had created the extra depth to his scent.

Dear Finley,

I enjoyed the sarcasm in your first sentence immensely. It really ~~ruined~~ made my night. I carried on reading with a ~~scowl~~ glow.

I spat out a laugh, settling back against the shaking birch to read.

First, and most importantly, your father's convalescence is fantastic news! I am so proud of you. I wish we could go back in time, because you would've been crowned as the best plant worker in the kingdom, I have no doubt. You and my mother would have had so much to talk about.

Consequently, why do you call him "Father" and your mother "Mom"? I picked up on that at your cottage but drugged your family and skulked off into the night before I could ask (...is that joke too soon?).

I am sure you will heal your neighbor, but if you turn murderer, I have heard that blaming cats can be useful in getting out of it. Hadriel provided that anecdote. I'm not quite sure how it will help get you off the hook, and in truth, at the time he offered the information, he was hanging upside down by one ankle in a costume I am pretty sure was meant to mock me, whilst heavily intoxicated. Nevertheless, it <u>bears</u> looking into.

Since we are on the subject of spelling mistakes, when you hoped I would "<u>bare</u> with you," it put a very different spin on the meaning. Soon thereafter, I read your favorite book on that list—the numbers I took to mean the number of times you had read them?

I giggled as I read, nodding. He'd figured it out.

Eighteen is quite a lot. After I read it, though, I think I understand. I'd love to see the physical book you have handled. I assume some pages have seen more wear than others, specifically the scene in which the couple is forced to escape the (rather tame) villain on horseback. I wondered why the author would have them outrun the villain so easily. And then we got the descriptions of his hands slowly gliding up her (milky) thighs and firmly palming her (luscious) breasts, and I *began to understand.*

I have never made love to a woman on horseback, but I am now desperate to try. The idea of a canter (probably a trot, actually—this author didn't seem to be an equestrian) pounding my cock deeper and harder into her tight, wet pussy is one I haven't been able to get out of my mind as I...bare with you. Wouldn't it be fun to try out the sex scenes explored in detail in the pages of your favorite novels? I wonder if I could give ~~you~~ (<—oops) someone as many orgasms as these heroes give their ladies. Likely not, but I am ever ready to learn. Given our current hopeless situation, I'll have to continue rigorously fucking myself instead. I seem to be getting worse at it, though, because I've been needing to do it more and more frequently. Maybe I should take a break from novels with passion and explore a book about bodies of water instead. Namely, cold baths.

Now who is babbling via parchment...

I twisted my legs together and fanned myself. Even when talking about deliciously crude sex scenes, he was well spoken. It was insane. The author of these letters did not sound like the gruff, rough-and-tumble, scarred beast I'd met and constantly fought with. It was like two different people.

Though I did remember the guy from the everlass field. The guy who'd opened up about his mom and easily worked past my angry defenses. That guy was fun to talk with. He was interesting and engaging.

Even that guy, though, hadn't been this eloquent. He hadn't sounded this regal. And while normally that might bother me…somehow, right now, it didn't. He was almost too charming to exist in this twisted version of real life.

If I had to guess, however, the horse-riding scene was not your favorite. Women would usually enjoy the declaration of love from the emotionally stunted hero. But given what I know of you, I wonder instead if it isn't when the hero falls down into the pit (miraculously without breaking a limb or his head) and the heroine outsmarts the trap and saves him. That sounds more like your speed.

My grin spread wider. He had me. That was a pretty epic scene. It was when the hero stopped treating her like she was breakable, and they started working as a team. It made the action more exciting and the sex scenes hotter. Still, the horse-riding scene was a close second. I wasn't going to lie. I'd also always wanted to try it.

After reading A Journey to Wastrel, *I under-stand why* Breakout *lost one exclamation point for its lack of romance. Thank you for opening my eyes. I see now that there is always room to squeeze in some fucking. I, myself, need at least some semblance of believable action and villainy. I'm going to say it was very good indeed!!!*

Shall I just continue through the list, starting with the books you've read most? Or would you like to adjust my next read to account for my (likely subpar) tastes?

As for your next read, I've included it here. I'm interested to see what you think of the ro-mance subplot. I've also brought you a book on dogs. I find them utterly useless, but I have been told (lately by a very drunk Hadriel) that I am a heartless bastard. However, most shifters do not like dogs, especially wolf shifters, unless they are of a certain power. Your village has the most dogs of all the villages, I believe, and that's only...five or so, right?

Regarding the connection between us/our an-

imals...

It's hard to know what to say. You say your animal is a surly cunt? Mine's a violent prick whom I wish would just fuck off. If it wouldn't doom the kingdom, I'd shove him so far down that the curse would probably take hold and suppress him as it ought. Suffice it to say, it wasn't his choice to break the connection, and he's been driving me mental. But I stand by what I did. You need to be free of me, Finley, for your own good. That's the only way you'll get a happy ending. Any idiot can see that. Protecting you means staying away from you. You'll see the truth of that in time. Until then, we have randy letters and fast, furious self-fucking to get us through our days.

Thank you for the elixirs and healing supplies. I will be passing those on as soon as I study the contents. You say your villagers are dense, but you are there to help them. You have no idea what the other villages are working with. And no, no one crosses between villages. Since the demons killed so many early on, everyone stays separated and with their heads down now. We don't have the ability to fight back. Only a few sneak out to meet me on a regular basis, always during the day, hoping it goes unnoticed. Lately it has. Hopefully that remains.

"First we heal," I murmured to myself, "then we'll have numbers to fight."

Thank you for looking after me. It means a lot that you'd brave my temper and try to heal me after my treatment of you. Maybe the ointments will stop the flow of scars onto my skin. Though I'm not sure there is much of a point. I am every bit as much of a monster as I appear to be. My days of vanity are long since done.

I would be <u>remiss</u> if I didn't diligently follow your landscaping demands (you had the use of remiss right). Hadriel and I will begin tearing out the plants you've advised, and I'll ask for more guidance once finished. I'll have a drawing made up of each stage of our progress to ensure we are on the right track.

By the by, I don't know whether you've discerned as much, but when my father was particularly angry with me, I spent time in that tower bedroom. Sometimes I was locked in there for days with only the servants for company (and they were only allowed to bring me food or bathe me). My mother used to work in her garden a lot during those times so that I could look down at her and not feel so alone, a service I, apologetically, didn't render to you. She had the wall constructed around her garden so that my father, passing by in the grass, wasn't the wiser. It killed me to lock you up in that tower. But I couldn't risk those demons infiltrating your mind and bending you to their will. I meant to apologize before now, but our discourse always resulted in fighting and then your tits or pussy in my mouth. So, for what it's worth, I am sorry about that.

Please stay safe. I think my dragon would work out a way to kill me if I let harm come to you.

I look forward to your book recommendations.

Your truly,

~~Dickhead~~

N

I sat with his letter for a while, not able to ignore my aching heart or the fire in my body. I didn't think I could compose a letter right now. Not after that. His apology and confession about the tower...

His delicious sexual comments…

His gratitude and the admissions about his dragon…

It was all so much to unpack.

I didn't want to leave him hanging, though. I didn't want him to think he'd overstepped. I definitely didn't want to stop this communication. Plus, night was creeping in quickly.

Dear Desperate to Fuck While Riding a Horse,

I need to get out of here. I just came to drop off more supplies and grab a few crowded plant leaves. I'll report back later tonight with a more thorough letter. Sleep is for dogs and other creatures you hate for no reason.

Yourssssss truly (this is me pointing out your previous error, in case it is confusing you),
Finley

P.S. My favorite part was definitely when he got stuck in the pit. Do not ruin that scene for me with semantics. It's fantasy. Sometimes you need a little make-believe to ensure a horrible fall doesn't kill the hero so that horse fucking is possible.

P.P.S. Goddess strike me down, I meant fucking

on a horse. Definitely a no to horse fucking.

P.P.P.S. I hate this fucking birch.

—Oh and I'll get that worn-in book for you. It's a library book, though, so you'll need to swap it for your copy. Probably for the best, because I have a feeling you'll be picturing ~~me~~ someone in the scenes and practicing your self-fucking while reading it. I don't want to subject other book borrowers to your sticky jizz pages.

The end of the letter has now officially come.

I hurried away with the new books and letter stored in my knapsack, along with more crowded everlass leaves. I needed to get that book for Nyfain. I also needed to read the ones he'd passed to me. Damn life for getting in the way of my new books!

I wondered what Nyfain would think of the next book on the list. If he'd thought of me in that last one, he'd definitely think of me in the next one. The main couple's relationship was turbulent, and they always ended up hate-fucking. It was the book I still had at home.

Probably time for a reread.

CHAPTER 4

Dear Finley,

Would you prefer a birch that sings in a shrill voice? Those were the only options available to me without leaving the kingdom.

I await your well-thought-out letter. I will bring the <u>clean</u> book to swap for the dirty one, since your comment was certainly the result of a guilty conscience and one-handed reading.

By the way, thank you for pointing out my mistake in my complimentary closing of the last letter. It's a lesson I'll take to heart.

Truly your,

N

P.S. I'd forgotten to return your dagger. Please find it here, polished and sharpened. Do you need any other weapons? As your prince, I'm happy to supply whatever you need in case I someday find myself in a pit and in need of rescue.

—The end of this letter has come, but not as hard as me the last time I thought of ~~you~~ <u>someone</u>.

(I apologize for being so crass. Give me the word, and I'll cease immediately.)

I laughed as I finished his letter and set down my own, as well as the rest of the elixirs and draughts I'd made up. In the letter, I'd told him about my father being strict with me growing up and his recent revelation as to why. I told him that Hannon had invited him for dinner or a midnight snack, and that my brother forgave him even before I explained why we'd been drugged.

And the details had kept flowing from my pen—babble about the market where Phyl gave me the dagger and withheld the finer rendition, saving it for *him*. What Phyl said about my mother and me. About James, and the way my feelings for him had completely dried up. About Jedrek's presumptuousness and threats. When I'd finished, the letter was nearly three pieces of parchment, front and back. I couldn't ever remember being so open with anyone. I hadn't worried about being embarrassed or saying something that might be deemed peculiar. I'd laid my life out raw and plain.

And yet, suddenly, it didn't seem like enough.

After reading his letter, I grabbed a piece of blank parchment that he'd left and penned a quick reply.

Dear Nyfain,

I'm happy to see that your letter had a second coming, or did you not finish off the second time? If not, yes, you must definitely work harder to be like the heroes of those stories. However, unless your dick game suffers compared to your mouth or fingers, I'd say you could give them a run for their money.

Yes to the crassness. After you read the second book on that list, I'd say it is unavoidable. I'm getting wet just thinking about you reading it. I'd definitely like to try a few of those sex scenes, especially the one... Well, I won't spoil it. I was going to do a reread, but instead I've left our library's copy of the book for you. Swap it out, please. I've written notes in this one for you about how one might go about re-creating those scenes in a modern-day (turned Dark Ages) castle. Maybe don't put it back in your library, either. I'd hate for an unsuspecting victim to find my sex letters. The notes are...quite specific to ~~you~~ <u>someone</u>. *I'm not incredibly experienced but have a great imagination. Still, they might find me hopelessly naïve.*

Actually, I AM hopelessly naïve. Other than our encounters, I haven't done much more than missionary without the candles lit and an occasional finger up his bum to make him jump/spur him on. (I never could tell which that unsuspecting finger would result in.) So please don't make fun of me. I'm suddenly regretful.

Many kisses,
Finley
The end.
The end.
The end.
The end!!!

I gathered the regular everlass I'd come to collect, stowed it away, and quickly headed out. I wanted time to read before I had to call it a night. The book on dogs would likely put me to sleep, and so that should be my book of choice, but the other promised to be full of action and fun and excitement, and I couldn't wait to get to it.

"Finley. It's time to get up." Sable slapped me on the

forehead.

I flinched before blinking my groggy eyes open, catching her staring down at me.

"Go away." I gave her a shove.

"No. Hannon said to make sure you get up. You need to be an active member of this household and village. People are counting on you. Get *up!*" She slapped me on the forehead again, then zipped away squealing laughter before I could get my foot out to kick her.

I rubbed my eyes and then stretched. I'd stayed awake way too late again last night. The book he'd picked this time was so much better than the last. The adventure aspect was unparalleled, and the slow-burn romance had me turning the pages like fire. I was halfway through, and there'd barely been a kiss, but the sexual tension leapt off the pages.

Groaning, I rolled out of bed and headed to the wash shed and my version of coffee.

LATER THAT DAY, after convincing Old Man Fortety that I *did* intend to end his suffering, though I neglected to say how, I gave him a weakened crowded nulling elixir and left Hannon to it. Just like with Father, I couldn't stand to see someone die from one of my supposed remedies. Call me a coward, but some things I wasn't sure I would come back from.

I used the waiting time to stop by the library. I couldn't stop giggling when I returned the book on trees, reminded of the way Nyfain had crossed out the word poison. He wasn't wrong. The author had slyly inserted information about various poisons in between the sections about trees.

I grabbed the book I'd be sending Nyfain's way next—after I knew how he liked my comments. Talking dirty—or writing dirty—was new to me, and while I was immensely turned on by it, there was a large possibility that I sounded like an idiot. Time would tell. I doubted he'd come out and tell me if he didn't like it, but I'd certainly be able to tell from his comments.

On my way through the village square to deposit my library book at home, I noticed a few of Jedrek's "bros" standing in a cluster near the open door of the pub. It was early for them to be crowded around like barflies, waiting to see which available (or not-so-available) woman they'd try to take home. As I passed, their volume dimmed, and their eyes shifted toward me.

Tingles crawled up my spine at their various expressions. Most were conniving and smug, like they knew a secret about me. Obviously this could be traced back to Jedrek, but I didn't like the fact that they looked so gleeful. One, a weasel-faced dipshit that was dumb as rocks, smirked before looking down my body in a suggestive but condescending way. It was the sort of look guys gave a woman when they thought their bro owned that pussy. One that suggested the woman held zero power in the dynamic.

What was Jedrek planning that these clowns thought would come to pass? Clearly he thought he had me somehow.

Cold dripped down my spine as I remembered his ridiculous talk about the demon king. He thought I'd tried to make a deal for my father's life, as if anyone from this village could even reach the demon king.

Sure, Nyfain had suggested that I do that very thing—bargain for an escape—but the how of it was still very vague and half-formed. I struggled to believe someone as dense as Jedrek could have figured it out.

Still, that didn't mean he hadn't consulted with the demons in town. And if they went to the castle to ask questions, the answers would lead right back to me.

The question was, would the demons care? Their goal was to torment Nyfain. Maybe I was only relevant when I was his captive.

Then again, they knew that I was an easy way to get to him. Maybe they'd thought he'd killed me. Hearing that I was still alive and had escaped, or, worse, that he'd let me go…

Inside, my guts were twisting, but I stalked away like nothing bothered me.

"Hey." I barged into Old Man Fortety's house, emotions roiling.

Hannon glanced up from the couch, cookbook in hand. He'd always been able to read me, so it came as no surprise when he immediately tensed. "What is it?"

"I don't know, maybe nothing. How is Old Man Fortety?"

"You tried to cure me, didn't you, you rotten, good-for-nothing little heathen," Fortety yelled out through the open bedroom door, crotchety as ever. "I'm feeling better, aren't I? Yes, I am! You lied to me! Never trust a woman. Haven't I always said never trust a woman? I thought you were different, Finley Mosgrove."

I smiled in at him and then closed the door. His ranting continued.

"It worked," I surmised, too distraught to feel happy.

"It continues to, yes, though if you were ever going to do an oops, he would've been the best contender for it. What happened?"

I explained what I'd seen and my worry about Jedrek.

"Or it could be absolutely nothing, and Jedrek is just spreading rumors to cover for his tiny ego," I finished.

"I really couldn't say. But I want to ask Nyfain—"

"Yes," Hannon said, standing. "Write a letter and go now. You can hunt tomorrow. We have enough to last us a few more days."

I nodded and jogged out, cutting through the back-yards of houses and trying to stay out of sight. The Jedrek problem might be nothing, but even if he didn't involve the demons, he could make trouble. If he tried to force the issue, I could take him with a dagger, I was sure of it, but what if he happened upon me alone and without weapons?

I stopped at home just long enough to hastily scrawl out the letter to Nyfain and snatch up my knapsack. Once at the birch, I found the bush and pulled out the mostly empty parcel, finding only a letter from him in it. I swapped it for mine and stood, contemplating whether to read his note here or back within the safety of my house.

But my house wasn't really safe, was it? Jedrek could barge in and force an audience any time he liked. He wouldn't do anything, surrounded by neighbors who would come to our aid, but he could scare the kids and threaten me.

Out here, however, I could evade him. If anything, with my animal's help, I knew I could run faster than him and his friends. I would run straight to Nyfain if I had to.

Or maybe I was overthinking this due to recent events and my fatigue.

I worked my way to the far side of the everlass field, and then climbed a tree and settled into the branches. Perhaps I was overthinking things, but safety first.

I pulled open the parchment and was surprised to see Nyfain's handwriting was messier than usual. The lines bowed in places and the ink was smeared in a few spots, as though he were pressing too hard. The second I started reading, I knew why.

Dear Finley,

You can deliver a warning to Jedrek on my behalf. If he so much as glances at you askew, I/the dragon will rip out his throat and feast on his entrails. He will die a painful, gruesome death before disappearing from existence.

If you are troubled by him again, tell me immediately. I will handle it. This I swear to you. Say the word, and the following night will be his last. I will not tolerate him or anyone else making you feel uncomfortable, and I certainly will not allow them to harm you.

Please send me a note to reassure me (and the dragon) that you (both) are okay. In the event it is you in the pit this time—I smiled because he was talking about the book he'd read— *I will bring you more weapons. I need to procure them from the royal armory, but you'll have them by the night shift. If I don't hear from you by then, I will break my promise and deliver them to you personally.*

Please stay safe. I'm sorry you have to deal with small-dicked arsepieces. Your refusal of his ridiculous proposal should've been enough. I'd be happy to teach him a lesson on etiquette.

At your command,
Nyfain

I blew out a shaky breath and my heart grew warm. I hated to admit my animal was right, but…she was right. Nyfain could and would handle any danger that I couldn't handle myself. He wouldn't balk, and he wouldn't back down. He'd fight until he bled out, for the kingdom, and apparently now for me.

I bit my lip, took stock of my surroundings, and worked down the tree. Back at the birch, I scribbled a hasty note and got out of there.

Dear Beast,

Thank you.

I'm okay. Your words have helped calm me. Please let me know about the demon situation— if the ones at the castle have heard from Jedrek about me. That's what has given me the most concern. I will try to make it here for the night shift unless things get weird.

As a quick aside, it seems I am still a healer and not a murderer. No cats will have to take the fall. Old Man Fortety is not amused.

The damsel most recently locked in your tower,
Finley

He'd be giving me some weapons. That was good at least. Ordinarily, I wouldn't accept a gift so easily, but the guy had a royal armory and didn't use weapons. He could spare a few things.

Halfway home, an owl screeched, warning its kind of my passing.

Every. Damn. Time. It seemed like it just hung around the area, waiting for me. It was nocturnal, for goddess's sake. Did it not have something better to do than watch its stoop for kids traipsing over its lawn?

"Sleep or something, you blasted thing."

Frustrated, at wits' end, I snatched a rock from the dirt.

"And if you can't sleep, hunt. Help your family out.

Unless you don't have a family, which makes sense, since you are obviously a rotten fucker who can't mind its own business."

I threw the rock, missed by a mile, and kept trudging toward home.

I'd told Nyfain that I was fine. That I was calm. Pure lies.

Because it made me nervous that Nyfain had focused solely on Jedrek and not said a word about James, who had also been a dick. Being an alpha whose duty was protection, he'd clearly sensed which one of them was a threat. He'd essentially confirmed my fear. And while I would love to snap my fingers and tell Nyfain to give Jedrek a hunting accident he wouldn't walk away from, I didn't want to do anything until I knew more about the blowhard's dealings with the demons.

I neared the edge of the wood and spied a shape walking past the perimeter. I pulled my animal closer to the surface, needing to further enhance my sense of smell and hearing.

One of the shitstains we passed in the square. A growl ran through her thought. *The dopey-eyed cunt with fuzzy eyebrows and a "dead man walking" tag stamped on his forehead. I put the tag there. Just let me help you collect it.*

Fuzzy eyebrows... That was probably Clautus,

Jedrek's right-hand man. He usually hunted in the communal wood on the other side of the village. The only time he ever came this way was to show girls how brave he was by walking five feet into the Forbidden Wood. That trick had stopped working a few years back when it became known that I went deep into the Forbidden Wood to get everlass. Deep compared to their reckoning, anyway.

Just the one? I thought, easing my new dagger out of its worn sheath.

Yes. He has traces of the others' scent on him, though. He hasn't been long out of their company.

He's looking for me, then.

By all means, let him find you.

I would.

I gripped my dagger a little tighter and then lowered it at my side, natural for leaving the Forbidden Wood at night. He'd have no idea that anything was amiss. Barren branches scraped across my shoulders. The warmth from the sun washed over my face.

Clautus saw me immediately, his brow furrowing and his lanky body pivoting.

"Finley," he called out too loudly. He was only ten feet from me and didn't need that volume—he was calling someone else.

A surge of adrenaline fueled my speed. Fire roared

through my blood, my animal providing me with power.

"I've got places to be, Clautus."

"We heard your dad is doing much better. Imagine that. Jedrek was right, I guess, huh?"

"About what, being a limp-dicked shit lozenge? Yeah, I'll say he was right."

He caught up to me as I reached my usual reading sycamore, angling past it toward my cottage. He pushed in close, trying to intimidate me. It was something he'd done in our youth, the older kid picking on the younger.

Then I grew up.

"Speaking of," I said, "what did you do in a past life to end up looking like you do? You look like a puckered asshole with a bad bleaching job. And if your eyebrows are like two bushes out of control, what must your balls look like? With a dick as small as yours, you should consider landscaping so the succubi can find your pecker. They probably think the damn thing fell off from inactivity."

"I hope Jedrek slaps that mouth off your face."

"I'd love to slap that face off your head. The village would look a whole lot nicer."

I reached my lane as Jedrek walked my way from the other end. He had a purposeful strut, screaming determination.

Clautus waved at him, silently communicating that he'd found the prize.

"He obviously knows you found me, idiot," I said, nearly at my door. "He can see."

"Finley," Jedrek barked, an unspoken command riding his words.

Unlike with Nyfain, though, I felt zero compulsion.

In measured steps, I walked to my door and laid a hand on the knob.

"It's been arranged. You'll be Jedrek's," Jedrek said smugly.

"What Jedrek wants, Jedrek gets," Clautus intoned.

"What's that, Clautus?" I asked sweetly. "I couldn't hear you with Jedrek's dick stuck in your mouth." I let my focus drill into Jedrek. "Leave me alone. That is a warning. You'd do best to heed it. I didn't meet the demon king, I don't talk to demons, and I will *never* marry you. Save some face and find someone who is willing."

He sneered. "Never say never."

I meant to turn the knob, but I had to pause for a moment. "Really? *Never say never*? First you talk about yourself in the third person, and then you drop that tired cliché at my feet? Seriously, bud. You're making a fool of yourself right now."

The door swung open, and Hannon stepped out, his face closed down and his eyes hard. His chest puffed up as his gaze beat into Jedrek.

"Is there a problem?" he said in a deeper voice than usual.

Jedrek tensed and narrowed his eyes. His smirk grew. "Not at all, Hannon. Or should I call you *brother-in-law*."

"Get off my property, or I'll make you my bitch," Hannon replied, gently taking my arm and pulling me into the house. "You're not welcome here."

Jedrek spat to the side, and then Hannon shut the door on them, his shoulders tense.

"I asked around," Hannon said, turning. "Jedrek was overheard boasting about making a deal. None of my friends know the details, but apparently he made it last night when a succubus and an incubus were getting him off. He was overheard saying it would be easy to live up to his side of the bargain, and then…" Hannon's face turned red with anger. "He said some not-so-nice things about you."

"What he'd like to do with me, right?" I rolled my eyes. "Guys like that are so predictable. They have to be loud and crass to puff up their egos."

"What are you going to do?"

"The few demons in town don't matter. Their power is weak. It's the demons at the castle I'm concerned about. Nyfain will look into it. If something is going on, he'll know what to do. He's been dealing with them for a long time. He knows how they work."

"It would be easy to say that Nyfain got you into all this, but when it comes to Jedrek, that's not even remotely true. I actually think you got lucky that Nyfain found you when he did. Because Jedrek would've always taken desperate measures to get what he wants. At least now you have someone powerful and knowledgeable in your corner. I shudder to think what would've happened if you didn't."

Nodding, I headed to my room. He was a hundred percent correct. Nyfain's actions in the beginning were strange and fucked up (in retrospect, I had to wonder how much of that had been fueled by his dragon), but at the moment, I was incredibly thankful for him. One thing I knew for certain: if there was a problem I couldn't handle, Nyfain would absolutely take care of it, and he'd do so viciously.

CHAPTER 5

"**I** DON'T LIKE this." Hannon stood in the living room in the wee hours of the morning with his arms crossed. A night bird called outside somewhere. The rest of the house lay quietly sleeping and had been for some time. "You shouldn't be wandering around on your own with what's going on with Jedrek."

I slipped the books I'd finished into my knapsack. "He's too much of a coward to go into that wood." I set the knapsack down and buckled my belt, the dagger's sheath resting against my thigh. "I'll be stealthy in the village and jog all the way there. Nyfain said he'd be bringing me weapons. Now more than ever, I need those weapons."

"At least let me go with you."

"There is no fucking way you are going with me, Hannon. Are you out of your mind? You're keeping this family together, and you're too much of a planner to react quickly to danger. No offense, but the Forbidden Wood is no place for you."

He followed me to the door, his eyes tight. "I have a bad feeling, Finley. Can't you get the weapons tomorrow?"

"When it comes to Jedrek, daylight is ten times more dangerous than three in the morning."

His jaw tightened. He couldn't argue with that.

I put a hand on his shoulder. "I'll be careful. I promise. That's why I'm leaving through the back. Jedrek is the best tracker out of all his bros, but he's not excellent. I'm a helluva lot more cunning than a deer."

Hannon yanked me into a tight hug. "Damn it, Finley. When will life be easy for us? Is normal too much to ask?"

I laughed softly. "Normal is boring anyway."

He watched me jog into the backyard and scale the fence. As soon as the night enveloped me, my animal pushed harder to the surface. I let her have plenty of room, needing her more than ever right now. Scents drifted on the breeze and tickled our nose. Coriander, thyme, a sweet floral scent, and the fading remnants of a decaying critter.

I could've done without that last one.

No people. No demons. Good news.

Still cautious, I darted between fences, tiptoed across yards, and broke for the tree line. In mere minutes, I was on my way to the birch, jogging fast. The wood lay quiet around us. My breathing and the rhythmic thud of my footfalls were the only sounds I could discern. Nyfain must have been through here and swept away all the riffraff, and none of the normal life had returned. It felt like a dead zone.

All I wanted was to see him again. The notes were no longer enough.

The birch shook and danced as I ducked around it and headed to the bush. The familiar yellow package lay in wait, tied with string to indicate Nyfain had been there. This time it wasn't a book shape, though, but a long rectangle. Hurrying, my animal keeping tabs on the sounds and smells around us, I untied the string and pushed back the material.

I couldn't help sucking in a breath.

A sword glittered in the starlight and the glow of the pale moon. A swirl like dragon scales had been etched into the double-edged blade, an accent to obviously fine craftsmanship. The hilt was leather-bound, the design punctuated by diamond cutouts and a curved hand guard with more dragon scale etching. I couldn't make out the colors in the dark, but the fluctuations of light and dark suggested there were many of them. It was beautiful. I bet he'd chosen the best one he could find. Actually, even the worst would likely be a work of art. Phyl had a ways to go before he could put together something like this.

I grabbed the note and unfolded the parchment, my heart speeding up for many reasons, only some of them concerning Jedrek and demons.

Dear Finley,

I had Hadriel ask around about the demons. I'm just back from checking in, and no one has heard anything. It seems the castle demons, which are their king's proxies within our kingdom, are not part of these schemes. At least, they are not advertising it. Hopefully Jedrek is blowing smoke and silencing him forever (which I'll gladly do) will be an end to it.

However, in the event that Jedrek has piqued the interest of your village demons, which are among the weakest in the kingdom, you will need to be on your guard. They enjoy drama and feed off the emotion of it. Don't give them what they crave. Give them pale emotion if you must, but feigning uninterest is best. They should lose interest.

In the event Jedrek is trying to make some

sort of deal (that they like the sound of), things will get a little dicier. They will need to request permission from the castle demons. Given the village in question, if the deal isn't interesting enough, the castle demons will likely grant the request without further inquiry. If the deal is interesting, or if the castle demons are bored or curious, they will command an audience with either you or Jedrek or both, depending on the nature of the trade.

Obviously you cannot, under any circumstances, be brought in. Your face is known here, your absence has been noted, and their games with me have intensified. If they gain access to you without my protection...

His pen ripped a hole in the parchment. Clearly the thought sent rage through his blood. Rage would've been nicer than the unease, disgust, and fear I was working with.

If they try to take you in, kill them all. It is within your power. Then run straight to the birch. Set it off three times consecutively, and I will come for you. Hide so that you aren't seen, and wait for me.

The sword you have seen. The rest of the weapons are hidden on the other side of the bush. Take them and go home right now. Stay on your guard. If you get bored, write more sexy notes to me. Or even if you aren't bored and have to squeeze it in with all your chores. Actually, even if you have to lose sleep, write me more notes about how we would accomplish those scenes with me under you, or over you, or inside of you. I've never been so turned on in all my life.

I digress.

If you feel danger for any reason and want my help, activate the birch (three times in succession), night or day. For <u>any</u> reason. I will always come for you, Finley. You have my word.

Yours always,
Nyfain

I couldn't decide if I was more touched or turned on. One thing was for certain, though: I was a little more nervous. It definitely sounded like Jedrek had made a deal, and he thought it was in the bag. Hopefully that just meant the demons would check me out, get bored, and leave it at that.

The finest bow I'd ever seen, etched with scales like the sword, waited beyond the bush. A leather quiver filled with arrows sat next to it. I picked up what looked like a set of throwing knives and took one out. Perfectly balanced and with an incredibly sharp point.

These weapons would be worth a sack of gold, at least. And he was just giving them to me. What must it be like to be that rich? To be a prince?

I wrapped up the books and my rambling letter before hefting my new treasures and doing as Nyfain had said. Once home, I'd continue to do as he'd said and write more sexy notes. My core tightened just thinking about it.

At the edge of the quiet wood, I peered at the outskirts of the village. Unlike earlier, no weasels patrolled, looking for me. All was clear and quiet.

I hefted my new things and took the stealthy route home. I was nearly there when a lightly pungent aroma caught my attention. Notes of musk woven with floral scents.

Demons.

The smell was fresh but not very strong. They couldn't have gotten too close. That, or their magic was significantly weaker than the demons at the castle.

I hopped the back fence and snuck into the backyard, pausing for a moment to listen. Hannon opened the door as I reached for the handle. He took me in for a moment, looking for damage, before he stepped aside so I could get in.

"All was quiet," I whispered, heaving a relieved sigh once I was in the living room and the door was locked behind me. "But Nyfain said that I could not allow them to take me to the castle under any circumstances."

"But he's in the castle."

"They'll use me in a game against him. I'll be a pawn. Lord only knows what they'll do to me to get at him. I'd rather not find out."

"Wow, Finley." Hannon took the bow gingerly, hefting it and then pulling it close so that he could sight and tug back the bowstring. "This is as fine a bow as I've ever seen."

"It's a beauty, right? And look at this…" I pulled the sword from its sheath on my left hip, where I'd secured it before leaving the field. "And these…" I grabbed the throwing knives out of my knapsack.

"This is a handsome gift," he breathed. "Or is it a loan?"

"Either way, he's entrusting me with them."

Fists rapped on the door. I froze with the sword in hand, my fingers wrapped tightly around the hilt. Hannon studied me for a second.

The knock sounded again, and I crept closer. A pungent aroma permeated the air. My heart was like a trapped animal in my chest. Demons. They'd come.

My glance at Hannon must've spoken volumes. He joined me at the door in a rush.

"What do we do? Should you run?" he asked.

"And have them wait here until I get back? That would only put you guys in danger." I eyed all my weapons. Then the back door. "Let them in. Nyfain said that they like drama. I'll act uninterested and hope they go."

"And if they don't?"

"I'll find a way to kill them. Then we'll drag the bodies into the wood and leave them there. No bodies, no questions."

It sounded great, though I didn't know if it was feasible.

We quickly stowed the weapons in easily accessible locations around the front room and backyard. As the third knock came, I pulled the door open, only belatedly realizing I still wore my day clothes. Clearly they hadn't pulled me out of sleep. Hopefully they wouldn't notice.

A tall man with long white-blond hair flowing around his square face waited on the stoop with a patient expression and dark, cunning eyes. Need stirred deep within me, quickly curdling my stomach as disgust replaced desire. An incubus, obviously, and my reaction was the same as it had been in the castle. Their magic, while still registering as sexy, now had the opposite effect on my body. My animal was running interference.

"Yes?" I asked in a mildly confused voice.

"Yes, it is you. I wondered." His tone was sleek and confident. Tingles of worry skittered across my skin. "I've seen you from time to time, hurrying home as darkness fell. Your beauty is so incredibly pleasing. You have many admirers."

"What are you, a dating service?"

A smile worked across his thin lips. He studied me for a moment. "You are so much more than that shifter could ever be. No wonder he is prepared to go to such extremes to have you." He looked beyond me to the inside of the house, then stepped back and glanced down the lane. "Were you born in this hovel? Or are you being hidden here?"

"Hidden here? What are you talking about?"

He was back to studying me, his eyes narrowing slightly. "Born here, then. Interesting. Monissa will want to meet you, I think. Come with me."

"Why? Actually, it doesn't matter. The answer is no."

His demeanor changed slightly, his shoulders squaring and a hint of power curling around him.

"Finley, what is it?" Hannon pulled the door open a little wider so he could fit beside me in the doorway, hand resting on the frame. His clothes were mussed, as though he'd recently put them on, and his hair stood on end. He was playing it like he'd just woken up. Which was not a great contrast to my fully awake vibe. His other hand stayed behind us, his side pressed to mine. "Who is this?"

"You are the older brother, correct?" the demon asked. "We have no need of you or your other siblings. We just want the girl. No problem." The demon was clearly reacting to Hannon's size.

Hannon's brow furrowed. "Here, come in. There's no point standing out on the stoop. I'll put on some tea."

The demon's gaze slid to me, and I could see him weighing this option. I crossed my arms over my chest in a pose that screamed *stubborn!* He'd be more inclined to accept Hannon's offer if he knew I didn't want him to. Bullies were predictable.

"Finley, come on. Let him in. I'm sure there is a reasonable explanation for all of this," Hannon urged.

"Yes, Finley. Be a good girl and do let me in."

Rage boiled within me at the demon's condescending tone. At his belief that he had power over me and my family. My animal surged forward and power lit me up, white-hot.

The demon's eyes widened. Surprise rolled across his face, followed by a look of recognition, like he'd fit a

K.F. BREENE

few pieces into a puzzle and suddenly knew what picture he was looking at. He reached for me.

Hannon shoved me out of the way with his left hand and swung with his right. The blade of an axe lodged into the demon's middle. Releasing the handle, Hannon grabbed the demon by the front of his fancy dress shirt and ripped him into the house like he weighed nothing. I grabbed the demon's flailing hands and wrenched them behind his back, holding his wrists.

"What's happening?" Sable asked from the edge of the hall as Dash ran out. My father stumbled out last, the wood legs of a chair screeching across the floor as he used it as a walker.

"Shut the door," I yelled. "Bar it."

Hannon threw the struggling demon down onto the floor, and I realized he'd already put down some water-resistant bedding. The demon crashed down onto the axe blade, driving it deeper.

"You couldn't have used the sword?" I asked, jamming my knee on top of the squealing demon before bending over and grabbing the sword from under the couch.

"What is going on?" my father asked in a weak voice. "What is the meaning of this? Finley, your eyes…"

"I don't know how to wield a sword," Hannon said,

86

jogging into the kitchen and returning with a carving knife. "But I know how to use an axe and knives."

"Good gracious, Hannon, and I thought you were the soft touch." I grabbed the sword hilt with both hands and drove the blade down into the base of the demon's neck. The demon spasmed and quickly stilled.

"I am, until my family is in danger. Should we cut him up and bury him, or…?"

I tilted my head at him with a small smile. "Who are you?"

He rolled his eyes and shoved me away. "This bedding only works for a while. I don't want to stain the rug. Let's get him out of here."

"There's the brother I know."

"Hannon…what…" Father hobbled in our direction. The kids stood at the edges of the room, watching quietly. If they'd had illusions of a cheerful childhood before this, that illusion was now well and truly dried up. I told them to stay in the house.

In the backyard, we dropped the demon onto his side in the dirt by the fence and extracted the weapons. Blood seeped out at first but quickly stopped. Dead things didn't bleed much.

"Wrap him up and we'll throw him over the fence," I said. "I'll jump over after him and carry him into the wood—"

Another rap sounded on the front door, barely heard out here in the back.

"I'll get it," Father called out.

"Of all the times for him to be feeling better," I said, hopping up and running for the back door. "Father, no—"

The door swung open to reveal a man and woman standing shoulder to shoulder. The woman opened her mouth to ask a question before she spied me at the back door. The man beside her was the first to spot the spray of blood across my shirt. He nudged her. It took all of a few seconds for her to put it together.

They surged through the front door, knocking Father out of the way. A burst of fire fueled me, and I turned and launched down the back steps. Before I reached the fence, I took a quick detour and snatched the sword from the ground. I hop-stepped as I labored to tuck it into its sheath. I'd need to practice that move.

"I'll take care of it," I yelled at Hannon as I jumped, grabbed the top of the fence, and hauled myself over. We really needed to think about adding a gate back here.

A hand caught my ankle. A grunt, and the hand released.

As I flung my body over, I caught sight of Hannon with his axe again, readying for another blow. The male demon staggered to the side, howling with agony as he reached over his shoulder to the center of his back.

"Go, Finley!" Hannon yelled.

My feet dropped down, and I hesitated for a moment. No way was I going to go if the demons stayed behind.

A moment later, though, small hands gripped the top of the fence. The female demon planned to pursue.

"I'll be back," I yelled, turning to run.

"Don't come back, Finley. It's not safe for you here…"

The words drifted into the night as I put on a burst of speed, hearing the lady demon drop down to the ground behind me. Adrenaline surged through me, but my heart caught on Hannon's words. *Don't come back.* But where would I go?

The answer smacked into me, but I didn't have time to absorb it. I ran through an alley and out onto the lane. I needed speed now, not stealth. The footsteps of the demon were fast on my heels, gaining.

Go, go, go, I urged my animal, pulling her as close to the surface as possible without letting her take full control. *I need more.*

This would be a really good time for four legs.

Power thrumming through me, we put on a burst of speed, tearing down the center of the lane. At the end, we turned right and blasted past my reading sycamore. The edge of the wood jiggled in my vision as we sprinted. The demon's boots behind me ate up the ground, hot on my heels.

Almost there, I said.

I still don't see why we can't stop and kill her here.

Because if someone sees me kill her, they will know I killed her. In the wood, any manner of things can happen, like the beast getting both of us. Hannon can say I've died, they can pretend to mourn—

Okay, okay. I get it. Almost there.

Took you long enough.

A branch scratched my cheek as I burst through the perimeter of the Forbidden Wood. I ran a pace, wanting to get in nice and deep. That blasted owl screeched, closer to the perimeter than usual. It probably held a grudge because I'd tried to hit it with a rock. One of these days I would get it, just to make it bugger off.

Breathing ragged, I got to a small, open patch and staggered to a stop, playing up that I was tired. The female demon slowed, her large bosom rising and falling. It had never occurred to me that they might not be able to go on forever. Her heavily lidded gaze took in my sword and my stance; she was probably correctly ascertaining that I'd had zero training with a sword and likely didn't know what I was doing with it. Little did she know that I didn't need a tutor to figure out how to stick the pointy end into her person. Still, I did wish I'd grabbed my dagger instead. I had more finesse with it.

"Nice blade," she said in a delicate purr. "No common girl has a blade like that. You must have rich friends."

"Common girls know how to steal. By the by, do sex kittens know how to fight?"

"Even kittens have claws." She wound closer with a seductive smile. Her magic curled around me, caressing, stroking. Bile rose in my throat.

"Gross. Stop that." I took a step toward her. Time to get this done.

"Your eyes are glowing," she said. "That means you have enough power to access your animal. Can you shift, as well?"

"No. You can, though, right? What sort of nightmare do you change into?"

She laughed. "Hmm. Sassy. I like that. Why don't you give up this tough-girl routine and succumb to me? I'll take good care of you, I promise. Have you ever had a woman lick your pussy? We're better at it than men. We know what feels good, how best to tease your orgasm until it explodes through you. You'll like it."

"A woman? Maybe. A demon? Y'all can go fuck yourselves."

"Oh, I do. Would you like to watch? Is that what gets you off?"

Damn it. I'd walked into that one.

"Come now, little pet," she said, five feet from me now, no weapon in hand. Her fingers probably turned to claws in her demon form, though. She didn't need weapons. "First I'll pleasure you…" Her magic pumped through the air, thick and syrupy, coating my skin and turning my stomach. "Then we'll go to the castle and see what is to be done with you. I bet the demon king would greatly like to meet you. He likes to toy with pretty things like you. Tell me, have you ever begged for cock? Crawled on your knees, desperate to be fucked?"

"Again, maybe. But not by one of you arrogant, fucked-up bastards. I want nothing to do with you." I lunged, stabbing forward with the sword.

She twisted and stepped to the side, easily evading me. I turned the lunge into a slice, but the sword was too big and cumbersome. She darted into my reach, her hip in line with the hilt of my sword. She reached out, and her body changed color to a mottled red and orange, like her scales were flaking off. Horns twisted from her head, and her face flattened with slits for a nose.

She slashed down with her long claws, grazing my skin. I grunted but held on to the sword until my senses caught up to me. I dropped it, reaching for my injured arm with my free hand. She smiled, exposing yellowed teeth, and her tongue slithered out and tasted the air.

Clearly I *did* need a tutor. Time for plan B.

"Good goddess, you are gross." I surged up and punched her in the throat.

She made a choking noise and instinctively reached for the offending spot. I grabbed her wrists and spun her, getting behind her. I clutched her head and twisted, trying to snap her neck. She cried out...but did not die.

What the fucking hell are you doing? my animal thought-hollered. *Just kill her already!*

That move seems a lot easier in books!

I probably needed a tutor for hand-to-hand combat, as well. I'd better start making a list.

The demon reached back and grabbed me, flinging me away with incredible strength. I rolled across the ground. A rock dug into my hip, sending dull, throbbing pain down my leg.

She was on me a moment later, clawing down my side, tearing flesh.

"Give in to me, girl." Her magic delved, punching me with disgusting desire. It curdled my stomach, sending bile up my throat. I convulsed, nearly vomited, and then squeezed the pads of my first two fingers and thumb together before jabbing her in the eyeball.

She howled and slapped a hand to her eye. I fisted her hair and ripped her head to the side. I really should've brought my fucking dagger! What the fucking fuck had I been thinking? Fuck!

I arched and bucked her off before trying to figure out how to kill someone with my bare hands. Books made this seem so fucking easy! Nyfain would have a lot of explaining to do, because the hero in that book he'd lent me did this all the time. He'd basically yawn and people would die. More realistic, my ass.

I punched her a few times, my hands, thankfully, strong from hunting and working the hides. What should I do, choke her? Try to, like…pound her head with a rock or something?

"Fuck, why didn't I realize I was so bad at this? Where's Hannon and his axe when you need him?"

I punched her a few more times and then ripped her toward me, hoping to get her by the neck again so I could strong-arm her over to the sword, where I might finally stab her and end this whole thing.

"It would be easier on both of us if you'd just tap out and die. Just give in to it," I said in a series of grunts, working my hand between her neck and the ground.

"Why…isn't…my…magic…working," the demon said through a strangled throat.

"Your magic *is* working. I just think it's gross. I

found someone sexier who doesn't need magic. So suck it. Come on now, stop struggling. You know I'm going to win. You know this! Stop making it so hard on me and just let me kill you already!"

My animal surged up, and a blast of fire crackled over my skin. My vision wobbled, blackening.

What are you doing? I demanded of her. *Too much power!*

A strong hand wrapped around my arm and shoved me to the side. A large, nude form stabbed down with my sword, the blade cutting through the middle of the demon. She cried out, the strength and volume of the sound lowering dramatically until it cut off.

Blotches of colored light throbbed within my line of sight, multiple small zigzags chopping up the image of Nyfain turning and crouching down beside me. My heart warmed, adding to the furnace in my middle, and prickles of pain turned into knife strikes, washing over my body and digging into my shoulders, head, and legs.

"Finley," Nyfain said, and hearing that deep, rough voice was like coming home. When had that started?

His power swept through me, a tidal wave quickly overcoming me and threatening to pull me under. The searing agony covering my flesh bit in deeper, and the inferno within struggled to get out.

"What the fuck are you doing?" Nyfain said, strain

evident in his voice.

"Couldn't...work...that sword," I struggled to say, my animal trying to kick me out of the way and take over. "Need...tutor after...all."

That was when I felt it. The strong, sure pulse beckoning my animal closer. Asking her to join hearts and minds and souls.

Nyfain's dragon was intent on protecting us. On dominating and claiming us. He called to my animal, and she was struggling against me to answer.

"She can't shift, you colossal prick," Nyfain said, picking me up and hugging me close. He bent and retrieved the sword as well. After a beat, he said, "No, I will not fucking shift with you in this state. You'll kill her. She can't shift with this curse! Stop calling to her animal!"

I wrapped my arms around his neck and pressed my cheek to his stubble, looking over his shoulder as he jogged. I squeezed my eyes shut and gritted my teeth against the pain. I didn't know where he was going, but it didn't matter. I trusted him.

Nyfain turned his head just a little, his lips brushing the shell of my ear. My animal purred in delight even as butterflies swarmed my stomach.

"Don't give in, Finley," he said softly, holding me tightly. "Don't give in to your animal. The first shift needs to be done in the best conditions, when the shifter is at peak power and in the presence of a guiding influence. This is the worst possible time for it. Talk to your creature. Pull her off my dragon's scent."

I squeezed my arms tighter around him. My heart beat strongly, and somehow it seemed like it was echoing through him before coming back to me. Like I used it, lent it to him, then got it back. One heart keeping us both going.

I slid my hand across his bare shoulder and up the side of his neck, to his strong jaw with prickly stubble. He stopped in his walk, suddenly silenced.

I turned my face just a little. Desire lazily crawled across my flesh and then soaked down through tissue to bone. It merged with the fire raging in my blood and calmed it, slow and syrupy, languid and delicious. All I knew was his touch. His heat. The feeling of that heart, bouncing back and forth.

"Nyfain," I whispered, needing something but not quite sure what. My animal goaded me. I was so tired of resisting her, of resisting *him*. "Nyfain…"

"No, Finley," he murmured, pained. His arms tight around me. His lips brushing the corner of mine. "Don't give in."

"Will you stop me?" I forced his face a little closer to me. We were on the trail, yes, but we had darkness for cover. People's fear of the beast for protection.

"I won't be able to. Please, Finley, resist. You deserve better than me. You deserve the world at your feet, and I don't have anything to offer you. I'm an uncrowned king of ruin. I am a prince of destruction. I am your worst nightmare. Please, resist and wait for someone better."

A sudden swell of power stole my breath. It rose within me, caught by my animal and held. More came, then more still—so much power, as though the two beasts were working together to create a storm. A rush of energy felt like it ate through my flesh. A command pulsed within me, all around.

Shift.

My animal wrestled me for control, eager to follow the command. Eager to get to his dragon.

No! You heard Nyfain. We can't! I don't know how!

We belong with them. You feel it. We all feel it. If you won't bond him as you ought, then I will push you aside, find my form, and do it for us. I am tired of the games of the two legs. It's time to bond. Stop being a set of saggy balls and help me!

Fire crackled across his skin—actual fire!—and seared across mine. The flame bit down, spreading tiny points of agony all over, Nyfain's dragon clearly helping push the issue.

My vision blackened further. My head grew light. With the dragon's help, my animal was winning. She was internally clawing me out of the way.

"You'll kill her!" Nyfain yelled. "You must stop!"

My bones twisted, dragging a strangled cry from my lips. My skin grew tight, itchy, like I needed to shed it. My animal pushed forward, growing in power, in might. She was preparing to shift, regardless of the danger to us.

Our beasts would not be sated unless they had this. Unless they had each other. They were forcing our hand. My beast was trying to break out of her cage to get to his dragon, who was helping her along.

If I was going to lose control, I'd rather do it sexually than face a shift I wasn't ready for.

I captured his lips in a rush and then roped my arm around his neck, squeezing tight. He groaned, and the dam burst.

He moved me easily, holding my weight with one arm while he used the other hand to cup the side of my face. He opened my mouth with his and then thrust his tongue in, sweeping it through. I wrestled my tongue with his, sucking a little, being sucked, the kiss taking me to a place that I'd never been before. I'd been kissed many times. Kissed well a few times, especially by him. But I'd never been kissed like this. It had never felt so deep. So consuming. Like my whole world was wrapped up into this one moment.

Electric currents sizzled across my heated flesh. Our joined heart sped up, pumping power into me, and then him, back and forth. Euphoria followed. My animal purred in delight. I felt the dragon's growl of dominance.

I ripped my head back and grabbed his chin roughly, looking into those glowing, smoldering golden eyes.

"Fuck me," I said, and fire blistered through me, turning it into a command.

A smirk pulled at his lips, and I could feel a shift in the energy around us. His dragon rose to the surface; I could feel it. His power surged and sparked, coiled and dangerous. My animal pushed forward as well, ready to meet it. I'd apparently issued a challenge, and his dragon would take it to the extreme.

Unexpected nervousness stole through me. A tremor of fear lodged in my middle. Suddenly it felt like my first time, a monumental occasion. My body trembled within the sheer force of his overwhelming masculine intensity. I wasn't sure I was ready for this. I was tired of resisting them, yes, and I wanted Nyfain more than I could express. But this was more than just sex... It was a game of the gods, and I wasn't sure I had the power to play.

"You can do better than that." His voice was rougher than usual. Excited. Dominating.

The dragon has come out to play, my animal thought, full of excited anticipation. *Let me handle this.*

Tingles worked over my flesh. Internally, I stepped aside and let my animal take the lead. This wasn't my moment. Nyfain's either. Something told me we'd have our own moment of truth, and our beasts' dalliance would fuel the fire.

Nyfain wouldn't be happy this had come to pass. Given his penchant for rotten moods, he'd likely take it out on me, but I'd cross that bridge when I came to it. Right now, two beasts were preparing to fight, and Nyfain's and my bodies were their battlefield. The first to an orgasm would win.

My animal intended to own that prize.

CHAPTER 6

"LISTEN HERE, SIR Alpha," she said in a husky voice dripping sensuality. Lust curled through our insides, throbbing warmth in our core. "You're *mine*," she purred. "So when I need that big cock in my greedy little cunt, I intend to get it." Our power gushed. This time, she put it all into her command. "Fuck me, dragon. *Now*."

Tell him to be gentle, I pleaded quickly. I'd thought I'd wanted it hard and fast, but now, faced with his size and strength, his enormous dick...I was chickening out. It was a moment of cowardice, I couldn't deny it. *Tell him to be easy. He's huge, and my ex was definitely not. I'll need to work up to it.*

There is no gentle in battle. We'll take it rough and brutal, and we'll say thank you when he destroys us with pleasure.

What the fuck is wrong with you?

All the best things. Hang on tight—it's about to get crazy.

He growled, his eyes hooded, sparking. "As you command."

He snatched our hair and ripped our head back, taking our lips in a bruising, dominating kiss. Excitement punched through us. He forced his tongue into our mouth and swept it through. His taste fizzed within our senses, decadent and delicious.

He dropped the sword before letting go of our legs and shoving us. She staggered back, about to fall, and then our back hit the nearest tree. She sucked in a startled but excited breath, and our pussy throbbed so badly that she wanted to slink down to the ground, open our legs, and beg him to ravish us.

Fear wormed through my gut at how rough this was starting. How out of control it seemed. But my animal was completely in her element. I'd never felt this sort of arousal pumping through us. It was raw and primal, completely devoid of thought and social niceties. It didn't rely on mutual respect or feelings or hearts or flowers. It was two beings utterly lost to their need for each other, and not giving a shit about anything in the world except how best to express it. They wanted to fuck, hard and long and without barriers. Without safe words. Without saying die. They wanted to take each other to the extreme and see who could stick it out.

And I was just a passenger. So was Nyfain.

I could either be traumatized by the whole thing, or get behind it and experience it for what it was—carnal, passionate, world-ending sex that would likely leave me a sore, hobbling mess in the morning. So be it.

The dragon in Nyfain's skin prowled toward us slowly, his movements sleek and agile. His broad shoulders swung with each step, his magnificent display of muscle tightening and loosening as he moved. His power pulsed in heady, dense waves that caressed our skin and turned our bones to liquid.

"Yes, alpha," my animal said, our voice wanton. "Take what is yours."

He closed the distance, taking his time. With only about a foot between us, he looked down at my clothes. He traced the line of buttons down our front and then dipped his finger in one of the holes. He ripped down little by little, popping off buttons. He pushed the fabric away and ran his fingers across the top of the waistline, dipping in just a little and tracing it around, identifying what belonged to him.

With a fast movement my animal wasn't expecting, he grabbed the top of my shirt and tore it the rest of the way. The rest of the buttons popped off. The shirt gaped open. He slowed down again, leaving us gasping for air, our chest heaving against the binding.

He pushed the fabric off our shoulders and down, throwing it to the side as though the garment was beneath us. As though a creature of our stature should only wear finery or nothing at all.

He traced a finger across my binding, finding a nipple and circling it slowly. With his other hand, he pulled the strip of leather on my sword belt taut before loosening it and letting it drop where it lay. Then he grabbed the middle of the binding and ripped it down. Fabric screamed. Seams tore. Our breasts tumbled out, bared to the night air. The chill immediately hardened our sensitive nipples, on display.

A growl of approval rumbled deep in his chest. The effect sent a thrill of pleasure slithering across our heated flesh.

He bent as he unbuttoned my pants, slanting his tongue across a nipple. He enveloped it in his mouth and sucked. A shock of pleasure teased a moan from our parted lips.

He undid the zipper and pushed my pants down, following them to our ankles before sliding them off with my shoes.

He fell to his knees and flung one of our knees over his shoulder. He tasted our inner thigh, licking gently, then skimmed his lips across our wanton flesh, stopping near our apex to harshly suck in sensitive skin.

Her hiss turned into a moan as his fingertip traced down our panty-clad center, morphing the feeling into pleasure. She clutched the tree with our nails.

He curled his fingers under the strip of fabric covering our pussy. With a harsh movement, he yanked it away. Fabric tore. He tossed it aside. His mouth worked inward, his tongue licking just beside our folds before he moved to our center and inhaled deeply.

What is he doing? I thought, the equivalent of a whisper.

He's savoring the scent of our arousal. Just shh *and enjoy it.*

I internally grimaced, trying not to get weirded out by the animality of it, and then mentally took a deep breath and sank back into the moment.

His tongue delved through our slick folds. Our body jolted like we'd been struck by lightning.

Her moan of delight rippled through us. He licked and tasted his way up to our clit before sucking it in, pulsing the suction. His fingers trailed along the inside of our thigh before finding our entrance and dipping inside, still exploring, now figuring out what made us tick.

This. This fucking made us tick. Her, me, it didn't

matter. This would make anyone tick!

She groaned and pushed our pussy harder into his face, but he backed off, looking up at us with a devilish smile. He made three *tsk*ing noises consecutively, telling her not to be so eager. He'd fuck us when he was ready.

My animal was deciphering all of this, of course. Reading his body language, understanding his unspoken assertions. I was just along for the ride. So far the ride was fucking amazing, and we hadn't even done anything yet.

He sucked harder, still pulsing. His fingers plunged through our wetness, hitting the exact right spot. She melted against the tree, groaning and tilting our head back. Those fingers. Those glorious fingers. We built quickly, breathing hard as our body gyrated against his mouth.

He stopped sucking and worked his tongue with broad, thick strokes. His fingers picked up intensity, his knuckles pounding against our folds. Our body tightened now, gulping for air as pleasure filled us like a vessel—caged, boiling, building, ready to explode.

He pulled his fingers out and backed off, that devilish look back. The rim of that wicked mouth shiny with our juices.

She whimpered in displeasure. We'd been right on the edge. Another couple seconds, and we would've found the goal line.

He pushed our knee off his shoulder and rose gracefully. With a large, scarred hand, he grabbed our shoulder and spun us before shoving. We fell forward, palms against the rough bark. His fingers whispered across our back and then the remnants of my binding fell loose, dropping to our feet. His fingers now spread across our skin, starting from our shoulders and kneading down to our waist. His lips followed, skimming, as though he were trying to familiarize himself with every single inch of our body.

His touch, his attentions, his slow movements and silence—the sensuality of this moment was like nothing I'd ever experienced. I was in rapture to see what would happen next, quaking with fear because of his ability for unbridled brutality, and anticipating the pleasure I knew we'd find inside of it.

His palm flattened against the center of our back, and he pushed, bending us farther forward. His lips skimmed lower, kissing and licking down each cheek before moving in. He spread our cheeks then, and his tongue traced along the outside of our asshole before feathering in the middle. Our mouth dropped open with these unexpected sensations, strangely ticklish and erotic. He prodded a bit, wetting the area, before dipping to taste our folds again. His thumb didn't leave that other hole, though, applying pressure before dipping in, a strange yet not unpleasant feeling, hinting at a level of fullness that we might hate or love, depending on the player.

He kissed our thighs, back to our cheeks, and rose behind us, two of his fingers dipping into our pussy and pumping. He added another finger, stretching to the point of pain. He pushed up harder, getting us ready. He seemed to realize he wouldn't easily fit, though. Not right away.

"Turn," he barked.

She made a sound like "Oohhhmmm," as the force of that command ripped through us. It danced on our nerve endings and whispered across our flesh.

I wanted to say, "Yes, sir," but thankfully she wouldn't let me. I was not in my right mind anymore. He'd blotted out reality and created his own world where he was the god and I was happy to learn how to worship him. Thank the goddess for my animal, who knew how to play these games without losing herself to them.

We stood naked before him, our six feet dwarfed by his size, his height a head taller and his breadth not even comparable. His frame rippled with muscle, hard-won from and continually conditioned by his nightly battles. His gaze roamed down our body, unhurried. He lightly traced each scar he found, old wounds too intimately placed for me to ask Hannon to treat them.

His head cocked to the side and his eyes drifted away, like he was listening. "I will take the time I need and no more. If demons followed her, we'll deal with them easily. Now shut up and let me get acquainted with my goddess. You've had all the fun. Without them able to shift, I have been left in the dark."

His focus back on us, he traced the little cleft in our chin with his thumb before running it along our jaw. He looked at our lips, the tiny freckles I knew were splashed across our cheeks, and then lingered on our blue eyes. Something in our middle stirred within that intense, focused gaze. It was like he was reaching through a window and peering down into our soul, shedding light on all the dark places and weighing what he found. In a moment his lips tilted upward, and pride lit his golden gaze.

"You are truly a remarkable specimen, Finley. The goddess sang when she made you. You are perfect in every way. You will never want for a home or protection. We will provide it, always. This I swear. The man has his own agenda, but it will never come between me and my oath to you."

He bent forward and kissed us lightly on the lips, an oath sealed.

"Now," he said when he pulled back. "Drop down to your knees. I want to see how deeply you can take my cock."

Excitement flurried within her, and a little bit of fear fanned higher within me.

We lowered gracefully to the ground, our hands sliding down his large thighs and then up, cupping his balls and taking his large cock in hand. He bent his knees a little, to make sure we weren't straining to reach, and then ran his fingers along our temple before tangling them in our hair.

This time my excitement matched my animal's, with no reservations. I'd done this before. I'd taken his monstrous cock all the way in and chin-bumped his balls. I'd liked the rough treatment. I'd known I could handle it.

Bring on the face fucking—I was all in. Which was good, since I wasn't actually the one in control.

She licked around the tip and flicked our tongue across the slit, lifting the precum and swallowing it down. He groaned in approval. She sucked in the tip as she massaged his balls, swirling our tongue around the tip again as she backed off. Then she blew softly, the opposite of what he was surely expecting.

His body went taut. That mighty form stood above us, hands in our hair, braced to fuck, one solid wall of muscle. His fingers slowly gripped, a hard, immovable hold, taking our face prisoner. His hips inched forward a little, rubbing against our closed lips.

"Hmm, yes," he breathed as she let him in oh so slowly, building up the anticipation, and then squeezing his balls tightly for some reason to make him suck in a pained breath and back off. His chuckle was dark and approving. "My alpha," he said. "My princess."

He wasn't using the name the way Nyfain the man used to, with condescension. The dragon's tone was reverent.

He pushed in harder, though she slightly resisted, forcing his way in, scraped by our teeth for his efforts. He must've known it would happen but obviously didn't care. He growled with feeling but didn't stop, hitting the back of our throat. She squeezed his balls, then twisted to force him back out.

"Fuck," he bit out.

What the fuck are you two doing? I said, bewildered. *You want to suck his dick. We both do. Why are you biting and twisting his balls? This is weird.*

It is a dance. He wants the pain. Because of his cock size and your relative inexperience, he knows he'll hurt us when he penetrates our pussy. He doesn't plan to give any pain that he won't readily take himself, my animal explained, and given what he was forcing on himself, that didn't make me feel any better. *He is a dragon of honor. We've chosen well.*

What's this we *stuff? I didn't choose a damn thing.*

Don't be dumb.

I intended to keep arguing, but the dragon pumped forward again, his cock scraping down through our teeth to the back of our throat. My animal still didn't let him through, backing him off again, sucking as she did. I watched in horror as she twisted his balls in a hard grip. Most men would've started singing in soprano, but he kept on, taking it.

He released the pressure on our head, giving us a chance to do this properly *(finally, for fuck's sake!)*. She took the base of his cock and sucked him down, massaging his balls instead of cutting off his baby supply. He hit the back of our throat, and she loosened up, gagging around that huge cock and continuing on anyway. Out and back she took him, getting into the rhythm. Feeling our lust rise as his sounds of pleasure drifted down around us.

She pulled our hands off his cock and balls and ran them up his outer thighs before curving around to grab his muscular butt. I didn't need to speak shifter to know what that meant. I geared up for it, excitement and desire running through me, remembering doing this with Nyfain. Remembering how much I fucking loved drawing out his pleasure.

He growled and slammed his hips forward. She clutched his ass, taking his onslaught deep. He pulled out as she sucked, then drove in again, picking up the pace. He angled our head and thrust downward, his balls slapping against our chin. Tears dripped from our eyes as she worked, sucking and gagging and owning his cock, knowing at any moment she could clamp our teeth down and severely ruin his life.

His pelvis crashed against our face as he fucked our mouth with hard, greedy thrusts. She reached down with one hand and fingered our pussy, adding to the pleasure of the rough, dominating treatment.

With a snarl, he ripped himself away, breathing heavily, the tip of his dick leaking just a little. He'd gone to the edge and stopped, tit for tat. He'd done it to us, and so he'd accepted the hardship for himself as well.

"Stand," he growled, still breathing hard, his fists clenched. He gritted his teeth, clearly fighting for control so that he didn't come.

She rose just as gracefully as she'd lowered, slinky and sexy. Our breasts jutted, eager to be licked and sucked. Our fingers still played between our thighs, rubbing our clit and eliciting soft moans.

He took a step forward and ripped our hand away. "If you need pleasure, you come to me. I will make sure you are sated and happy at all times."

Yeah, right, as if that's feasible, I thought as arousal licked higher.

Just go with it. The dragon is trying to figure out his duty to us. The man will sort all that out. Let's just agree with everything so I can get that big cock in me.

He stepped closer still, his fingers taking over for hers, rubbing at exactly the right firmness and speed. Exactly like she'd been doing.

I'm now on board for hoping it's feasible... I thought desperately, sinking into the decadence of his ministrations.

He bent and kissed our lips softly, his fingers moving to our wetness and pushing inside, stroking as his thumb moved against our clit. She whimpered, running our hands up his arms and over his shoulders. He angled his head and deepened the kiss, his tongue thrusting in time with his fingers. His thumb moving.

She tightened her hold around his neck. Stood on tiptoes to get more of that kiss. Our toes curled within the divine sensation; we were lost to the feel of his lips. His fingers. His heat. I wished Nyfain and I were in charge, not our animals. I wanted to take him like this, to lose myself in his body. I didn't care about the consequences right now. Our stations hadn't changed, but right now I didn't care about being a royal side piece. I doubted either of us would ever get a chance to settle down with someone else anyway. My fate would likely be dark, as would his. I wanted a little slice of light before the world started burning.

Something in our middle clicked, like a key turning in a lock. It tugged before sending a shot of hot magma running from him to us. It thrummed within us, and she closed our eyes in utter ecstasy.

His kiss deepened still. One hand gripped the back of our neck and the other moved from between our legs and smoothed down our back and to our butt, pulling us against his hard cock. He ground into us, no room between our bodies for us to grab it and stroke. He walked us backward toward the tree, his lower hand slipping down and cupping our cunt before lifting, two of his fingers dipping inside as he hoisted us up to his waist.

"Such a dainty little thing," he murmured against our lips, and it was the first time in my entire life I'd ever been called that.

He rammed our back against the tree before leaning in. The bark scratched, fading into the background as his fingers rubbed.

"You're so fucking wet." He reached farther, getting our clit and massaging, his kiss dominating.

She groaned into his mouth. Rolled our hips against

him.

"Fuck me, Nyfain," we said, her or I, I didn't know. It didn't matter anymore. I was on board with this, and I no longer cared who was leading the charge. It might hurt at first, but he had shown he wouldn't take it for granted. "Fuck me, *now*," my animal said.

"As you command," he said.

He pulled back, dragging that dull tip through our slick folds. His tongue thrust between our lips as he rocked his hips.

My world stopped turning as his plunge seared into our wet depths. The dull ache competed with the explosion of pleasure. He stretched us full until we couldn't take any more, not able for his size.

She gripped his shoulders to stop him for a moment, whimpering with the onslaught. All the sensations around us heightened. The rough bark rubbing against our back, his smooth hips under our knees, our tingling lips swollen from his kisses, and the soft, chilled night moving around us. Our body became pliant, our arms looping around his neck.

"You need to take more of me," he growled, pulling out before thrusting again, working in deeper. "Take all of me, my princess. Take it all."

Our eyes fluttered closed as she let our head fall back against the tree, relaxing around him. Willing our body to accept his size.

He reached between us and massaged our clit, small movements now, pushing in deeper. Unsatisfied until we'd taken all he had to give and then some. The dull, burning ache morphed into a building pleasure. He kept going, working faster now, working deeper. Nearly fully sheathed.

"That's right, princess." He leaned forward, pushing us harder against the tree. His hips moved rhythmically now, rocking forward in steady, firm thrusts. He caged us in, keeping our body put. We couldn't get away from the burning, delicious onslaught. We didn't try. "Take it all."

He held us tightly as he gave one last hard thrust. She cried out, squeezing our eyes shut against the pain.

"There you go," he cooed, pulling us away from the tree and lowering to the ground. He sat, firmly lodged within us and cradling us on his lap, our legs to either side. He held our face in his hands, gazing into our eyes. "Are you ready?"

My animal purred and rolled in anticipation, and suddenly I knew what he meant. He was asking if she was ready to be claimed by the dragon.

No, no, no, no! I shouted at her. I clawed at her, trying to yank her away. Trying to stop it.

A smile curled his lips. "The man does not want us

to do this, my princess. What do you think?"

"Neither does the woman. Very short-sighted, then, to leave us in charge of their skin…"

Nyfain—the dragon—laughed darkly. "Yes, I think you're right. But I do not wish to break her trust in you. You are newly experiencing each other in troubled times. It would be wrong to damage your soul-bond as it is forming. Besides, it will be much more explosive when they agree to it as well. Maybe we'll wait until they are further along. We have extended the soul-bond into the foursome. That is enough for now, don't you agree?"

She made a disgruntled sound, and he nuzzled our neck. He kissed and sucked gently, tickling and enticing, working her back into a good mood and me into some sort of fervor I didn't understand. Our body was so hot that I could barely stand it. Our pulse raced, shared with Nyfain and his dragon. The strong connection in our chest—apparently that was the soul-bond—pumped power and euphoria and pleasure, making me want to smile so big it cracked my face. His cock burned within us but in the best of ways, deep and raw and consuming.

"You are mine," the dragon told us. "Nothing will change that. The two legs will come around. They'll have to. I'll want to be in you every chance I get, and I'll force the issue if the man won't agree."

She made a pleased sound, and he kissed us, deepening it until it stole all our focus and made the world drop away around us.

"How is the ache?" he asked. "Subdued? It is taking all my power to keep from pounding into that tight little cunt."

"Since you won't claim me..." She rose slowly, dragging his cock out of our pussy and wrapping our arms around his shoulders. He shuddered and groaned, his hands splayed across our back. "Does that mean I can join the sex parties and fuck everyone in the castle?"

He yanked our hair and thrust upward from the ground, banging that cock back fully inside of us before dragging us back down to sit firmly on his lap again. The tightness sent shivering pleasure racing across our heated flesh. Our eyes fluttered closed, and she moaned.

"Only if you want a trail of dead bodies in your wake."

"Hmm," she said with pleasure, and I was torn between wanting to claw my control back so they wouldn't keep inciting each other and doing nothing so that they *would* keep inciting each other. It felt fucking amazing having him inside of me. It felt better than I could've possibly (and had) imagined.

She moved our hips in a circle and then lowered

back down, grinding down onto him. Back up, nice and slow, and down, working him in until all the ache was gone.

He leaned back on his hands, eyes closed, breathing deeply.

"What are you doing?" Our voice was husky.

"I am hanging on to every spare shred of control that I possess while you play and get comfortable. It is not easy. You feel so good, my princess. So good. I have been waiting my whole life for you. Use me. Use me however you want. Take what you need from me. I will stay strong until you are ready to get destroyed by my cock."

She smiled with his rough words, liking it. Liking how he mixed sex with violence, violence with gentle words and pet names. It was like his torso, cut up with scars and inked with tattoos. It didn't diminish the perfectly sculpted abs and mouth-watering pecs. If anything, it made the whole package hotter.

She traced a nipple with our thumb and slowly rose, our body loose and tight at the same time. Coiling but languid. New points of pleasure sparked and then soaked in, building. Ever building, but slowly. Thankfully, my animal had listened to me, and she was warming us up. Or maybe she realized with the first thrust that we weren't ready to be pounded yet. We weren't ready to let the alpha out of his cage and see what destruction he could do. After he was done, I knew we'd be sore as fuck for a while. We needed to do the delicate work now.

She rolled our hips while massaging our clit. Liking the feeling, she slowly rocked back and forth, working him inside of us. Feeling the brutal torment of teasing up the gloriously slow build.

He moaned softly. "Yes," he breathed out. His whole body was flexed, his legs shaking. We were driving him to the brink.

My animal grinned wickedly.

Shit. Here came the games.

"Because of all the stress to get you inside of me," she purred, rocking forward and massaging our clit, "I'm going to come on your cock, and you're just going to sit there and take it."

He laughed softly, his abs shaking. She traced them with our fingertips.

"I take it back," he murmured. "It wasn't the goddess who made you—it was her evil twin."

"Watch me, Nyfain."

His eyes opened slowly, hooded and soaked with lust. They slid down our front, taking in every inch. Every detail. His gaze lingered on our fingers massaging our clit and our hips rolling slowly, taking him in deep before releasing him. His cock shone with our wetness, disappearing once again into our tightly stretched pussy.

He sucked in a tortured breath. His fingers curled into fists.

"I can't... I..." His jaw clenched, and my animal laughed, delighted.

"Ladies go first. Didn't the man tell you? He must've learned that from the books he just read."

He groaned and squeezed his eyes shut, rolling his head. His hips bucked, searing into us. Pleasure blistered. We moaned, running our hands down our front and lightly pinching our sensitive nipples.

"Watch me, Nyfain," she whispered. "I like when you watch me."

"Fuck," he murmured, glowing eyes blinking back open. "You will pay for this."

"I hope so." She smiled languidly, because she held all the power right now.

She worked a nipple as she moved on his cock. Up slowly, tantalizing, then grinding back down. His hips gave little thrusts he clearly couldn't control. We had him on the absolute edge, and it was driving us insane with raw lust.

She breathed hard now, working faster. She rose on his cock and then crashed back down, a tiny bit of pain morphing into the sort of pleasure that couldn't be put into words or sung about in songs. It was pleasure gifted by the goddess for which mortals would endure the trials and tribulations of mundane life. A pleasure the demons tried to mimic and got completely wrong.

"Suck on my nipples, Nyfain," she said, rolling and bucking, massaging our clit. The pressure was incredible, filling every inch of our body and burning hot in our core. Every sensation pushed us higher. Every movement sent a vibrating blend of incredible bliss rolling through us. "*Now.*"

Nyfain's mouth enveloped our nipple and sucked aggressively. The world slid sideways.

"Oh shit!" She drove down onto him, suddenly out of control. She bucked and labored, on fire with pleasure. She gripped his hair tightly and pushed our breasts at him, holding him to our right nipple. "Bite a little."

His teeth pinched just perfectly. His hands held our waist, his fingers digging into our flesh, trying to hold on for dear life. He'd said he'd stay strong, and she was taking him at his word. Pushing him to see if he'd break. Hoping he didn't.

She rode him hard now, lifting and dropping down with all our weight. The dull ache was back, but fuck, it was glorious. He rolled his tongue around our nipple then bit again.

We exploded with the orgasm, crying out our pleasure. She yanked his head back and kissed him, hard and needy, out of breath. Broken. Everything in us had fractured, and now we needed him to put the pieces back together.

He caught us as we melted around him, boneless and in ecstasy.

He didn't speak for a long moment, and it occurred to me that he was holding his breath. He sucked in air, holding us tightly, obviously still trying for control.

"I have never, in my life," he whispered hoarsely, "received a command that was as hard to follow as that one. You better prepare that little pussy, my evil goddess. I'm about to unload all my frustration."

He yanked our hair back and thrust with all the force and power that we knew he was capable of. His cock slammed home. We cried out, not expecting the delicious brutality—and liking it.

His hips crashed against ours. He rolled us, his arms around us to stop our back from grinding into the hard dirt. He rammed his hips forward mercilessly, pounding his cock into our body. His kiss tore us away from this world and thrust us into a different plane altogether, where the only thing that existed was his presence. A dozen hard, brutal plunges, and he was up again, swinging us around.

She clung on for dear life, stretched around him, trapped in his arms. He slammed us against a smooth-barked tree, pulled out, spun us around, and shoved us forward. Our palms slapped the tree trunk. She barely had enough time to suck in a startled breath before he thrust again from behind. His cock pushed deeper into our hot depths, hitting new heights. She cried out, full beyond belief. We couldn't take all of him. We couldn't take all of this.

"Nyfain…" my animal whimpered.

This was a terrible time for me to say, "I told you so."

He yanked us back by our hair and licked along the shell of our ear. We shivered, bearing down against the onslaught. Struggling to hang on.

"Fight back," he growled. "Use me."

I had no idea what he meant.

My animal didn't need to be told twice.

Fire roared through our veins. Power pulsed, her sucking it from him, then pulsed harder, fueling us. Invigorating us. The pain dimmed. His hard thrusting wasn't so overwhelming. She pushed back onto it. His skin slapped ours. Our harried breathing echoed each other. The connection within us sparked and boiled, turning to flame. It burned hotly, and within it, we could feel the dragon and the man's longing for us.

Their desire. There was something else, too. It was so strong and potent that I couldn't even put a name to it. It vibrated within their whole being, like a heartbeat that took up ninety percent of their body. The dragon might be expressing his desire for us, body and soul, but the man felt it as well. If I'd had any doubt, that feeling would've put it to rest.

He kept at it like a rutting animal, completely without reason. Without thought. He pounded our cunt, claiming ownership in action if not in title. He slid in easily now that we were so wet, the sound of our rough sex slick and wild.

I fucking loved it.

She shoved off against the tree, still in control of our body, knocking him back. She stepped forward and off his cock and turned, launching at him. He caught us without skipping a beat, and she wrapped our legs around his middle. He growled his approval, an ass cheek in each of his large hands, and moved us up and down his cock.

She raked our fingers down the sides of his back, over the scars from his wings. He hissed, gripping us tightly, falling with us against the tree. Our back hit, and she reached around and gripped the trunk to keep from sliding down to the ground. He pulled his arms from around us and braced them against the trunk. His chuckle was dark and vicious.

"Well done, my princess. It takes an alpha to know an alpha. The divine goddess has chosen well. Do it again. *Harder*."

She raked our fingers down his scars again, using nails this time. His tortured groan set our core to blazing, my animal loving pushing him to his limits. His cock worked us. His hipbones would leave bruises on our battered flesh.

She left our fingers against that sensitive area and kissed him, the world going taut between us. Our body was so keyed up we couldn't stand it. It was too much. The battering. The incredible pleasure without release. The—

She cried out our climax, the waves of bliss vibrating through us, leaving us utterly speechless. The orgasm lasted and lasted, wave after intense wave hammering us with exquisite pleasure. He groaned and shuddered, emptying inside us, giving a few final thrusts as he came.

He fell forward, breathing the same air. He put his hand behind our head and kissed us, delicious and full of feeling. Our new bond sparkled between us, between *all* of us, and we could feel his supreme satisfaction.

"That was incredible," he said softly, not pulling out yet. He crushed us to the tree, and we didn't mind.

He put his hand against our cheek, his gaze delving into ours.

"I have to allow the man his skin back. He is eager to attend to business. I will see you again, my princess," he said reverently. "One day I will help you through your first shift, and I will finally get to see you in your true form."

His eyes fluttered, closing for a moment. When they opened, the pupils contracted. Anger.

Nyfain was back.

That's my cue, my animal thought. *Enjoy the fallout.*

It felt like I was putting on a skin suit as I stepped back into the ownership role. The world tilted and righted, and Nyfain's cock was still inside of me. His chest brushing against my nipples. His heat bracketing my skin.

His eyebrows sank, and he pulled his hand away from my face. Without a word, he pushed off the tree, yanking his body from mine and leaving behind a feeling of emptiness.

CHAPTER 7

H E PAUSED AS he turned, almost looking back, and I wondered if he'd felt it too. Or maybe he was feeling my turbulent emotions with what I knew was coming, given that I'd liked what we'd done. I'd liked giving in to the rush, as crazy as it had been. I liked his body filling mine.

Then again, I wasn't exactly sure I liked the strings attached. I might've disregarded being a side piece a moment ago, but sometimes the mind could ignore crazy things when she needed to get a little ass. And his moods weren't amazing...

"Get your stuff," Nyfain barked. "We need to move. We've wasted too much time."

I could hear the seething anger writhing beneath his words.

"What was I supposed to do, lose control of her and

let her shift?" I demanded, grabbing my ruined slip of panties. Those wouldn't do anyone any good. Looked like I'd be going commando.

He didn't comment, waiting for me to grab my pants. I paused when I had them in my hand, though, looking down at my legs. His release mixed with a tiny bit of blood trailed down my inner thigh. *Ugh.* I hated the cleanup. Women got the short end of the stick when it came to this stuff.

I tramped into the brush and found the largest leaves available. They'd have to do. It would've been nice if he had some clothes I could steal, but given he'd clearly gotten here in his dragon form, he was rocking the skin suit.

"Are you drinking the tea to ward off pregnancy?" he asked gruffly, having noticed what I was doing.

"I haven't slept with anyone in a while. So no. It doesn't matter, though, does it? When I was first at the castle, Hadriel said you can only knock up your true mate, and true mates have to be the same animal. Not to mention they're rare. We're good."

"The curse has many hidden features, and no one understands them all. My father didn't even understand them all. He slipped into a brain fever shortly after my mom died. The demon king preyed upon him when he was weak, twisting their dealings. Or so I was told. I was not here at that time. To hear tell, it was a time of great confusion after my mother died." His voice dripped with pain and regret. "It's hard to know what is fact and what is fiction. Regardless, after the curse was laid, the exact details of whatever my father worked out went with him to his grave. I was not strong enough by myself to save him from the magical gag." The demon's curse prevented those who knew the details from sharing them with those who did not. It literally stopped them from breathing if they attempted to speak of it. "There could be hidden facets to the curse that might mean you're susceptible to getting with my child—"

A shock of emotion blasted through the bond, cut off so quickly that I didn't get a chance to figure out what it meant. What he was feeling. I just knew his dragon was suddenly roiling and tearing within the bond, possibly trying to take the skin back.

Strange tingles worked through my body, and a worrying soft heat unfurled within my middle. My animal felt like she was rolling over, purring softly and aching down deep. She was responding to his admission. To his possibly being able to get me with child.

Holy fuck, why the fuck was I feeling longing, too? Was I insane? Before him, I'd mostly resigned myself to a life as a spinster. I was going to fly solo. This new change of pace was not welcome. Not with him, at any rate. Not with our setup and the obvious fact that we could never be together! I had enough problems without liking the idea of him knocking me up.

I shoved away the thought and let logic reign. He was clearly just playing it safe, or possibly freaking out a little because he'd just banged after a long streak of celibacy. Unlike the rest of the (very promiscuous) castle, he clearly hadn't adjusted to the idea of his coming no longer directly relating to babies.

It just didn't stand to reason that he could knock up any old person. He was part of the magic that affected the castle, and I knew from before that none of them could get pregnant. The women didn't have their periods and the men's swimmers didn't work. It would stand to reason that he would need a fated paring to beat the curse. Some things were stronger than magic.

"When we get back to the castle," he said, "I'll have Hadriel give you the tea. Take it all month, just in case. I don't intend to take any chances with you."

His hard stare said he wasn't just talking about pregnancy anymore. Regardless, if it would get him off my back, fine. It wasn't the best-tasting tea, but it had to be better than this rotten mood.

His words before all that struck me, though. His pain. His regret.

The breath went out of me for what he must have suffered. He'd lost his mother, someone he'd been close to, and then watched his father die, unable to help him. I knew exactly the kind of stain that left on the soul. We shared that bitter agony within our pasts.

I gulped. I'd never heard those details about the mad king. About the brain fever or how he'd died. I was too young to know the confusion Nyfain was speaking of. One thing I did believe, though, was that the demon king would prey on the weak. His minions certainly loved to, at any rate.

I smoothed my hair, thinking about where I'd need to go. "Is there any other choice for me other than going back to the castle?"

He turned his back. "You had a demon chasing you. I assume you were on your way to the birch?"

"No, actually. I was luring her into the wood so that I could kill her." I pulled on the binding, much looser now than before. It would work, though. Kinda. At least it would keep my breasts covered. I tied my ruined, gaping shirt into a knot at my waist.

"Then what were you doing?"

"Killing her softly."

I quickly told him about my interactions with the demons tonight, including what the woman had said regarding the demon king.

He shook his head as I affixed the belt and then grabbed the sword. The blade was still bloody, so I went to use my ruined panties to wipe it off.

"Stop."

I froze at the bark of command.

Nyfain walked over and grabbed the panties out of my hand.

"Despite what our beasts just did, and what they want, I will not fuck you, Finley. I will not claim you. I can't help what just happened, and I know that you can't either, but this is where it ends." A nerve in his jaw jumped. "That being said, I won't take you for a fool and pretend that I won't be dreaming of that precious little cunt wrapped around my cock. Or that I won't read the notes in that book you gave me and think of you playing the role of the heroine to my hero. I will dream of that horse ride. So save those panties for me. Don't spoil them with the demon's blood. I'll use them instead of you."

Staring at me, he roughly tucked them into my pants pocket. Clearly if he'd had pants, he would've shoved them into his.

Heat stole through me as I held that troubled, fiery gaze. He'd just laid himself bare, not hiding his desperation for me. Not his animal's...*his*. Giving him my panties...it awakened a strange kind of arousal I couldn't explain. I nodded mutely.

He turned and started walking. "Let's go. When you get too sore to walk, let me know. I'll carry you."

I looked down at my sword as I jogged to catch up. "I think I'm numb right now, actually. Except what do I do with the blood on the tip?"

"We'll use the demon. I want to look at her before we fake your death."

"Fake my death?"

"It'll be a show for your village so the demons there—and that dead man—will think I ended you and them. Of course, it'll only work if Hannon dealt with the other demons."

"We can count on him. He'll probably cut them up and bury them. I had no idea that guy was so hardcore. I feel bad about saying he's bad in crisis situations."

"You'll return to being my captive. The story will be that I found you in the wood and retrieved you. That is, of course, unless the demons at the castle knew their kind were bringing you in. In which case, I'll thank them for flushing you out." He paused for a moment. "I wondered if you would stand out enough that the demons would notice and consult about what to do with you. That's one of the reasons I took you in the first place, to ensure you were under my control and not theirs. I shouldn't have let you go back to your village."

"Why did you?"

He tensed, and a storm of emotions colored our bond. Like a moment ago, they were so jumbled that I couldn't tell what the overall vibe was other than "turbulent."

"I didn't, as you'll recall. You snuck away on your own. I merely tracked you down and saved your life."

"We're going to be pissy now, are we? You're going to turn on the charm like when we first met?"

"I wouldn't want to disappoint you."

"Aren't you used to disappointing people by now?"

I hadn't meant to be so cutting, but I was still dealing with the sharp sting of his rejection. I couldn't help lashing out to cover the confused, hurt emotions.

And then I didn't feel bad at all.

He turned, grabbed me by the collar, and yanked me toward him. I remembered when he'd grabbed me by the throat and reacted in kind, just in case he got any ideas.

I stabbed forward with the sword, aiming for his side. He'd heal.

He swiveled his hips, and the sword slid past. He slapped my hand, and the weapon fell to the ground, utterly useless.

"You were better with that pocketknife." He pulled me in closer, getting right in my face. Imposing. Dominating. "I am used to disappointing people, yes. Which is why I have no problem locking you in the tower when we get home and keeping you there until the demon king eventually comes for you."

Anger boiled through me. I moved my lips, as though I were trying to talk and couldn't. A crease formed between his eyebrows, and he leaned in a little closer so he could hear me, pulling his focus from everything else.

I swung my foot and connected with his already bruised balls.

His left eye squinted, and his face turned red as he wheezed and dropped, letting me go. He landed on his knees and bent over, the muscles rippling across his broad back.

"Do not"—I picked up the sword, thought better of it because it would be embarrassing if he just slapped it away again, and jammed a fist to my hip—"manhandle or threaten me. Look, we fucked. It happened. I enjoyed...most of it. But if you don't want to do that anymore, fine. I'd rather not deal with all the strings attached with you, either. If I'm going back to the castle, though, we're going to have to work together. You need to drop this temper-tantrum bullshit, got it? Try acting like a team player. You're going to need more everlass elixir to help your villages, and I'm here to help. So let's just be acquaintances without all the drama, yes?"

He lay on his knees and forearms with his head down. "What the fuck were those beasts thinking shoving my dick between your teeth and twisting my ballsack? My cock and balls are on fucking fire. Your kick crippled me, I think. How's your pussy?"

This guy's mood could sure pivot.

"Still mostly numb, I think. It's a little sore but not throbbing yet. It's also leaking our combined orgasms. So that's unpleasant for me."

He groaned and dropped his head a little more. "I enjoyed it, too. I've wanted to thrust into you since you left your family to save them and stared me down in the wood. Your fearlessness, your bravery, the feel of your animal, your smell... I wanted to lay you down right there and have my fill."

He pushed painfully to his feet, holding his junk.

"But it's not meant to be," he said.

"I said okay. I hear you."

He nodded. "I'm also a broody bastard. I don't make excuses for it. I wasn't born with charm."

"That didn't need to be said."

"So don't sass me." He grinned a little and looked up at the starry sky. "What sort of mess have we gotten ourselves into?"

"A big one?"

He sighed and nodded, finally looking at me again. His eyes and the bond held remorse. "A big one." He glanced at the sword in my hand. "Why'd you bring that with a demon on your heels if you don't know how to use it?"

"I stupidly thought a sword wouldn't be that much different than a dagger. Or that all you really have to do was stick the pointy end in the creature you're trying to kill."

"That *is* all you have to do. It's just the way in which you do it that matters."

"Yes, thank you. I hadn't figured that out when she easily evaded me and then raked her claws down my arm."

He glanced at the arm in question. "Flesh wound."

"Yeah. It stings. She could've really gored me, but she kept it light."

"She probably thought she had a prize for the demon king. I wonder what that dead man offered as a trade."

I wondered the same thing, and it delighted me that he kept referring to Jedrek as a dead man. Any remorse I might have had about unleashing Nyfain on him had dried up after this stunt. The only problem was that I was wary about siccing the beast on someone so popular in the village. The demons would surely hear about it, and they'd probably tattle to those in the castle. It wouldn't take long before the whole kingdom full of demons knew that Nyfain could now easily slip past the magical barrier and get into the villages. I didn't want to spoil things for him because of a grudge. I'd have to, annoyingly, tell him to let Jedrek be. It wasn't like Jedrek could do anything at this point, anyway. As far as the demons were concerned, Nyfain had ownership of me now.

Nyfain hobbled a little until we reached the demon's lifeless form. He turned her over with his foot and glanced at her face. "I don't recognize her. She's low on the hierarchy. She won't be missed." He picked her up and threw her deep into the brambles as though she were nothing but a stone. "Come on. Time to fake your death. Your family will know it isn't real, correct?"

"Hannon will know, yeah. He told me I couldn't go back. He'll know why we're doing this."

He nodded and backed away from me. Confused, I followed.

"No." He held out his hand. "You stay there. I need room, or I'll crush you. The dragon is very big, remember?"

"You just said 'come on.' How was I supposed to know you're about to change into the thing that just took my second virginity?"

Heat kindled through our bond. He muttered something, but I didn't catch it.

He grew into his massive creature, half as tall as a tree. Dull black scales covered his body like armor. His back sloped down, with longer front legs than back, and a tail ending in wicked spikes. A dragon without wings, ground-bound.

His head bent toward me, mouth open, large teeth staring down at me. Instead of grabbing me in his maw, like before, he inhaled deeply.

"Gross," I muttered with a scowl. "Save that for my animal. We two-legs don't do shit like that."

His teeth clamped over me a little harder than was purely necessary, so I swung and clanged the sword off his armored face. A rumble that sounded suspiciously like a chuckle issued from deep within his chest as he ran toward my village, the branches thwapping me and the wind tossing my hair. In a moment, we were at the edge of the wood. He stopped quickly, and I screamed.

He dropped me to the ground gently and roared—a deep, rumbling, fearsome sound that turned my blood cold and sent a peal of desire working through me. I really needed to sort out my issues involving fear and arousal. He grunted a couple times, snatched me up again, and waited.

I looked out at the quiet village, no candles at all

burning near the edges. Given the disturbance earlier, everyone was lying low.

Nyfain shook me, clamping down a little harder. I squeaked and tried to clang him with the sword again.

He wants you to scream, dummy, my animal thought.

"Then loosen up. I can't breathe," I wheezed, clanging the sword off him again.

The pinch of his teeth lessened, and I tried to ignore the large tongue pushing up against me. Before, it had been touching me in a functional way, shielding me from the sharpest parts of his lower teeth, but now it moved a little, the tip running against my leg.

"Gross. Stop it! It's only okay if you're in the other form."

He's doing it for me, because he knows I can feel it.

"I don't care who he is doing it for—it's gross, and no thank you."

I screamed again, was put down, and listened to his mighty roar echo. A moment later, I was back between his teeth, and we were running in the direction of the birch. Once there, Nyfain changed and caught me as I fell, hugging me close for one solid moment. I thought I heard him inhale, his face in my hair, his thumb stroking my shoulder. My eyes fluttered shut as I soaked the moment in.

And that's not gross? my animal asked.

What?

He just sniffed our head.

No, that's not gross. It's our hair.

It's the hair on our head. The dragon sniffed the hair on our cunt. It's the same thing.

It is not, even remotely, the same thing.

The birch shook to a start and then sashayed in place. "Ugh!" I said, nearing my wits' end.

Nyfain looked at me funny.

I gestured to the birch. "Don't you find that annoying? And my animal is annoying. What's the difference between smelling my head and my…" I pointed at my crotch. "Really? Big difference."

"I'll take smelling your pussy over having my balls twisted any day. Or trying to sheer off my cock skin with your teeth. What the fuck was he trying to prove? He told me to shut up when I asked, then called me a terrible lover."

I let out unexpected laughter. "My animal said that your dragon knew you were going to hurt me because of your size, and he was showing that he would take as much pain as he would give."

He glanced upward as he walked around the birch.

"Ah," he said, bending and reaching into the bush. "That makes sense. Though working into you nice and easy would've been better for everyone instead of scraping my cock and battering the hell out of your almost-virgin pussy."

"I mean…" I cocked a hip in mild embarrassment. "It's just that I wasn't used to your size. I'm definitely not a virgin. I know things."

He laughed as he pulled out a yellow package from the bush. "Reading those books, I am sure you know plenty. More than me." He handed the package off to me, not meeting my eyes. "There's a letter in there, and another book, though I guess you can pick books at your leisure now."

"I thought we had a deal?"

His eyes cut my way. He didn't speak.

"You pick a book for me, and I pick a book for you, right?"

He studied me for a second. "With notes?"

I blew out a breath. "I might need more than notes on yours. I tried to snap that demon's neck, and she just yelped. I should have enough strength, but…"

"How's this?" He took my sword before finding a leafy plant and wiping off the blade. He'd been too pissy to do it earlier. "You write me notes in the books—"

"Or how about on paper so we don't ruin the books?"

"On parchment, then. You write me notes"—he slid

my sword into my sheath—"and I'll teach you how to fight."

My belly fluttered. "Deal. What about pleasuring me?" His eyes darkened. I put up my hands. "Your dragon said that I wasn't allowed to pleasure myself, and that I should go to him for all my pleasuring needs."

"Fat fucking chance," he murmured, stepping around me. "You have fingers. You can take care of that."

"At least I'll have my own space. Since you've claimed my panties, I guess I can admit that I was wet reading your letters. And I had to find places to hide and masturbate outside when writing those notes in that book to you."

"I know. I smelled your sex on the pages," he growled. His power thrummed within me, and desire flooded the bond. "I smelled your arousal near the birch, too. I knew I was the one who'd caused it, and it drove me wild."

"And we can't just have sex without all the claiming because...why?"

He glared at me but didn't answer.

"I mean, look," I continued, walking with him toward the everlass field, still holding the package. "I'm not going to bang any demons or staff. Let's get that straight. I'm good with being a one-man show, and I get that this isn't going anywhere. So why can't we enjoy ourselves? A little good-morning bang-bang never hurt anyone."

He bent to the plants, running his fingers along them, giving them love, while stripping away the shriveling or wilting leaves. I set the package down at the edge of the field and chose the row beside his to help.

"Oh, hey!" I grinned at him. His scowl was in full effect. "I broke your dry spell. My body did, at least. How'd that feel after sixteen years?"

He stepped into a different row, putting more distance between us.

"I'll tell you how I feel," I said, working my way through the plants. "I'm starting to feel awfully sore, and that was weird as fuck, but wow, those orgasms were amazing. And the kisses. And the feel of you inside—"

"Stop talking," he barked, power riding the command.

"Just tell me how it was after sixteen years, and I'll stop. That's all I ask."

"First, those sixteen years feel like one long month of misery. Nothing changes from month to month, and the only thing that changes within the month is the size of the moon and the number of battles. I look back over that time, and it is all a blank. A blur. It's like it never happened. It's like that amount of time is just a wasted black hole in my life."

"Except you stopped aging, right? So after the curse, you should resume life as a twenty-five-year-old."

"I wasn't nearly this tired and jaded when the curse began. And if you'd told me at the time that I could be any more tired and jaded, I wouldn't have believed you."

"So then breaking your dry spell was nothing special."

A pang hit my heart. I hadn't expected to feel sentimental about sex with him. I hadn't thought being his first since the curse would mean anything. But now, hearing that it wasn't exceptional in any way made me feel lesser. Naïve and inexperienced. Because it had blown my mind. As weird as it had been, letting the beasts take charge, it ended up being sensational. I only wished it could've been Nyfain and me, maybe doing the nice and easy approach like he'd suggested. Going slow and sensual, allowing feeling to cradle us as we made love.

I ran my fingers through my hair and straightened. I needed to snap out of it. All of this buildup with him—the foreplay and the letters and the sex—had turned my head. But no good could come of this. I liked the guy, yes, I couldn't deny it, but it wasn't meant to be. There'd be no forever, no babies, no future. These feelings would need to die on the vine.

"Hey..."

I jumped and spun, fumbling with a sword that was way harder to get out of its sheath than a dagger. The thing got stuck halfway through. I needed a wider arm span or something.

Nyfain glanced down at my efforts, his brow furrowing. He'd snuck up on me. "You really are bad with that."

"Oh, you noticed, did you?" I dropped my hands.

He stood close, his breath dusting my face. He ran his fingers down my jaw and gently cupped my chin.

"It was unconventional," he said. "My dragon has never pushed me aside so completely without shifting. And some things were not at all pleasant..."

"The smelling, right?"

A little grin tweaked his lips. "It was the best sex I've ever had, and I wasn't even in control. It more than broke my dry spell. It ruined me for other women."

"Oh..." I let the word linger, suddenly embarrassed and not sure why. I tried to pull away.

He held me close. "I felt you through the bond just now. I don't want you to think you were—are—

anything other than extraordinary. You and your animal. My dragon wouldn't be this adamant about any other."

"But you still don't want to knock boots even without claiming?"

"No."

"What if it's just a partial claim? Or a claim and a takeback—is that a thing? I'd be in for that."

"No claiming. No fucking. We've satisfied our beasts, and that is enough. I'll have the memory of your touch and the feel of your body, and that has to be enough."

"Why?"

"Because I will have to let you go, and if I give much more of myself, I won't be able to."

CHAPTER 8

"S ERIOUSLY, STOP WITH the tongue," I ground out as the tip of the dragon's tongue prodded my knee. The dulled tips of his teeth bit into my side, highly unpleasant when I wasn't afraid for my life.

Fuchsia streaked the sky. Muted yellows and oranges highlighted the horizon. Dawn was just around the corner, and I was now officially moving into my new home for the foreseeable future. The only way I'd get to leave was if the curse was broken (and war was afoot, since the demon king would be able to kill Nyfain as soon as we were freed) or if I made a deal with the demon king to grant myself a ticket out of here. My fate was not looking so great.

He's just messing with you, my animal said, chuckling. *It wouldn't be our knee he licked if he were serious.*

"Gross. Why can't I just ride on his back like normal people?"

What normal people?

"Well, *me* for a start."

At the edge of the wood, he didn't cross the threshold toward the castle. He veered left instead, putting on a burst of speed and rushing through the trees. We crested a large knoll, and then he climbed a rockface about seven feet high. The land leveled out on top, the trees not growing on such rocky terrain. There he changed, dropping me from the sky. I fell with my eyes closed and hands tucked in, trusting he'd catch me.

Strong arms enveloped me, and Nyfain's familiar smell gave me a little thrill. He held me for a moment, walking toward a little bench at the edge of the rise. Finally, he put me down and took a seat on the bench, just high enough to give us a clear view of the horizon.

I lowered beside him, inhaling the fresh, chilled air.

We sat for a moment in silence as shoots of canary yellow cut through the blues and violets in the sky.

"I often come here after a night of battling," he said, his voice subdued to match the hush of the dawn. "When I'm not hurt too badly."

"Speaking of." I stood and walked around to his back. The four slashes from the attack that nearly killed him had all but faded, leaving nothing but jagged pink lines through his flesh. They looked similar to my arm and legs. "These won't scar if you keep using the healing ointment I gave you. I can make some more, too, if you've run out."

"I've had to have Hadriel or Lena apply it. I wonder if you would do them the favor of taking over…"

He let the words trail off, as though he wasn't sure I'd say yes.

"Of course I will." I slid my hands over his shoulders, giving in to the urge to touch his heated skin, always warm despite the chill.

"You mentioned making more of that nulling elixir. I was able to replicate it—I had to; I didn't want to be thought dense—but it is time-consuming, and time is my most important resource. I wouldn't trust any of the staff with it." He paused. "Truth be told, until they stop fornicating with the demons, I don't want any of them to know about it. I want to keep this from the demons for as long as possible. The demon king would not look favorably on losing one of his torture devices."

"I'll have nothing but time, and after all these years of hustling, I'm incredibly proficient at it. I can make loads. What about the crowded nulling elixir? What can we do about that?"

"Let's distribute the regular stuff first, so the villagers can see how it works. They are not quick to trust. After that, we can sneak you into various areas in the village to see the sickest patients."

I didn't mean to make an *ugh* sound.

He glanced back with an arched eyebrow.

"I'm not a big fan of nursing," I explained, kneading his tense shoulders.

"You nursed me quite thoroughly." His tone held innuendo, and I knew he was thinking about the morning after he took the crowded elixir, plus our encounter in the washing shed that afternoon…

Heat wormed through me. I slid my hands across his shoulders again, stopping one where his shoulder met his neck and continuing to explore with the other, sliding up the front of his throat and applying a little pressure. I made him lean back against my legs, his head just under my breasts. Now I pushed my first hand down and across his delicious pecs, feeling his scars, lingering on a nipple.

"That was different," I murmured.

"How?" he whispered, allowing me to maintain the firm hold on his throat with one hand as I glided a thumb over his nipple before rubbing in a circle.

My core tightened, and I leaned over to run the edge of my tongue along the shell of his ear. Goose-bumps covered his flesh and a shiver ran through his body.

I smiled, my ardor rising. Through the bond, I

could feel him reacting the same way. Not that I needed that hint. His cock was standing at attention. He was not bashful in the least about his body, something I appreciated. I was not bashful in the least about staring at it.

"I don't know how, to be honest." I tightened the arm that was draped down his front, curving closer to his body. I licked and kissed down his jaw line, my core so tight I could barely stand it. "I would say that I cared about you getting better, or that I worried I'd lose you, but I cared about those things with Father, and yet I couldn't bear to be the one nursing him."

"Maybe you could...*bear* it if I died, and so it didn't matter whether you nursed me." He tilted his head a little, his eyes closed, and I noticed his hands gripping the edge of the bench with white knuckles.

He was referring to my spelling mistake in our letters.

He was thinking about my body being bare.

A surge of warmth ran down my inner thighs, the effects of intense arousal and our earlier fucking session. His nostrils flared, and though I knew he wouldn't mention it because of my issues with his pussy-smelling dragon, he was clearly aware of what was happening. A soft growl sounded in his throat, and he turned his head a bit more, angling his lips toward mine.

I kissed the corner of his lips, over his scar. He jerked, as though to pull away, and I tightened my hold on his throat, my fingers digging in a little. It wasn't nearly enough to cut off the air, but it was a firm expression of what I wanted.

I let the kiss linger and then adjusted the angle so I could brush my lips against his.

"That isn't it." I nibbled his lips, tingles washing over me when he gently sucked in my bottom lip. The man was an expert kisser. He could read the tone and match it perfectly, taking me to a place where the only thing I knew was his taste and his touch.

"I do wish it could've been you and me on our first time together, going easy like you said," I whispered, stepping back a little so he would be forced to lean more weight on me.

His words weren't much more than a sigh. "I know. I'm sorry it has to be this way."

I deepened our kiss, my tongue flirting with his. The muscles in his arms flared, and it reminded me of his dragon earlier, lying back and holding on to control so that my animal could play. Could do what she wanted. This time, Nyfain the man was the one holding back. He was allowing me access, but he clearly did not plan to bring things any further.

That was definitely for the best. My pussy ached

with need and soreness both. I needed time to recuper-
ate.

"How's your dick?" I murmured against his lips.

"Not in need of more teeth, I can assure you. My
balls hurt like a motherfucker."

I chuckled and leaned back to laugh harder. "That
was so weird."

"Yeah. I can think of other signals to back a dick out
of a mouth than corporal punishment."

I kissed his cheek and moved my hand away from
his throat to around his collarbone, hugging him from
behind.

"Like what?" I straddled the bench facing him,
pushing his arm up and around me, letting me in closer
to his body.

His hand landed on the top of my butt, and his arm
constricted, making me scoot closer still. I threaded a
leg between his knees and angled a bit so that our sides
were nearly touching. He slanted his face down to mine,
his gaze on my lips.

"Like the sounds of her—"

"Me. We're talking about me."

"The sounds of *someone*..." He smiled, and my
heart fluttered. "The sounds of you gagging, for a start."

"I gagged with the blowjob in the wash shed and
you didn't seem to notice."

He leaned down quickly and captured my lips, sucking before thrusting his tongue in. I moaned into his mouth.

"Fuck," he breathed, backing off with tightly closed eyes. His entire body tensed, his muscle flaring. His fingertips dug into my back. "I don't think I'm strong enough for this."

"It's okay." I straightened up and reached around, hooking one arm around his neck and the other hand on his opposite cheek, pulling his face back to me. "I'm getting really sore now. I won't be trying to swindle sex."

Eyes still squeezed shut, body taut, he let me pull his face back to mine. "I'll nurse you when we get back. It's my turn. I'm going to have to jack off first, though, or I'll explode."

"I can do that for you."

"Please don't use your teeth," he whispered, his lips tweaking into a mouth-watering smirk. "You know, it's considered a challenge when a shifter grabs the throat of another shifter."

"What kind of challenge?"

"A challenge to the death in most cases. If a male grabbed my throat, I'd kill him, no questions asked," he growled. "If a female did it, I'd make sure she never thought to do it again. With you…it's a challenge not to throw you down and fuck the sense out of you."

The violence in his voice, the malice, was like a delicious caress. I remembered his hard thrusts earlier, pounding into us. Telling us to fight back when it became too much. How glorious it had been when we did.

"That's a trigger, then, touching your throat?" I let my hand slip down, firmly tracing the line over his Adam's apple.

His chuckle was dark and promising. "Only you would be turned on by my threats."

"That didn't sound like a threat."

"Only to you, princess. No woman I've ever bedded could or would handle me when I'm in a temper."

"No hate-fucking, then?"

"No. No hate-fucking. Not even with scrappy whores."

I felt my eyebrows lower dramatically. "Don't call them that—they are working like anyone else, regardless of the profession they chose, and they should be respected. And don't mention other women to me again."

Fire lit in his eyes, and approval came through the bond. "As you command," he whispered.

I snuck a kiss, then let it deepen as I moved my hand to fully cover his throat.

K . F . B R E E N E

"I *am* turned on by that threat," I whispered.

He shook his head, keeping his mouth close to mine. "My control is firmly in check right now. No rage-fucking. I'll need to make do with the notes in the book you sent. I like this one much more than the other, by the way. I can picture you on every page."

"But no horse rides."

"If there were a horse ride in that book, it would be"—he brought a hand up and kissed his fingers—"perfection."

"I'm sure you're just being dramatic." I let my hand trail down his chest and leaned over and licked one of his nipples. I sucked in softly as I felt the rolling surface of his abs. "Women before the curse—especially noblewomen—were softer than people are now. Reality now doesn't allow for someone to be that affected by your anger."

He tilted his head back and laughed.

I frowned at him and sat up, running my palm along the inside of his thigh. He slowly spread his knees, allowing me whatever access I wanted.

"What? It doesn't," I said. His smile softened all the harsh lines in his handsome face. "Your staff doesn't count. They have to fear you—you're their boss."

"Women before the curse, especially noblewomen, were some of the most courageous shifters I have ever known. They were not the kind to back down, and yet they still recoiled from my anger."

I rolled my eyes, very lightly touching his balls. Just a graze of my fingers, knowing they were probably as sore as my vagina. She'd put up the white flag.

"You were their prince. They wanted to please you."

"What does that have to do with cowering from my anger, or freezing up when even a little rage soaked between the bedsheets?"

I sucked in a labored breath and closed my eyes, my body suddenly pounding to know what it was like to have rage seep into a hard fucking with Nyfain. To have that level of passion and strength slamming into me. His firm grip in my hair. His dominating touch punishing me with his anger. I'd punish him just as thoroughly until we both climaxed in a heap.

I wrapped my hand around his girth and stroked firmly, reaching the top and smearing the bead of precum over his tip. I tightened my arm around his neck and grabbed his jaw, forcing him to bend farther and kiss me hard. I angled my head the other way, stroking faster, and he moaned into the kiss, his tongue thrusting. Me sucking it in.

He pulled back a little, breathing hard, sharing my breath. "See?" he got out.

"It wouldn't be much different than with your dragon earlier; it would just be us in control."

He pushed forward and bruised me with a kiss as I stroked, faster and faster, wanting his cock in my mouth but wanting his kiss more. I groaned and tugged at him, making him lean closer. He tightened his arm around my back, holding me tightly.

He sucked in a breath before kissing across my jaw and down the side of my throat. I pumped his cock, my grip tight, the desire to fuck so strong it nearly took control. My animal was right near the surface, basking in the sensations. His was there as well, and I could feel him straining to get out, his power searching for my animal. His desperation to be with her again unmistakable, uncompromising.

"Oh goddess, Nyfain," I murmured, squeezing him tightly, stroking. My animal pushed forward. My control wobbled for a brief moment, enough for her to get out, "Bite me!"

His teeth sank into my neck, and a strange thrill sang through me. *Mate,* it seemed to say, pooling hot in my core. Wetness dripped out of my pussy.

"I need to lick your cunt," he growled, standing in a rush and yanking me with him. I had no idea if it was him or the dragon. I did not fucking care.

He tore at my pants in a frenzy. He ripped them down and over my boots. They snagged partway down, but he'd already granted himself plenty of access, so he laid me on the bench and pushed my knees wide, bending between them, licking up my center. I moaned his name and arched, straining up to his mouth. He sucked on my clit before going back to lick and suck my core.

My desire surged. I raked my fingers through his hair, rocking my hips up into his mouth. Knowing our combined releases were on my skin. Knowing he was getting off on it as much as I was. His tongue traveled through my folds, erotically filthy and delicious. His fingers put pressure on my back door. The taboo nature of it threw me into a new place. A place without limits. Without boundaries. A place that was just sex and trust and passion.

"Hmm, yes," I breathed, arching into him.

He pulled his fingers up again and plunged them into my pussy. The ache from earlier vanished. He lapped at my pussy and then sucked on my clit again, hard.

I bucked and cried out, shattering. I pumped against his mouth and shook with my climax. I came long and hard, my whole body locked up and vibrating.

He pushed to standing and leaned over me, bracing his hand behind my head. He lifted me before feeding me his cock. I took to it eagerly, held by him and bobbing on it hungrily. He thrust into my mouth, deeper now, growling with pleasure. Another pump, and he exploded, filling my mouth and throat. I sucked it down greedily, something I'd only done with him.

He pushed back and sat down hard, panting, catching his breath.

"You're so fucking sexy, Finley. It should be outlawed."

I smiled, completely relaxed. "Then what fun would you have?"

He gathered me up into his arms and settled me onto his lap, my pants still stuck over my shoes and now trailing in the dirt.

"I am definitely going to need a cleanup after this," I murmured, resting my head on his shoulder and looking up at the lightening sky.

"You'll get it. I promise. Let's just let the demons go to bed first. I don't want to have to do too much acting when we get back."

"What does that mean?"

He stroked my hair and leaned his head against the top of mine. "We need to act like you're a captive being taken back to your tower prison. Remember when I first brought you in?"

"You were all rage and impatience and annoyance."

"I was going for brutal and ruthless, but yes. You

were…confused and frightened?"

"Confused and…wary."

"Right, of course." He chuckled. "You were not comfortable, we'll put it that way. Things are different now. You know that I mean you no harm."

"Aside from pounding into me when I'm not used to your size."

"Within reason, right. But we need to act the part. You need to seem scared. And, while this is grotesque, probably try to act violated. I've bitten you. My smell is all over you. In you. Your smell is all over me. The higher-powered demons will know that we've had sex. It's best to sell it like I've taken you. Like you mean nothing more to me than a pair of spread thighs."

I curled up closer to him and felt better when his arms tightened around me.

"Which we both know is not true," he whispered against my hair, stroking my cheek with his thumb.

"I played the wilting flower last time. I'm sure I can do it again."

"I'll put on a small show for the staff, but it can be very limited. I'll just throw you over my shoulder and march you up to the tower."

"Really? You're going to lock me in the tower again?"

"No." His voice was a low hum. "I apologized for

that, and I meant it."

"But you said—"

"I said that out of anger. I don't have a very even temper. We were just talking about that. I don't always mean the things I say. You're right to kick me in the nuts when I get out of hand. I'd expect no less. The dragon is proud of it."

"What if the demons wait outside my door, and my animal goads me into going out and trying to kill them?"

"After the display you put on with your sword earlier, I doubt she'd goad you into it. I rather think she'd tell you to hide and wait for me. If you have a dagger..." He shrugged. "I've seen what you can do with a dagger. Or a pocketknife. If you need to kill a demon that is harassing you, then do it. Soon they'll get the picture."

"I didn't bring a dagger."

"We have plenty."

"Why the tower, though? Why not a normal room? I know there must be some. Even one of the rooms reserved for staff."

He took a deep breath. "Two reasons. One, because past rulers built in extensive secret passageways to either spy or bring their lovers to them without being detected. Or, in my father's case, get drunk and accost the staff."

"Ugh," I said.

"Yes, exactly. There were many reasons why I tried to leave, and that is one of them. It didn't happen often, but..." He squeezed me tightly, anger coming through the bond. "The castle has many dark secrets, from my father's reign on back. Power corrupts, even for a species as noble as mine."

"Don't sell yourself short or anything," I mumbled with a smile.

"Anyway, most of the rooms in the castle also have multiple sets of keys. One is held by the room owner, another by the cleaners, and yet another by the head house staff to look in on the underlings...on and on. The only room in that castle that only has two keys and no secret passages is that tower. It is the absolute safest place for you to call home."

I took his hand and threaded my fingers in his. He'd been looking out for me even when he seemed to not care about me.

"And the other reason?"

"I spent a lot of time in it as a child, and then used it as my sanctuary when I got older. I could hide up there for days, and my friends wouldn't know to look for me. It was a prison turned refuge."

"And you hoped my prison would turn into a refuge within the castle?"

His breath fanned over my hair. "Something like that. I'm not sure, Finley. I don't really know what I'm doing anymore. I feel like I'm blundering around in darkness. This half-life has gone on so long. I've latched on to my immediate duty, and anything else…"

He shook his head, and it sounded like he'd cut himself off. I wondered if it was the magical gag.

I let it drop.

"The tower it is. Will I still be able to work that garden? Will that offend you, given it was your mother's?"

He pulled one of his hands from around me and placed it on his chest. "It would honor me. I will tell you what I remember of it, and if you could do something even remotely similar, I'd be forever grateful."

"That's settled, then. I'm going to make that the best garden in the magical kingdom, regardless of whether anyone else sees it or not."

He rubbed my back without comment, acceptance that no one probably ever would. The touch filled me with sadness. He didn't think he'd ever see any kind of salvation. He expected to die in this role without the curse ever being broken. He expected me to try to flee to save myself.

Frustration and anger filled me, but I pushed it away. I wouldn't dwell on any of that right now. I wouldn't let his misguided thoughts on the future affect me. Clearly he needed rescuing. I'd just have to add that to my list of things to do.

He must've felt my turbulent emotions through the bond, because he said softly, "So fierce. You will fight your way to freedom, I know it. It's what your kind does."

"My kind?" I asked, taken aback. "Do you know what my animal is?"

When he shook his head, my stomach sank in disappointment.

"No one will know your animal until you shift and she shows herself to the world," he replied. "Not even she knows what she will become. Right now she is just an essence, waiting to take shape. Waiting to embody her own space without having to fight you for control."

"Do you ever fight your dragon for control when in the dragon form?"

"I did once." His smile was fond. "I wanted to fly. I caused us to fall out of the sky and into a lake. Thankfully, he took over again before we drowned. That was the first and last time. And usually he doesn't step into my skin. It's just... Well, he is not overly fond of how I am handling things with you."

"Because you're a terrible lover, that's why."

"Obviously, yes. You've hit it on the nose."

I laughed, not bothering to look at the changing sky,

as beautiful as it was, nearly full morning now. I traced his chin instead, finding a little scar hidden in the dark reddish-brown stubble.

"I didn't feel it before," I said.

"Feel what?" he asked.

"The bond. I didn't feel your dragon's touch inside of us. Me."

"It was only half realized. Only when both parties agree and establish the bond does it manifest. It's then you feel each other intimately through it. After that, if there is intense love and devotion, the couple imprints, solidifying their bond for life."

"But my animal said she accepted the bond last time."

"But you didn't. I didn't."

"And now?"

He gave me a long look. "You feel it, don't you?"

"Was it you just now, or did he take over again?" I asked.

"Me."

I let my eyes close, and a smile budded on my lips. "My animal pushed me out of the way to ask you to bite me."

"Hmm."

I couldn't tell what that meant, but passion washed through the link.

"Biting is a shifter thing, huh?" I asked.

"Biting is marking, and yes, marking is a shifter thing. She asked me to bite you because marking you where the shoulder meets the neck is traditionally a shifter way of claiming a...person."

Butterflies filled my stomach. It almost sounded like he'd been about to say "mate." Which was the exact feeling that had come over me when he bit me on the middle part of my neck—that he was marking me as his. I knew it wasn't an actual claim, but I had felt the sentiment.

I went ahead and filled in the blank. "A mate?"

"Yes," he said softly.

"So if you claim someone, you are basically mating?"

"If a shifter claims someone, that person usually becomes their mate. The reason is because it usually happens in moments of strong feeling and blind love, and the couple then needs to figure out what to do about it. The effects of claiming are forever. A person can be claimed by multiple parties, but the scent of each is always there. However, mating itself doesn't require love, like imprinting does. It really just needs the agreement of both parties. If the claiming didn't happen before the mating, then it will traditionally happen after to further establish their agreement."

"If I were claimed by five people—" He stiffened and dipped his head, running his teeth along my neck. I shivered but continued, "I'd smell like all five?"

"Yes."

"And that's it?" I asked. "You just bite me on the shoulder, and I'm claimed?"

"No. With my dragon's help, I...secrete sounds bad, but... I secrete a pheromone that will soak into your skin. It'll ensure my scent weaves in with yours. Other shifters will know you've been claimed. That you are mine, and if they flirt or touch you or...whatever, it is a challenge against me."

"And you'll..."

"Kill them," he growled. "Swiftly. With pleasure."

I bit my lip. That admission shouldn't have been so hot. "And then, what, you just get to flirt your way through the castle?"

"You would mark me, too, if you wanted to lay a claim on me."

"Why wouldn't I?"

He adjusted his position uncomfortably. "A mate's mark isn't always welcomed."

"People lay it on others against their will?"

"No. That is forbidden. The punishment is death. But with arranged matings, a couple might mark each other without sharing a true connection. Sometimes the male will mark the female to claim her, trying to ensure she doesn't bed anyone but him, and she does not desire to return the mark."

"Your mother didn't mark your father," I guessed.

"Correct, and it was a source of great contention because it showed the world that she did not want him. That she was there out of duty and nothing else. He tried to beat her into doing it, and she would not."

"He beat her?"

His expression turned hard and rage lit his eyes. "Yes. Another dark secret. She tried to hide the bruises, but I have excellent eyesight. I could see her bruised face in the garden when I was locked in the tower. She did not bend, though. I respected her more for it. I just wished I could've helped her."

"Did you try? Not that I'm judging you, I'm just wondering—"

"I was only a teen then. Late teens, but... I asked her how I could help. She told me to leave. To find someone I loved, without the weight of a kingdom on my shoulders, and be happy."

"But then..." I pulled away so I could see his face. Sorrow shone in his eyes, and guilt ate through the bond. "But why would you think you killed her if she told you to go?"

He tucked a strand of hair behind my ear. "Because

I left her here with a monster." His eyes glossed over as he stared out into nothing for a moment.

I stroked down his face, my heart aching for him.

His eyes fluttered, and then his gaze zipped down to me. All at once, his expression hardened. His body tensed. Anger rushed through the bond to cover the softer emotions. He was trying to erect walls to keep his pain inside.

"Get off," he barked. "It's time to go. We've dallied long enough. Your lady's maid can clean you up."

He pushed me off him and walked to the edge of the rockface, clearly waiting for me to put on my pants.

I sighed, still aching inside, but not because of his rough treatment. His words and actions didn't affect me as much now that I understood more of his pain. His *turmoil*. His behavior was a symptom of a greater problem, and while I wouldn't let him go overboard with it, I would tolerate these little outbursts. It was human, this side of him. I welcomed that.

"Yeah, okay." I worked my pants back on and felt my face sour. "Gross."

He glanced back, saw that I was ready, and changed into his beast.

Back to reality.

CHAPTER 9

N YFAIN HAD DONE a very convincing job of dragging me back to the castle, which had involved throwing me over his wide shoulder and a lot of growling and grunting on his part. Back in the tower, Leala had come to me as I was stripping off my disgusting pants, and she'd started a bath right away.

After I'd been scrubbed from head to toe, Hadriel waltzed into the room. "My darling." He wore a purple robe open at the front, revealing a bare torso covered in sparkles and tiny pink briefs showing off the outline of his flaccid cock. Fuzzy blue slippers covered his feet, and the pungent aromas of smoke and alcohol drifted off him.

"Hadriel, she's bathing," Leala snapped, waving at him to get out.

"Yes, clearly she is bathing. That is what one does in

the tub." He sat on the edge of the large copper lip as I hurried to cover everything up. "Finley, my love, I would've been very angry at you if you hadn't sent that fantastic potion along with the master."

"Oh yes, milady," Leala gushed as she shoved Hadriel to make him get up and out. "Blocking the demon's magic, even partially, was fantastic for clearing the head. This place is—"

"It's a nightmare. Cheers!" Hadriel put up his hand, scowled, and said to Leala, "Be a dove and get me a drink, would you? It's needed for that toast."

She gave him a disapproving look. "I was going to say that this place is *less* of a nightmare—"

"Cheers!" he said with a grin. "Still works. Where's that drink—Would you quit shoving at me, you tramp? I might fall in!"

"Well, get out. She doesn't want visitors right now. She's naked!"

He rolled his eyes and looked at me. "Sweetie, don't worry about that. I've seen it all. You ain't got nothing the other ladies don't have. Except you are much hairier."

"She's natural," Leala said with a fist on her hip.

"And currently embarrassed," I muttered, ducking my head to hide my red face.

"Nonsense." Hadriel waved it away. "We'll get that

sorted. Now, I have a bone to pick with you. I got in an awful lot of trouble the other day when you locked me in the tower. The master was not pleased."

"Are you still drunk?" Leala asked him.

"Yes. But I haven't stuck my dick in anything unsavory since Finley gave us that potion. Things are looking up. Speaking about that, dear girl." He smoothed his wisp of a mustache, which currently resembled patchy moss growing on his upper lip. "Do you have any more? We've run through it already."

"Can I maybe get dressed before we have this conversation?" I asked.

Hadriel scoffed and stood. "I forgot about your modesty. That won't stay long."

He wandered out, and Leala set a towel down on the cold tiles so I could comfortably step out of the tub. She wrapped another around me, rubbing to dry, and retrieved my robe.

"I can do it, Leala, really. I'm not accustomed to being waited on."

"Yes, milady, except I've gone so long without having anything to do. This is my job. You must let me do it."

I pushed my hands through the sleeves of the robe and allowed her to lead me into the bedroom. Once there, she pulled out a seat near the window and sat me down so she could work a brush through my hair. It felt like being pampered. Like being looked after. I couldn't say I didn't like it.

"Now, all better?" Hadriel sat on my bed with an ankle over his knee, giving me an unwanted view of his crotch.

Leala hissed at him, pulled out another chair, and gave him a dirty look.

"Goddess spread her thighs and squirt, this is ridiculous." Hadriel grumpily lowered into the chair. "Now, as I was saying, we need more of that potion. It is magnificent." He leveled a finger at Leala. "Don't tell anyone we are getting more. Make up an excuse why we can't—Finley cracked her head and can't remember it or something. We have some loose lips in this castle, and we need to start picking and choosing who gets the potion or the demons will surely be all over our asses for more information. I don't know about you, but I've had just about enough demon ass-play to last me for a lifetime."

"You aren't supposed to speak to me while in front of the miss," Leala said stuffily.

"Really?" Hadriel shot back. "We're going to try to go back to the old customs? Because I'll be honest, I don't know them. I was not trained for this job."

Leala sighed softly.

"I can make more of it," I said. "Did you say it only partially worked, though? I made it stronger than normal, but it still wasn't strong enough?"

"It mostly works—that's what matters, milady," Leala said. "It leaves the head much clearer when the incubi and succubi are around."

"I mean...I can just make it stronger. It's no big deal." I closed my eyes as Leala ran the brush through my hair. "I can make enough for everyone—"

"No, no," Hadriel said. "If we all suddenly didn't respond to the demons, they'd know something was up. No... Wait, is that..."

I opened my eyes to find him staring at my neck. I covered the bite mark with my palm, my cheeks warming.

"It's nothing," Leala insisted, draping my hair over the mark. "She slipped and fell."

"On the master's teeth?" Hadriel quirked a brow. "Who are you trying to fool, Leala? I'm not one of *them*. I know to keep my mouth shut. The master said he'd pull off my arms if I didn't"—his eyes widened—"and I believe him."

"You're drunk. You are a horrible gossip when you drink and don't have a dick in your mouth," she mumbled.

"Not about the master's affairs, I'm not. So, doll, tell

me everything. I know he got hurt saving you, and you nursed him back to life." He braced his elbow on his knee and his chin on his fist. "Then what? He's a closed book, that one. I'm *dying* to know how you ended up back at the castle. I honestly thought he was going to let you go, what with the way he was moping around, snapping at everyone, scaring the staff half to bits. The demons thought it was because you got away. So that's good, at least. And you did, except now you're back. Tell me, did you miss him, is that why?"

"Hadriel," Leala said with a note of warning in her voice.

"I'll tell you everything after I get a few hours' sleep," I said.

Hadriel made a disgruntled sound. "I hate when the party has to end."

"I don't know why, with the amount you party," Leala said, putting the brush aside and moving to turn down my bed.

"What else do I have to do?" Hadriel stood and staggered as he put the chair back.

"Help me with the garden, for one," I said. "Play-time is over. There's an entire kingdom that needs our support, and you're going to help me cater to them. Nyfain can't be expected to hold this place up on his shoulders alone. It's time we pitch in and do our part."

"I suddenly think I need another drink," Hadriel muttered as he wandered out.

LATER THAT AFTERNOON, I did as I'd said and put Hadriel to work. Nyfain had already started him on the garden, with help from some of the other staff, so I let them continue that. I visited the small herb garden on the east side of the castle, something the cook apparently took care of for the food and what little supplies Nyfain needed to add to his subpar healing remedies.

"This is it?" I asked, standing at the edge and looking it over.

Jessab, a round-bellied man with a white mustache and thin lips, puffed out his chest. "That is all I need to make the food. You want I take care of plants I don't need so that I don't make the food?"

He was clearly not from this kingdom, but I didn't want to waste time asking about his past. It didn't matter in the present. Also, I had a feeling he'd say something unsavory about my nosiness.

For some reason, it felt like I was on a timer. It felt like I had to get the kingdom healthy before doom struck us. Again. I had no idea what form that doom would take, but I had a suspicion it had to do with the demon king.

"Don't you have a gardener? I thought someone

told me there was still a gardener left in the castle."

"The gardener, he tends the everlass plants with the master. He has no need to be messing with no herbs for cooking."

"Right. Well, I'll need some starter sprigs from you. I'll be creating a larger herb garden for elixirs and whatnot."

"Listen here, honey. I no answer to you. If you want starter sprigs or whatever, you ask the master—"

He cut off as I leaned toward him, a few inches taller and a whole lot meaner. I dropped my voice and upped my menace.

"I will take what I need, and I'll do it as I need to. Do we understand each other?"

He turned a little and pulled his arms up, as though my words were poisonous darts and he was trying to protect his chest. He didn't answer. Not that I'd expected him to. I gave a last look at the herbs and headed out to the everlass field. I'd plant an herb garden in the queen's garden so everything was in the same spot. There was no sense wandering all around the castle trying to keep everything watered, when I could do it all in the one place. She'd had space for it anyway, I seemed to recall.

The everlass shed was clean and immaculately organized. Leaves had been set out to dry, and a cup sat in the middle of the first worktable, halfway full. I picked it up and smelled it. The nulling elixir, I'd know that scent anywhere. Cold, though. Old. It wasn't good anymore.

I turned toward the door to toss out the contents and jumped. My hand jerked, and liquid sloshed over it.

Nyfain stood in the doorway, watching me. The guy was incredibly light of step for having such a big frame.

"Hey," I said with a shaky release of breath.

"Well?" he asked, clearly still in a shit mood.

I ignored it. "It's great. It'll definitely work. This batch is old, though. It does best when it's fresh."

"It'll work…meaning it's not quite right?"

I brushed past him and poured the contents out. I set the cup in the wash station and looked over the spread-out leaves. "When were these dried?"

He walked up behind me, pointing at the first batch. "At dawn to try that out…" He pointed down the way. "In the evening."

"Great. And you've collected the other ingredients?"

"Yes, but we'll need to start a larger herb garden if we plan to make a lot of this. I can also ask the villages to supply me with what we need."

"I already told your grumpy cook that I'd be taking sprigs for my own garden, and yes, the villages' help would be good to get us started." I looked at the cold ash below the cauldron in the corner. "How do we intend to transport all of this?"

"I am having a staff member create a harness fit for a dragon so that I can transport large quantities. Was mine not quite right?"

He clearly wasn't going to let it go. "Yours would be great for almost all cases. But it was a little acidic smelling, which likely means you didn't grind the leaves enough. It's almost there, and it'll work, but for the toughest of jobs, it'll fall short. It won't hold someone back from the beyond. Don't take it personally—most of the people making the elixir can't do it as well as you did, and they've been attempting for years."

He grunted but didn't otherwise comment.

I familiarized myself with all the supplies. "Given the distance you'll have to travel...the elixir is going to lose potency anyway. We're fighting an uphill battle."

"Can you find a workaround?"

I sighed and sagged against the table. "I'm going to have to, right? People are dying."

He slid his hands over my shoulders, kneading the tense muscles. "At this point, anything will help. What about that potion for blocking succubi and incubi magic?"

"It's a draught, not a potion. Potions are stronger, temperamental, and require faerie magic. Luckily, draughts are incredibly hardy, so preparing that to travel is no problem. Hadriel implied that the one I gave you to pass on didn't fully work. I need to make it stronger. The demons in my village weren't packing the same power."

Suddenly I felt incredibly overwhelmed, but he continued to knead my shoulders, his touch comforting me.

"I'll help," he said softly. "We have some time. We stopped the lower-hierarchy demons from bringing you to the demons here. With you back and…how you'll act toward me in public, they'll be content to play with us for a while."

I nodded and thought about leaning back into his warmth, but he'd already moved away, going to stand by the door.

"I'll join you here tomorrow," he said. "You can show me the proper way." A ghost of a smile flitted across his lips. "I already gave the last batch to the hardest-hit village. I haven't heard the results yet. We'll put together small batches for the other villages to try. As soon as they request more, as they will, we can put together larger batches while they try to make it themselves. You might have to show them. I don't have the patience to teach. Before you do, though, I want you looking…" His gaze slid over my body, and regret bled through the bond. "I want you looking the part."

I was wearing his old clothes again because he'd ruined mine and I didn't have anything else. Before, it had aggravated me to wear his things. Now…I kinda liked it. It brought a bit of comfort to my turbulent life.

"You're going to try to put me in dresses?" I asked with a sinking heart.

"You don't like dresses?"

"I like them just fine, but they have a time and a place. Working is not that time or place."

"What is that time and place, then?"

I shrugged. "A nice dinner. A ball. A date, I don't know. Things we don't have anymore."

"First, I didn't mean put you in dresses, no. I meant that you should wear clothes actually made for you with a certain finery of fabric that the villages will expect from a representative of the royal court. You've already been measured; we just need them delivered and you wearing them. You'll have to resign yourself to wearing my old training clothes just around the castle. Second, we can certainly plan a nice dinner. I get a least a night off a month. I'll look forward to being your date."

My belly flipped over as he left, the sun showering down on the white shirt spanning his broad shoulders. Talk about hot and cold.

I shook my head and looked around. He'd said he would help me tomorrow, but that didn't mean I had to wait. Might as well get started.

BY THE TIME evening descended, I was sweaty and tired, having worked feverishly all afternoon. I'd hunted down some canisters that would work and prepared them for Nyfain's evening departure. He found me almost as he'd left me, standing within the shed, staring.

"It's time to go in," he said in a dark tone, his gaze sliding across the workstation. His brow furrowed. "What is this?"

"So." I unstuck my hair from my sweaty face. "I think I've solved our traveling issue. I've prepared and mashed the ingredients. Come here, I'll show you."

He glanced behind him, up at the sky. Without comment, he came around the table and stood beside me.

I took the pestle out of the mortar and held it up for him to smell. He leaned down and did so.

"Do you smell the difference between yours and mine?"

He nodded, straightening up.

"Okay. I've sectioned the prepared ingredients into these canisters. I've scratched a line on each one to indicate how much hot water should go in. All they have to do is fill it, mix it, wait until it cools enough to drink, distribute it into ten equal cups, and feed it to who needs it. It doesn't matter how far along the person is in their sickness. This is safe for anyone to drink. It'll be as potent as it gets if they just mix it themselves."

Nyfain chuckled. "Incredible."

"What?"

He shook his head. "The rate at which you problem-solve. This is perfect, and it'll be much easier to carry. Thank you. The villages will thank you."

"Yeah, and they'll also witness firsthand what it's supposed to look and smell like. That should make it easier for them to re-create it."

"I am constantly wowed by your giving heart. Most people would become wealthy by selling or trading this elixir. There is no reason that your family should struggle."

I put lids on the canisters and piled them up for him to take when he could. "People don't have much in my village. It isn't fair to profit from people who don't have the money to pay when there are lives on the line. Living shouldn't come with a price tag."

"A sentiment not many people share."

"That's their problem, not mine."

He stepped away and waited for me to follow.

I hesitated, uncomfortable with leaving a job unfinished. "I didn't get a chance to do the demon draught." I glanced at the dwindling day, the light leaching from the doorway. "I'll get to it tomorrow, I guess."

"You don't have to do everything in a day, like I

said. Relax for a moment. Maybe try to enjoy yourself. There is a lot to learn at the castle. I hear watercolor painting is fun."

I laughed, thinking of Hadriel's story about painting a bunch of dicks for that class.

"Maybe I'll go and mess with Hadriel's puzzle set-up," I said. One of the rooms was full of half-completed puzzles—every surface covered in loose pieces—and Hadriel was apparently their star.

"There's dancing, too." Nyfain's tone turned somber. Quiet. "I used to love to dance. I haven't done it in so long."

We crossed the grounds toward the back door. "I can dance, a little. Hannon taught me. He was impatient, though, and also my brother. It was weird. Maybe I'll try that just to see what it's like with a proper partner."

"I need your choice of book, too. I've read the last one twice."

"Yes, but I hear there's a tight-ass guarding the library, and I have to be shown the proper way to check out a book."

He flashed me a mouth-watering grin as he pulled the door open for me. "True. I'll show you the ropes tomorrow, I promise. You can use the library at your leisure." His gaze turned serious, and I stalled in the doorway. "All I have is yours, Finley. You have but to ask."

"Well…" I put out my hands and looked down at my attire. "It looks like I'm already taking the shirt off your back, so what are a few books…"

He laughed and slid his hand across the small of my back. It was time to pretend we were a "happy" couple—one kidnapped and held captive, the other a horrible beast who wanted to use her at his will.

Desire whispered across my flesh. Nyfain moaned softly.

"What did you just think about?" he asked as we walked into the castle and down the quiet hall.

"You using me sexually," I whispered, pushing in a little closer to him. His side rubbed mine. My nipples tightened.

"Would you like that?"

"Yes," I breathed.

A pungent whiff drifted across my senses. A demon.

Nyfain veered, pulling me with him. He spun me around and changed his hold, wrapping his fingers around my throat. He slammed my back against the wall and leaned over me, his body inches from mine.

"Try to look scared," he murmured, his gaze roaming my face.

I did try. I really did. But my core tightened up, and

my new panties (again taken from Leala) were quickly doused with wetness. My pussy ached from what we'd done last night, and yet it craved more. I was desperate to be filled by him again. To be bent over and taken from behind. To feed him my pussy and arch with the pleasure.

He squeezed my throat before bending down and running his lips over mine.

"What does it mean when a male grabs a female by the throat like this?" I whispered against his grazing kiss.

"It is either a challenge or foreplay, depending on the woman. If foreplay, the female is inviting the male to exert his dominance. Only if and when he overcomes her will she submit, and then they fuck explosively. If a challenge, the male will try to physically dominate, possibly kill, and the woman must overpower him first. Typically a male's power is in his strength, and a female's power is in her magical will, a will that can be manifested physically if she is powerful enough. When they mate, the strength blends with the will, and they create an unstoppable team. In theory."

"So with you, I would command you to step away."

"No. With me, you'd likely command me to fuck you. With others, you wouldn't get the chance to kill them or use your will because I would have already ripped them away from you and twisted their heads off."

"Right. And so what are we doing now?"

"Waiting to see if that demon is going to come this way."

"And if it does?"

"I haven't gotten that far yet. Probably grope you. How's your pussy?"

"Really, really sore. Please don't touch it. Unless you want to touch it, in which case, please put your cock in it. I'm sure the soreness will go away…"

He smiled and kissed me, a hard, consuming kiss, with his hand still squeezing my throat. The whiff of demon increased. He grabbed my other hand and pushed it to his hard bulge.

"Don't kiss me back," he whispered, barely heard. Louder, he barked, "Rub my cock."

I whimpered, closing my eyes and clenching my jaw, so fucking turned on by him ordering me to do sexual favors for him I couldn't stand it. Who would have thought I'd be into that? I held my breath to hopefully make it look like I was uncomfortable.

I rubbed, stroking firmly. Wanting to undo his pants to get at that smooth skin.

"That's right," he said in a rough, dominant voice. "Tell me you want me to fuck you."

I opened my mouth as his hand left mine and braced against the wall next to my head. He was leaning over into my space, trapping me there.

"I want...I want you to f-fuck me," I said in a somewhat quavering voice. It was the best I could do, trying to hide my need.

"That's a good girl." He licked my bottom lip, obviously a show of sexual dominance for the demon, but damn if it didn't zing through my body. "Maybe when I get back."

"Or maybe I could fuck her for you..."

Nyfain jerked away from me, his hand still on my throat. A succubus I hadn't seen before sauntered down the hall with a little leather whip in hand, a tassel at the end. She wore a tiny thong and no shirt, her full breasts bobbing as she came to a stop. Her brown hair had been pulled back and fastened on top of her head.

"She is *mine*," Nyfain growled, power whipping through the hall. Another burst of wetness soaked my panties.

"Yum." She curled around him so she could get a better look at me, still some distance away. "She responds to her fear, it seems. I can smell her arousal. You've had her, then, Nyfain, hmm? How was she?"

She inhaled the scents, and I grimaced.

Nyfain yanked me closer, his arm coming around

me possessively. "If you touch her, I will end you."

"Is that so?" She smiled wickedly. "We shall see. Guard her, Nyfain. Or I will show her how good sex can truly be."

She continued down the way, turning right to go down a different hall. She glanced back as she went, that seductive little smile just for me. She tapped her whip against her shoulder before turning.

He let out a breath. "Let's get you back to the tower. I am sorry it has to be this way. It can't be pleasant for you... Though..." He cocked his head.

Yeah. He could smell my arousal too. That had to be confusing, given he was trying to be a villain.

What he didn't understand was that he was a villain on my side. A monster in my corner. A beast that would kill for me. It was so incredibly hot that I couldn't stand it.

Possibly that made me unhinged. I'd just blame this newfound desire on my animal. Conscience cleared.

"I don't like pretending I don't like it," I murmured, curving my hand around his forearm. "Can all creatures smell when a woman is turned on?"

"Demonic creatures who feed off emotion can smell that emotion. She feeds off lust and desire, so she can smell arousal. But normally shifters cannot, no. Not unless...they are in tune with the person they are smelling."

"And you're in tune with me."

"Yes. You are in tune with me, as well—you probably just don't know what you're smelling."

"I don't really want to know."

"Exactly."

A middle-aged woman with a dirty blond bob streaked with gray walked toward us. I staggered, caught and held up by Nyfain, as I cataloged her situation. Her face was etched with lines, around her eyes and across her forehead. She wore a chain choker, a leather bustier that exposed her breasts, and tiny leather briefs over fishnet stockings. Around her crotch was a holster of sorts, holding in place a large purple cock.

"Master, you're here late." She stopped in front of us casually, as though her tits weren't hanging out in front of the prince and a large purple cock wasn't strapped to her person.

"Missus Smith," he said indifferently by way of greeting. "Yes, I was helping Finley finish up with the everlass. I'll be leaving shortly. She will need a bath and dinner brought up."

"Yes, of course. Leala has been expecting her return. I believe the food has already been prepared. I'll make sure cook knows to take it out of the warmer. And for you?"

"I had a bite to eat earlier. I'm fine, thank you."

"Yes, sir. I'll see you tomorrow."

She bowed to him, smiled at me, and excused herself down the hall.

"Was she wearing... I mean..." I rubbed my hand down my face. "I know she was wearing a big purple dildo. Why was she wearing a big purple dildo?"

"It's called pegging." He guided me toward the stairs. "She is more alpha than many, and she likes to dominate. A few men in the castle enjoy it when she fucks them. The women do as well, I assume."

I lifted my eyebrows and glanced back as we rounded the first set of stairs and headed for the second. "So she screws them in the ass with her big purple dildo?"

"Yes."

"Huh. That's..." I couldn't tell if it was crazy or hot or crazy or... "I feel so naïve."

"You are handling it a lot better than I did when everything started to devolve. A lot better. That is one pairing I have never wished to try, though it's interesting to watch."

"You've watched?"

We got to the tower, and he opened the door before following me in and closing the door behind us. He leaned against it, watching me as I stopped and turned, suddenly bombarded by his delicious smell. Balmy and light with a hint of extra spice, heavier than normal. Heady, almost.

"Yes," he said softly. "Some things in this castle are...interesting."

I remembered the admission he'd made in my bedroom when he was basically forced to hump my bed in uncontrolled desire.

"You've wanted to try some things," I murmured. His bulge was pronounced, and I knew he was rock hard.

He didn't answer, his eyes liquid gold.

"The demons have smelled you on me. *In* me," I said softly, stepping a little closer. Wariness clouded his eyes. Lust flooded the link. "Eventually that smell will wear away. If you're being so obviously sexual with me in their presence, they're going to wonder why you've stopped banging me."

"The thought had occurred to me," he whispered.

"While I could always jack you off and let you come on my pussy, that wouldn't be nearly as fun as you coming inside of me."

His Adam's apple bobbed as he swallowed. "Food for thought," he said in a strained voice, and then left, closing the door behind him.

I let out a breath and leaned against the bedpost. That guy was a hard nut to crack.

I had bigger things to consider, though, like my curiosity about the crazy things that went on in this castle and what, exactly, Nyfain was interested in trying.

CHAPTER 10

THE NEXT COUPLE weeks passed in a blur. I was supposed to get access to the library, Hadriel kept prodding me to get me into the seamstresses to try things on, and I wanted to find the dancing instructor to see if I remembered any moves. But reports from the villages had come in by way of Nyfain, and they were crying out for more nulling elixir.

The elixir had worked, as I'd known it would, but their everlass plants hadn't been maintained and their ability to make more elixir was apparently nonexistent. They weren't getting it done. We would need to pick up the slack until Nyfain and I could help them with their plants and I could physically show them how to make the elixir, all without the demons being the wiser.

The draught to cut out the reaction to the demons' magic was also in high demand, both within the castle and in the villages. It gave people the clarity they'd been missing, and it made a casual stroll after dark less treacherous. And then there was my coffee substitute. I just didn't have enough hours in the day to make it a priority, and thankfully Hadriel was fine being a stingy bastard, so I just made enough for those closest to me. It wasn't a healing elixir, after all, so I could stomach not sharing.

From what I could see out my window, the garden was coming along nicely. They were still ripping out things that didn't belong. I hadn't been able to get in there and work in person, though. I hadn't had the time. Hopefully soon.

Each day passed in a rush of everlass leaves and other ingredients. There just wasn't enough daylight to learn a new hobby or put in a proper inspection of the library. Nyfain made sure books were delivered to me, and I was satisfied to relax in my room after the tough day to eat, bathe, read, and sleep.

Poor Nyfain had been doing double duty. Maybe even triple duty. He would work with me during the day before heading out to the wood at night.

He was soon making the elixir like a champ. Mixing the draught like he'd been doing it all his life. He also hunted for meat to deliver to my family in stealth since I couldn't. The exhaustion was starting to show on him.

Dark circles had developed under his eyes, and his shoulders drooped.

Finally, one day, I snapped.

"Get out." I pointed at the illuminated door in the work shed. The midmorning sun shone strong and warm, hinting at spring right around the corner.

Nyfain stopped in the doorway. "What?"

"Get out. You're exhausted, Nyfain. Go to sleep."

He shook his head and started forward again. "Three people were expected to die this last week in one of the villages. Because of your elixir, they are hanging on. This is important, what we're doing."

"I know. But they need you in that wood. I can handle this. You handle that."

He stalled at the end of the table. "I can do both, Finley. Finally I feel like I'm doing some real good. I see hope flashing in people's eyes. Just wait until you make the other elixir for them."

"I get that, Nyfain. I do. But a body needs sleep. Go to bed. I'll see you in the afternoon."

His jaw set stubbornly. "I'm good."

I straightened up and squared off with him. "*Go to bed*," I growled. Power whipped through the shed. My animal turned over within me and stirred.

His muscles flared. He swayed a little, his eyes hard. I pulled more power, my animal pumping it out for me.

"Now," I said in a firm voice.

He took a step back that he clearly didn't want to, judging by the jerkiness of his movements. Humor filled the bond.

"As you command," he finally said, turning for the door. "And Finley?" He stopped and glanced back. "Please join me this evening before I leave. I'd like to show you the library. You've been reading, and I have not. I miss it."

I pushed the hair out of my face. "Okay."

"And get those clothes sorted out. We need to get the villages up to speed so you can do…other things."

I frowned at him, but he left.

What other things?

BY LATE AFTERNOON, I'd made all the elixir starter, as I was calling it, that I could with the leaves we'd dried and harvested. We'd need to harvest more. The problem was, because I wasn't directly seeing the effects of the elixir, I had no idea if the one harvested at dawn worked any better than the usual. Though I supposed it didn't matter. It was the crowded plant that would provide the cure, if there was one. The slight difference in potency of the drying times wouldn't make enough difference to matter.

I walked to the wall around the queen's garden and

hopped up. I knew how to get there through the castle, and Nyfain had given me a key to access the room, but I was dirty and tired and didn't want to go through the trouble of traipsing through the castle when it was faster to reach it from outside.

At the top of the wall, I paused before walking around the side. A crew of three were working diligently, Hadriel the only one I recognized. The blackberry bushes were long gone, the vines and brambles had been cleared away, and now they were weeding and tilling the ground.

"Wow, you guys." I jumped down, marveling at the transformation. "This is great!"

Hadriel looked up from his patch of tilled dirt, his face red and sweat streaming down his temples. "I haven't worked this hard in…" He puckered his lips in thought.

"That's the reason you're still alive," a grizzled older man said. White whiskers hung down the sides of his brown, wrinkled face. He wore a faded denim shirt and dirt-stained trousers.

"This coming from the only gardener still going, Jawson?" Hadriel drawled. "I wonder how we can possibly explain that? Mediocrity, maybe? Hmm…" He tapped his chin in a pantomime of deep thought.

"Because I know how to keep my head down, that's

why. I don't parade around the castle in nothing but a fancy thong screaming about goddess knows what."

"Ah, you noticed how fancy my thongs are." He waggled his eyebrows. "Caught you looking…"

"I never did see a butler who does so little butlerin'," a ruddy-faced man said. He wore a wide sun hat punched through with holes in the bill. I wasn't quite sure what the point of it was. "We're gettin' real close, miss." He straightened up with a wince and put a hand to his hip. He didn't look a day over thirty-five, but he stood like he was eighty years old, stooped a little, somewhat crooked.

"That's Gyril, the horse master." Hadriel hooked a thumb the man's way. "He's gotten thrown a few times. No one wonders why he's still alive."

"The horses are all spooked about the curse, that's all."

"What were they before the curse, then?"

"Awful cunts," Gyril grumbled.

I hazarded a guess that he hadn't been the horse master before the curse. He'd probably stepped into the role because everyone else was gone. That seemed to be the situation around here.

I wandered around, getting a feel for the space. The rosebushes lining the back were still wild, big, thick bushes with shoots every which way. All the other flowers and plants had long since died.

"I have a map of what it looked like back before the queen died," Jawson said, leaning on his shovel. "Don't know if that would be any help to ya."

"It would, actually, thanks. What do we do for seeds and things around here?"

"I have a store of seeds up at the shed. The master can get some starter plants from the wood or the other villages if you need those," Jawson answered. "We don't have a nursery anymore. Everything kinda fell apart when the curse came and the king died."

That was understandable. I nodded, turning toward the queen's quarters.

"Wait, love." Hadriel followed me.

"You should call her miss, milady, or Miss Finley," Gyril said.

"You should learn not to stand behind temperamental horses and scratch your nuts. Besides, you don't know what we've been through. We're on friendship terms now."

"We know what she goes through every day having to deal with you," Jawson said. "It's enough to drive someone to drink."

"Nice working with you peckers," Hadriel called out over his shoulder.

"Lick rust," Gyril yelled back.

Hadriel and I walked through the glass doors into the cool room. The enchanted rosebush continued to wither in the middle of the floor, only two buds still in bloom and one branch moderately healthy. The kingdom was in bad shape.

"Great guys," Hadriel said as I peered down at the dome for a moment. "They had a soft spot for the queen. We all did, but they volunteered to help bring the garden back. It's nice, actually." He held out his hands, the dirt crusted on his fingers and ground into his palms. "I've never gardened before, but it's much better than watercolors or half of that other crap people around here are into."

"Well, there is still a lot of work to be done, so I appreciate the help."

He nodded as I made for the exit, intent on heading to my room to change. I wanted to get down to the library finally and take a nice, long look around.

"We need to visit the seamstresses," Hadriel said. "You are in dire need of clothes."

I groaned. "They already took my sizes."

"Yes, lovely, and now they have to fit you. You're long overdue. The master requested we get a move on. You can't go waltzing into the most influential villages wearing…that. If you do, it won't matter that you're on the prince's arm—they won't take you seriously."

"Does Nyfain put on fancy clothes?"

"No. He doesn't need to. He's the prince. You, however, are a nobody. As far as they are concerned, anyway." He put his hand out flat, his pinky pressing against my arm. "You knew he was the prince, right? You've figured that out? I can't remember what stop we're on in the drama train. I'm no good at secrets. They give me indigestion."

"I know that, yes. And yes, they will take me seriously. Healing a loved one tends to open people's minds."

"Yes, sure, but when the master isn't looking, they'll treat you like garbage. Wear something nice and wow them. They won't even notice your surly 'fuck off or I'll cut you' attitude. They are very shallow, those people. Back in the day, the nobles were the worst. Always walking around with their noses stuck in the air. Arrogant bastards. They thought that they were the prizes of the kingdom because they were dragons."

"They were, though."

"Yeah, but hello? Maybe a little humility? Anyway, let's get washed up, and we'll visit the seamstresses. I'll go find Leala."

"I can wash myself. I don't need to bother her."

"Sweetie, you need to let her do her job. She loves it. She's one of the few people left who likes to work. Let her help you. It has put a hop in her step and a smile on her face."

I sighed. "Fine. Tell her to hurry up. Nyfain is finally showing me the library, and I want all the time I can get in it."

Hadriel took off at a run, the first time I'd ever seen him hurry this much. Up in my room, I'd barely gotten undressed before Leala bustled in with a pleasant smile.

"Hello, milady, how was working the everlass? Did you get it all done?" She stood behind me and helped get me out of the very intense binding.

"Yes. Done for now. Demon draught is done, too. I'll probably help with the garden until we can harvest some more."

"Oh yes, the garden." She gestured me into the washroom and poured a bowl of warm water for quick washing. On the way, she stopped at the windows and looked down. "It really is coming along. I remember the queen's garden back in the day. It was beautiful. Those roses are really overgrown. Will you be able to tame them, or will you need to pull them out and replace them?"

"Just prune them way back in a way that allows for new growth. Like a haircut. The only way to tame them is to strip the thorns from their flowers and decorate your table with them. I wouldn't dream of it. Decorating a table is a job for daisies or tulips or something. I'll keep the roses outside and wild."

"I think the master would be happy to hear it."

I knew he would. The roses reminded him of his mother, and I wanted him to view them with fondness. With pride. I was positive I could make that happen—I just needed tools and time.

After dressing me in a plain, flowing dress with no shape and no undergarments, Leala led me out of the room.

"I was told to escort you down to the seamstresses. They'll have undergarments ready for you. You can stop using mine."

She meant that I could stop ruining hers. Nyfain wasn't kind on panties.

"They're excited to unveil their work for you," she added, her words sending a shock through me.

"I'm just a commoner from a poor village."

"Every great person started somewhere, milady. Just because you grew up common doesn't mean you need to dress common. You'll be going onto the battlefield soon—the social battlefield—and you'll need your armor."

We first visited Eliza, the good-natured seamstress who smiled and cooed about all the wonderful working attire she'd made. There was not a single dress in sight.

Instead, she'd made formfitting trousers with a little stretch to them and blouses that cinched at the waist but gave ample room around my bosom. They fit like a dream, and I could move with ease in them.

I absolutely loved them all! They were feminine while still being tough, pretty but usable and durable. The material was as fine as I'd ever seen, soft and supple on my skin, and decorated with lovely, flattering designs—flowers along the sleeves, vines twining along the seam. The binding around my breasts was tight but still flattering, and a sort of wire had been sewn in so I had two boobs and not one flattened uni-boob across my chest.

Hadriel and Leala both agreed that Eliza had out-done herself, and she'd better keep a very low profile for a while or her expertise might get her noticed by the demons and killed.

While we were on the way to the seamster, some-thing occurred to me.

"That tower used to be Nyfain's retreat, right?" I said, noticing the light starting to dim through the arched windows overlooking the grounds. Hadriel and Leala nodded. "Well, whose dresses were those, then? They were too small in the waist and shoulder to be something Nyfain played dress-up in."

Hadriel and Leala exchanged a look, and I got a

weird pang in my chest.

"Spill it," I said.

"Those were his ex-fiancée's dresses," Leala said. "He had the dresses made to her measurements because he was planning to bring her home to meet the king and queen. He wanted to surprise her, I guess. But the queen died before the trip, and so he had to rush home for the funeral. The fiancée—"

"*Ex*-fiancée," Hadriel corrected her.

"Right, the ex-fiancée was supposed to follow, but then…the curse."

The breath went out of me. It felt like a horse had kicked me in the sternum and I should be walking crooked like Gyril. I'd known Nyfain had wanted to marry for love. I'd conveniently forgotten about his probably having a fiancée before the curse.

My eyes stung with unshed tears. I blinked profusely to keep them at bay. "I guess that makes sense."

"What's that, milady?" Leala asked softly.

I shook my head. I didn't really want to talk about it, although that didn't keep my brain from thinking about it.

Of course he didn't want to have sex with me. He was already promised to another. A non-shifter, which was why his dragon was leaning my way. But Nyfain's heart was probably still with her, and I was playing hell on his self-control because he'd been abstinent for sixteen years.

I felt like such an asshole. I'd been goading him on. Our animals had done the same. We'd been preying on a guy who was clearly losing hope. All that "I'll ruin you" stuff made so much more sense now. Goddess forbid I fall for him, only for him to rip my heart out by leaving me for another woman the moment the curse ended (*if* it ended). That would kill me. I knew we couldn't be together in the long term—he was a prince—but I didn't want to see him move on so soon. That had already happened with my ex, and it wasn't fun.

"This situation is so fucked up," I said, lost to my thoughts as we entered the chaos of the seamster's workroom.

"Well, it is about time you showed up," Cecil said. His apron hung down his front, not tied, smeared with various stains and stuck through with needles. How he got stains from working with fabric, I did not know. "I have been waiting for you for ages."

He stepped to the side, blocking me from walking past him.

"Uh-oh, you're sad. No, this will not work for my designs. Get happy, immediately."

"You can't tell a woman to just change her emotions

in a moment." Leala took my arm. Gently she said, "Come on, milady. And don't fret about the master. He's never mentioned her since the curse. Not once."

"Who?" Cecil put his closed fist on his hip, the measuring tape sticking out on either side. "Who has done this to her?"

"It's fine." I waved them away. "I just didn't know they'd been engaged, that's all."

"Finley, love, no." Hadriel rubbed my back, stepping in the way of an inquisitive Cecil. "It was nothing. Truly."

"You don't propose to someone if it was nothing." I rolled my eyes. "But it's fine. It doesn't matter. He was always going to marry a princess or a noble or a queen or something. I've always known that."

"Oh, you're carrying on about that plain faerie lady I made all those dresses for, eh? Is that what this is about? Bah!" Cecil batted at the air. "What was he doing with a faerie, anyway? I'll never know. Especially one who tried to cover up her plainness with hideous dresses. I saw the pictures. My eyes bled making those dresses. They bled. I had to take breaks just so I could see again, they were so clouded by the terrible designs."

"Okay, overdramatic, calm down a bit," Hadriel mumbled.

"Overdramatic? What do you know about it, you

wispy-haired fuckbumper? You were stuck in the back stables trying to suck your own dick when this was all coming to pass. You didn't know what was going on."

"And I would've been able to suck my own dick if I'd been lounging around as much as you do," Hadriel replied.

"No. The master did not want that woman for himself—he wanted her to spit in his father's eye, that's what he wanted," Cecil went on, shooing the others away and herding me toward the stand in the center of the room.

"I don't think he expected the faerie noble to spit in his father's eye," Hadriel drawled.

"It is an expression, you no-love-monkey-punch. An expression!"

"I have only had a no-love-monkey-punch once, you awful jackass, and it wasn't on purpose." Hadriel held up his fist, his face turning red. "How was I supposed to know he'd called my name just so he could shoot jizz on my face! I didn't know why he'd pulled out and then called my name, so I looked back. Anyone would've done it! Just that one time, though. I don't care what you've heard. It was just that one time! I learned my lesson, damn it!"

Cecil leaned back and guffawed.

"Wait…a what?" I asked. I wasn't sure I wanted to

know.

"The master was just rebelling," Leala said, looking through the dresses hung on a stand in the corner. Not a frill or flourish could be found on any of them. They looked like plain fabric waiting for the seamster's touch. I hoped that was the case, too. It meant I wouldn't have to wear them anytime soon.

"Yes. Rebelling. I heard all the gossip from the ladies in waiting." Cecil winked up at me. "That faerie had her own motives. She wanted his touch with the everlass. His song. If he resided in their kingdom, the everlass would follow. He has a special way with it. It responds to his touch, his song even more than it did to the queen. He was always the golden son, and it showed with the everlass."

"Well, she might've been using him, or so people thought, but he wasn't using her." I tucked a lock of hair behind my ear. "Anyway, it doesn't matter. He's been very clear on where he stands. I just need to accept the truth."

"What truth?" Leala asked, and the others slowed their chatter, looking at me.

"There is nothing between us," I said.

"But he bit you," Hadriel said.

"No." Cecil straightened up and leaned way too close, grabbing the plain dress I'd worn in at the shoulder and pulling it wide. "No bite…"

"On her neck." Leala tapped her own neck. "The mark is gone now—it wasn't a claiming mark. He's done it twice, though. The temptation is there."

"The neck?" Cecil's face pinched. "Why the neck? The neck does no good."

"He will not be claiming me," I said. "Can we hurry this along, Cecil? I want to get to the library."

"Why not?" Hadriel asked. "He likes you. I've seen how he looks at you. How he treats you."

"Because he has a fiancée." Anger was starting to rise, and my animal roiled within me. "Because I don't want him to. Because I'm common. Because this could never work. Take your pick. The only reason anything has ever happened between us is because of our animals. The animals want each other."

So do the humans, my animal thought, and I ignored her.

"Well, that is good. Our beasts always know." Cecil grabbed my dress at the bottom and started to work it up over my head.

I clutched at it. "Um…no."

Cecil paused. "What do you mean, no? I need to see my dresses on you. You can't wear some sort of…artist smock while I fit you."

"It's one of my outing dresses, thank you very

much," Leala muttered. I curled my lips under, not having known that.

"I need to see your form," he persisted.

"Then use a slip or some undergarments like Eliza did," I said. "I'm not getting naked in front of you."

He rolled his eyes. "I have seen it. I have seen large breasts, small breasts, breasts that hang down low, man breasts, hairy man breasts…all kinds. I've seen vagins, too. Do you want to know all the vagins I have seen that I didn't want to see these past…too many years? Bald vagins, hairy vagins, vagins with strange designs—"

"Vah-gine-*ah*, you illiterate prick," Hadriel said, looking at his nails in the corner of the room. "Get it right. It's the toughest body part in the known world. It takes a beating, grins, and says *more, please.* Straight guys trying out men for the first time hammer into your ass like they have a vendetta. No, thank you. I am sensitive, unlike the mighty vagina."

"You *are* a vagine-*ah*," Cecil told him.

"I wish I were, I'll tell you that much. I wouldn't fear the demons then. I'd get bloody and be like—come at me! I can do this for days, no problem. Bleeding does not mean I'm dying; it means I'm readying to duplicate and come at you with an army!"

"Just…here." Leala bustled over with a lacy thing that looked like it would cover most of my torso while revealing all of it. There was no crotch, either.

"I...don't think that is better?" I said.

"Amateurs." Cecil stalked across the room and grabbed a tiny little slip of red silk. The bust was red lace and nearly see-through, and the hem would barely reach beyond my crotch. It was slinky and sexy and felt divine in my fingers. "There. That will cover you. It is for when you bed the master."

"Are you hard of hearing? She isn't bedding the master." Hadriel flashed his teeth at Cecil.

Cecil stared back with a flat face. "If the master were to employ a sack of shit, would he have to pay it as much as he does you?" Hadriel narrowed his eyes. "She can use it to seduce the master, then, whatever. Put it on. I will turn around."

I pulled it on under the dress, removing my arms from the dress sleeves so I could hike it up. Leala pulled the dress off over my head, and I put my arms through the slip while Cecil waited with his back turned, sighing in annoyance.

"I have seen all the stomachs. Fat stomachs, skinny stomachs, stretch-marked stomachs, bulbous stomachs, stomachs with no ab muscles that men want me to pretend have ab muscles..."

"Please stop. Seriously," Hadriel said. "You've seen a lot of naked people. We get it. She doesn't want to be one of those people. *Move on.*"

"Asses," Cecil said. "The problem is asses…"

Leala gave me some sparkly thong underwear, and it was definitely clear that I would need to do something about the lady beard growing up out of it. That was embarrassing.

"I cannot create a good pair of slacks with asses that do not exist," Cecil muttered. "I can clothe wide asses, or saggy asses, or bubble asses, but no ass? What do I do with no ass? Men come in with no asses all the time. I wish I could turn them away. Are they afraid of ass work?"

"I need to visit the salon, I think," I whispered to Leala. "But, like…not for the demons. Just to…landscape things a bit."

She winked at me as Cecil moved on to penises.

"Men have no shame when they come in here. They do not even wash the peen half the time. They swing it around, they play, they laugh when they get hard while I try to measure—it is annoying, dealing with the peen. And the big peens?" He made an exasperated sound. "One of the dragons had a peen so big, I had to make extra room in the clothes. I had to make them extra durable. And he got hard *all the time.* It nearly poked me in the eye when I measured his legs."

"Are you talking about Nyfain?" I asked.

"The master—Can I turn around now? How long does it take to put on a teddy? This is a problem. Any person will lose interest if it takes you this long to undress."

"Yes, you can turn around," Hadriel said. "We would've told you sooner, but you were having such a wonderful time commenting on all the body parts you've seen."

"Not the master, no. He needs a bit more room, yes. He's bigger than the average dragon."

"And the average dragon is a lot bigger than the average anyone else," Hadriel said. "It's an eye-widener."

Leala nodded with a small smile.

"Yes, but the master is not terrible," Cecil said. "He has a good ass, too. Good, strong bubble. Easy to design for him. No, this was another dragon—he's dead—with a huge peen. It was a job hazard. My eyes!"

His dead-serious tone made me giggle helplessly. The guy was a trip.

"Now. Here. You try this." He held up a slip of material that didn't look like anything special. The second I put it on, though, I knew I was working with a genius.

CHAPTER 11

HADRIEL LED ME down the quiet hallway on the second floor. Everyone had wandered off, having finished their hobbies for the day. Most doors stood open, the rooms dark. At the end of the hallway, the wide double door stood mostly closed, only showing a slice of what lay beyond.

"I'm surprised it took you so long to get down here," Hadriel said. Leala had stayed behind in the tower to put everything away and order up a tray of bread and cheese for whenever I wandered back up. I hadn't wanted to be rushed. I'd brave the demons in the hallways to spend more time perusing. "I'd thought it was the one thing you wanted above all else in the castle."

"In the castle, yes." I felt the nervous excitement coiling in my belly. "In the world, no. Making the nulling elixir was more important."

"You're a good human, Finley." His tone was uncharacteristically serious. "You're a good reminder of what life outside of this accursed castle could be."

"We'll get back to that someday."

"We can't return to something we never had. The nobles were pompous assholes, and the king was a tight-fisted ass. They worried about themselves and their kind and looked down on the common man. We would've been taxed for a cure."

I remembered Nyfain's comments about my generosity. I shrugged. "Desperate times, as they say."

"Indeed."

Hadriel put out his hand to stop me and then walked into the library and turned around, pushing the door mostly closed. I heard something click, and then he pulled both doors open at the same time, a grand gesture. He stepped to the side and swung out his hand.

"Milady. Welcome to the library of your dreams."

I beamed, crossing the threshold.

My stomach dropped out of my body. My smile slid off my face. I had to squeeze my legs together so that I didn't pee myself.

"Oh…" That was all I could get out.

He led me forward on my suddenly wooden legs. My face had lost feeling. I simply could not believe what

I was seeing.

First, the sheer size of the space was incredible. It was bigger than two of my house, one stacked on top of the other. Much bigger. The ceiling arched over the enormous room, and there were little pockets within the beams covered in hand-painted murals. Shelves lined the walls, decorated with wood columns between each of the stacks. A ladder attached to a metal rod at the top could be slid along to access the top shelves. Above that, a balcony constructed of the same polished wood ran around the room, the walls lined with more books.

The wood floor was covered in plush rugs, and comfortable seating options abounded, from recliners to piles of large pillows that lay everywhere—on the furniture, in piles on the ground, and in little cushioned corner nooks, or cleverly positioned between the stacks. It wasn't just a place for browsers—it was a place for readers. It was a place to settle in and stay for a while.

The deliciously sweet, musty smell of old books wafted toward my nose. It was a smell of comfort, of knowledge, of fantastic adventures and faraway places. It worked into my mind and relaxed my body.

"Where would I even start?" I breathed, trailing my fingertips down my mostly bare chest.

I'd decided to wear one of Cecil's dresses. The neckline plunged to my sternum, collected under my freely hanging breasts, and from there the material skimmed down my stomach. Five straps fit over my shoulders, two on one side and three on the other, each of them holding the dress a little differently. A slit ran up my right side and the bottom dragged against the floor in the back. It was elegant and plain and comfortable, and I felt slinky and sexy when I wore it. Underneath I wore no underwear, mostly because I was still embarrassed about the wild lady beard that definitely needed to be tamed. I hadn't dusted my face with makeup or bothered to change my hair from the messy bun. I'd just wanted the feel of the soft, flowing material against my skin.

"How about with finding the place you will read?"

His sandpaper voice flowed over me. Goosebumps coated my skin. My animal eagerly sat up and took notice.

Hadriel drifted to the side as Nyfain walked toward me from around a corner deeper in the library. Clearly there was more to it. His gray T-shirt, though a bit looser than the white ones he usually wore, stretched across those impossibly broad shoulders. His jeans hugged that delicious bulge.

"Goddess have mercy on us mere mortals," he said as his gaze roamed over me. "Cecil does not disappoint." He glanced to the right. "Hadriel, that will be all. Close the doors after you. We are not to be disturbed."

I smiled, dropping my gaze in sudden embarrassment. When Nyfain reached me, he fitted his hand below my chin. Pressure had me looking up, meeting his golden gaze.

"You are a vision, Finley."

I ran my hand alongside my face, then touched my hair. "I didn't dress up or anything. This is a lounging dress, he called it." I shrugged. "It's comfortable."

His smile was soft, and his gaze hadn't left my eyes. "You don't need your hair and makeup done. Your inner beauty radiates out of you, enhancing what nature gave you. The dress blends into the background. Your fire, your strength, your unyielding power... You are... You take my breath away."

He bent slowly, grazing his lips across mine. I placed my palms against his chest and then slid them up and hooked them around his neck as the kiss deepened. His tongue swept through my mouth, his taste delighting my senses. His smell beat that of the books, balmy and comforting and sensual, like a lazy afternoon in the sun beside a high mountain lake.

When he backed off, he slid his tongue down the side of my throat. He kissed softly where he'd bitten me on the neck in the past. He moved down then, his lips lingering at the base of my neck. My heart sped up. My core tightened.

"This dress would show a mark very well," he growled. He sucked in my fevered skin to the point of pain.

"Hmm, yes." I tilted my head, outside of myself, not thinking about anything other than the heat of his mouth and how desperate I was for the sharp stab of his teeth in my flesh. "Please."

He pulled off, my skin popping out of his mouth. The air caressed the new mark, chilling it.

No, don't let him stop now! my animal thought desperately. *He wants to mark you, I can feel it. The dragon is desperate for it. Urge him on!*

"I can't," Nyfain said, as if hearing her. Or maybe he was talking to his dragon. "I have to…stop."

He put his arms around me, his palms flat, feeling the soft fabric against my flesh. He cupped my butt then slid his hand across to the other cheek before coming back. The other hand reached up along my front as he nibbled my lips, his kiss sending me into a state of anticipatory bliss. I moaned softly, my pussy pounding, needing to be filled.

He pulled back, his eyes dark with arousal. The bond blistered with it. He stared at me for a long time, indecision coloring the bond. Once again, his eyes seemed to be reaching down through me, searching for answers to undisclosed questions.

"Come." He took my hand, threading his fingers through mine. "Let me show you around."

I staggered a little, and he waited for me to regain my composure. In a moment, I followed him, trying to ignore the wetness sliding down my upper thigh, my animal's cry of frustration at his change of pace.

"I'll take care of you before I leave, I promise," he rumbled, pulling me around the corner.

"What do you mean?"

"My dragon promised that we would fulfill your carnal needs, right? I haven't been holding up my end of the bargain."

As he should, my animal purred.

Shivers coated my body, and heat pounded in my core. I didn't trust myself to speak. Thankfully, my brain took over, overriding my body's tightness.

Nyfain walked me through the various sections of the library, showing the little metal plaques that identified each area by genre. They were tasteful and inconspicuous, blending into the overall beauty. We walked all the way around the room, toured the second story, and Nyfain paused frequently for me to brush my fingers across a spine or take out a book and look it over. At the end, he led me to a darkened corner in the very back. A forward-facing lounger sat behind a large hanging tapestry. The table beside it held a leafy green plant that seemed to block the view.

"If you sit a certain way, you can see most of the library. I'll show you in a bit. Right now..." He gently tugged me deeper into the corner. Behind a squat shelf, a collection of volumes chronicled the historic laws of foreign kingdoms. He reached behind one of them and flicked a switch. A door popped open within the bookcase.

"Your mother's secret library," I said with an excited grin.

"I'm still waiting on a letter from you."

The hidden space was about as big as my living room back home, crowded with all kinds of books in no particular order.

"She liked to hunt for her reads," he explained as I browsed, biting my lip. "She liked to pull down books and leaf through them. If something caught her eye, she'd read the book. If not, she'd try again, and again, until she finally decided to pick something." He stood by the open door, watching me look. "I remember being so annoyed by how long it took her to pick a book. That was before I knew about this room. She did it with all books. Later on, I'd settle in and read while she hunted for a find that would appease her in that specific moment in time. She said that there was a book for every single moment, and she was not satisfied until she had found it."

"That's so cool. I haven't heard of anyone else doing that." I ran my hand across the books. "So in here, where there was no rhyme or reason, she didn't even have to limit herself by genre. She could just pick at random and had no idea what she would get."

"Yes, exactly." He waited a while for me to look them over, trying her method.

"I think I'd rather read the synopsis."

He laughed. "Me too."

"Maybe I'll try her method when I'm indecisive."

I wandered toward him, my hands behind my back. My breasts popped out. He glanced at them and then did a double take. Hunger flared in his eyes.

"What will you choose for me to read?" I asked.

He shook his head slowly and reached out, cupping a breast. His thumb circled the nipple, and I closed my eyes as pleasure speared through my body. "I won't pick right now. You need to roam and explore. Pick a few for yourself."

"So what is the system for checking things out?"

He kissed beside my lips, then on them. "There isn't one. Not for you. Use this library as your own. I know you'll treat it with the respect my mother would've wanted." He sucked in my bottom lip and nibbled. "I wanted to show you the library myself because of the secret room. No one else knows about it. Not even the staff. Not anyone left alive, anyway. Keep it closed when you're not in it. Or when you are, if you'd like. It's hard to see this corner from the rest of the library, and the books kept here, right outside this room, are the most boring in the kingdom."

"I'll read them anyway. One day."

His smile was sad. He didn't respond.

I wanted to ask about his past, about his ex-fiancée, but he was already pulling me out of the room and settling me on the lounger.

"Check out the view while I lick your pussy. Or would you like some other means of pleasure?"

He didn't wait for an answer as he slid his hands up the outsides of my legs, gathering the material with them.

I watched the fabric shimmer as it bunched, revealing more and more of my thighs. He pushed the dress up to my waist and growled when he saw that I wasn't wearing any panties.

"I need to go to the salon before I wear the panties he made me," I whispered.

"You don't, but if you would like to, we can book you into the salon when we have time. How's that?"

"We?"

"Yes. No one will be touching you but me. I'll take care of whatever you need."

He trailed his lips up my inner thigh.

"Spread your legs," he commanded, and I whimpered as lust came over me.

I did as he said, gasping when his hot mouth went for me immediately. He sucked in my clit and thrust two fingers into my pussy, stroking just right. I arched into him, moving my hips in rhythm with his fingers, with the suction of his mouth. I gripped the lounger, no staying power at all. I hadn't been self-pleasuring in the evenings. It had been some time since I'd felt something this good in a place so intimate.

I groaned his name. Pushed up to his mouth. My body tensed, so tight. So hot. Right there—

The climax tore through me. I shouted his name, vibrating in bliss. He licked up my middle, tasting my release, and then pushed up, his knee between mine, his kiss on my lips. I tasted myself on him and threw an arm around his neck.

"My turn," I murmured against his lips.

"I wish. I have to go. The demon king's creatures must've been released by now. You can stay here for another hour, at the most, then head up to the tower. No one is supposed to use the library for their sexual adventures, but the parameters I've set are often over-looked when I'm gone. I don't want a demon to find you here. Not until we can start some long overdue combat training."

I snuck in another kiss with a smile. "Awesome. I badly need it."

"Yes. I am aware." He gave me another kiss before parting. "I'll see you tomorrow. Just an hour, okay? I'm trusting you."

He really should've known better than to trust a bookworm in a library.

TWO HOURS LATER, I sat at the edge of the lounger, ready to close the book and walk upstairs. A small pile of volumes sat at my feet, one for every mood. One of them was about frogs. *Frogs.* But it was colorful and eye-catching, and I'd leafed through it and decided I wanted to know more. I had two books for heavy reading, plus one adventure story I was reading at a lightning pace because it was so good. There was also a picture book for children about shifters in my pile. I figured that would help me learn about my people, about myself, and then I could go on a deeper research mission.

I finished a paragraph, and then decided I'd just as soon finish the chapter before I closed it and went upstairs. I would've gone up sooner, but the lounge was so comfortable, the library so beautiful, and the little reading nook was nice and cozy. I had every reason to believe it would become my favorite place in all the world very, very soon.

Voices bled through the images dancing in my head. I ignored them, flipping a page. They got louder, and then a woman laughed in a seductive way.

I turned my head a little to maybe look and see what was happening, but the villain had a knife to the hero's throat, and it just wasn't a great time to clue into reality.

A deep baritone spoke, and then another, and it became obvious there were other people in the library. I ignored them, nearly at the end of the chapter now. It was time to get going, anyway. I could continue reading in my room, undisturbed.

A feminine moan brought me up short. I cranked my head around and then leaned back on the lounger to look through the little space between the plant and the tapestry. From there, I could see most of the entrance, tinged green on one side.

A woman sauntered farther into the library, a red dress flowing over her shapely hips and cutting across the top of perky breasts. Two guys walked behind her, one closer than the other, both wearing dress shirts and black slacks. There must be a fancy dress party on tonight. Or maybe they just wanted a reason—or needed no reason—to dress up.

"This room is off-limits," said the guy in the back, glancing up at the second story. "If the master finds us in here, he'll rip our throats out."

"He's never around at this time of night..." She stopped by the couch and fanned her arms across the back.

The first guy walked around her, putting his back to me, and the other stopped a bit away. "I don't know..." He messed with his spiky white-blond hair as if nervous.

"I thought you both wanted to plug my holes. Isn't that what you said, Thomous?" the woman said, sticking out her chest.

The guy closest to her, with hair down to his shoulders, leaned a hand against the back of the couch. "That is what we said, Thomous, don't you remember? How long has it been since we got to fuck our fair lady here without the demon magic messing with our heads?"

"We can do it anywhere, that's the thing. The master—"

"Is a little less rigid lately now that he's got his captive to fuck. If he's here, which he isn't, he'll be with her." She licked her lips. "Besides, it's more exciting because he might catch us. Maybe he'll take a turn with me, too."

The first guy ran his hand down her bare arm. "Come on, Thomous. We don't want to keep her waiting."

The woman looked at Thomous as she ran a hand across Long Hair's shoulder. He pushed in a bit closer, angling so I could see better. His hand drifted up her side and then over the swell of her breast. He bent to kiss her neck, kneading.

She moaned and tilted back a little, now reaching for Thomous.

I stared, horrified. I shouldn't be watching this. This was an intimate moment that was clearly about to get sexual. I needed to remove myself and give them some privacy.

Except...there were only two exits in the library, and they'd see me if I tried to use either of them. I could slink back into the secret room, but what if the movement caught their attention?

Of course, I could also go now, before anything happened. They'd talked a dirty game, but no one had exposed themselves—

Long Hair pushed the top of the woman's dress down, exposing her breasts, and there went my chance of a non-awkward escape.

My core tingled with uncomfortable arousal. This

shouldn't be turning me on. It absolutely shouldn't be. Fuck, though, it totally was.

Long Hair bent and fastened his mouth to one pink nipple.

"Hmm, yes, baby," she said as Thomous finally ventured closer, the outline of his rigid cock filling his trousers.

He palmed her other breast and bent to capture her lips. She felt down with both hands, one for each cock, stroking through their pants.

"Yes," she said again as Thomous kissed down her neck and gave her a little nip. "Hmm."

Long Hair bent, pushing down her dress as he did so, and it stretched over her hips and fell to the floor. He knelt in front of her and rubbed between her thighs, kissing her navel.

She reached over and undid Thomous's zipper. He cupped the back of her head as he kissed her, his tongue delving into her mouth while Long Hair pulled down her panties and put his hands on her upper thighs, spreading.

Instead of complying, she pushed away. With a sultry smile, she stepped out of her dress, still in red high heels. Her hips swayed as she walked around the couch on the left, in full view of me. She'd just made this a spectator sport.

My core pounded, and a gush of wetness made me decide to push my limits. What was a little voyeurism among friends?

I pushed the plant back just a little and settled in, pushing a knee wide and bending my leg. I dipped my hand up into my dress, brushing my fingers across my wetness. I pushed in a finger as I continued to watch before lazily circling my clit.

Honestly, they were the ones doing it in public. She'd even said there was a thrill in potentially getting caught. Besides, hadn't Nyfain admitted to watching the goings-on of the castle? He hadn't been the least bit bashful, and given all the stuff Hadriel had said, no one would care one bit.

Game on.

The woman sat on the couch, her thighs spread, giving me an eyeful. Her pussy was completely shaved, not a tuft of hair in sight. Long Hair met her there quickly, stripping his shirt and pulling down his zipper. He put a knee on the couch beside her, his crotch at her eye level.

She reached in and took out his cock, eyeing Thomous as she licked the tip. Long Hair reached over and caught her nipple between his first finger and thumb, rubbing and pulling. She sucked him in as Thomous reached them, his own shirt off. He didn't pull out his cock yet, though. Instead, he bent between her thighs.

She leaned back to give Thomous more room but also sideways so as to reach Long Hair's cock. Positioning was clearly the key to having multiple partners. I could just see Thomous lick through her folds, reaching her clit and fastening his mouth. He slid his fingers into her, eliciting a heady moan.

Long Hair pushed his cock into her mouth. She fisted the base and sucked him in in greedy slurps, her cheeks hollowing as she did so. Long Hair groaned, tilting his head back in bliss for a moment. He looked down between her thighs, where Thomous was sucking her clit and using hard, heavy finger strokes, beating into her pussy—happy to do a little voyeurism himself.

"Make her squirt," Long Hair said as he kneaded her breast. "Make her squirt, bro."

Thomous rose and took a battle stance, it looked like, with his hard cock poking out of his pants. He slammed his middle and ring finger into her glistening depths, slapping her pussy with his palm.

She groaned around Long Hair's dick before pulling away, still pumping with her hand. Her mouth gaped in ecstasy at Thomous, who was finger-banging her aggressively. Her upper body lifted off the couch and tensed, straining, her mouth hanging wide open now, reaching for that orgasm.

"Yeah, baby. Come on, baby," Thomous goaded,

working his cock with the other hand. He increased his tempo, his fingers slamming into her, leaning over a little to get more muscle behind it.

"Oh goddess, yes, *yes*," the woman said, pushing her knees out further, her whole body tense. She let go of Long Hair's dick and gripped the couch. "Yes, yeee—*aaaaah!*"

She shuddered with a loud cry, leaning her head back and arching. Her pussy erupted, spraying her orgasm over the edge of the couch and onto the floor like a fucking waterspout.

My fingers stilled. I'd never even known that was a thing, and I...I wasn't sure how I felt about it. I mean...that was a mighty powerful orgasm, but now it was everywhere. I definitely would *not* be sitting on that couch.

Thomous peeled off his pants and shoes and sat down beside the woman, his knees wide and his shaved balls on display. The woman repositioned herself and knelt between his knees, taking his cock into her mouth. Her head started bobbing.

Long Hair came around behind her, and in one fluid movement he pulled her ass into the air and threaded his cock into her waiting cunt. He took hold of her hips and pulled back as he thrust, his skin slapping against hers. She moaned, taking more cock now, her hand pumping.

I made circles around my clit, pleasure starting to build inside me. I ran my fingers down my slit and returned, everything slick. I wanted Nyfain here with me, a partner in crime, watching the others while we fucked in tandem. Naughty and sexy and titillating.

Long Hair pulled out as she was still bobbing on Thomous. He knelt behind her and spread her ass cheeks wide. He bent between them, and though I couldn't see exactly what he was doing, I got the impression he was circling or prodding her asshole with his tongue. He was getting it ready. This was about to get real.

"Hmm," she said, stilling on Thomous for a moment to take a little *her* time.

Long Hair bobbed a bit, clearly now fucking her ass with his tongue. My core pounded, and I dipped my fingers deep into my pussy while half frowning. Great goddess, that was erotically filthy. But somehow incredibly hot, because I knew he was about to fuck her ass and also likely didn't give two shits about anything else. If it wasn't my tongue, who cared?

I worked my fingers hard, breathing fast now.

He put his face in her cheeks, really going after it. She was moaning hard, stroking Thomous, who had reached out to palm her breast.

Long Hair pulled back and stood, stroking his cock a little while repositioning himself.

I slowed, wondering what would happen next. They all seemed to be enmeshed in some sort of erotic dance, the steps known, the players clear on what to do and when. No bumbling around with various holes for this experienced crew. They were masters.

Thomous stayed where he was, receiving a scorching kiss from the woman before she turned around, using the back of the couch for support. She planted her feet on the couch cushions on either side of Thomous's legs. Thomous grabbed the sides of her butt and held her for a moment.

Long Hair rifled through his discarded pants and came back with a little canister. He scooped out something that looked like gel before pocketing it again. Whatever it was, he smeared it down Thomous's cock, stroking a couple times while he was there, running his thumb across Thomous's tip.

"Hmm, yes, boys," the woman said.

Long Hair leaned forward and kissed her, his hand leaving Thomous's cock and finding her asshole. He rubbed the gel across and then in, pumping a couple times with his fingers.

"Yeah," Thomous said, lowering her again.

"Fuck her in the ass," Long Hair said.

Thomous rubbed the head of his cock around her asshole before pausing at the opening. She lowered herself down slowly, the tip getting resistance at first. She backed off before sitting down a little more, leaning forward. Up and then back down, a little further. His cock pushed into her ass, deeper and deeper. As she lowered this time, he thrust up, clearly unable to contain himself, fully seating within her ass.

"Oh fuck, baby," she said in a throaty moan. "Hmm, yes."

I bit my lip harder. Holy fuck, this was hot. Crazy but hot. My fingers moved faster. Gleefully. This was so wrong and exciting, for all of us!

She rose on him, his cock pulling up a bit before she sat back down. He pulled her hips as she did, thrusting into her. Long Hair bent to her clit, licking and sucking while she worked her ass around Thomous's cock. In a moment, Long Hair rose and pushed forward, and I wanted to run closer and get a better view. As it was, I leaned up a bit more on the lounger, peering around the plant.

Long Hair crested her opening with his cock, paused, and then slowly but firmly threaded it into her pussy. She groaned, he groaned, I groaned—we all groaned!

He fully sheathed his cock, and I wondered how

incredibly full she must feel. Give her one more guy, and she'd have some serious dongage on her hands.

Long Hair pumped forward, and she leaned back a bit farther, pushing with her hands and feet to bridge off Thomous a bit. In a moment, I saw why. Both guys were pumping into her, Long Hair more than Thomous, and I bet they were kinda rubbing against each other inside of her body, getting more friction. The bottom dick moved in and out of her ass, good and deep, and the top thrust hard into her pussy.

I rubbed my clit, watching in awe, my body taut. The guys kept going, grunting, the woman moaning long and loud. Everything sped up, their cries louder, my breathing faster. They were right there, I could tell. I was right there with them, Creep-O-Meter going off big time.

The door slammed open and a roar filled the space. Everyone froze in terror.

CHAPTER 12

THAT WAS, EVERYONE froze in terror...except for me.

My body turned pliant as arousal licked higher. My animal leaked fire into my already scorching body.

Nyfain looked like one of the dragon gods of old, come down from the heavens to smite the land. Dirt and blood streaked across his chest. A fresh gash sliced his right bicep. His dark brown hair was wild, and an impressive display of muscle corded down his robust body.

He rushed in, his presence emanating strength and raw, vicious power. He clapped eyes on the three on the couch and growled, terrible to behold. He was upon them before they could get untangled.

"Where is she?" He grabbed Long Hair by the throat and launched him across the room.

"Not the books, Nyfain, be careful," I yelled. Maybe I should've been worried about the guy, but ink before kink. The books were the priority.

The others didn't look my way, not with the mighty dragon prince leaning over them. *He* did, though. His head snapped up, his eyes on fire. He grabbed the back of the couch with his hand. He yanked, overturning it, dumping the two onto the floor.

"Get out," he snarled, his feet pounding against the wood as he stalked my way.

Long Hair took off at a hobbling run, not bothering to grab his clothes on the way out. The other two managed to disentangle, his dick popping out of her ass, and they hurried along after him. Nyfain came into my little den, as I thought of it, his eyes scanning, landing on my leg pulled wide and my dress pulled up. His eyes flashed, rage and hunger running through the bond.

"I was being a voyeur," I blurted, my face flaming heat.

In embarrassment, I moved to fling my dress down my leg, but he dashed forward and grabbed my wrist so fast I gasped in shock.

"Did one of them touch you?" he said. Possessiveness rang in every word.

My animal rolled and basked in it, purring in delight. *Hmm, alpha,* she thought.

His brutal intensity crashed down on me, soaking deep into my flesh. I arched within it, wetness trickling out of my pussy. I wanted him to take me. To ride me hard, to explode me into pieces and then meld me back together before destroying me again.

"No, I was back here by myself," I said huskily. "I was going to leave, but they got naked really quick, and they would've seen me, and then..."

"And then?" he asked in a dangerous tone.

"And then I didn't want to leave because it was hot to watch. I wanted you to be here with me, watching and fucking, but you weren't, so..."

He brought my hand up slowly, his eyes on mine. He sucked my first two fingers into his mouth. I barely dared to breathe as I watched him taste me. His cock stood straight and proud, the tip shiny, ready for me. I licked my lips, catching his heated gaze.

He flung the other portion of my dress up to my hip, exposing me fully. He knelt on the lounger, pushing my knee up and then hooking his hand on my hip and pulling me closer.

"What am I going to do with you?" he asked, eyeing my neck now. "I try to refrain, but you keep getting sexier and sexier. It's killing me."

He grabbed my wrists and pinned them above my head.

"I felt your desire through the bond," he said, keeping my wrists in one of his large hands and then feeling down my chest with the other. He slid a thumb across my nipple before reaching lower and pushing two fingers into my pussy. "And then I felt your passion, as if someone was fucking you. You were so into it. I thought for sure one of the demons had gotten a hold of you. I ran from the other end of the kingdom, ready to tear the castle apart. And here you are, in your little hideaway, touching yourself as you watch a threesome. Fuck, you're so wet."

He smelled up my neck before nipping my jaw.

"You have an uncompromising hold on me, princess." He plunged his fingers in faster. "I dream of you. I think of you always. My dragon begs to be back in control so he can feel your animal. It's tearing me apart."

He bit down on my neck, puncturing skin, and a thrill exploded through my body.

"I have never felt this strongly about anything in my entire life. It's not natural. It's certainly not normal. And yet I live for it. I'd die for it. I *will* die for it." He ran his tongue across the fresh wound before grazing his teeth down lower, to my shoulder. "What would happen if we just gave in?"

My chest heaved. I couldn't get enough air. I pushed

my head back and away, giving him all the access he needed, knowing it was a terrible idea for so many reasons but not wanting to think of them. My animal uncoiled within me, desperate for him to bite. To finally do this. To claim us as his.

He stroked his tongue across my flesh. Scraped his teeth.

I yanked at my hands to get loose. To reach down and grab his cock. To guide him into my desperate body.

"Fuck, Finley, I want to," he whispered, skimming his lips to the crook of my neck and then up to my lips. "I want to so badly."

His kiss was deep and possessive. His hold on my wrists was firm, almost painful. He grabbed the base of his cock and lined it up before driving it into me. I cried out, gloriously filled, and then melted into the lounger. He pulled out and then rammed in again, starting fast, getting faster. He kept his lips on mine as he drove in deep. His balls slapped against me. His hipbones banged against my flesh.

I called his name, trapped in his grip. My eyes fluttered, flickering light dancing across my lids. His body moved within me, the glorious friction setting my everything humming.

He sat back onto his knees, his erect cock shiny with

my juices. He was dirty and bloody and raw and incensed, and I turned into liquid within his heated stare. In that moment, he could mold and shape me however he pleased.

"Come here and sit on my cock," he commanded.

Fire pinged through my body. My animal was right near the surface, not taking control but not wanting to miss a single thing. She liked the look of this alpha as much as she liked the sound of him. The feel. One day we'd battle, he and I, and I'd make him prove his physical dominance while I proved I had a will of steel, but not right now. Right now, I was drunk on lust. Raw on need. Right now I wanted to be his fuck toy.

I pushed to my knees gracefully, mindful of my dress.

"Take it off," he said, realizing it and thankfully not wanting to damage it.

I pulled my hair from the bun and let it tumble down in a messy collection of waves. I then swept it to the side and turned, allowing him to find the few buttons. He unclasped them, his fingertips whispering against my back. Goosebumps spread across my skin in their wake.

I turned to him again, on my knees now, and pulled the straps from my shoulders. I let the dress slide down my body, catching on my breasts before falling to my knees. I sat back and pulled it out from under me before dropping it in a beautiful cascade of fabric to pool on the floor.

I waited for him to tell me to climb on. He paused, though, to look at my exposed flesh, reaching forward to trace the backs of his fingers down the slope of my breast and over my nipple. He then ran them down my cheek, and his eyes softened as his fingers trailed my jaw and gently traced the line of my throat.

He took my hand and pulled me closer. Intense emotion rolled through the bond—warmth, reverence, devotion, and something stronger that took my breath away. My animal basked in it, and I could feel his dragon through the bond pumping out power to enhance it.

"Fuck me, Finley."

With a surge of desire, I climbed into his lap, my arms around his neck, my lips on his. He wrapped my legs around his hips as I settled down onto him. His cock drove up into my body, deep and delicious. He grabbed the sides of my butt and lifted before crashing me back down, jutting up with his hips as he did so. Pleasure speared me. I dropped my head back and sighed out his name. He did it again, and again, plunging so deep it filled my whole world. I dropped my hand to work my clit as I bounced on top of him.

"Finley," he said, his fingers tangled in my hair, his cheek pressed to mine. It sounded like he was begging. Like he was pleading for something. Emotion bled through the bond. I didn't know what he was responding to, I just knew something deep inside of me was flowering. It felt like he was opening himself up a little more, and as he did, I was cracking open with him.

I kissed him deeply, rocking on top of him. Nearly there. I draped my hands over his back and ran my fingers down one of his wing scars.

He growled, suddenly bucking frantically, ramming me hard. I hit a peak and cried out, shuddering. He pushed forward onto the lounger, putting me under him, still going. Still fucking me like a man possessed.

The sensations overwhelmed me. Dragged me under. I kept going, jerking my hips to meet his downward thrusts. The slap of our skin echoing. Our moans competing. Harder he strove. Harder still. I ran my fingers down his scar again, applying more pressure. Putting some nails into it before the sensations became too much. The thick slide of him inside me set me further aflame. I hit another peak but didn't tumble over. There I stayed, at the top, my body strung out beyond anything I'd ever felt, desperate to pitch over.

"Please, Nyfain," I cried, tight all over, more pleasure rolling through me. His thrusts were hard and brutal, his pleasure incomparable. "I need to come!"

He kissed me, bruising. Dominating.

The wave crashed, and I came violently, shaking against him. But still he strove, his teeth scraping against my shoulder. I came again. And again, a constant stream of pleasure that I couldn't seem to escape. That I didn't want to.

"Come with me!" he commanded. His power shocked through me. His teeth pierced the flesh on my neck.

I screamed out my orgasm, nearly blacking out, clutching him with everything I had. He shook against me, finishing with two hard thrusts, and then stayed buried inside me.

His chest heaved, and he pushed his weight onto me, not asking if I could take it. I kissed his neck and draped my limbs around him, liquifying into the lounger.

We rested for a long moment in silence, limbs entwined.

"Did you honestly think I'd enjoy myself with a bunch of demons?" I asked softly. "What were you thinking?"

"They can make a person enjoy themselves."

"Not me. Not anymore. I don't even need the draught—when they put that magic on me, it makes me nauseated."

He stroked his fingertips down my arm. "That's good to know."

"Your response was a bit overkill, though. Are all shifters that possessive?"

"Dragons are incredibly possessive when they...feel strongly," he said, and butterflies spread through my stomach with that hitch in his words. I wondered what he'd been about to say. "Being that I'm an alpha, and me, I am worse than most."

"What's going to happen with your fiancée when all this ends? The curse, I mean."

His brow furrowed. "My fiancée?"

"The one who owned the dresses in the tower. The faerie."

He shook his head. "She has certainly moved on. As soon as the curse went into effect, we were scrubbed from everyone's minds. This kingdom doesn't exist to anyone but us and the demons right now."

"Yes, but...after. Would she not meet you and care for you?"

His smile was grim. He lay beside me and gathered me into his arms. "I'm not sure she ever cared for me, in truth. She wanted certain things from me, and I wanted certain things from her. To escape, for one. We were compatible, and I've thought of her from time to time in these last agonizing years…" He paused and continued in a subdued voice. "But then you came. You told me that you saw your ex again, after you left, and felt nothing for him. It's the same way for me. Suddenly, those feelings were just gone. There was nothing there. Not even a memory of anything there."

"So you're not cheating with me, then? And yes, I realize that was a question I should've asked before this, but… Well, I'm terrible, I guess."

He chuckled. "She has certainly married another. Probably has children by now. She was a noble in high demand for her healing abilities. I would've helped her grow the plants that she used. I'm sure she found a noble faerie to take my place. So, no, I'm not cheating. That had absolutely nothing to do with my abstinence. I already told you why I was celibate."

"Yes, but you lie."

Hadriel ran in wearing an open white dress shirt and black slacks. He looked around wildly.

"Finley! Finley, are you in here? Knock once or something if you are."

Nyfain tensed. He got up and walked around the tapestry as I hurried to put my dress on.

"Oh!" Hadriel sagged, a hand to his chest. "Master, it's you. Thank the goddess for her mercy. Finley hasn't returned to her room, and she didn't take the draught earlier, and…"

"She's fine. But she'll need to go back to her room now. It's past time."

"Yeah." Hadriel looked at the couch lying on its back. "What happened here? Did you guys battle for dominance or something?"

Nyfain didn't answer. Apparently he wasn't a kiss-and-tell kinda guy.

"Knock once or something?" I grabbed my books and walked out from behind the tapestry. "Why wouldn't I just yell for you?"

Hadriel spread his hands with his eyebrows raised. "Maybe you had a gag or something, I don't know. It's the only thing that came to me. Come on. I'm actually enjoying myself for once. I've had three demons ask me to engage in sexual relations, and I have turned them all down." He puffed up his chest. "I feel like a new man. Did you hear me just there? *Sexual relations.* I didn't even say *fucking.* My mama would be proud."

"Their lack of effect on the staff will be noticed," Nyfain said softly, taking the books from me. He looked at the titles as we walked toward Hadriel. He paused on the one about frogs before sliding an inquisitive glance my way.

"What? I opened the book, and there was a pretty frog. I thought I'd read it."

Nyfain gave me a lopsided grin. He didn't say anything as he gave the books to Hadriel.

"Oh good, I get to be the donkey. Fantastic." He took the books. "And not everyone is immune. Only the people who aren't huge blabbermouths."

"Finley showed up, and things changed. It'll be noticed." Nyfain kissed me before turning. "Stay safe. I'll see you tomorrow."

When he was gone, Hadriel walked me to the tower.

"Did you guys get it on when he was in that state?" Hadriel asked.

"Yeah," I said, my voice breathy. "He looks super hardcore and sexy right now."

"Finley, love, that wasn't his blood streaked on his chest."

"We fucked in the blood of his enemies."

Hadriel turned to me with wide eyes and a crooked smile. "My goodness, look at you! I like it. That man is absolutely nuts, and anyone that is with him has to be nuts as well. I am much too sensible for a guy like him. But crazy is a good look on you."

I rolled my eyes as we reached the tower.

"And that dress looks gorgeous on you. It's really fitting. Your hair is an absolute mess, but besides that, you're very striking."

"Enjoy your party."

"Well, thank you. I think I might this time. I really think I might."

He lit two candles for me and then wished me good night.

LATER THAT NIGHT, I startled awake. Strange sounds had permeated my dreams—a growl followed by snuffling noises. A spark of pain had ignited in my middle, and my animal had jerked and rolled. I sat up in the stillness, listening, taking a deep breath.

The growl was soft, ending in a strange ticking noise. The snuffling sounded at the base of my door, down by the crack.

Tingles of apprehension lodged in my chest. I pulled back the covers and draped my feet over the side before standing. My nightgown slid down my legs to stop at my calves.

The snuffling came again, and another flare of pain blossomed in my middle.

What is that? I asked my animal.

How the fuck should I know? I can't see through doors any more than you can.

I mean the pain. That's not from the bond, is it?

How are you this obtuse?

If you were a separate being, I would punch you right in the mouth. Also, is that a no?

I could feel her rolling her eyes. *It is a no. It's being caused by that creature outside of our door. It needs to be killed, but not by you, because it won't wait around until you drag it by the neck toward a sword.*

I shook my head and crossed the room to the dagger Hadriel had brought me from the armory. It was a little smaller than the one I was used to carrying. A little lighter. A lot sharper. I could wreak all sorts of trauma with this little baby.

Still, I'd learned my lesson. I was not going out to meet that thing if I didn't have to.

As I went to turn, movement caught my eye. Two people were walking outside my window, beyond the garden area. A man and a woman. They were probably ten yards apart, walking the same direction at exactly the same pace. They stopped when I noticed them, staring up into my window. There they stood, watching me watching them.

The creature at my door laughed in a low, terrifying tone. Somehow they were connected, these creatures. They could feel each other, or maybe they could feel the effect they were having on me. Whatever it was, their teamwork would have me outnumbered, and their goal was fear-based pain.

My heart sped up. Something clicked in my mind. Locked into place, like when Nyfain had first entered me. Like when I'd handled my first everlass plant as a ten-year-old.

I tightened my grip on my dagger. The creature at my door snuffled. It might've been smelling my fear, which was rolling off me, but I wondered if it could also smell my determination.

Because I was done with the wilting flower routine. Done with it. I had never been a wilting flower. I would not strive for mediocrity. And if that got demons on my ass, then I'd kill them. Let the demon king come. Fuck him. We all had to die sometime, and I would die taking a stand.

I just had to learn how...

CHAPTER 13

"COME AT ME."

I gripped the very pretty sword in my dirty hand and faced off with Nyfain. The late-afternoon sun shone down on our mock battlefield, the greenish weeds trampled underfoot, the everlass field not far away, and a sweaty me doing a terrible job at sticking the pointy end into Nyfain's person. He was so convinced I was crap with a sword that we weren't even using a practice one.

He was right. I hadn't even scratched him. I hadn't even gotten close.

"Can we go back to the dagger?" I asked him, short of breath. I'd proved very useful with a dagger, as we both knew I was.

"The sword is longer, giving you—"

"A longer reach, I know."

"Right. Come at me."

I assumed the stance he'd taught me. This was our second practice session in three days. I'd told him about my visitors. They weren't regulars at the castle, apparently, but visitors from one of the more fear-based villages. News about his "captive" had gotten around, and given the snuffing at the door, they knew he was intimate with me. He wasn't sure what kind of risk that posed, but he'd been adamant that we start training right away.

I took a deep breath and then *flowed* through the movements, bending like a crane, stabbing like a monkey or some such thing.

This is ridiculous, my animal said as I swiped at him and missed entirely. He barely even moved. *It's a waste of time.*

Big words from someone who has yet to show her face. Until you can come out and actually do something useful, this is all we've got.

She made a disgruntled sound and went back to crouching within me and watching. I had her strength, and her speed, but apparently not her prowess.

"You're doing the stance perfectly, you're doing the movements perfectly, but you're forgetting to actually try to stab me until the very end." There was a twinkle of humor in Nyfain's eyes.

"It's not funny."

"No, it shouldn't be."

The twinkle of humor didn't diminish.

"So, like...I don't get it. These movements I'm learning basically go in a straight line, but people move. What, am I supposed to hop from side to side to get lined up and then charge?"

A deliciously crooked smile worked up his face. "I don't remember anyone in my classes having that complaint. This is why we start very young, before we know to ask logical questions." He put out his hands, obviously thinking. "You'll master a bunch of stances and movements that go with them, and you choose the one best suited to the moment. So, for right now, we are learning this one."

"Fine. Don't move so that I can stab you."

He laughed helplessly. "That's not how it works. The enemy will move."

"Then I'm not going to be in a straight line," I yelled, wanting to throw down the sword and just give up. It didn't make any sense to me.

"Okay, let's try it without the sword and see how you do."

It turned out that I did very well without the sword. I'd flow through the very fancy movements, get close, and randomly launch at him and try to kill him. I got to his body every single time, and then usually found myself hugged tightly to his chest while he gave me a raspberry against my neck or something else equally childish. He was mocking me, obviously, because I didn't know what to do with him when I got to him.

"Next time we'll start with hand-to-hand combat, then," Nyfain said as we finished up, grabbing a towel that Hadriel had brought out before returning to the garden. It was still his favorite activity, weeding and getting everything ready. Soon we'd be ready to plant, and I'd start working on those roses.

"We need to harvest some everlass," I told Nyfain as we started back to the castle. "Or...I do, I guess."

"We do. And yes, I know. Within the next few nights, I should have the time to do that."

"Are you still keeping up with the everlass field near my house?"

"Yes. They are using it. I want to make sure they have what they need."

I slipped my hand around his arm and walked close. He'd continued to deliver fresh kills to my family, and now he was taking the time for this, as well. We hadn't been giving the people of my village starter elixirs because they knew how to do it on their own, but soon I'd need to make up a few batches for those who didn't have the ability. It was their turn to be looked after.

"I was thinking I could work that field while you clear out the riffraff. The other field, too. All the fields, if you need. I can help with that to free you up."

"You can't sing."

"No. But my crop at home was just as vibrant as yours, and I never sang to the plants."

"Did you speak to them?"

"No. I muttered to myself a good bit, though."

"That's probably good enough. My mother always said that there was power in words. I was shy and never knew what to say to the plants. That's why I started singing."

"The seamster said you were better than her at growing them," I said, glancing at him. "At making them happy. He said the plants thrived whenever you worked with them."

"My mother always told me that. I think she just said it to make me feel good about myself. All of the women sang and spoke to the everlass. Look at you— you can do it, too."

"Except I'm hanging on to the dream that I would've been good enough for you to introduce me to her one day, and if you say I'm not special, then I'll never forgive you."

He laughed and put his arm around me. "Sorry. Yes, we are very special, you and me. More so than anyone."

"That's better."

He opened the back door for me and waited until I went through before he followed. "I wondered." He nodded to Lena as she passed, fully dressed and prim-looking with pursed lips and a bustling walk. I would've never guessed that she strapped on a dildo and toured the castle at night. "In a couple days, I should be free. I wondered if you'd have dinner with me?"

"Yes. All my clothes have been finished, so I have something to wear. Wait! No. I need to visit the salon first."

"Well, then. Maybe we'll incorporate that into the date. We can have dinner once you're...how you want to be."

"How do I want to be?" We climbed the stairs. "That girl the other night was shaved completely clean. We didn't really do much of that in my village. That I know of. Not like anyone would tell me about their pubic hair situation, but..."

"It doesn't matter to me, Finley. You can leave it as it is if you'd like."

"You don't have a preference? I noticed yours are trimmed."

"Trimmed, then, if you like."

I shrugged. I definitely wanted less to fuss with down there. If I weren't so vain, I'd do it to my head hair as well.

He stopped at the tower door and waited for me to get out my key.

"What will you do tonight?" he asked.

"Read, as usual. Work on the notes for your next book."

"Hmm. Yes, please." He wrapped his arms around me and kissed me.

"Or I could help you with the everlass."

He shook his head. "Too dangerous. I don't want to leave you out there alone. It doesn't take me long to tend to it, anyway. And since you've been working the field on the castle grounds, you've already lightened my load."

Hadriel crested the stairs, took one look at us, and about-faced.

"I was just leaving, Hadriel," Nyfain said, then stole one last kiss before stepping away from me. Regret rang through the bond.

"Don't leave on my account, sir. I was just getting lost, anyway."

"No, no. I have things to see to." Nyfain stroked my cheek, his touch soft and intimate, his eyes delving into my soul. "I'll see you tomorrow."

"Or…tonight, when you get back?" I asked.

He hesitated, and a grin pulled at his lips. "Tonight,

then. Wear something slinky."

A thrill ran through me. He clearly felt it through the bond, because he smiled.

Before he left, he asked, "You still have what you need for the tea, correct? Should I gather anything from the other villages?"

"We're good for a while. Hadriel isn't passing it out to everyone."

Nyfain's brow furrowed as he glanced at Hadriel. "Why are you—Ah, no. Not the draught for demon magic. The regulator tea. To prevent pregnancy."

"Oh." *Shiiiit!*

I belatedly remembered the conversation we'd had in the woods. Since returning to the castle, though, I hadn't thought a thing about it. It had literally never crossed my mind. I'd had it in my head that he was just being cautious, and there had been so many other things going on, that…I'd forgotten. Fuck.

Goddess help me if his caution wasn't unfounded. Please, please let Hadriel have been correct and knowledgeable and Nyfain was just nervous and overreacting.

Whether it was the look on my face or the feelings through the bond, he clearly read the situation.

His demeanor changed in a moment. His eyes hardened. He turned to Hadriel.

"Tell me you've been giving her the tea," he demanded.

Hadriel's face paled. "I… I…"

Nyfain grabbed him by the shirt and yanked him closer. "I specifically told you to make sure she was drinking that tea."

"Y-yes, sir. Except that was the first time, and you guys hadn't…you know…and then she came back, and… I…"

Nyfain growled and lifted him off the ground. "Go make that tea. Right now. Watch her. I want to know when she bleeds."

"It's not supposed to happen for…" I looked downward as I thought frantically. As I struggled to remember the moon's current fullness.

Nyfain's terror bled through the link.

"*When?*"

I jumped at the ferocity of his tone. The hardness of his gaze. An inkling of fear wove through me as a pang hit my heart. I'd been ready for this temper when we first met, but I'd grown used to the other guy lately. The guy who showed everyone else this side and not me.

Tears filled my eyes, but I straightened up, refusing to bow under his stare. "Not for another few days," I said in a rush, and I was pretty sure that was correct.

He blew out a breath and stuck a finger in Hadriel's face. Then he turned his back on me and jogged down the stairs.

When he was gone, I sagged, shaking and suddenly exhausted. A tear slipped down my cheek, and I batted it away. A few more followed, my heart aching. I hadn't been ready for his rough treatment. I still wasn't. It would take a second to harden myself toward him again.

"You said he could only impregnate his true mate, right?" I asked Hadriel, my hand shaking and the key pinging off the sides of the lock.

Hadriel hugged me from behind and then took the key from me to do it himself. He butted it against the door, then the side of the lock, then off the metal of the keyhole. He was worse off.

I took the key back as he said, "Yes, as I understand it."

"Then what is his deal? We obviously can't be true mates because he's a dragon and my animal purrs. Purring is probably a big cat. Well, hopefully a big cat. Being a tabby cat will be a bit embarrassing."

For all of us... my animal thought.

"If we don't have the same animal, we can't be true mates. And if my parents were dragons, I wouldn't have been allowed to live. So…"

Hadriel shrugged. "I don't know. But he's adamant, so we better do it. I'll get that tea."

NYFAIN DIDN'T SHOW up that night. I lay awake at about the time he was supposed to come in, feeling the strangest emotions through the bond. Anger and fear and anxiety and self-loathing and regret and determination and...hopelessness. I had a feeling the anger was his dragon's, over his sudden change of heart, but I couldn't understand why he'd been so adamant, so ugly.

Was it something in his past that had set him off? Or maybe he had an irrational fear of fatherhood because of his problems with his own father? A man could go to extremes not to be like his dad.

Or maybe...Hadriel hadn't known the full extent of how the curse worked, like Nyfain had said.

Tingles washed through me, and I turned my head to look out the window. The moon hung heavy in the sky. I'd been right—it should be a couple days or so until I bled.

If I bled.

A storm of emotions accosted me. Warmth seeped into my middle, and suddenly it was hard to breathe.

You want this as much as I do, my animal thought in the equivalent of a soft tone. *As much as the dragon does.*

No, I do not. Are you crazy? It would be incredibly bad timing—the worst possible timing in the history of bad timing—to get with child right now. A strange tickling of anticipation and longing quickened my heart. I shoved it away violently. *This kingdom is dying, demons are threatening our very existence, and if the curse ends, the demon king will likely wreak havoc. I need to fight. I can't do that with a child in my belly.*

Timing aside, you want a child with the man. You want a future with him, just like the dragon and I do. Admit it.

I trailed my fingers across my flat stomach, and a tear bled out of my eye and down my cheek. I stared out at the night sky. Goddess smite me, I did. Despite our differences in social status, our differences in upbringing, his horrible temper and bad moods...I could see myself happy with Nyfain. I was no longer content with the thought of a solitary future. I was no longer fine envisioning myself alone as I got older. The desire for a family had reasserted itself. A home. A loving mate.

Nyfain had brought about that change.

I wanted to feel for a mate the way I felt for him. I didn't want to live the rest of my life without intimacy or someone to share my thoughts with. I didn't want to lose the fire I felt when lost to Nyfain's touch.

I blew out a breath. These were dangerous waters to tread.

I pulled my hand away from my stomach.

It doesn't matter, I thought. *I should bleed in a cou-*

ple days. Even if Hadriel was wrong, and logic says he probably isn't, I'm sure the timing was off. I know how these things work, and I doubt I'm with child.

What sort of logic exists in a demon-created curse?

Please shut up. You're giving me a headache.

My animal huffed. Try to brush it aside if you want, but I know your true feelings. And I know that taking the tea now won't do a damn thing. Right? At this point, either you are or you aren't.

She was right there. All I could do now was wait.

Don't tell the dragon that, though, she thought, and it felt like she was mulling something over.

Why?

Because the thought of his getting us with child creates this...need in me. It's deep...and consuming...and primal. I feel it all through me, pulsing. It's like I'm dizzied, desperate to demand his seed. I feel almost frenzied when I think of his claiming us and putting a child in us. For some reason, when I dwell on it, I can squeeze more power through this cage the demon magic has around me. It's because of the primal urges, I know it. I can feel it.

So what does this have to do with the dragon?

He's more powerful than me. He's been working on escaping the confines of this cage for a lot longer. Before us, his resources were tapped out. The only primal survival mechanisms he's been able to pull on these last years have been those earned in battle. Fear, rage, adrenaline, etc.

I screwed up my face. *I'm not following.*

What is more powerful than a species' biological need to procreate? It's built in. And an alpha like him, with the attraction he has for us—he's going to feel it incredibly strongly.

So you think his desperation to procreate is somehow going to break through the curse? I asked.

She took a moment, and it felt like she was gathering herself.

This is what I know, she finally thought, and I could tell she was trying to work things out. Trying to figure out her own constraints. *Of all the shifters in this whole kingdom, only one was powerful enough, and headstrong enough, to batter his way through the curse's hold and force a change. That shouldn't have been possible, and that dragon took great damage, but they still managed it. Their will to remain together was stronger than the curse's magic.*

She paused, and I waited for her to continue.

When I gather enough power to shift, intent on forcing your hand to do something I want, that happens by drawing on the primal urges within me. To shift. To mate. To claim and be claimed. It's all primal. It's all built in. The dragon showed me how, and drawing on it shaves away the hold the curse has on us. Now there is this frenzy to mate, to build a family, and the compulsion is ten times stronger for some reason. I can feel it. I know he can. He will move mountains to see it done. He will be an unstoppable force. The man needs that if he is going to survive. We need it. The kingdom needs it. Plus, I want it. I want him.

I shook my head and stared at the ceiling. *Why all of a sudden is this a thing?*

Because all of a sudden it became a possibility, idiot. Someone didn't bother warding off pregnancy with the tea, and that fact has incited the dragon. I doubt he knows the details on how this stuff works, so he's going to try to load you up with his seed to make sure it takes.

Ew, I thought. I might want a family someday, but I did not want to think of it in those terms.

It was the dragon that set me off, and now I'm buzzing with the frenzy to mate. Or maybe he's buzzing with it and I'm all for it? It's all one big, delicious, turbulent jumble of need and longing, and I want to sink down into it and lose myself.

I thought back to Nyfain's anger when he realized I

wasn't taking the tea. To his outburst. To how that made me feel.

Well, don't, I thought, another tear slipping down. *I won't try to incite him with this.*

Not even to give him desperately needed access to more power?

I shook my head, suddenly exhausted. *Nyfain doesn't want to claim me. He sure as shit doesn't want to get me with child. I'm sure I'll bleed soon, and that's the end of it. The way past this curse isn't fucking with that dragon's head. He's crazy enough.*

My animal settled down grumpily, and I continued to watch the sky.

Regardless of his reasons, Nyfain had handled that situation badly. I had to own that it had hurt, how he'd treated me. I might make allowances for some outbursts, but that one had crossed the line. I planned to make sure he knew it.

THE NEXT AFTERNOON, after preparing everything for a harvest that night, I stepped into the garden by way of the wall. I did not plan to go through the queen's chambers in case Nyfain was in there for some reason, probably staring at that wilting rosebush and brooding. He did that well, the brooding. It was his trademark.

"How goes it, boys?" I asked, sizing up the rosebushes. Soon I'd be ready to tackle those suckers. I wanted to attend to the everlass, but after that, these bushes were going to get my full attention.

Hadriel straightened up and grabbed his back. "Good, I think. But Jawson doesn't think this soil is the best."

Jawson was on his hands and knees weeding the area by the wall. He used the wall to straighten up to his knees so he could look at me.

"It's a little too acidic, Miss Finley, if I had to guess." He took a handful and let it run out the side of his palm.

"He is definitely guessing," Gyril announced, hacking at a blackberry root. "He hasn't brought out any of his little machines or anything."

"I've been doing this all of my life, young man, and I know about soil."

"Yeah, but given you are still alive, you've been doing a mediocre job all of your life," Hadriel said, looking over the ground. He bent to scoop out another couple of weeds he'd missed.

"Mediocrity ends now," I said, and power rode my words. I wouldn't be hiding that, either. I was letting my lady balls hang out, and they were big and beautiful, and, unlike a man's, they liked it rough.

I stopped near a tilled patch and dropped down to a crouch. Closing my eyes and centering my mind, I soaked in the sensations around me. The soft sunshine beating down on me. The cool breeze ruffling my hair. The frigid smell of winter clung to the air, but within it I caught the sweet smell of spring not far off. It was the perfect time to be planting a garden. Luck was on my side in this one thing.

I dragged my hand through the soil, meeting plenty of resistance. It wasn't...soft enough for plants. Yielding enough. It was bitter, this soil. Slightly angry. It wouldn't help me grow things.

"Yeah." I stood and smelled the dirt clinging to my fingers, turning my face toward the Forbidden Wood. "The demon's filth has infiltrated it. I wouldn't be surprised if one of the vines you ripped out carried their magic somehow. Some plants have a way of ingesting the magic around them and transferring it to the soil. The everlass does that, but they are partial to dragon magic. Let's..."

I visited various patches of dirt, tilled and not, sticking my fingers in and assessing the vibe. Every natural space had one. I'd learned that early in life. Spending time in natural spaces helped me center my mind and forget about an awful day or the sickness around me. They rewarded me with a sort of soothing current. Unless something was amiss, of course, and then I couldn't quite connect.

"I need to hit the library. There's something…not quite right here, I think. Something more than demonic magic." I closed my eyes again, letting my mind drift. Letting the feelings soak from the ground into my fingers. "Something…sad, almost."

A swell of emotion hit me, rocking me to the core. The ground seemed to sing a sad tune, one that would wilt flowers.

Aching pain. Utter hopelessness. Guilt.

I fluttered my eyes open as a tear dripped down my face. I turned, looking in through the glass at the darkness beyond.

Nyfain.

"Does the prince sing in this garden?" I asked, my mind working.

When I turned back, it was in time to see the three exchange glances.

"I'll take that as a yes. He's causing the problem." I shook my head and laughed. "That rat bastard. He's not special, huh? All the women sang to the plants?"

"I love guessing games usually," Hadriel said, "but not when the clue giver has a manic gleam to her eye that makes my blood curdle. Mind telling us what you're talking about?"

I shook my head, remembering my conversation with Nyfain the other day. "He's a Syflora. He must be.

It hadn't even occurred to me because it's a sort of magic usually gifted to faeries. No wonder they were happy to welcome him into the fold. It's talked about a lot in gardening books. He can help plants thrive, force them to falter, affect the soil...all with his song. His mom must've known. She used to call him special. He was either playing modest or lying."

Jawson was nodding like he'd known. "The queen never did tell him. She didn't want to upset the king. He wouldn't have wanted it getting around that his son had a special 'woman's magic' or, worse, faerie magic."

I fisted my hands in a sudden flash of anger. The more I heard about the late king, the more I hated him. I couldn't imagine being stuck with him as my father or my mate.

Jawson nodded again, reading me. "I'm the one that told the queen about it, but she asked me not to speak of it. All the ladies knew, and they played it up like it was totally normal to sing to the plants. They included him so he would unknowingly hone his gift. He probably knows deep down that he is different, but I doubt he'll admit it."

"I mean, but...read one thorough gardening book and you're bound to see them praise the work of Syfloras."

"Love, I doubt he spends a lot of time reading gardening books," Hadriel said. "Did you see the state of this garden? If he were a master gardener, I'm sure he would've fixed it up himself."

That was true.

"Not to mention," Jawson said, "in the grand scheme of things, a prince has more important duties than singing to plants."

There was that.

Still, the plant workers had welcomed him; he'd found a calling there. He was more than the mighty warrior—he was a bringer of life. Those two qualities in one man...he was perfectly suited to be our king. Too bad he was a miserable bastard half the time. If he didn't try to push me away constantly, I could help him more.

"What a waste," I said, running my hands through the soil. "So many growers would kill for that gift."

"Now you have it." Hadriel winked at me. "And look, you actually know what to do with it."

I blew out a breath and looked around the garden. I supposed that was true, in a way. For now.

I smoothed my hair back over my head, tightening my ponytail. "Regardless, I can undo the damage if he doesn't know how. It'll just take time. It'll take working the soil. I'll start the day after tomorrow."

"Do you have the magic?" Jawson asked, and I braced my hands to my hips.

"No. I have run-of-the-mill gardening gifts." I headed back to the wall. "I can get the same results—it just takes a lot of hard work and determination."

"Those gifts are still magical, Miss Finley," Jawson said, and all three guys turned toward me, keeping their shoulders squared with me. "Some gemstones are created from the crush of time. Buried deep in the bedrock, they grow stronger to resist the temptation to turn to dust under the weight. When they finally emerge, they are as strong as they are beautiful. You are such a gem, I should think. Your best magic isn't going to be in the books, Miss Finley. Your magic will write the books to come."

His words punched me right in the feels. I gave him a sappy smile. "Thanks for saying that, Jawson. It's nice of you."

I turned and jumped up and grabbed the top of the wall.

"What are your plans for this evening, Miss Finley?" Hadriel called.

I paused in swinging my legs over. "Did you just call me Miss Finley?"

He rolled his eyes. "I apologize. What came over me?"

"Sense," Jawson drawled.

Hadriel shot him a scowl. "I was going to say I got

swept up with these nitwits, but sense left them years ago."

"Keep talking, shitstain, and we'll get to that wrestling match," Gyril muttered.

"Suck a rock, Gyril." Hadriel gave me a grin, a twinkle in his eye. "Forgive me, my love. I lost the color in my personality for a moment. What a boring butler I would be then. What are you doing this evening?"

I laughed, much preferring this Hadriel to the stodgy butler variety. "I'm going to go clean up, and then I'm going to visit the library until curtain call." I didn't mention harvesting the everlass. He'd just tell Nyfain, and Nyfain would either forbid me or follow me around in brooding silence, grating on my nerves. I had my dagger, and I had a few new moves. I'd be fine.

"The library." Gyril nodded. "That is the best place for a young woman such as yourself. Read all you can, Miss Finley. Improve that mind to match your courage and strength of personality. You'll be unstoppable."

Hadriel put his finger in the air and tilted his head. "Gyril, did you just call her dumb?"

"What?" Gyril's eyes widened. "No! That's not what I meant. I meant—"

"You just called the prince's captive dumb, Gyril," Hadriel taunted. "What would the prince say? You know that he isn't in his right mind when it concerns her. He might pull your arms off for that."

"No, no! That's not what I meant, Miss Finley. You must know that. I just meant that any young woman should improve her mind through vast reading, and there is that big library now—"

"Maybe stop talking," Jawson murmured.

I laughed. "I know what you meant, Gyril, and I intend to. Wait…should I call you Mr. Gyril?"

"Well, actually, you should call us by our last names," Hadriel said. He spread his fingers across his chest. "But I will gladly be on a first-name basis with you, since we are becoming the best of friends."

Gyril rolled his eyes.

"You're in limbo right now, Miss Finley," Jawson said, rubbing his arm across his forehead to wipe away the sweat. "Once you find your place, you will know what is right."

I doubted that somehow. I nodded anyway and smiled at them as I hopped off the wall and onto the brittle ground. It would be nice to get some grass in here, and to take down that wall. I wasn't sure why the plant life could grow and age but the people couldn't— probably the specifics of the curse—but the beauty of this place should be shared. The queen had had her reasons for keeping it private, but now it seemed like a shame to keep the garden closed off.

All in due time.

Right now, I had to practice my new fighting moves in case I needed them later on. The question wasn't whether I would run into demons—it was which ones, and how they'd react when I didn't have a surly dragon escort.

CHAPTER 14

T HE HUSH OF the library greeted me, carrying that sweet must of books yet unread and journeys yet untaken. I'd brought two books back, the one I'd just finished and the one Nyfain had left in my room before his freak-out about the tea.

I climbed the ladder in the fantasy-adventure section and slipped the book Nyfain had given me into its home, organized alphabetically by the author's last name. Once there, I looked down the rail and wondered if I could move the ladder while on it. That would be handy.

I climbed down and put away the other book, near the bottom, before sliding the ladder over and pausing. I didn't feel like another adventure. Instead, I might try...

I lifted my hands and moved them through the air, turning a little as I did so, feeling light and carefree.

Damn it, I loved this place. It spoke to my soul. The pages whispered to me, begging me to pluck them from the shelves and settle in to devour them.

"How about a good mystery?" I murmured, finding those stacks and pulling the ladder to the center. "No. A cozy mystery. Maybe a little humor might do the trick."

Who are you talking to? my animal asked. *It better not be that invisible crowd again.*

I'm talking to myself. Butt out.

If you crack up, what happens to me?

You'll feel right at home, I thought dryly.

I'm bored.

Well, tonight we go into the snake pit. I'll need you on deck.

I know. I can't wait. Let's go find that woman with the dildo and see what she's up to. Or Leala. She's obviously wild. I want to see. Although curiosity is only okay if it won't get us killed.

The demons wouldn't kill us.

I slid my hands across the volumes, taking one out and skimming the pages. I stopped, reading a line. Too somber. I put the book back.

"I'm going to need to keep track of the ones I've read. I'll never be able to remember all these titles," I murmured.

The demons don't care about us, my animal said.

They care about Nyfain. And despite his current, rather peculiar issues, he cares about you. They would absolutely kill you to piss him off.

I hadn't thought about it that way.

I pulled down another book, and then another. Not finding anything that way, I started reading synopses. After all, that frog book was fantastically boring. I was reading it, just to know more about frogs, but I wasn't enjoying it. I was mostly using it to put myself to sleep.

Hadriel's voice floated through the space, coming from around the corner. "Knock once if you're in trouble, twice if you're dead."

"Hilarious," I called out, descending the ladder with a book in hand. In the end, I'd just grabbed one.

Hadriel wasn't smiling like I'd expected, his expression instead flat and his lips drawn.

"What's the matter?" I asked.

He lifted his eyebrows. "Nothing. Find something?"

I handed it off and headed to the second story. "I want to see what information I can find concerning plants. It can't hurt to expand my plant knowledge. Something might help me flesh out the crowded nulling elixir."

"Over there is where I got a gardening book." He pointed down the way. "But for everlass, they might keep it somewhere else. I don't know. I'm not an expert on this library."

"Don't even suggest I ask Nyfain."

"I wasn't going to. I hate suggesting things that are then ignored. How much failure does a person need in his life? I don't need any more complexes."

When I didn't find it with the gardening section, I searched my brain, came up empty, and realized I might have to draw a map of the library laying out the different sections. It was simply too large to keep track of everything otherwise. What an amazing problem to have.

I didn't allow Hadriel's glance at the darkening windows to rush me. I took my time, looking at the spines and trying to date the books based on their appearance. I randomly pulled down volumes and leafed through them, just to feel the breeze from the pages. A sublime grin settled on my lips, and I continued mooning around the balcony of the large room like a lovesick dummy. This library was literally to die for. It was absolutely amazing. More than anything, I wished I could meet the queen who had clearly put such love into this corner of her world.

Anger burned in my gut at the thought of the king mistreating her. Of him squashing her will and her dreams. I obviously couldn't be sure about that, but it stood to reason. Then, finally, she threw in the towel.

Now her son was trying to do the same thing. He fought each night, not hoping to one day lead, but waiting to die.

I wiped away a tear that slipped down my face. The story of the kingdom hit me right in the gut. Nyfain's pain squeezed my heart. He hadn't done anything to deserve all this. None of us had. It wasn't fair that we had to endure it, no end in sight.

No, that wasn't true. There was an end in sight. Because I was going to do what I'd set out to do long ago—cure this kingdom of that demonic sickness. When I did, the demon king would surely show up. And then we'd see what I was made of. I wouldn't escape to free myself as Nyfain hoped, though. I'd figure out a way to save this place for good. I wasn't the type to run. I was the type to fight. And I'd do so for all.

"What's happening?" Hadriel asked, following behind me as I reached the section on magic and magical types.

"I'm looking for a book."

"You are pumping power out all around you, and it's waking up my wolf, and it feels really great, but he is incredibly frustrated and confused at being trapped."

"Is he an asshole like mine is?" I put the book back and kept looking.

"He's not an alpha, so no. He's more helpful than

anything. I never knew what it was truly like to be alone until he was suppressed. I think that was the hardest to bear at first. And now…there are other things to fill the gap."

"Like gardening."

"Exactly like gardening. And looking after you, doll, which is not proving to be the easiest task I have undertaken."

"Milady?" Leala walked into the library. "Oh!"

I glanced down as she turned toward me, smiling.

"I wondered if you wanted dinner delivered to your room?" she asked. "Or, if you leave now, you could sit for it, if you like."

In all the time I'd been in the castle, I had never sat at a table and eaten dinner like a normal person. I'd always been racing the clock, trying to get everything done before the demons came out. And while I was about ready to take a stand regarding that, tonight wasn't the night. I wanted to get to bed early so I could be up at the right time to harvest.

"Up to my room would be great, thanks. I won't be too much longer."

"Yes, milady." She gave me a fluid curtsy and walked from the library.

I took down another book to read the synopsis.

"Well. If you don't need me for anything?" Hadriel

stepped away.

"No, you're good. What sort of party is on for to-night?"

"I don't know, and I don't care. I'm exhausted. I brought up that book on gardening earlier, and I'm going to read that before I hit the sack."

"Quite the fuddy-duddy lately, Hadriel."

"Thankfully." He hefted the book I'd given him. "I'll drop this by your room."

"Thanks."

"Yep." He headed off, leaving me alone. I continued to peruse, finding two more books of interest, and made my way back to the lower level. Night was brushing against the windows. Soon the demons would emerge, ready to cause mischief and feed on the emotions of their prey.

I took a last wander through the stacks, thinking about going into the hidden room for one more book. I still had the one that I'd planned to write notes about for Nyfain. I hadn't finished, having kept so busy these last few weeks, and didn't really want to. I actually didn't want to think about romance at all at the moment.

As I turned, a faint whiff caught my attention. A hint of pine infused with lilac, sprinkled with honey-suckle.

My head snapped around so fast that I thought it might fall off. Two golden eyes looked at me from between the plant and the tapestry. Suddenly Hadriel's flat expression and Leala's surprised "oh!" made all kinds of sense. He'd been here the whole time. Why hadn't I checked?

He didn't speak. I lifted my chin, not planning to, either. But, damn it, curiosity got the better of me.

"What are you reading?"

He glanced toward his lap, where he surely held a book. "*Destined Hearts*. From my mother's book room."

My muscles locked up. I'd been ready to head out of the room, but now I wanted to see what the book was about. Curiosity got the better of me again.

I crossed to him with brusque movements, moving around the tapestry. He lay on the lounger with a throw blanket over his legs, pulled up past his waist. His customary T-shirt was black today, faded from years of use, with little holes dotting the seams in the shoulders. The blanket tented over his cock.

"It's steamy, then?" I put out my hand for the book. He held out his free hand for the ones I was holding.

I rolled my eyes, but I made the exchange.

"No," he answered, that delicious voice scrambling my thoughts. "No on-page sex in this one. It isn't the book that has caused my hard-on. It's you. My cock has been like this since you entered the library." He said it matter-of-factly, no opinion on the subject.

I took the cue and didn't engage, reading the back of the book. A sweeping love story of two people from different worlds.

Fantastic. Nice reminder.

"Your mother's garden has a problem with the soil," I said. "You've been singing in it, right? Lamenting her loss?"

His jaw went slack. He looked like a man who'd just heard a fortune-teller reveal a secret that no one knew. Confusion bled through the link. Unease.

"If you want a real thrill," I said, "grab a book about Syfloras. You'll find it in the gardening section. You might pick up a new trick or two."

"How did you know?"

I grabbed the books back and hefted them. "I read. I know things. Why didn't you tell me?"

He shrugged uncomfortably. "My mother clearly kept it from me for a reason. I figured I wasn't any good at it. I only knew what it was from the faeries. They'd planned to teach me to use it, but…"

"Not any good at it…" I huffed. "You and your lies. Is all your life one big lie?"

"It's starting to feel that way. I honestly didn't think it was worth mentioning. The faeries thought I had untrained talent, at best. They looked down their noses at me, only agreeing to teach me because I also brought the everlass with me."

"Well, the singing works. Please stop singing sad songs in the queen's garden. If you need to lament, do it in the Forbidden Wood. Or, better yet, think of happy times. That would probably help more. Good night. I hope your dick rots off."

Okay, sure, that last bit was childish and overboard. I knew that. But he hadn't even acknowledged what an ass he'd been yesterday, and now he was reading that book and talking about hard-ons and... I mean...who the fuck was he kidding?

My dinner was waiting for me in my room, Leala with it, ready to set it up and make sure I was taken care of before she left the key and excused herself for the night.

"Thank you, Leala," I told her as she opened the door. "For everything. You've been a blessing."

She smiled at me. "Thank *you*, milady, for showing up and disrupting our lives. I can't express how much it was needed."

I ate dinner in silence and then stared out the window for a while, unable to read. My thoughts boiled. Flares of rage and aggression pushed through the link, Nyfain out hunting, his dragon taking control. My animal crouched in her blackness, saying very little.

Why are you so quiet? I asked as I readied for bed.

I'm saving my energy. I've felt the change in you. You're about ready to take your fate into your own hands instead of letting the alpha lead you around by the nose. You're going to need me.

I thought you liked the alpha leading me around by the nose.

Sexually? Yes. Very much. But this feels like something different. I'm ready.

I gazed out the window as stars twinkled overhead. The moon was half-full, a reminder of my status. Any day now and this whole "with child" thing would be behind us. All of us.

I tucked myself into bed and set the little wind-up clock to wake me when it was time to do my job. Not my duty, not the thing that had been affixed to me without anyone asking for my opinion on the matter, but something I chose for myself. It meant more that way.

THE CLOCK CHIMED at three o'clock in the morning. It took a mere moment for me to become fully awake.

I ate the last of the bread and cheese from dinner, the bread heading toward stale at this point, and drank down the rest of the water. Hydration, very important.

I grabbed the clothes I'd set out before bed, Eliza having made a few garments that could conceal various weapons. These, with their pretty little flowers and a few dizzy patterns, would draw the eye away from the side of the thigh where the dagger hung. I didn't want the demons to know that I was armed. The hunter used different tactics when he knew the prey could fight back.

The pocketknife went into my pocket, just in case. The throwing knives would have to stay home with the sword that I was utter shit with.

I listened at the door before I clicked over the lock. My animal waited near the surface, bleeding power through my bloodstream.

The dragon will know something is up, she said as I pulled open the door. Nothing waited for me.

Will he suspect what I'm up to?

He won't. Not sure about the man.

Likely. It was early for him to return, though. He wouldn't want to leave part of the kingdom unchecked. Which meant I'd best hurry. I really didn't want him to play hero tonight. I was tired of feeling like someone was always looking over my shoulder, no matter how dangerously sexy he was.

A shout and a squeal drifted my way on the third-floor landing. Merriment. On the second floor, I heard singing drift up from somewhere below. A guitar strummed a clusterfuck of chords. They needed more classes.

It wasn't until I was halfway to the back door that the unmistakable sounds of people getting it on caught my attention. Grunting and panting followed the slap of leather.

I slowed and flattened against the wall, looking both ways down the hall to make sure no one else was wandering around. I edged toward the slice of candle-light spilling out into the hallway and peeked around the corner, wanting to ensure no one was around to follow me.

A woman stood in the center of the room, her hands spread up and wide, bound above her head, and her ankles apart and secured to the ground, the ropes affixed to other parts of the room. She was only given a little room to bend at the waist, which she did now, dangling with a large blindfold covering her eyes and half her face. An incubus stood behind her with a leer and a leather tool of some kind in his hand, the end a collection of little leather strips.

As I watched, he slapped her ass with the whip thing, the crack ringing out.

"*Oh!* Yes, Daddy," the woman said in a sultry voice, and holy shit, it sounded like Leala.

"You filthy little slut," the man said huskily, swinging the tool again. The leather tips slapped her ass again, and she jumped.

"Hmm, *yes*."

Crack.

"Oh, Daddy, more. I've been naughty."

Great goddess, my animal thought.

I stared with wide eyes. Where were the imaginary pearls I'd brought to the castle? I needed to clutch them.

The man with the leather strap advanced on the woman who had to be Leala, dipping low, his cock erect and ready. He thrust up and obviously in.

"Take it all, you greedy slut," the man said. He reached around and grabbed her nipple, twisting it, rough and vicious. The action drew sounds of pain from the bound woman…but they quickly turned to whimpers of pleasure.

She slackened against her binding, her mouth pulling into a smile. "Hmm, yes, Daddy, punish me."

The man licked his palm and then slapped the woman on the ass. A moment later, he reached around and did the same to her breast. She cried out, and then the sound reduced into a heady moan.

"I think we'd better get the nipple clamps," he said, thrusting rhythmically.

"Or how about the hot wax…"

Nope, I thought. *I'm not cut out for these shenanigans. I need those pearls.*

The second he pulled out and ducked to the side to grab whatever torture device she wanted, I hurried by. She couldn't see me, and he had his focus elsewhere.

Down the hall a ways, the door came into sight—but so did shapes off to the right, in a shadow by the bench. This must've been a favorite spot, because this was where Nyfain and I had seen the people in furry costumes. That, or it was the same couple and this was their hangout.

A nude man was on his knees, bent over a bench. The head housekeeper crouched behind him, wearing that leather halter that exposed her boobs and the briefs with the strapped-on purple dildo. Given she wasn't directly getting pleasure, she was free to pound him while looking around the hall. I'd be noticed in an instant.

Side door? I thought.

Just go. Who is she going to tell? Leala is tied up, and Hadriel isn't out. Nyfain probably already knows, and he's not here anyway. Unless you think she'll tell a demon?

I doubted she'd tell a demon.

I took a deep breath and went for it. Worst case, she'd go find Hadriel, and he'd come out and try to talk me into going back to my room. Which wasn't going to happen.

I walked forward as if I owned the place, my head held high and my steps purposeful. The man's grunting and moaning didn't stop, a good sign.

Outside the door, the night air cleared my mind. The slow throb of crickets rose and fell all around me. Closer to the everlass field, the trees shook gently within the light breeze. Moss covered stumps and a light floral aroma filled my senses. No unusual scents wove through the natural tapestry.

"Okay, friends," I murmured to myself, feeling the tension drain from my shoulders. "Let's get to work, shall we?"

Can you just talk to me rather than your imaginary friends? my animal thought. *I mean, fuck, woman, did you have no friends growing up?*

Very few, actually. They all thought I was too weird and played too rough. Even the boys. Then we got older and I was definitely *too weird and played too rough, so they buggered off.*

Have I ever told you what a sad sack you are?

No, but you've sure hinted at it plenty of times.

She grunted as I grabbed the trays and set them out next to the field. When everything was set up, I let my mind drift as I harvested, pausing near the crowded plants to run my fingers over their leaves.

"I think you might be my favorite type of everlass," I told them, taking a note from Nyfain and his mom and talking to them directly. I felt ridiculous. I was sure my animal thought I sounded foolish, too. "When the situation is dire, you save the day. Mess with you, though, or use you without caution, and you kill a bitch. If I had a mascot, it would definitely be you."

I moved on, picking the healthiest leaves and pulling and dropping those that were losing their luster.

"Don't get me wrong, I like the rest of you, too. How dare the faeries call you weeds, am I right? Nyfain's ex planned to mate for the privilege of having you at her disposal! And they call you weeds? Fuckers. They're just jealous. If I had my way, I'd rub your awesomeness in their faces and withhold you until they gave you the respect you deserve." I paused in thought. "I wonder if they even get you anymore now that the demon king has hidden us with the curse. Nyfain is the one who looks after everything. He wouldn't willingly help the demons, and even if he was forced to help unwillingly, he doesn't seem to put anything to the side for the demons to take. Though I suppose..." I filled two trays and started working on the third. "The demon king wouldn't want to give the faeries access to a healing plant. He'd prefer to thin the herd, so to speak. Though

I'm sure they figured something else out. Besides, there are dragons in the wolf kingdom—one of the wolf kingdoms, anyway. I can't remember if Nyfain said which one. I wonder why they are there and not here? Seems strange. I have to go digging through the library to see if there are any recent histories or anything. The queen would probably want a book about her homeland. Or maybe the king wouldn't let her…"

Third tray done, I picked one of them up and headed off to the shed. I didn't have the strength Nyfain did. I couldn't carry two at a time.

"Crazy about a dragon's dick size, am I right?"

Are you talking to me? my animal asked.

I shrugged. I had always talked to myself when working gardens and plants and things. It was nice to break the silence. Having someone who actually heard the thoughts was a new thing.

"Sure," I said.

Great goddess, you're weird, she replied.

New, but not necessarily great…

"Nyfain is huge. I don't think I could handle any bigger. Fitting him in my mouth is a trial. And he's just a little above average for a dragon? Can you imagine the monstrosity of a big-dicked dragon?"

My animal stretched in delight, clearly picking and choosing the parts of my speech she cared about.

Namely, fitting Nyfain in my mouth.

Lust sparked down deep, because now I was thinking the same thing. Soon the feeling turned into an uncomfortable knot of longing as I remembered him earlier, all snuggly on the lounger, reading. He'd looked content in a way that bespoke many hours in that exact spot, his little reading nook. And now, because of me, he was reading a new genre, a genre I hadn't known many men to enjoy. Not even Hannon read my books. It was so...sweet, a word I wouldn't normally associate with him.

I missed the letters we'd exchanged when we were apart. If we could just communicate that way, maybe things would smooth out a little.

Then again, I missed touching him, also. Kissing him. Letters wouldn't be enough. It had only been a day, and the longing ate through my middle. His very presence was an aphrodisiac, and being at odds with him dampened my spirits.

Stupid brooding, moody men prone to hysterics. He was messing with my mojo.

A hoarse scream rang through the night. I paused halfway to the workroom with the tray in hand, tilting my head to listen. Another scream, followed by a shout to stop.

I set down the tray and jogged back out, listening.

At the next shout, I was running. It sounded like Hadriel, and it was not because of pleasure.

"No, no, no, no, please!" he yelled, blind terror in his voice.

Around the corner, I saw the issue. Hadriel was leaning backward out of a third-story window, held by someone. If that someone let go, he'd fall. Given he'd be falling headfirst or near enough, he wouldn't survive.

"No, please! I'm just taking a night off. I'll be back to shame-fucking tomorrow, I promise," Hadriel said in a clumsy string of words, fear slurring his speech.

Demons, then, not pleased about the change in status quo.

Fire rolled through me. I increased my speed to a sprint for the back door. Once inside, I ran through the castle, straight for the stairs and up. I'd never been to Hadriel's room, but I could gauge his location from where I'd seen the window. Down the hall and around the corner, though, and his shouts were all I needed.

Two men and three women crowded the hall outside his room, looking frightened and wringing their hands. Their faces were vaguely familiar, but I hadn't officially met them. They clearly didn't plan on helping.

I slowed to a stop just outside of the room, breathing heavily.

Protect him, my animal growled, dumping power

into my body.

No shit. But I can't just barge in or they might let him go.

I assumed a casual air and walked in, pushing the door open wider as I did so. A male and female demon had their hands on Hadriel, holding him outside of the window. Another male stood close by with a big grin on his face. He snuffled, soaking up Hadriel's terror.

Recognition unfurled within me as I registered their scent.

The demon from the other night, my animal said, meaning the creature on the other side of my door. The other two were the ones from the grounds.

"What's going on in here?" I asked in an unaffected tone.

The demon that had been outside of my door startled and looked my way. He hadn't heard or smelled me come in.

Red eyes in a waxy oval face gave him an inhuman quality. His nose was mostly flat and his hair resembled a bird's undercoat of feathers.

"Your human shell needs work, buddy. You look a mess," I said.

The other demons slowly pulled Hadriel back into the room. His chest rose and fell quickly, his face incredibly pale and his eyes rounded. They didn't give up their hold on him, and my animal coiled in rage.

I sauntered in farther. If they tried to flip Hadriel out, I wanted to be close enough to grab him.

"I know your smell…" Feathers snuffed the air, his smile resulting in pointed teeth.

"Yuck. You're ugly." I stopped and looked around the quaint interior. "Not much to this room, huh, Hadriel? Not even a fitting reading chair."

Feathers kept his eyes on me as he crossed to the door. He closed it, his eyes gleaming.

"I smelled your fear the other night, little girl," he said, and a spark of pain flared in my middle.

My animal answered with a gush of power. She snarled just below the surface. Shit was about to go down, and if I didn't rise to the challenge, she would.

I had no problem rising to the challenge.

"You might want to lock it, too." I winked at him. "I wouldn't want you escaping."

"You wouldn't want *us* escaping…" he repeated, apparently thinking that was just hilarious. He twisted the lock on the door. "I will feed on your fear and your pain as you slowly die."

"Promises, promises."

CHAPTER 15

I POINTED AT the other two, their faces both square with the same dark brown eyes, the same points at the tips of their long noses—they looked like identical twins with different-length hair. One male, one female. "You two, let him go."

They offered me the same sort of smile, delighted and condescending. They thought they were at the top of the hierarchy in this room.

"I don't think we will," Male Twin said. "He is giving us just the right amount of terror."

"Hadriel, if you get access to your animal, will it make you stronger?" I asked.

"I think I do have access…" he answered in a quavering voice. "I feel him."

"Will it make you stronger?"

Feathers drifted against the wall, trying to trap me

between him and Female Twin. He moved slowly, as if I were a flight risk. I ignored him for now.

"Y-yes," Hadriel answered, palming his chest. "Yes, it will."

"Good. Don't let them throw you out of that window."

I fell into the fire pooling in my body, pulling it up and yanking it through my being. More power gushed in from Nyfain's dragon—he'd clearly sensed our activity through the bond and was quick to help. Full to bursting, I ripped out my dagger and launched at Male Twin. He thankfully let go of Hadriel, who then tried to rip out of Female Twin's grasp. As long as he didn't go out the window, I didn't care. I'd be on hand to help him when he needed me.

Male Twin pushed forward, reaching for me with outstretched hands. Claws curved down from the ends of his fingers. He was clearly trying to grab me. What an idiot.

I sliced his forearm as I happily accepted his open-armed embrace. Once within his reach, I stuck my blade into his side and ripped across. Skin parted and insides dumped out. I stuck him again in the breastplate and used my other hand to shove him back.

His expression was one of surprise. He staggered and then slumped, falling to the floor.

Hadriel struggled with Female Twin, slapping at her hands. It was a very odd fighting style. Great for distraction.

Feathers ran at me, his claws out and face a mask of violence. I stepped in at a diagonal, closing the distance between us. He slashed through the air, and I dodged the blow easily, faster by far. I struck, missing the kidneys. It would still hurt like the bejeebus, though.

He squealed like some sort of wild boar, bending and slapping his hand to the wound. I left him there and darted to Female Twin, who had just about gotten Hadriel turned around and her arm around his neck. That was exactly what I wanted to avoid. We didn't need a hostage situation.

I ripped Hadriel away. He rolled across the floor, not much better at falling than he was at fighting. I shoved Female Twin against the wall and laid into her, stabbing multiple times in quick succession.

I felt the presence of the other being closing in behind me. A glance revealed that he was readying to slash me with his claws. In a moment of pure genius that I couldn't have planned if I'd tried, I ducked and rolled. His hand sailed through the air, nearly raking across the slumping center of Female Twin. I popped back up and stepped forward, stabbing him in the back and dragging my blade across his spine. Steel hit bone. Damn, it was good to be super strong.

I pulled the blade free, adjusted my positioning, and got it right this time, sinking the blade into Feathers' kidney. Then, because this was good practice, I dropped the dagger and palmed his chin the way Nyfain had taught me. I grabbed his head with my other hand and ripped up and to the side. The vicious crack gave me chills. He bonelessly slid to the ground.

*Nice! m*y animal thought. *Now you're not so embarrassing.*

I had to agree.

I retrieved my dagger and advanced on Female Twin. She groaned, struggling to stay to her feet. Fire still pumped through me. More power came in steady gushes—Nyfain's dragon was going a little overboard, and my animal was not sending any back. The thrill of it sang in my blood. It filled me to bursting, stretching my skin.

I let out an inhuman sound, like a baby animal roaring, and struck her again with my dagger. It wasn't enough violence, though. The rage burning in me was almost a palpable thing. Was this what the dragon felt all the time? Because it was intense.

I pulled the dagger back, dropped it to the ground, and grabbed her person. I ripped her into the air, held her over my head—because it basically felt like she weighed nothing—and tossed her from the open window. She didn't even scream as she sailed, likely already dead. I rounded on the others, thinking of doing the same thing, when my heart fluttered. It left my body for a moment, then returned to beat. Left it again, and returned.

Nyfain was on the scene. He was coming in hot.

"Unlock the door, or it'll get busted," I said, a thrill of excitement coursing through me. I grabbed my dagger, used one of the demon's shirts to clean it, and stowed it in its sheath.

Hadriel stopped staring at me with a slack jaw and moved to get up.

Too late.

The door blasted open, ripped from the hinges. The wood thunked as it crashed down, nearly hitting him.

Nyfain's powerful frame filled the doorway. His eyes glowed, and I felt his power fill both of us. His dragon lurked near the surface, his presence throbbing. Man and beast set eyes on me as he crossed the space in a rush and wrapped me in his arms.

"Are you hurt?" He pulled me away a little to look down my front. Blood splattered my new top, heavier in some places than others.

"No. It's not mine."

He half turned me to look at my back before nod-

K.F. BREENE

ding and pulling me tightly against him again. I felt his shudder as he took a deep breath.

"Come on. Let's get you back to your room." He swung me up to carry me. "Get this cleaned up," he told Hadriel. "Dispose of the bodies. Try to conceal their deaths if you can."

"Easy for you to say," Hadriel muttered, looking at the bodies. "They aren't bleeding all over your floor. Hey!"

Nyfain stopped in the doorway and turned.

Hadriel met my eyes. "Thanks, Finley. I don't know if they would've actually killed me, but they were certainly considering it. You saved me from a really bad night."

"No problem," I said. "Next time you get in trouble, just go ahead and scream again, and I'll come help."

"Oh great, yeah. Rub salt in the wound," he muttered.

Nyfain walked past the onlookers that had pushed to the other side of the hall with wide eyes. Continuing down the hall, he held me tightly. My eyes drifted shut, our combined power still thrumming in my middle. His scent tantalized my senses, calling to me. His heat bled through my flesh.

I grazed my lips from the base of his neck on up, stopping by his ear and doing everything in my power

312

not to run my tongue along the outside of his earlobe. He took the stairs quickly, and anger burned through what was left of his fear. He'd been afraid for my safety, something I hadn't felt when in the thick of things. And now…

At the tower, he didn't put me down, but held his hand out. He wanted the key.

"I can do it," I said, coming to my senses and wriggling in his hold.

His anger fanned higher, burning through the bond. He left his hand out, waiting, not commenting.

"Nyfain, I can do it. Put me down."

He dropped my legs, and my body swung down after them. He caught me before my feet hit, set me down incredibly gently, and then slammed me against the wall. He grabbed both of my wrists, pinning them above my head in one of his hands, and shoved his hand in my pocket.

"Are you serious right now?" I demanded, struggling to get out.

"When are you going to learn?" He found my pocketknife and moved on to the correct pocket.

He dragged me sideways against the wall so he could reach the lock and open the door. That done, he flung me over his wide shoulder and marched me through the door.

"When am I going to learn that you're an overbearing prick?" I parroted. "I've already learned that lesson, actually."

He shut the door behind us and then fit the key in the lock. He didn't turn it, though. He didn't lock us in. He crossed to the window with me still draped over his shoulder.

"Put. Me. *Down*," I commanded through gritted teeth. My power pulsed.

His body froze, and the muscles flared on his large back. His arm came away from me slowly, struggling against my command.

"Now," I said, adding more power.

His arm continued to peel away. He shook with the effort to ignore my command. I just pumped in more power, receiving an extra boost from his dragon.

Why is his dragon helping me boss him around? I asked my animal.

Probably payback for something Nyfain pissed him off about. Or maybe he thinks it's hot. I get the feeling alpha dragons like their females strong. This one does, at any rate.

Nyfain's whole body quivered now, but his arm still pulled away. His body bent to the side, and I slipped off, catching myself on the ground to keep from sliding along my belly and onto my face.

I stood and released my power, squaring off with his big body. He turned as well, his eyes golden furnaces. Rage blistered through the bond.

"What the fuck did you think you were doing leaving this room?" he demanded.

"Oh, nothing, just possibly saving the life of one of your staff."

"I'm not talking about that. You were out with the everlass, weren't you? Alone."

I lifted my chin a bit. "Yes. We need more leaves, and you're being a dumpty cunt. The job needed to be done, so I did it. I'm not in the habit of men escorting me around like I'm breakable."

"Finley, your involvement with me has made you a target. Anything could happen to you out there. It's not safe. I trusted you to stick to your room at night. If you continue to defy that trust…"

"What?" I curled my hands into fists. "You'll lock me in here? Keep me hostage until your mood improves? Because you've been in a terrible fucking mood for sixteen years and counting, and I don't want to wait another sixteen for you to get your thumb out of your ass."

A vein throbbed at the side of his jaw. He stared at me with barely contained aggression. His imposing presence hammered into me.

I ignored the fear sparking within my gut. Fuck, he was intense. Instead, I wrapped myself in power and held my ground.

"You will let me escort you out," he ground out.

"I will do what I want, and you will fuck all the way off. If I hadn't been out there, Hadriel might be dead. Those demons might have moved on to terrorize someone else. I will *not* live in fear, Nyfain. I will not cower in my room and wait for you to hover around me like some sort of poltergeist fart. I can handle myself, and you need to step out of the way and let me. If you can't live with that, tough."

He leaned toward me a little, invading my space. Rage bled hot through the bond, spicy sweet. Electricity crackled between us, running across my flesh and pooling hot in my core.

"You will do as I say," he growled, his rough voice tickling me just right. My breathing sped up, and liquid heat throbbed between my thighs.

I leaned a little toward him, our faces now inches apart. Rage and lust pushed its way through the link to me. From me.

"No," I said through my teeth.

We stared at each other for a solid beat, and then his lips crashed onto mine. He ripped at my shirt desperately, yanking it over my head. With harried, desperate hands, I unbuckled my sheath and let it drop to one side, quickly working at my pants. His tongue swept through my mouth, and I tilted my head, keeping the contact as I bent and pushed my pants and underwear down. He spun me around and worked at the binding around my breasts. It was fashioned after my older set, something I could put on myself, and he got me out of it easily.

It fell down my front, freeing my breasts, as I bent to undo the laces on my boots.

He couldn't wait.

His hands slapped down on my hips and he swung me around and forward. My palms hit the wall. He instantly thrust his cock into me, searing into my wet depths. He used his hands on my hips for more momentum, pulling back as he rammed in, slamming into me with hard, bruising thrusts. Taking out his anger. Giving in to his rage.

Tingles ran through me. Primal urges surfaced—the need to flee or fuck.

I chose fuck.

"Yes, Nyfain. *Harder,*" I said as I fell into my own anger and rage, basking in the unfinished violence of a moment ago.

Power bulged within the room. Our beasts pumped it higher.

He snarled savagely, pulling me closer with his hands as he thrust in deeper, his hips slapping off my butt. I used the wall as leverage to increase the pushback. The sound of skin meeting skin filled the room. His cock pounded, and I dropped my head as I soaked in the delicious friction.

One of his hands curled around my shoulder, and he held me against him while his other hand reached around and down, his fingers finding my clit. He massaged me, and his grunts of pleasure slithered across my flesh, heightening the rapture building within my body.

I arched, reaching back for him. He pulled out and pushed me toward the bed. My pants around my ankles tripped me up, and I stumbled. He was there, lifting me and throwing me onto the bed. He made quick work of discarding my shoes and tearing off my pants before kneeling between my legs and pushing my knees up. He punched his cock back into me savagely, rocking his body forward to get more strength. The jolt hit me just fucking right, and I arched into it, running my palms over my breasts and stroking my nipples.

His growl was soft and sexy as he pushed my hands away and paused in his thrusts to fasten a hot mouth to one of my nipples. He lifted his head as he sucked in a breath, leaning more heavily over me and hammering his cock home.

Crying in delight, I grabbed his shoulders and pulled so I could get my hands on his back, could scrape my nails ruthlessly down his incredibly sensitive scars.

He groaned, lifting his head back and roaring. His dragon clearly helped, because the sound echoed through the room. He laid his body on mine, pumping his hips, sucking in my bottom lip.

"More," he groaned.

I scratched down his back again, moving against him. He snarled, his hips swinging wildly.

He pushed back to sitting and pulled me up with him. I sat down on his cock, and he squeezed me closer with his strong arms, kissing me fervently. I bounced on him, reaching down to work my clit. The pressure increased. My ardor rose. Our movements got smaller and smaller until I could barely stand it anymore, so wound up and in need of release.

"Come with me," I said against his lips, rocking my hips, fingering my clit. Pleasure pounded through me. The feelings were so fucking amazing that I could barely stand it. And then, inspired by my animal, no will to trap the words behind my teeth, I said, "Come inside me."

Our animals rose in a frenzy, blasting out their power. Fire flowed over his skin and sizzled across mine. He crushed me to him, snaking his hand through my hair and gripping tightly to keep me put.

"Fuck, I want that so badly," he murmured, and it sounded like it was to himself. "Why can't this nightmare ever end?"

He buried his face into the hollow where my neck met my shoulder, his lips flush with my skin. His teeth played with my flesh but did not push down. He pumped into me reverently, longing rolling through the bond, along with something else. A softness, almost. A sweetness that broke my heart and brought tears to my eyes.

He thrust again and groaned, shaking as he finished.

"Finley," he said softly against my lips, holding himself deeply inside of me. That feeling from before washed through the bond again, followed by a longing so intense my tears overflowed. My animal's power pulsed, feeling his dragon's need to mate. Despite my thoughts on the subject, with their fervor filling me, I couldn't help but come violently again, shaking and vibrating against him.

"Your animal is riding you," he whispered against my lips, breathing heavily.

"Yeah. Ever since the whole tea thing. Don't worry, though, it'll totally be fine. Even if we were true mates, which we obviously aren't, or there was some hidden thing in the curse, I doubt the timing was right. Or wrong, I guess. It'll be fine, much to her dismay."

"My animal is riding me, too. I'll admit…if it were a different time, I'd tell you not to worry about the tea and just see what happened. But we aren't living a life where that is possible, Finley."

A breath whooshed out of me. Something tight and knotted within me loosened a little at his admission. His reaction the other night had been about timing, the same hang-ups I had. He hadn't been rejecting me. Nothing changed about our situation while everything changed. Somehow, his admission made this all a bit more bearable, made me feel like I wasn't alone in waiting for a verdict. He'd still been an ass, and he'd deserved my anger, but he wasn't leaving me hanging out to dry. We were in this, all of this, together.

I clung to him tightly. "I know."

"And our animals shouldn't be in a breeding frenzy, anyway. That only happens between dragon true mates when they've imprinted and the female goes in heat."

That stopped me up short.

I tried to pull away from him a little, but he held me firmly, his cock still deeply inside me, his body glued to mine.

"In heat? Okay, I know we're shifters, but using terms like 'breeding' and 'in heat' is crossing the line."

He laughed softly. "It wouldn't be if you'd grown up around such talk. The animal parts of us can be…"

"Gross? Pushy dickheads?"

"Intense. Anyway, yes, there is a heat cycle, basically, where the female isn't satisfied unless she's getting the male's seed in her constantly. I've only ever heard of a couple of dragon true mates, and apparently the men were not complaining about being needed constantly. The ones I've heard about walked around with tired smiles. Growing up, everyone thought it was an urban legend, but *everyone* wanted to be the guy to experience it. It almost always results in a young one, though, I've heard. Otherwise dragons don't produce as much as some of the other shifters. Wolves, for example. They have numbers, and we have more power. It balances out in the long run."

He rolled to the side, laying me on my back, pressing me into the mattress. He kissed me languidly.

"Our animals are feeding off each other, I think," I said before nipping at his lips. "Yours seems like a headstrong jackass, and mine is eager for him to get his way. They don't really give a shit about logic. They just want to bang."

He chuckled. "I think you're right." His mood sobered. "I worry about you going out at night without me. It's why I act the way I do. I've never been good at dealing with vulnerability, and you are my greatest weakness. I don't want to lose you."

I ran my fingers across his muscled arms, utterly spent in the best of ways. An aftershock shivered across my skin, and I let my eyes drift shut.

"You can't watch me all the time, Nyfain. You can't be everywhere at once."

"I know," he whispered. "But...can we compromise? Clearly I can't force you to my will. But I can't handle making another mad flight across the Royal Wood because I think you're in trouble. It rips my heart out. I'm a strong man, but I'm not strong enough for that. It's a danger to me as much as to you, if you care about that. I'm never focused on my surroundings when I'm running to you."

"Of course I care about that."

"So meet me halfway. Please. Tell me what you plan and let me try to at least be close by in case something goes wrong."

I opened my eyes and took in his golden gaze—his expression, open and expressive, imploring me to see sense, or his version of it. I kissed his soft lips and slid my knees a little farther up his sides.

"Fine. But if you're in one of your moods, you might need to settle for finding out in a letter."

"A letter is fine. Send Hadriel if you need. Whatever."

"I wouldn't do that to the poor guy."

He smiled, his gaze roaming my face. "Did you harvest?"

"Yes, but I didn't get a chance to put them in water to keep them from drying. I also didn't get a chance to pick from any of the crowded plants."

"We'll pick from them tomorrow."

"I thought you were just going to stay close."

"I will. Very close." He pushed off me with a smirk, quickly bending to run his tongue up my folds and then flick my clit. It was so decadently filthy that I couldn't help getting turned on again.

In that mood now, wanting to see where it would go, I reached down and ran my fingers through my deliciously used pussy, biting my lip. I moved the wetness up to my clit and stroked lazily.

"Fuck me," he whispered, grabbing the bedpost. His eyes flashed with heat, and his cock started to rise. He glanced at the bared pink flesh between my spread knees and groaned.

"Maybe just come back and spend what's left of the night…"

"You're going to be the death of me," he murmured, and shook his head. "I do want to stay, but there are still a few things I have to do."

He leaned down over me and kissed me, long and slow, rubbing his fingers over my clit and down, dipping them inside me.

"Pleasure yourself when I leave," he whispered, his lips against mine. "I want to feel it through the bond. Think of me licking your pussy when you do. I want to hear all about your filthy daydreams when I see you next."

His fingers pumped a little faster, and I arched, my breath hitching.

He swore softly and pulled his fingers away. "I do have to go. I'll put those leaves in water. Sleep, princess. I'll see you tomorrow."

"Will you ever spend the night with me? Or, you know, what's left of it?"

He paused next to the bed. He ran his hand up the side of my thigh, over a hip...and then his touch skimmed my stomach, longing ringing through the bond again. Our gazes locked, our connection so deep that I fell in and lost track of the world around me. My heart squeezed at the warmth I saw.

I wrapped my fingers around his muscled forearm just to have that connection. To ground myself in him. I knew then that he felt the same way as me. Wanted the same things. Was equally cockblocked by the difference in our situations and maybe fate itself.

"I wish things were different," he whispered, his thumb stroking across my belly.

I nodded mutely.

"But for now, I take delight in knowing that this…" He ran his hand down and rubbed his fingertips firmly at the base of my pussy, collecting our combined release and gently pushing it back into my body. He left his hand on me, and his eyes lit with a possessive gleam. "This is *mine*."

My heart fluttered. It was hard to breathe. My animal purred in ecstasy, basking in his words and tone, in his possessive dominance. His dragon, very near the surface, flooded the bond with pride and approval.

I didn't grow up knowing the shifters' ways, but clearly I was getting a crash course.

"Yes," I said softly, not able to fight it. Not wanting to anymore. My animal nodded in approval. Maybe now she'd get off my back.

He bent and kissed my lips, his fingers trailing back to my stomach. "I will stay with you soon, yes. I want more time to properly fuck you. Rage-fucking is fun, thank you for that, but I want the next time to be slow. I want to take care of all your needs and destroy you for anyone else. I might not get to keep you in the end, but I'll make sure my memory is etched into your body, if not your mind."

"Do me a favor?"

"Anything."

"Stop bringing up that you won't be able to keep me. I know you'll have to move on, but I don't want to hear it until I have to face it."

He shook his head slowly, pain eating through the bond. "You have it wrong. I won't be the one who moves on. Not ever."

"More lies, right? Of course you have to move on. You're a prince. You'll find a noble girl of good standing and fashion and whatever else you social elite do, and either I'll get lost or I'll be your side piece. I'm definitely not going to be the side piece, so…"

He chuckled darkly and ran his fingers through his unruly dark brown hair. "You're daft sometimes, you know that? My side piece? As if your animal would stand for that. As if my dragon would allow me to lie with someone else instead of you. No, princess, that is not how this works, which I have explained to you repeatedly. Do *me* a favor and take it in this time. I refuse to be your ruin, and if you stay here with me, that's exactly what will happen. The second the curse is broken, the demon king will move in and kill me and everyone close to me. He'll take some of the villagers as indentured servants and likely kill the rest, or give them to his demons as playthings. He'll either move his people into these lands, or strip them of any value and leave them to rot. To stay with me is death." His voice took on a hard edge. "I will not do that to you. When the time comes, you will leave me to save yourself and anyone you can take with you, and I will let you. Do I make myself clear? You are not trapped with me. But *I* am trapped with you. I refuse to claim you because I worry that the demon king will be put off by my scent and it'll take away your only chance at a better life. I worry that I'll become too selfish to give you up. I refuse to claim you because I…" He paused, his gaze intense, as though stopping himself from saying something. "Because I respect you too highly to drag you down with me."

My heart ached and more tears filled my eyes. My animal did the equivalent of pacing, unsettled at hearing him say he wanted us to leave him. For her to leave the dragon.

"What makes you think the demon king will barter with me?" I whispered, so many emotions flying at me that practicality was the only thing I could latch on to.

"Because you are everything he will want. Fierce and determined and smart, as well as incredibly beautiful. Furthermore, you're a shifter, and he likes taking proud magical races and demeaning them. He will make a trophy of you."

"Fantastic, yeah. That sounds amazing. What an incredible future you have chosen for me, Nyfain."

"That isn't your future, Finley. That is your means to an end. You'll barter with him to get out, you will endure unwelcome treatment within your gilded cage, and you will escape and find freedom. It is within your power. That is the only way you can stay alive. Above all else, you must stay alive."

"Why does it matter to you so much?"

His eyes grew hard. He stared at me with a set jaw. "Because I will not see another prickly rose torn out by the roots. This time, I will not take the easy road while the people I care about suffer and turn to dust. This time, if there is to be a funeral, it will be mine, and I will die happy knowing I could at least give you the chance at a better life. I couldn't save my mother, Finley, but as the goddess looks down on me, I *will* save you."

CHAPTER 16

THE NEXT MORNING, I finished the notes about the book for Nyfain. After the speech he made before (once again) storming from the room, I'd decided he'd get as many write-ups as he wanted. He'd get blowjobs every day. His words had been beautiful and heart-wrenching and *confusing*, and his devotion had rung through the bond loud and clear. He honestly thought that the only way I would have a chance at happiness was to sign myself over to the demon king with the hopes of escape. It sounded ludicrous. The whole thing would obviously blow up in his face, but we'd cross that bridge when we came to it. Until then, I was going to brave his terrible moods and bang the living shit out of him.

Letter in hand and new trousers and blouse hugging my curves, I trekked down to the library. On the way, staff members loitered in the halls or on the landings. They turned to me as I passed, bowing, curtsying, and smiling. Jessab, the cook, stood at the bottom of the stairs and shook his fist with a smile.

"Thatta girl, eh? Give 'em what they got coming to 'em."

"What in the goddess's bustier are you lot doing?" Hadriel said to the loitering staff as he walked up, wearing a jacket covered in sequined flowers and a newly trimmed mustache. His bright pink velvet slippers didn't match any part of the hideous jacket. "Don't you have work to do? Leave Miss Finley alone."

"Oh, look who's a big man now suddenly, eh?" Jessab said, patting his stomach. "Go fall out a window, why don't ya."

"Hilarious, you backwater dish jockey." Hadriel glared at him. "Go suck a wheel spoke."

"You'll have to get your dick out of it first." Jessab turned slowly.

"Back to Miss Finley, then?" I smirked at Hadriel, heading to the library.

"Only to keep the status quo. Don't worry, love. I haven't suddenly gotten good at my job."

The smile dripped off my face. "Yet they still went after you."

"That's because I was alone. Those types find the

outliers. There aren't many of those left in the castle. Now you see why."

I shook my head as we walked down the hall. Doors stood open, and soft noises issued forth as people got started with their hobbies for the day.

"I can't stand by and watch stuff like that happen," I said. "It's not in me."

"The master said that in the beginning, too. The thing is…if you kill them all, the demon king just sends more. Worse ones, too. We lost a lot of people in the beginning because of people fighting back. If you have to kill, do it in secret."

I stopped at the library door and put up a finger. "Stay here."

"Why?"

Because I had the book and the annotations for Nyfain, and I intended to leave them in his mother's secret book room. But I could tell no one about that room, so I settled for, "Because Nyfain gave me a secret, and I intend on keeping it."

"How could you do that to me? You can't just dangle something like that in front of me and not tell me the secret! I love secrets!"

"I doubt it is a secret you'd care about."

"What a shitty hint. I need more than that!"

I rolled my eyes and hurried into the library, slow-ing as I passed the lounger. Nyfain's smell permeated the area. I sat down, pulling the blanket up around me. I longed to just grab a book and lie there until he wandered in. Then maybe we could make love in our reading nook before curling up together and talking about books. What a dream come true that would be!

After a deep breath, I folded the blanket and got up. Maybe we'd be able to do it one day, after everything slowed down. Dare to dream.

I found a folded-up piece of parchment on the little table in the corner of the secret book room, right where I'd intended to put my book and letter. My name was written in Nyfain's beautiful scrawl, and I snatched it up and opened it immediately.

Dear Finley,

I'm sure by now you are well versed in my bad tempers and worse moods. It seems sixteen years of being trapped in a pit, with no fair maiden to spring me out, has made me unpardonably surly. I wasn't the nicest of men before the curse, and now I am generally considered unbearable. I applaud you for trying to keep up with my hysterics, as I know Hadriel calls them. You are a strong woman, and I value that quality more than I can say.

I do so apologize for my outburst the other night. I handled the news about the tea badly. Please see my note in the beginning about moods and tempers. I understand your point about a pregnancy being unlikely, but I do not wish to take any chances. You are already a target. I shudder to think what it would mean for you to bear my child. The demon king would kill him or her as quickly as he'd kill me. I wouldn't be able to protect you. Either of you. And if you think I am possessive now, it is nothing compared with how I would act regarding my child.

So please, keep up with the tea and forgive me my alarm. By now you understand your situation. And if it is too late, and you carry my child, please know that it would fill me with such incredible reverence. I would be honored. I would also need to figure out a way to hide you both. I warn you, that might entail breaking the curse, accepting my fate, and making sure you both escape this kingdom to my mother's village, where I hope they will harbor you. But we will cross that bridge when we come to it.

Regardless of what comes, you will *have a future. I will make sure of it.*

Very apologetically yours,
Nyfain

I leaned against the edge of a bookcase and read it again, smiling. Fuck, he was charming in his letters. If only the two sides of him could be united at all times—the charming prince and the brooding, possessive alpha who raged over my wellbeing. I would never be able to say no. I'd just fall onto my back, spread my legs, and say, "Have at me."

Though, in fairness, I wasn't all that far from that now…

Taking a deep breath, I folded up his note and slid it into my pocket. I replaced it with the letter I'd written and the notes with the book before roaming the room for a moment, reading titles.

Before I'd been taken to the castle the first time, I wanted to read about hate sex and hardcore fucking. Now, though…

I picked out what looked like a love story. I needed a sweet, happy ending. I needed to believe they were possible.

"Staring is rude, Cathrin," Hadriel called out as I emerged from the library.

"Your ugliness is eternal, Hadriel," a middle-aged woman shouted back as she slipped through an open door down the way.

"That didn't seem to bother you the other night, when you all but begged me to fuck your face—She's gone. I'm talking to myself." He lifted his eyebrows as I appeared beside him. "All set?" He glanced down at the book. "Ah. Okay, let's run up and put that away, check out the garden, and then get you a dance lesson. The master asked me to arrange it the other day. He is thawing a little, and it's really helping my stomach."

"Dare I ask how it is helping your stomach?"

"He's less scary, and when I am less afraid, my bowels aren't quite so watery."

"Gross."

"Yeah. Maybe don't ask next time. That's on you. Speaking of, we need to schedule you two a dinner. What kind of food do you like to eat?"

"Hello?" someone called as we neared the stairs.

Hadriel and I stopped, glancing at each other. The voice had sounded young, like a female child.

"Hello?" she called again.

Hadriel frowned and took the stairs to the first floor, stopping at the bottom step with his hand on the banister. I walked out a few more steps, looking toward the front entrance.

A girl of about fifteen stood in the open doorway, a slip of a thing with baggy, dirt-stained clothes hanging off her bony frame. Her stringy hair dripped beside her sweat-lined, flushed face. She rested her hand on the doorway. Her arm trembled, but her head was high and shoulders squared. She was clearly terrified out of her mind.

"What in the hell..." Hadriel said under his breath, starting forward. "Hello," he offered cordially, closing the distance between them. I followed like a little duckling. "How can I help you today? To what do we owe the pleasure?"

"You sound like a man who got his voice out of a can," I whispered. "Act natural."

"I don't know what natural is for a butler!" he said in an undertone. "I'm used to acting like a gobshite to stay alive!"

"I'm looking for the prince," the girl said with a tremor in her voice. "It's my momma. She needs some of the potion that the prince has been dropping off."

"Oh, thank the goddess for her tricky ways. You're up, doll." Hadriel motioned me on.

I stepped forward, pulling the girl's focus from Hadriel. "We don't have any more ready just yet. I'll be drying the leaves tonight and making more starter elixir just as soon as I have all the ingredients. Does your village not have any extra leaves or elixir to share?"

Grief lined her face and bowed her spine. She held

her shoulders rigid against the desire to reduce down into the fetal position. I knew, because I'd been there myself, countless times.

"They didn't have enough for us. They are treating the village leaders first. Please, we have two everlass plants. Just tell me how to make it. I can make it."

"Don't you have the recipe? It has been passed out to all the villages…"

A line formed between her brow. She clearly didn't know what I was talking about.

"Things seem to work much differently in your village than elsewhere," Hadriel murmured, his hand on my arm. "Most of the villages have a very distinct class system."

And she was definitely not high class.

Anger burned through me.

"I made that elixir for everyone, not for snobby cunts who think they are better than their peers." I put a finger up to the girl. "Wait there. I'll be back in a moment. I will personally see to your momma, okay? If she is alive when I get there, she'll be alive when I leave. I will make sure of it." I about-faced. "Hadriel, wake Nyfain. He'll be taking me to this girl's momma—and explaining how this was allowed to happen."

"Yes, my darling. I am loving that idea, truly." Hadriel ran to catch up as I took the stairs two at a time.

"Except remember that bowel thing? It would be really unfortunate if I shit myself. It's an issue. How about, instead, I go and get some horses saddled up and ready to go. Wouldn't that be a better idea?"

I blew out a breath. "Fine. Where is Nyfain's room?"

"All this time, and you still don't know? A travesty." Hadriel walked me along the second floor and pointed down a hall. He gave me directions before hurrying away.

I jogged now. It must've taken great courage for that girl to venture through the Forbidden Wood, even in the day, and approach the castle of the beast. While she might have known the beast was the prince, she'd probably also known the castle wasn't a place where poor waifs would be welcomed. I knew all of that from experience. Her mother must be on her deathbed. I knew what *that* was like from experience as well.

Nyfain's scent called to me, pulling me along. Intoxicating me. I wouldn't have needed directions at this point. I took a left and two rights to a grand room with a wide double door beneath a great arch. Quite a difference from a one door, squat-ceilinged tower.

The door opened easily, and I wondered at him not locking it. Maybe, for all his blustering, he wasn't pestered like the rest of us were. The things we learned…

The first room was similar to the queen's, with private sitting and eating areas and wide glass doors leading out to a veranda. Through a door in the side, a great bed sprawled out on a little dais. I ignored the lavish furniture in the rest of the room and took the two steps to the royal bed, as it were. He lay in the middle on his stomach, his arms spread out wide and the covers pulled down around his hips. His muscular and inked back was on full display, the scars of his wings cutting down each side in horrible slashes.

"Hey." I shook his shoulder, noticing a fresh flower on the little table by the window and his clothes set out near the dressing table. His door had been opened by a man's maid, or whatever they called the prince's servant, and that person had left it unlocked, clearly. "Hey!"

I leaned over and pushed his shoulder, inhaling his balmy scent and feeling my heart flutter.

He groaned and turned his head, a golden eye peeling open and noticing me.

"Hmm. Dreams do come true." He turned and grabbed me in a rush of movement, pulling me into the bed and pinning me beneath him. His lips captured mine before he licked along my bottom lip, trying to coax me to open for him. His hardness pushed against my apex, thick and delicious. He dragged it down before sliding it back up, rubbing me in a way that did not fit the moment.

"Hey!" I slapped his face.

"Hmm. Is that how you'd like it this morning, princess? Rough?" His kiss bruised my lips now, and his hips pumped aggressively. I'd forgotten that little issue with dragons—getting smacked around was foreplay to them.

"Stop, Nyfain!" I pushed at his shoulders.

He kissed me again, pushing my hands up above my head. "What?" he mumbled, trailing kisses beside my jaw and down my neck. "Why are you clothed, baby girl?"

Heat pounded in my core. His rubbing was making me delirious. His familiar and erotic scent was threatening to drag me under.

"Stop!" I said again, and this time I put power behind it. My animal rolled inside of me, shoving her own force through the bond, the equivalent of claws digging in. For once, she was on my side when it came to resisting him.

Nyfain pulled back, blinking his bleary eyes. He focused on my face for a moment before rolling to the side and sitting up.

"I apologize," he said.

I crawled off the bed. "Someone from the village

showed up just now, begging me to help her mother. I'm going. You're coming, too."

"What?" He pushed off the bed and straightened, a fresh slash trailing down his thigh. I hadn't noticed it when I saw him last.

"Do you need—"

"No," he cut me off, crossing to the clothes that had been laid out for him. "I attended to it myself last night. It's nothing. What is this about a girl?"

I waited by the door and quickly relayed our encounter. He stepped into his jeans and then shook his head.

"The villages have their own way of doing things at this point. It is how things have evolved—or maybe *de*volved—throughout the curse. The throne used to delegate to the nobles, and they would work with the governing bodies of each village. Most of those groups were killed or have died from the sickness throughout the years, however. Not to mention I was shut out from the villages for a long time, and they clearly grew to like not having a ruler. I don't have the resources to properly govern them all anymore. Or the military might to subdue them when they refuse my rule. I can only assert my influence through broad strokes, and lately, that has often turned into a fight. Basically, they'll distribute the elixir to her family when they have enough."

I widened my stance, white-hot rage rising within me. I opened my mouth to tell him what I thought of his comments, and of the villages leaving the poor to die, something sure to impact the whole kingdom, but instead I just snapped my mouth shut again.

I smirked without humor. "You don't need military might when people are dying. You need a cure and brass lady balls. Luckily, I have both. Let your people die if you want. I will not. Try to stop me, and our battle won't be sexual."

I slammed the door shut behind me. A staff member in the hallway jumped and backed up to the wall. I walked by with a trail of power behind me.

"Finley, stop," Nyfain called.

At the stairs, I jogged down. He caught up at the bottom and grabbed my arm, whipping me around. I let out a thrum of power, blasting into him. His hand ripped away and he staggered backward, his eyes widening. My animal stretched within me, just getting started.

Looks like our will can manifest into actual blows, she said, and I could feel her grin.

Or maybe I was the one who was grinning.

"Fuck with me when I'm trying to help people, Nyfain," I snarled. "I dare you."

He stopped dead, staring at me with a flat expression, surprise clear in the bond. This was probably unusual for some reason, but I didn't stop to find out why. The blast of power had worked. I'd roll with it.

"Come on… What's your name?" I asked the girl as I strutted toward the door.

"Dabnye." Her eyes were as wide as Nyfain's as she looked at him standing where I'd left him.

"Tell me your mother's symptoms."

With a last look at Nyfain, she turned and hurried after me.

As we crossed the grounds to the stables, I listened to her description of a sickness we all knew very well. Her mother was on the very edge, but she hadn't been there for too long, it sounded like. Of course not—she hadn't had the elixir to prolong the inevitable. She certainly didn't have the crowded elixir to pull her back from death.

Hadriel and Gyril waited with four horses, two that looked older and a little rough around the edges, a small one that was likely a pony (that one was hopefully for me; I was no horse master), and a great big black stallion with crazy eyes that was obviously Nyfain's.

"Nyfain isn't coming," I said as I neared. "Why the fourth?"

Hadriel tilted his head at me, a look of alarm on his face. "What do you mean he's not coming? Then why is he marching across the grounds like he plans on killing someone! It's not me, is it? You wouldn't save me from demons last night just so the master can kill me today? That's not the sort of joke friends play on each other, Finley!"

Nyfain eyed the girl when he neared, glancing at her clothes and finally her shoes, worn through in patches.

"What village, girl?" he asked.

"Great bedside manner, dickface," I muttered.

"Orchard Blossom," she responded, her voice subdued and her face tilted downward.

"Don't let him scare you. He's actually warm and gushy inside," I said, eyeing the horses. "No saddles?"

"We don't use them. Don't need them," Nyfain said, looking at me closely. "Can you ride bareback?" He ran his palm along his stallion's neck, then down to its shoulder.

"I guess we'll see…"

"She'll go with me." Nyfain jumped up gracefully and threw a leg over the back of his horse. He reached down for me.

"Right, but…" I eyed the options again. "Your horse isn't going to want to handle two of us."

"He's more than capable. He's had to carry me with a wounded dragon double your weight."

Apparently the horses here didn't age any more

than the humans did.

Hadriel hopped up onto the next largest horse like he'd been doing it all his life.

"I have never ridden," Dabnye said quietly.

"No problem, little darling. You can ride with Uncle Hadriel, the best horse whisperer in the kingdom." He walked his horse forward a bit and put out his hand.

She took it shyly, and he swung her up behind him.

"Hold on tight and don't fall off the back," he told her, walking the horse forward a bit more. "We're not quite sure just how good of a healer Finley really is."

"She made that look really easy," I muttered, taking Nyfain's hand.

"It is." He pulled me around, and I swung my leg over.

My weight was going too fast, though, and I slid off the other side. I hit the ground on my side and rolled away quickly, lest the stallion decide he wanted to step on me.

"Maybe it isn't," he added.

I hopped up and dusted myself off before trying again. This time I managed to stop myself while still on the horse's back, clutching Nyfain's robust body and hugging him tight. He put his hand over mine for a moment, apparently to make sure I was on, before kicking the horse's sides and clucking his tongue. We quickly sped up to a trot, heading toward the Forbidden Wood.

"What made you decide to come with us?" I asked as I twisted to look at the others behind us. Hadriel held the bridle with two hands and sat with a straight back, looking like he'd been born to ride. Being a butler was a waste of his efforts. Dabnye held her skinny little arms around his waist, tighter than they probably needed to be. I knew how she felt. Riding bareback and behind someone was a little daunting.

"A few reasons. I didn't want you to barrel into the village, knocking heads, and cause problems until you got your way. I also didn't want you to accidentally kill anyone. I definitely didn't want you to reveal that you have the power to unsuppress their animals. It's been happening a lot lately. Last night when you were in Hadriel's room, I could feel your power pumping out into the hall. Everyone there stood around in wonder, gripping their chests, reconnecting with their animals. I'm not the only one who's noticed you." He sighed. "But I'm tired, and sticking my nose in the villages' business will be incredibly unpleasant, so I might've made excuses for why I didn't need to bother. In the end...I followed my dick."

"You want to fuck on a horse."

"Yes. I certainly won't need to rescue you from a pit.

You've shown that you are more than capable of getting out of a pickle. Unless you have a sword, obviously."

"Damn sword. It's really pretty, too. It would look good hanging down my side."

"It was my mother's."

We ducked as the horse trotted under low-hanging branches.

I didn't know what to say. In the end, all I could get out was "Why?"

"Because I knew it would look good hanging down your side."

I leaned my cheek against his back. "I don't know what to say. I mean, there is the obvious: I'm not worthy. That just rolls off the tip of my tongue. And then there is the fact that I'm not trustworthy with it. I've dropped my pocketknife, I've dropped my dagger— I might lose it! And then, you know, we barely get along. I'm not the right sort…"

"Finley, you are exactly the person she would wish to have it. It's not that we don't get along, it's that you call me on my shit. You always push back. She would've wanted that for me. It keeps me grounded."

I blew out a breath, my cheek still pressed to his back. I moved my hands so that they were gripping right above his pecs, more of a hug than a precaution against falling.

"Well, I guess I'm going to have to get good at using the sword now."

"Obviously. We have a lot of work ahead of us."

He slowed the horse to a walk as we neared some rocky terrain. I ran my hands across his muscular chest and down his bumpy stomach. How lucky was I that I got to touch his stellar body? That I got to feel it moving against me in the height of passion?

"I read your letter," I said as I continued moving my palms downward.

"Oh?"

"You're very charming when you write letters. Very eloquent." I wrapped one arm around his stomach and slid the other over his bulge. "Are you always hard?"

"Around you? It seems so. It's incredibly distracting."

I rubbed up that hard length, closing my eyes for a moment. "Thank you for explaining yourself. It helps to know why you freak out."

"I never freak out. I, instead, express my concern. Without emotion, of course. Men are not emotional."

"Ah, yes. Men love to sell the idea that they are not emotional, as if anger weren't an emotion. But it's not that you aren't emotional, it is that you store that one emotion up until you explode with it. It's ridiculous, really."

"It must seem that way to someone who calmly waltzes into a three-against-one battle and proceeds to slice everyone up and throw one of them out the window."

"Talked to Hadriel, did you?"

"Yes. I was speaking to him, very unemotionally, about you being in danger."

"It wasn't his fault."

"Which is why he is not black and blue today."

I shook my head, pulling my hand away lest he make a mess of himself. "Is it the curse that says you can only impregnate your true mate?" I asked, back to rubbing his chest.

His muscles flared under my palms and across his back. He didn't answer.

"Magical gag, huh?" I murmured, though if that were the case, how could Hadriel have told me? Then again, Hadriel had almost died when he let too much slip, so maybe Nyfain was trying to stay on the cautious side. I didn't blame him.

I tried to go a bit broader in questioning. "Do you know how to end the curse?"

His muscles flared again, and he adjusted his seating in discomfort. Clearly a yes. At least partially, I waged, if there was such a thing.

I rested my chin against the center of his back and

rubbed up and to the outside of his shoulders, my mind working.

"If there'd been no curse, would you have been able to mate a person like me?" I asked, and regretted it when I felt his emotions through the bond. I knew what was coming.

"Likely not with my father's blessing. You're gifted enough that you would have been invited to eat at his table, maybe even join the court, but without a dowry or any connections, you'd have only been granted a lower noble to mate. My father was not one to flout custom for any reason, hence my current—the *kingdom's* current situation."

I wondered if true mates tended to also be of the same social class, then remembered that they had to be the same animal, and dragons here were all noble. Clearly in other kingdoms as well, since his mother wasn't from here and she had still been a noble. Of course his father would want to bake that into the curse. He'd want to force his son into a "proper" alliance, as befitted the kingdom.

"Your true mate, then, would be a noble of good standing," I said in a small voice, mostly to myself.

His muscles flared again, and he struggled to take in a breath. Alarm bled through the bond. His dragon yanked power from mine, pulling everything we had.

Fire flooded me as my animal generated her own power to give to him.

"Nyfain?" I clutched his shoulders and tried to look around at him.

He sucked in a noisy breath and then coughed, pulling on the reins to stop the horse. He bent over and coughed again, palming his throat.

"Stop asking about the curse," he growled. "I can't answer. You'll do the demon king's work and kill me."

"Sorry," I said, remembering the flare of his body, his unspoken yes.

For a moment there, I'd half wondered if maybe, against all odds, I *could* be his true mate. If this deep, damning need for him was indicative of something greater than lust and affection.

Then again, true mates were rare, and plenty of people loved their mates without that connection. My parents weren't true mates, and they had been head over heels for each other. I needed to pull my head out of the clouds and hear what Nyfain was saying, actually *hear* what he kept telling me and let it sink in.

If the demon king came, I needed to barter for as many lives as I could, using the thing that I had always shrugged off, my beauty. I might not change the stars and keep the heart of my prince, but I could damn well keep this kingdom alive. Some of it, at least.

I blew out a breath and blinked away unshed tears. Time to strap on my iron tits and get the job done. It was the hardworking lower class that had built this kingdom, and it would be the hardworking lower class that would save it. I'd make sure of it.

"Everything okay?" Hadriel called forward as we got going.

I gave a thumbs-up and pretended not to feel my heart twisting. Pretended not to feel the hollow opening in my middle. This was the problem with all those stories about happily-ever-afters and dreamy men—reality seemed much bleaker when you realized you wouldn't be playing a part in one of those stories. That they were called fantasies for a reason.

At least the orgasms were real for me, though. I'd take it.

"You good?" Nyfain asked, and I could feel the regret in the bond. The somberness of his tone.

"Perfectly. I just needed a little reality bitch slap, and now I am ready to go."

He didn't comment as we pushed past the tree line and into a village that blew my mind.

CHAPTER 17

S UDDENLY THE WHOLE social class issue made a lot
more sense. Large houses rose before us, two stories
and surrounded by large plots of mostly cultivated land.
Lovely flowers bloomed beside cobblestone streets and
lamps with candles nestled inside hung from light
fixtures. Clearly someone walked around at night,
lighting those and replacing them. Who paid for it?

More roads intersected up ahead, a maze of a
neighborhood.

Hadriel trotted up beside us, looking at Nyfain,
clearly wondering how to proceed.

"I'll need to see their town council and discuss my
presence," Nyfain said, his tone resolute.

I swung a foot over the stallion and jumped to the
ground before he could grab me. I motioned for Dabnye
to jump down after me. "By the sound of it, her mother

doesn't have too long. We'll walk from here."

Nyfain turned on his horse so he could look down at me. "You are accompanying me. There are certain protocols each village has devised since the curse…"

"No offense, your royal highness, but stick it up your hole. As we've just gone over, I'm not a noble for you to command. I'm just a common girl." I shrugged and grabbed Dabnye, jerking her to the side. "Let's get out of this neighborhood. It's giving me hives."

"Sir…" Hadriel looked between Nyfain and me.

"Go with her. Make sure she…" He rolled his shoulders. "On second thought, come with me. You can hold the horses. You couldn't help her anyway."

"There's the spirit, sir. Insult my masculinity whilst forcing me to spend prolonged time in your presence, which will likely make me shit myself before the day is through. Fantastic. I will look forward to my eventual demoralization."

"Less talking, Hadriel," Nyfain growled. "It's giving me a headache."

"Yes, sir." Hadriel showed me his teeth with wide eyes and a *help me* vibe.

I didn't waste any time. I plucked Dabnye's sleeve. "Let's hurry. I'll need to gather some supplies, but I want to see your mother first."

We jogged around the outskirts of the nice neighborhood. Slowly the houses diminished in size. The yards didn't look so nice. The shutters weren't so picturesque. Across a dirt lane pocked with ruts and holes, the dwellings weren't much more than shacks.

"Goddess help me, that was a steep decline," I muttered, turning down a small lane that would barely fit a horse, let alone a wagon.

"You're probably from somewhere fine. We don't have much in this part of town."

"Was this the most influential village in the kingdom before the curse?" A child stared out a window, her face dirty and hair disheveled. At least they were still producing kids.

"Second most, I think? I haven't ever seen the others. I can't imagine it being nicer than this. I mean…up near the village center."

"You have a center, huh? My village is the poorest one, I think, and we just have a square. We don't have much, but the poorest of us have more than this. This is…" I gritted my teeth as anger ate through me. It was unacceptable, that's what it was. This village wasn't a unit. They hadn't come together to look after each other. They had cut the weakest members off and turned their backs on them, not even giving them medicine for the sick.

"Fuck this shit," I said as she turned down a trodden

collection of weeds and stepped over a hole in the porch of a ramshackle structure. It wasn't much more than a lean-to. "Fuck all of this shit. We have some empty places in my village. You could go there."

"We can't visit other villages. The demons will kill us. Only the prince moves between villages, from what I've heard, and he does it within the shadows."

"I doubt the demons will give two shits about you, to be honest. No offense."

She looked at me like I'd grown a third eye, then glanced down at my clothes. "I've never heard such a fine lady…"

"With a mouth like mine?" I grinned and waved her away as I pushed open the wobbly door. "Don't mind my clothing. The prince insisted that I dress up before visiting the villages. I was wearing his childhood clothing for a while. I was wearing plain men's clothing before that, made by my mom or brother."

"But you're so pretty."

"You can't help the face you were born with. It doesn't make me who I am. Now, show me your mother."

She led me through the dimly lit interior and into the back bedroom—actually, the only bedroom. It held an empty cot and a sickbed. A woman lay in the bed, her arm thrown to the side and her breathing shallow.

She didn't open her eyes or show any sign that she knew someone had come into the house.

I felt her pulse, then her head. Burning up. Her face wasn't sallow, though. She wasn't wheezing. No coughing.

"She's got time. It's not going to be fun for her, but she's got…a couple of months, at least."

The girl sucked in a shaking breath and held it, her eyes shimmering with emotion.

I put my hand on her shoulder. "Sorry. I'm not the bedside nurse of my family. I'm the jerk who talks to herself out in the yard and hands off the nursing to others. You can see why. A couple months is very good news. I'd thought the situation was dire. It isn't. We'll save your mom for the time being, no problem, okay? Then we'll save her for good. You're not going to lose her."

A tear leaked out, and she wiped it away, nodding.

"Okay." I patted her. I needed Hannon. He was the other half to this healing team.

I braced my hands on my hips, looking around. No fireplace in this room.

Out in the living room, the ground beneath the small pot in the hearth was cold. I pointed at it.

"What's the deal with no fire?"

"We don't have money for fuel. With Momma not

working, and me not getting much for my sewing…"

I nodded and stepped out of the house, looking down the lane. "What about your neighbors? What kind of situation are they in?"

"Um…"

I stepped forward and went to the next house over, opening the door without ceremony and popping my head in. "Official business. Right ball of the prince." No one sat in the living room. The single bedroom in the back held three beds, one of them occupied by a man who could barely take a breath. Liquid had collected in his lungs. He didn't have long. "Crap."

I pushed my way out, heading down to the next house. Dabnye followed, probably not knowing what else to do.

"How many in this village are sicker than your mother?"

"I don't know. There are about a dozen in this section."

I pushed my way into the next house. A little boy looked up from two blocks on the floor. His eyes took in my clothes and he froze.

"Where's your—"

"What is this? We've paid our rent." A woman in a mustard-yellow apron thundered from the kitchen so quickly that she still had flour on her face. Her scowl etched deep lines in her face, and bags circled her eyes. She wiped her slick forehead. Someone groaned from the back room.

"Damn it, you're sick, too. Is this whole fucking village sick?"

Her demeanor changed, her expression turning desperate. "It's not me. We don't need the potion for me. It's for Rufus. Please help him."

He was in one of the two bedrooms, coughing into a napkin. I stopped by his side and took the napkin away, startling him. No blood. His cheeks were flushed and his eyes reddish.

"Nah, he's good for a month or more." I walked by her, ignoring her confused expression, then stopped at the door and turned back. "Does anyone in this area have access to a large fire? We need a cauldron over a large fire, inside or outside, doesn't matter."

"Uh…Maryanne down at the corner house. She has a cauldron in her backyard. They say she dances naked in the moonlight. She's not in her right head."

"She sounds like she's about to be the most liked person in this area of the village, actually." I met Dabnye at the door. "Show me to her house."

No one was home in her three-room house. The back door was open, a screen covering the doorway. Beyond, most of her backyard was covered in healthy green plants, reaching up to the stark, white-yellow sun. To the side, a large cauldron hung over ashes. Over it, a little roof held up by four posts was embedded in the ground.

"Maryanne, is it?" I asked from her back door.

She startled and stood, a woman a little older than me with large brown eyes and a small nose. Beads of sweat shone on her rich bronze skin, and a large hole in her tatty pants gave me a glimpse of her knee.

"I already paid rent," she said with a lovely cadence to her voice. She could sing, I bet. Probably when she was dancing naked in the moonlight.

I looked down at my outfit. "Man, this is great. I wonder if the people in the expensive part of town would hand over rent if I just wandered into their houses. When's rent time?"

Her eyebrows sank.

"Yeah, I'm not from here. Listen, you have a lot of sick people in these parts." I pointed to the cauldron. "Do you use that for brews or draughts or anything more useful than dancing?"

Her expression soured further, and she turned more to face me. "Look, I'm not trying to summon the demon king or practice black magic or anything. I don't even dance around it! I just make a few natural remedies to try to help with the sickness. It doesn't even work! I'm not doing anything wrong."

"Clearly you are doing something wrong if your remedies don't work." I walked out into her extensive garden, identifying the various plants. Dabnye pushed up next to the screen door, watching.

"Who…who are you?" Maryanne asked me.

"Someone who could use your help." I pointed down at the everlass. "Where did you get that?"

Guilt crossed her expression before it cleared and she lifted her chin. "It grows everywhere around here. I replanted them from the edge of the village. They were wild. I didn't do anything wrong."

"Crap on a cracker, this place has done a number on you. Look, lady, I'm not here to get you in trouble. Don't let these fine clothes fool you." I bent to the everlass and plucked off the dying leaves. She made a sound and stepped forward, but ultimately held her tongue. It wasn't because she realized I was pruning.

That done, I stood and glanced back at the dead fire. Then at the house.

"Have you harvested any of this everlass?" I asked. "Have you dried it?"

Her face closed down. "No," she said.

I smirked. "You're a terrible liar." I crooked a finger at her. "Come with me."

With a straight back, she did as I said. I had to hand

it to Nyfain, these fancy clothes he'd insisted on had set me up great.

In her kitchen, by the small, round table, I waited for her to enter. Dabnye filed out of the way.

"I need parchment—or something to write on—and something to write with," I said.

Maryanne frowned at me, moving slowly to make it clear that she didn't want to do any of this but realized she had no choice. I could not wait to barge in on the fine people who'd made the rules in this establishment so I could give them a taste of chaos. My anger was rising with each passing moment.

She slapped some homemade paper down on the table, parchment clearly way too expensive and labor-intensive for her resources. The paper was oddly brown and misshapen, but it would work. She followed it with a quill and a small container of ink.

"First, I like your pushback. Good on you. Second, I hate these things." I picked up the quill and sighed. "Don't you have a fountain pen?"

"Some of us don't have the money for an actual fountain pen."

"I don't have fuck all, and we have a fountain pen. Fine." I sat down at the table and scratched out the recipe for the nulling elixir, including when to harvest the leaves and dry them. I gave her a few options there, just in case. That done, I wrote out the demon-sex-magic-be-gone draught.

"Now, here's the thing," I said when I pushed it away. "You need to baby those everlass."

Confusion bled through her scowl as she looked down at what I'd written.

"She's the one," Dabnye said quietly. "I went to the castle and brought her back to see Momma. She's the one that makes the potion. She made the prince come and everything."

Maryanne's eyes jerked up, taking in Dabnye. Then me. "What?"

I pointed down at the paper. "I've written out the recipe for the nulling *elixir*. It's an elixir, not a potion. I'm not magical in that way. This was given to your village already, but clearly it wasn't passed down to you for some reason. My whole village has that recipe, though some aren't good at making it. Some are just too sick. If you follow those instructions to the letter, you should be able to re-create it. Now, here's the thing. You need to baby that everlass plant. You're treating it like all the others, and that just won't do."

As her face went slack at the news, I explained how to better work the plant. Then we talked about when she'd harvested, how, and how much of the dried plant she had on hand.

"It'll have to do for now. Get it to the sickest people you know. Don't worry about using rainwater for this batch. Just use normal water. You should have everything else in your garden. Start with small batches and see if they work. Once you get the hang of it, use that cauldron. Keep them from dying."

"But this recipe..." She studied it in disbelief. "It's so simple."

"Using everlass is always mostly simple. It's how you treat the everlass that determines what results you'll yield." I stood and stepped away. "Another thing...do you have anything that can be used as fuel? I need to make a different sort of very dangerous elixir for the few who are barely hanging on. No one seems to have a proper fire around here, but you look like you have a couple pennies to rub together. Nyfain can ensure you are compensated...however that happens. I'm sure he has gold or wood or something, I don't know. Go cut some down during the day from the Forbidden Wood. There's plenty there. I know a birch that needs to go..."

"Who are you?" Maryanne said with wonder.

"Someone without any fucks to give." I pointed at her. "Fuel?"

"Y-yes."

"Good. Get it going. You have someone down the lane at death's door." I walked out through the front door and waited for Dabnye. "Show me how to get to the council. This shit show has gone on long enough." They would be convening because Nyfain was here, and I had some choice words for them.

We stopped in quite a few houses on the way so I could assess the damage. The shanties were clearly the hardest hit, their lack of good diet and probably hard labor taking a toll. As we neared the center of town, their market a sprawling affair within wrought-iron gating, things turned a corner. People were up and moving around for the most part, shaking off the worst effects of the sickness. They'd gotten the nulling elixir.

It hadn't helped everyone the same, of course, the worst of them only rebounding a little. They'd need more doses and quicker, and it didn't seem like they'd be producing it themselves. This village was apparently relying on me to supply everyone.

The council convened in a small white building with a spire and carefully cultivated grounds. A little play structure existed for well-fed and clothed children, who played with smiles on their faces and not a care in the world. Quite the difference from the other side of the village. Or from my entire village.

Dabnye stayed very close to me, pulling gazes to her like bees to bright flowers. I marched through the village center, rage pumping through me, power barely kept at bay. The crowd parted, confused, then scowled at Dabnye.

"Excuse me, but what is the meaning of this?"

A man with a large mustache and dark circles under his eyes stopped in front of me. Clearly he'd gotten some of the nulling elixir. The signs of weakness showed, but he was bouncing back. For now.

"What is the meaning of what?" I stopped for a moment, topping his height by a few inches and beating his scowl from experience.

"Well…" He chuckled softly, trying to hide his sudden wariness. "This little girl looks like she is far from home. Is she troubling you?"

"No."

He waited for more. I didn't provide it.

"Yes… Well, you see, the thing is, we don't allow beggars—"

I slapped him in the dick. Not too hard—just enough to bend him over and quickly release his breath. I could've gone for the face, but that wasn't unique enough. I wanted him to remember me. Now he would.

"She's not begging," I told him in a firm tone, loud enough to carry. "She is looking for the nulling elixir that is her due. And *I* am wondering why she has not gotten it. Now, if you'll excuse me." I grabbed him by the shoulders and bodily moved him out of the way, a little rougher than was absolutely necessary.

Surprised gasps sounded from the quickly gathering crowd, and I sure hoped it was because of my violence and not because they could feel my power. Still, I wasn't totally naïve—I'd firmed up my place in the rumor mill. Oh well. A reckoning with the demon king was inevitable anyway, right? What was the difference if he came sooner or later?

I cranked the bronze handle in the wide double doors and shoved them open, walking through. A little kitchen sat off to one side with two women busy preparing pots of water and tea sets. How quaint. On the other side of a half wall, eight men and women sat in couches or chairs, facing Nyfain, who sat seemingly relaxed in a seat a few paces before a stage. Various musical instruments waited on the stage, and I assumed this was a place for dances or concerts or the goddess knew what. We didn't have anything like it in my village.

Nyfain looked up from above steepled fingers. Intense wariness flowed through the bond. He knew this wouldn't be good. Amazingly, though, he wasn't getting up to stop me.

Hadriel was nowhere to be seen. He'd probably stayed outside with the horses.

The council members turned or glanced my way.

I wasn't sure how to start. Yell? Throw something? Try to overturn one of the couches they were sitting in? My rage begged for all of those things. My animal wanted violence to match my mood.

"Hello." I put my hand up for Dabnye to stay by the door. She didn't need to be a prop in this.

My boots thunked against the wood as I made my way to Nyfain. He watched me the whole way, not offering any emotion.

I stood next to him, where everyone could see me.

"Do you know who I am?" I asked.

"What is the meaning of this?" a middle-aged woman said in an outraged voice. Her fine dress said she had money, and her attitude said she was not used to being interrupted. The others were one and the same.

"I'll take that as a no." I braced my hand on the back of Nyfain's chair, shaking because I was so angry. I tried to stay calm and give them a chance to do the right thing. "I am Finley from Lark Crest village." A few narrowed their eyes, looking at Nyfain for the meaning of this outrage. My village clearly wasn't looked upon favorably. "I am the creator of the nulling elixir."

Surprise lit their faces. Delight.

"Oh, that potion is genius—"

"It has saved countless people—"

"We are so thankful—"

"Enough!" I barked, and power pulsed through the room. This time I knew the gasp was because I'd revealed my hand.

A few faces went slack.

Not much I could do about it now.

"I gave you that elixir in good faith. It was supposed to be distributed to the sickest among you. Why wasn't it?"

"Well, it was," the middle-aged woman from before said, her stupid hat propped high on her coiffed head. "We cured all the sickest we had, and it worked like a charm."

I pointed to the door—I was doing an awful lot of pointing in this village. "The guy I just ran into out there was not the sickest in this village. Not even remotely. There are people on their deathbeds in the cheap section. You should've given it to them first."

An older man with a pressed suit and a gray comb-over offered me a slick smile. "Ah, but you see, young lady, his highness gave us the...elixir in good faith, not you. And his highness knows that in our tithe we have a certain way of doing things. The villagers who offer the most to the village will receive it before those who offer the least."

Rage boiled and bubbled. It coiled within me, a living thing.

Brain him, my animal said. *Twist off his head and kick it around.*

No. Physical violence won't work here. They think with their pockets. They don't like sharing.

"Fair enough," I said, and I felt Nyfain's surprise. "There are a couple of things you should know. First, the nulling elixir doesn't work forever. It's a patch. A good patch, but a patch nonetheless. It doesn't cure. You will never stop needing it, and eventually they'll die anyway. When they get close to death's door, you'll need it more often—stronger, if you can get it—with the best leaves available."

Slick spread his hands. "We understand. We thank the prince for his generosity."

"Second," I said with a smile, "it isn't *his* generosity. It is mine. And now that generosity will come at a cost. If you want more, or if you want instruction, you will pay for it. I'll accept your coin or your trade on an as-needed basis."

His expression froze. Everyone else's eyes darted around. Smug pride rolled through the bond.

"You should also know this," I continued. "I will be donating my time and services to those less fortunate. I will personally help them create and distribute the elixir, and I will be working with an experimental recipe for those on death's door. I will do this for free until this council decides to create and distribute the nulling elixir as I have requested. If I hear that any of you have ventured into the poorer areas to take what they have made, or to interfere in any way, I will kill you."

The room froze now, all eyes on me. They hadn't heard threats like that before. Before long, their gazes drifted to Nyfain.

He dropped his hands to the arms of the chair. "I am declaring this demon-created sickness a kingdom-wide emergency. Internal village rents and taxes are to be frozen until such a time as we have rectified the issue. If that decree is ignored, I will withdraw the crown's aid and leave you to succumb to the sickness." He stood and placed his hand on the small of my back. "I back the royal healer's efforts and stand by her decisions. I will be her broker if you decide to go that route." He paused for a moment. "Stand," he commanded, and power pulsed through the room.

Looking around as though they'd been slapped, they slowly got to their feet. None of them uttered a peep.

Nyfain stared them all down, and I wondered why he got to wear jeans and a T-shirt when I had to wear tailored finery. Though I did have to admit that the effects of these very comfortable clothes were worth looking like a snobby noble.

One by one, they offered stiff bows.

"Come," Nyfain said to me, his hand applying pressure.

When we stepped outside, he led me around to the back. Dabnye followed at a distance, probably nervous to be in the presence of the prince.

"I'm impressed," he said. "I thought you were going to explode."

"I felt like it."

"This was the better way. The professional way. You'll get the same results, but they'll respect you more for this approach."

"It wasn't nearly as fun, though."

"No. Not to fear—at least one of them will defy you. You can set the example then."

"We're not done yet," I said as the horses came into sight.

"I figured. How bad is it?"

"Very. And I am incredibly disappointed in you that you didn't know."

He stopped me in front of his horse. Hadriel glanced over from the corner of the building, where he stood talking to a buxom woman with a ruddy face. He straightened up quickly and smoothly put a mug of what was probably ale behind his back. I wasn't sure who he thought he was fooling.

"Finley, as I said, this village operates a certain way,"

Nyfain said. "They all do. Since the curse, this is a fractured kingdom. They won't let me get too involved in their day-to-day affairs, and I don't have the resources to push the issue. Just there, I did what I could. I froze taxes and rent so that they can't siphon the extra money from people you'll be helping for free."

"I get what you're saying, but Nyfain, you are the only person still able to shift in this entire kingdom. You turn into an enormous beast. You have more than enough might. You keep telling me it's your duty to protect all these people. Well, part of that is protecting them from themselves and each other. This isn't like normal times. *Nothing* right now is like normal times. These people are stuck here. They can't get out and find better treatment. They can't change their stars if they are constantly kept down. And they are definitely kept down. If you don't push the issue and do something for them, who will?"

His eyes sparkled and warmth seeped through the bond. He ran his thumb along my chin.

"You will. *You* will do something for them. You will be their savior, and I will be your muscle. Together we will cure this kingdom."

He kissed me slowly, nibbling on my bottom lip. "Now I must go to the other villages and warn them of your coming. This village had to learn the hard way.

Hopefully the others will start working a little more diligently on spreading the wealth. Hadriel will take you where you need to go. I assume it is to get supplies to help the slip of a girl who likely reminds you of a younger you?"

I put a hand on his chest and then leaned in a little, wanting his arms around me. He complied immediately. "Obvious, is it? She looks about my age when I first had to go into the wood after everlass."

"I remember. But she isn't that girl. She won't have to do it on her own, because of you. Where will you go right now?"

"Home. I need to get some dried crowded everlass and steal Hannon while I'm there. If the kids weren't in school, I'd grab them, too. We need someone with bedside manner and experience. I only have one of those things."

He nodded. "We must be long gone before the demons emerge. When you are through for the day, I'll escort you to the castle."

Tingles spread across my flesh at the promise in his tone. I could barely breathe as he kissed me again and turned.

"Hadriel, hurry now. The royal healer has places she needs to visit."

Hadriel took a step toward us, bobbing his head in a

strange sort of bow. He showed his back for a moment, upended his mug, and passed it over to the woman. He waved and jogged my way.

"At your command, sir. We will ride!" He untied his horse and swung up onto it in a smooth, easy motion.

Nyfain gracefully jumped onto the back of his stallion, gave me a nod, and kicked with his heels. Man and horse cantered out of the area.

"Oh." Hadriel stared after them. "Uh…what?"

"He's going to warn the other villages of my coming, I guess." I waved my hand at him for help up. "I don't know what he's so energized about. The fight has just begun."

"He's a dragon. A fight is what he's so energized about. They live for starting fights." He reached down and grabbed my hand, not nearly as great at hoisting me up as Nyfain was.

"Great goddess, Hadriel, lift a weight once in a while."

"How dare you! That would ruin my wiry physique. What would all the boys say if I couldn't bend just right?"

"Guys don't give a shit about the details, you know that. They're just happy for a ride."

"Truer words have never been spoken. Right, where to?"

I turned to look at Dabnye, watching off to the side. "We'll be back, okay? Your mom will be fine until then. Help is coming."

She nodded slowly and took a step back. "Thank you," she said, and I could hear the relieved tears in her voice.

A lump formed in my throat, and I tapped Hadriel. "Go," I whispered, grabbing around his body, much smaller than I was used to.

"Frog in your throat, oh great healer?" He kicked the horse's sides and said, "Hah!"

"Feels good to be back on a horse again, huh?"

"Yes, actually. Butlering is boring. One day I'd like to be the stable master. I've always wanted to be. So, what all happened since we parted?"

I explained the state of the village. After describing the council meeting, I said, "That village greatly needs Nyfain's help, and he barely did anything."

"What do you mean *he barely did anything*? He gave them you. That is everything."

"I shouldn't be taking charge. He's the prince!"

"No, doll, you have it all wrong. Royalty delegates. That's what they do. To avoid looking like tyrants, dipping their fingers in everyone's affairs, they section off their power. They manage the managers. Given everything has gone to shit, there hasn't been a manager to delegate to in a while. But now…there is you.

"Nyfain elevated you to the position of royal healer. He has delegated the control of the elixir to *you*. Plus, he has a built-in threat to get everyone to step into line, since he said he'd support you, and you threatened to kill anyone who interfered with your operations." He laughed with glee. "He's probably tickled pink with you, my love. I doubt there is a prouder dragon in all of the world."

"And he will show his pride by pushing me at the demon king."

I hadn't meant to sound so bitter. Or hurt.

Hadriel patted my arm as it wrapped around his middle. "Yeah, I heard about that. He thinks he's saving your life. And honestly…he probably is. I am absolutely going to try to go with you. Though Leala will probably have a better chance because she's your lady's maid. I chose the wrong job. The bitch of it is that I would've rather worn the maid's outfit than the stupid butler outfits. These things are hideous."

I laughed despite the situation and looked away. "He wants to fight for everything else, so why won't he let me fight, too? It'll suck, but I'll step away when he meets his noblewoman."

The hush of the wood around us lent weight to Hadriel's words. "He *is* letting you fight. He's letting you fight the greatest battle, actually. He's hoping you'll save his people before you get out. It's a rare honor for him to put so much trust in someone. Since the curse—maybe before—he's shouldered burdens on his own. Give him some credit."

My eyes clouded with tears, and I bit my lip, jerking my head in a nod and staring out to the side.

"It doesn't seem like reality, that suggestion," I admitted. "Make a deal with the demon king? Leave here for his kingdom? There is no—" My voice hitched. "There is no way. I've only recently, for the first time, lived away from my family and my village. And then I had Nyfain to protect me."

He left his hand on my arm. "That's it, I'm going to commission a maid outfit. I'll be your second maid, how's that? I'll be with you every step of the way, doll. I won't leave you to brave the demons on your own. You need a damsel to keep you level. I'm the best damn damsel there ever was. I scream right on pitch."

I wiped away a tear, laughing.

He patted me. "It'll all work out in the end," he said softly. "I have faith in that. The prince has been playing hero, keeping the kingdom cranking, waiting for you. Now you will take over for a spell. When you two come together again, it'll be explosive."

"How are we going to come together again if I'm

carted off to the demon kingdom?"

"I have no fucking idea, my darling. Not a clue. But you must, or we'll all perish. No pressure."

"Fantastic. Great pep talk, as ever," I said dryly.

"I know, I know, I should stick to screaming."

CHAPTER 18

A S WE APPROACHED the tree line of my village, I
patted Hadriel's arm. "Okay, stop here. We can't
bring the horse. We'll be noticed immediately."

"Sweetie dove, I am wearing a flower-patterned
dress coat and velvet slippers with thin soles, and you
are wearing a lovely outfit designed by a master in the
finest of fabrics. How in the literal fuck will we not be
noticed on foot? We might as well arrive in style."

I patted him again. "We're going to sneak around
the back."

"Need I remind you about the thin soles? I see a lot
of dirt and stone out there. I doubt I'll do much sneaking. Do you know what *can* sneak? Horses. They sneak
super well. I'll even bend over a bit so that the horse
looks lost and I look drunk. No one will notice."

I rolled my eyes and slid off the side, stepping away.

"Either stay here with the horse, or come with me on foot."

"Ugh!" He hopped down and tied the horse up to the nearest tree. "No one is going to steal him, right?"

"And go where?"

"Lovely lady, again, I am wearing thin-soled *slippers* right now. I will admit, I wasn't thinking when I started this venture. It's been a long time since I've left my post. I don't give a shit where someone might take Mr. Chompers; it'll be farther than I want to travel in these shoes."

"No, no one will take him. They are afraid of this wood. Will you come on?"

We crossed the threshold and worked around to the side, but while I started to jog, he picked his way carefully, not bothering to keep up. I slowed because the last thing I needed was for a guy dressed like him to wander down the lane, peering in windows, looking for me. The village would think they were hallucinating.

As it was, Chrystal from down the way spied us passing by the back of her fence, enough boards missing that she could identify my face.

"Finley?" she called out, shielding the sun from her eyes.

I kept moving with a grimace. Maybe it wouldn't be so bad if they thought they were hallucinating…

"Finley!" She hurried toward us, realized that I wasn't stopping, and headed the other way.

"Go, go, go…" I grabbed Hadriel and yanked him along.

She appeared at a gap in the fence. Her washing basket was held firmly to her hip, and her ample bosom strained her threadbare shirt, only barely covered by a brown apron.

"Oh my stars, it's you," she said. "Praise the goddess, you're not dead." She hustled after us.

"There is some sort of washerwoman following us, Finley," Hadriel said, glancing back. "She looks mean. Does she bite?"

"That's just her face. She always looks like that." I neared the corner as she overtook Hadriel. We weren't going to get away. I stopped and faced her with a bland smile. "Hey, Chrystal."

"Oh, Finley!" She threw her arms around me so effusively that my back cracked with the pressure. "We all thought you were dead. There have been a few sightings of the beast loitering around the general area, too."

That must've been Nyfain bringing meat for my family.

"I'm okay." I put out my hands. "It's not as you think."

"My goodness, look at you!" She ran her gaze down

my front. "Oh my—you are the spitting image of your mother in that outfit. Well, she never wore pants. It really suits you, Finley. Tell me." She leaned forward. "I heard you got tangled up with the demon king. I also hear he is very handsome. Is he holding you hostage and making you pay your rent with your body?" She leered.

My mouth dropped open.

"I did *not* expect that coming from her," Hadriel said with a grin. "You really never know, do you? I thought it was just the castle that was filled with sexual deviants, but apparently this whole kingdom is kinky as fuck."

"It isn't the demon king," I said, turning. "Stop listening to Jedrek."

"But—"

I put on a burst of speed. Hadriel would just have to figure it out.

At my house, I hopped the fence and crossed the backyard, exactly as I'd left it. Well...before the dead bodies. Hannon had cleaned up.

At the back door, I knocked softly before turning the handle. Hannon met me on the other side with a furrowed brow. In a moment, his face cleared and a big smile crossed his face.

"Finley." He wrapped me in a tight hug. "You're

okay." He pulled away and looked down at my clothes. "He's treating you well?"

"As well as a broody fucker like him is capable of, yeah. Listen, I need the dried crowded everlass. I've been positioned as royal healer to help the masses. The other villages, Hannon…" I shook my head and whistled. "Not great. We got lucky. They are all basically fighting over the elixir."

"Why?" Hannon moved into the kitchen and reached above the cabinets to a jar on the top. A little skull was affixed to it. "I realize not everyone can make it, but there should be enough of them to ensure it won't be in short supply if Nyfain comes through with everlass."

"That's just it." I took the jar. "They aren't even giving out the recipe! They're actively hoarding it."

"But…why? Aren't people sick?"

"Yes! Honestly, I have no idea—"

"Power." Hadriel walked through the opened back door. His pocket hung down, ripped from the rest of the jacket. He had another tear along his thigh. "Holding the elixir gave them power over others. But Finley has just stripped them of their power and claimed it all for herself."

Hannon gave Hadriel a once-over, lingering on the slippers. One was missing.

Hadriel noticed and pointed back the way he'd come. "The fucking fence, am I right? What's the problem with using doors? I don't stand out *that* much. Not in a place where people feel comfortable wondering aloud if the royal healer is lending out her body to the demon king as a means of paying rent."

Hannon quirked an eyebrow.

"It's nothing. Don't mind him." I gave a dismissive wave. "How is Phyl? I told him I'd make him elixir, and then fucked off."

"Well, actually, you allegedly got eaten, but close enough," Hannon said. "We're taking care of it. Sable collects the leaves from the field in the Forbidden Wood, and Dash makes the elixir. She can't go at night, obviously, and Dash is not as good as you, but it'll have to do. Nyfain is continuing to tend that field, so we have plenty for the village. We have a few people who are dwindling, though."

"What about Father?" I chanced a glance at the back bedroom, not having done it sooner because I was a coward.

A smile spread across Hannon's face, and something loosened in my middle.

"He's right as rain, Finley. He's making a full recovery! He's obviously weak from lying in bed for so long, and his lungs still aren't quite right, but he is at the market now, selling a pelt he made. Nyfain has been keeping us in plenty of meat."

"Oh good," I said on a release of breath. "Thank the goddess. It works, then. The crowded everlass actually cures."

"Wait..." Hadriel stepped closer and leaned in. "What's this now? You have an actual cure?"

"It's looking like it, but it's dangerous. I wouldn't trust anyone else to make and distribute it just yet."

"But...a cure." Hadriel continued to stare. "Does Nyfain know?"

"Not conclusively." I looked at the top of the cabinet. "How much dried everlass do you have, Hannon? The regular kind. I'll take what I can. You can easily dry more, since you know how to work with it."

Hannon pulled out a box, took out a few leaves, and held the rest out. "Given Dad doesn't need it anymore, we're just the emergency fund at this point."

"Well, tickle my balls, your family is incredibly giving," Hadriel said. "How are you real? This was never the way before the curse. Not that I knew of, at any rate."

"Who is he again?" Hannon asked.

"The mediocre butler. Long story. Thanks, Hannon. Also..." I glanced around. "What are you doing right now? There's a village in very bad shape, and you know my bedside manner…"

Without a word, he walked to his bedroom.

"Deliberation before the verdict, I like it," Hadriel said, watching him go.

"He's just getting his stuff. He doesn't waste energy on idle chitchat, unlike *someone* I know…"

"The master, then? Is that who you're talking about? I know. That guy just will not shut up. If growls were words, you know what I'm saying?"

I chuckled as Hannon returned wearing a light jacket discolored in places, worn shoes, and two-day-old scruff on his face.

"At least he'll blend in if shit goes sideways," Hadriel muttered.

"In that place, I'm not so sure that's a good thing." On our way out, I told Hannon what Chrystal had said to me.

"She's been visiting the pub a lot lately. New demons moved in, realized the space was unoccupied, and decided to stay. They came from some other village, I guess. I don't know which one. They aren't used to so many people ignoring them."

"The draught?" Hadriel asked. I nodded.

"They've been pushing their…magic on people pretty hard," Hannon continued as we reached the fence in the backyard. "Some people are getting a little weird around here."

"You have no idea, Hannon." I motioned Hadriel up. "Come on. Chop, chop."

He sighed dramatically, jumped, and caught the lip of the fence. He labored to pull himself up, scrabbled with his feet, and lost the other slipper.

"Ouch!" he hollered. "I think I got a splinter!"

Hannon put his hand on Hadriel's butt and pushed him to the top. I reached up and shoved him over. Hannon threw the slipper after him.

Hadriel hollered again, ending in a grunt. "Some fucking family!"

Laughing, I handed off the jar of everlass before climbing over. Hannon handed the leaves over before following. No one noticed us sneak around the houses, and while a couple of people were on the lane, they didn't look toward the wood. Within the tree line, Hadriel quickly jumped onto the horse. He eyed us both.

"There's no way we're all sitting on this horse. Hannon is too big. It is Hannon, right? We weren't properly introduced. I'd say that was because Finley was raised in a barn, but that would disrespect both of you. You're too big to disrespect, and she's too mean."

Hannon and I started walking at a brisk pace. Hadriel followed along behind us on the horse.

"How has it been?" Hannon asked me.

"Busy. I've been supplying the starter to make the potion—dang it, now they have me doing it—the *elixir* and demon-sex-magic-be-gone draught, and trying to get a garden sorted... I'm not allowed to go out at night, so I only have the daylight hours."

"You're not *allowed*?"

"Yeah, that sounds bad. I mean, it's true, I am not allowed to go out at night. The other night I did anyway, but it turned into this whole thing, and it's not worth the annoyance, honestly."

"Saving my ass is an annoyance, is it?" Hadriel said. "And here I thought I was the light of your world."

I rolled my eyes and continued. "Plus...the castle is pretty crazy at night. I don't really want to get caught up in it."

"Wow." Hannon's lips turned down. "I would not have thought anyone could tell you what you were and were not allowed to do."

"Just so we're clear," Hadriel said, "she doesn't typically do as she's told. This is more of an instance of her knowing what's good for her."

"If you were there, Hannon, you'd get it," I said. "The demons there are a lot more powerful. A few of them nearly threw Hadriel out of a window. Nyfain doesn't rein me in otherwise, though, not even when dealing with the village earlier. It's literally just at night that he gets crazy protective."

"Just so we're also clear, he is *always* crazy protective of her," Hadriel said. "She just hasn't tested him. If anyone touched her the wrong way, that person would soon be missing a throat. But no, he doesn't seem concerned about reining her in." Hadriel huffed. "Dragons. They are always asking for trouble."

"If he wants trouble, he found it," Hannon muttered with a grin.

"I haven't had time for trouble. The kingdom is in a bad way and, come to find out, they aren't even properly using all my hard work." I pulled my ponytail in irritation.

"Yes, about that. What are we walking into?" Hannon asked.

I talked Hannon through the situation as we made our way. I clearly didn't do a good job of describing the houses in the richer area, though, because he gaped at them as we arrived.

"These are enormous," he said as we trod along the cobblestone.

"These are, yeah."

"This place is way richer than our village." Hannon looked off in the direction of their village center as I led us around the outskirts.

"Overall, yes, probably. But their poor people have it really bad, and our poor people—us—have all we need."

"Barely, and that's because we all work our butts off."

"You'll see."

And he did see. His expression darkened, and his fists started to clench.

"It sounds like they get hassled a lot," I murmured as we found Dabnye's lane, Hadriel still following us on the horse, drawing plenty of attention. Horses clearly weren't usually in this area of the village. "Maryanne, the woman we'll see now, acted cowed over a bunch of stuff that I've always taken for granted. I could've pulled the everlass out of the ground and she would've let me. Can you imagine if someone from our village tried to do that to my plants?"

"No, I cannot," Hannon said.

"No. Because I would rip that bastard's face off. A lot of the wealth here is kept with a select group of people who are deemed important, and the rest just…die slowly, I guess. I don't know."

I rapped on Maryanne's door. Her lovely face appeared in the window, her hair escaping her bun and frizzing on top of her head. She opened the door a moment later, a sheen of sweat coating her face.

"You came back," she said. Her eyes took in Hannon, lingering for a moment, and then darted to Hadriel behind us, sliding off the horse. "And you brought a clown."

A crooked smile worked up Hannon's face.

"Of course we came back." I walked into the house and went straight through to the backyard. "Why such a big house—in the scheme of things—for just you?"

"How do you know it is just me?"

"Because there is only one scent in it, and it belongs to you."

She'd set up another little station nearer the back door, wood burning within a ring of rocks under a pot on a hook. A little table sat beside it, holding a mortar and pestle. It was perfect for smaller batches, which was exactly what she was readying.

"I lived with my gran and granddad when the curse hit," she said. "They did okay for themselves. My cousin lived here with us, as well. But the sickness got my gran and granddad, and my cousin…" She smoothed the hair on her head. "He went into the royal wood to help disband one of the demon's creatures…and didn't come back. The prince wasn't actively patrolling in those days. I've tried to house the orphaned children, but the council puts them in the workhouse. I have this big space, and no one will help me use it."

"Your council has to go." I picked up the mortar, bringing it to my nose. A slightly acidic smell wafted from it.

"They didn't used to be so bad. That's what my gran and granddad said, anyway. But the demons killed the old council members, and the sickness killed a bunch more people, and so this is what we're left with."

"You don't have anyone to push back against them," Hannon said, standing off to the side.

Her gaze lingered on him again, zipping to his shoulders and chest before zipping away. "No. Those who could push back benefit from the existing power structure."

"Of course they have someone to push back." Hadriel walked into the backyard.

"Who?" Maryanne asked with an attitude.

"Me, apparently," I muttered.

"Oh, you dirty little goddess, look at this garden!" Hadriel exclaimed. "Finley, look at this. It's amazing. Is this what we're going to make?"

I put the mortar down, shaking my head. "Something is wrong with the everlass. Show me the dried leaves."

She disappeared into the kitchen to get them, and I took stock of the situation with the cauldron. The fire under it was burning, but the water hadn't heated up enough yet.

"I'm actually going to use the pot." I put the jar on the table and raised my voice so she'd hear me in the house. "We'll make a big batch for the cauldron. I'll use the smaller pot for a very dangerous, very concentrated batch."

"Dangerous?" She emerged, a crumpled sack in her hand.

"Oh no." I took it from her, knelt beside the table, and emptied the contents onto the dirt ground. "No, no." I picked out withered leaves that she'd dried instead of throwing away, then the oddly shaped leaves that had apparently dried in a cluster. Only a few leaves looked in decent shape. I smelled them and grimaced. "This whole batch has to go. You're not working the plant right."

She put her fist to her hip but didn't say anything.

"It's my clothes," I told Hannon as I took the box of regular leaves from him. "She is afraid to talk back because of my clothes."

"No, it's because you clearly know what you're talking about, and I want the knowledge," she replied. "I don't want to scare you away with my personality."

"She's got one up on you," Hannon told me quietly. "You wouldn't dream of holding back for the sake of knowledge."

"I would! I just wouldn't need to because I know everything." I grinned.

"Are you two related or something?" Maryanne asked.

"With him." I hooked a thumb at Hannon. "Not with the clown."

"Oh, I'm a clown now, am I?" Hadriel straightened up within the garden.

"It's the shoes," I said as Hannon said, "It's the jacket."

"Why is she wearing finery and you're wearing…" Maryanne was back to looking at Hannon's shoulders.

"He didn't have the unfortunate luxury of being kidnapped by the prince," I said. "Now pay attention. Playtime is over. It's time to work."

I gave her detailed instructions on how to care for the everlass plant, from pruning and picking the leaves to showing it the love and care it craved. Finally, I used Hannon's leaves to demonstrate making the nulling elixir, cluing her in to the various smells she was looking for and the right temperature of the water. When I was finished, she took a deep breath.

"That was…not as simple as I thought," she said.

"Yeah, but I guarantee, if you treat the everlass right, it'll save lives. It is worth going to the extra effort for that plant."

"It must be, or you wouldn't be looking like that, talking to me. Am I going to get arrested for this, by the way?"

"No. I've told your council that if they interfere with me, I'll kill them. Nyfain—"

"The crowned prince, his royal highness, she means," Hadriel cut in.

"—told them he supports me. He gave me his blessing to handle the situation. So if they bother you, or harass you in any way, get a message to me."

"How do I do that?"

I shook my head. "I don't know. We'll figure it out before I leave. That batch is ready for water, and then we need to distribute it. Hannon, you know how much water. You guys take care of that. I need to work with this crowded plant. Do you have another mortar and pestle?"

"What's a crowded plant?" Maryanne asked as she got me what I needed.

I started explaining as I picked a leaf out of the jar and put it into the cleaned mortar. Remembering Nyfain's account of his mother's experimentation with crowded everlass, I added some lilac to smooth it out and a bit of ginger to help the stomach. Those additions wouldn't mess with the potency, but would help with the body's ability to handle the end result. I ground it all down as much as possible and then stilled, taking a breath.

Okay, folks, here it goes, our third trial, I thought, and my animal, thankfully, didn't reply. She knew the stakes.

"What's the matter?" Maryanne asked softly.

"She is wondering if that elixir will heal or kill," Hannon replied.

"Then I better give it to…whatever poor sap needs it." Hadriel reached out. "I am a master at shit jobs. I literally shoveled horse shit before the previous butlers were murdered and my standing was elevated. This is a job for me."

"I'll do it. I know what to look for." Hannon held out his hand for the mug. "How far is the house? Should we pour the water there, since this particular elixir is…touchier?"

"Probably. One of the bad cases is right next door, but…" I grabbed a potholder and pulled on my animal's power for extra strength.

"Whoa," Maryanne said as I picked up the pot and followed Hannon out the door.

"She has access to her animal," Hadriel said. "Which is a secret, love. Let's keep that—maybe all of this—between us, what do you say?"

I gave two knocks on the house next door, where

the man had been alone in his bed, on death's doorstep. I startled when the door opened. A woman looked out, sadness pulling at her gaunt features. This wasn't sickness, it was a crushed soul, helplessly watching a loved one die.

"I'm here to help," I said softly, heat pricking the backs of my eyes as I remembered that struggle.

"Who are..." She glanced down my front. "Who are you?"

"I'm the creator of the...potion that is helping people. I have something stronger for the man in this house. I'd like to talk to you about it."

"The...potion?" She glanced down at the pot in my hand.

"Yes. I am working on something that will help...your husband?" She nodded, picking at her nail. "There are three options. The first is a very potent elixir—potion—that could cure him. I've tried it on two others, and it seems to have cured the sickness. One of them was my father, so please know that I do not take any of this lightly. However, it is also incredibly dangerous. If it doesn't work, it'll kill him immediately. That's option one."

Tears came to her eyes. She nodded without comment.

"Option two is the normal elixir—potion. It is

weaker. It will help him a little, but it won't help him for long. It's not a cure. It'll essentially give you a chance to say goodbye to him. The third option is doing nothing, and he'll die quite soon, I would think. Those are your choices."

Her tears overflowed, and she wiped them away. She took a deep breath. "You made the potion that the prince gave the village?"

"Yes."

"They won't give it to Rufus because they don't have enough. We need to wait our turn."

My heart broke for her. To see a loved one in such bad shape, know there is something to help, and be told to wait was a torture unlike any other. I couldn't imagine her grief, waiting and hoping the help came before she lost him. Possibly losing hope by the day.

I swallowed down an uncomfortable lump in my throat and focused instead on anger. There had been no need for this continued suffering. Rufus should've been one of the first.

"They aren't in charge. I am, and I say it's your turn. I'm going to make some right now. Which kind should I make? The kind that'll let you say goodbye, or the kind that will either cure him or kill him?"

Tears continued to slip down her face. My heart shattered because I knew what I was making her choose.

But then, we all had to choose eventually. The mad king had made sure of it.

"He's suffering," she said, breaking down. "Please, help him if you can. Try to cure him. If it doesn't work, at least he'll have a timely death."

I nodded.

Here we go.

Beside the bed, I poured the water into the mug and mixed it, waiting until it cooled and the smell hit the notes I was looking for. With a deep breath, I held the mug out for Hannon and walked out.

"Where is she going?" the woman asked.

"She's done all she can. Now it's my turn," Hannon said gently.

Outside, I sucked in a deep breath and went back to Maryanne's house. I would mix the other elixir now and start passing it out. All we could do was wait to see if I'd hurried a man into the beyond.

AN INDETERMINATE AMOUNT of time later, a delicious smell caught my attention. I knew it right away, and my animal perked up in pleasure, desperate to drag me that direction.

Nyfain's large black stallion walked down the small dirt path. He sat astride it in the same T-shirt as earlier, stretching across his mouth-watering chest. The sun sank behind his head, creating a golden glow on his unruly hair.

I stopped in my trudge back to Maryanne's to check on the supplies and see if I could make more elixir. We'd been lugging the stuff to every house in the whole neighborhood, it seemed like. So many people were in various stages of affliction. It wasn't like my village at all. I realized that we'd had this under some sort of control for years. I now saw what happened when that wasn't the case.

He caught sight of me immediately. Anyone in the vicinity stopped and stared, gaping up at the marvel of the prince, one of the last remaining dragons.

He stopped beside me, looking down. "It's getting late. Time to go. Get your team, and let's get out."

"Oh, it went well, thanks for asking! Really good, actually. We got a ton accomplished." I walked on, passing him.

He reached down at lightning speed and caught my arm. I squealed as he pulled me up and dragged me in front of him.

"You have revitalized them. Now it's time for me to revitalize you," he growled, kicking forward toward Hadriel and Hannon, who were walking down the way with empty mugs in their arms. "Hadriel, take Hannon back and head for the castle. Tonight is the lull. I'll be spending it with Finley, as previously discussed."

"Yes, sir. Of course, sir."

Maryanne trailed after them, her eyes wide and mouth agape. She gracefully fell to a knee.

"Your highness, it is an honor. Thank you for bestowing your royal healer on us."

"You have her to thank for that, not me. Take her pot. We must be going."

"Yes, sir." She rose and reached for it eagerly.

With a scowl, I handed it back, looking at Hannon. "I'll see you soon, okay? The other villages will likely need looking after as well. Tell the others I said hi."

He nodded at me, then tilted his head at Nyfain in hello.

"You will definitely see him soon," Nyfain said as he kept the stallion moving. "The other villages are much like this one. I asked for a tour of the hardest-hit locations. It was…eye-opening. I hadn't realized it was so bad. I've failed them."

I leaned back into him, resting against his chest. He held the reins with one hand and wrapped the other around me.

"You didn't fail them, Nyfain. You protected them from the monsters all this time, and you helped me find a cure. It worked again!" I put my hands on his strong thighs. "I have it, I really do. I brought one guy back from the brink of death. I helped several more who were a month or two out. It works!" I beamed, so relieved. "We used all the crowded plant I had dried. I'll need to harvest more. I might need to pick from other fields, since we have a short supply of crowded plants."

He squeezed me as we left the perimeter of the village and entered the wood. "You're the miracle these people needed."

"I couldn't be the miracle alone. We did this together."

He slid his lips down my neck and over my shoulder, applying pressure with his teeth, and a thrill arrested me. I groaned, wanting to be closer. Wanting his skin on mine.

"How did it go at the other villages?" I asked in a breathy murmur.

"I lost my cool a few times. At each village. I have a few triggers, it turns out."

I smiled, rubbing my cheek against his jaw. "What are those?"

"I don't much like when people call you common. Or when they say you don't have enough experience to be valuable—it was the 'valuable' part that set me off. Or that you're incredibly beautiful. Or that people from your village aren't to be trusted—"

"So all your triggers involve disparaging remarks

about me."

"It seems so, yes."

"Except the beautiful one..."

"His eyes flared with lust. I didn't much care for it."

My animal purred in delight, and it felt like she stretched out through the bond to connect with his dragon. I reached back and hugged a hand around his neck.

"That must've been the guy I met in the wood after you drugged me and left my house in the middle of the night."

"Yes," he growled, obviously remembering the exchange in the village.

Ask him how he handled it, my animal goaded me. *Ask him what he did.*

I rolled my eyes, pretending the little thrill was all hers, and relayed the message.

"The reactions varied relating to what they said. Tables were flipped, chairs were thrown, doors kicked in... I didn't have a firm handle on things."

"And the guy?"

He growled and raked his teeth down my neck and across my shoulder. Pleasure curled through me, and the thrill from a moment ago intensified. Suddenly my every nerve was firing electricity. It felt fucking amazing, like I'd just gotten a shot of adrenaline and energy and power and lust all at the same time.

"I threw him across the room," he said, his power pulsing, taking on a keen possessive edge.

I fluttered my eyes shut and leaned my head back and to the side, exposing my flesh for another bite. His intensity curled around me, and a delicious feeling crept across my skin, like claws made of velvet.

"Why does that turn me on so fucking much?" I asked huskily.

"Because you want me to claim you," he whispered against the shell of my ear. "You want me to dominate you and take you as mine. You want me to fill every hole you have and leave my mark all over that tight little body."

I groaned as he said it, suddenly incredibly wet, my pussy begging for his hard shaft pounding into it.

His hand drifted up my chest and cupped my breast. He pulled back on the reins and let go for a moment, reaching around me and unbuttoning my pants.

"I'm not sure this is possible, but we'll give it a try." He pushed down the zipper before suddenly swinging me down from the horse.

I gasped as my feet hit the ground.

"Lose the pants," he commanded.

I wasted no time, peeling off my panties as well. He

laid them in front of him before undoing his fly and pushing it down as much as he could, pulling out his large, hard cock. He put out a hand, and anticipation and excitement tore through me.

"Face me, I think," he said, making a circle with his finger.

I took his hand and let him pull me up, laying my legs over his thighs with my butt resting on my pants. Before I could crawl up onto his shaft, he grabbed my nape and pulled me forward for a bruising kiss. I moaned into his mouth, loving his taste, loving when his tongue tangled with mine.

He hooked his arm under me and lifted, pulling me tightly to his chest. I rose, bracing myself, while he ran his fingers across my wetness. His growl of desire coursed heat through me. His fingers entered me, plunging deeply and rubbing all the right places. He pulled them out and then guided me on top of him, his dull tip pushing at my opening.

I slid down onto that hard cock, sucking in a breath as it parted my folds and slowly filled me. My wet depths hugged him tightly.

"I think they did it the other way around in the book," I murmured, sitting all the way down on him, grinding against his hipbones.

"How the hell would we manage that, though?" He

let go of my back and grabbed the reins. "Hold on. If you fall off, chances are you'll take my cock with you."

"You might be able to lose one of those things, but it would be a pure travesty to lose them both."

His kiss turned urgent, and he sucked on my tongue before nibbling my lips. He let go of the reins with one hand and grabbed my nape again, keeping me against him as he kissed me like a starving man. I lost myself to it, swept away entirely.

He moved his arm to curl under my butt and lifted me before sitting me back down, his cock sliding within me. He did it again, but then had to use both hands on the reins to guide us over a bit of rocky terrain.

"Maybe cantering in a field," he murmured, his breathing labored.

"Or maybe I can get off, and you can just suffer…" I brought a hand between us and massaged my clit, moaning in delight.

He swore under his breath, directing the horse.

I leaned against his shoulder as I worked myself, not needing him to move to get where I was going. I licked and sucked his neck before running my teeth across his flesh. He shuddered in delight, his groan soft and tortured. My body wound up as I rubbed, my pussy muscles flexing and releasing as I took myself higher.

"Oh fuck," Nyfain bit out, leaning forward a bit and

forcing me to cling to his shoulders with one hand.

He kicked with his heels, and the stallion sped up to a trot, the trail flattening and widening for a stretch. I jostled on top of Nyfain, his cock driving up into me. It wasn't entirely rhythmic, but the hard punches of his cock speared pleasure right through me.

My mouth hung open, the sensations so extreme they were almost unbearable. I worked my clit and slid up and down on Nyfain's cock, my pussy so wet it leaked down his shaft and slicked his balls. Another hard jolt, and my climax tore me apart, blasting through me.

"Fuck. *Fuck*," Nyfain said as I cried his name, slumping on top of him. The horse slowed to a walk again, the trail narrowing up a berm between large trees. "Oh fuck, this is torture."

I smiled silkily as I ran my lips along his jaw. "It was good for me. Pity about your blue balls." I nipped his chin.

"You're going to pay for this," he wheezed, leaning hard against me. "Fuck, fuck, *fuck*. I can't even hear myself think. My dragon is going absolutely fucking crazy. He wants me to pull you off this bloody horse, bend you over, and fuck you senseless."

"That wasn't in the book, though."

"Whose stupid fucking idea was it to act out the sex

scenes in those books? I just read one that faded to black. Let's fade this to black, get off here, and then *get off* here."

I laughed delightedly, tightening my legs around him. "It was your stupid fucking idea, so I think you need to pay the price for it. And what's a lull, anyway? You told Hadriel it was a lull tonight."

"I get two nights a month off usually. Sometimes one and a half. For whatever reason, nothing comes through the portal. It's not always like clockwork, but it's usually within a couple days of when I expect it. That's tonight and maybe tomorrow. I am going to wine you, dine you, finally give you your salon treatment, and then pleasure you to within an inch of your life. We'll fall asleep when we're too exhausted to move, and lie together until neither of us can stand the bed anymore. Then we'll get up, be fed in my rooms, and maybe take a bath, or something else luxurious. I've been craving you, Finley. I want more of you. I intend to get it."

"And what if I don't want to be wined and dined, bathed and pleasured?" I asked with a sensual smile as I started stroking my clit again.

"You're my captive. You will do as you're told."

CHAPTER 19

DOMINANCE RANG IN his tone and blistered through my body. I rubbed a little faster, dropping my head back in delight.

"We're getting close now," he said.

"Yes, I am." My breathing sped up, and my pussy clenched around him, getting ready for a second release.

He growled, his shoulder hard under my palm.

"Hang on for just a—Hah!" He kicked his heels into his stallion's side.

His cock drove into me. I was weightless for a second, and then it drove into me again. My jaw went slack. I slapped against his balls, wet from my orgasm. His cock pummeled me in hard, uncompromising jolts. It was the best fucking thing I'd ever felt—and probably one of the most dangerous things I'd done, given our speed and his divided attention. That made it even better. Death while fucking. Dick of death.

We ran across the castle grounds, his cock deep in my pussy, my legs wrapped around his middle. I held on to his shoulders as I slammed down onto him, was lifted, and then slammed down onto him again.

"Holy fuckity cunticles—" I didn't know what I was saying. Couldn't do anything but swear. "Arsehole twat trolley!"

The glorious friction nearly undid me, the merciless pounding branding my body with his cock. The pleasure built, and built, and built. I bit down hard on the base of his neck as his cock speared me. I didn't know how to claim, but I knew how to mark. My teeth tore flesh.

He growled in pleasure, hissing out, "*Yes!*"

Apparently he wanted a claim as well.

The thought spiraled me higher. I hit a wall and then a gush of pleasure tore through me, so intense that I blacked out for a moment. I screamed and shook on him, my pussy clenching him tightly. But the ride kept going. His cock kept ramming into me with each hard landing. Another wave came. I came with it. Another, my teeth tearing at his skin, the thought of claiming him making me dizzy with lust. I came, and came, and came, almost unable to fucking stand it.

"Fucking *fuck*," I swore, vibrating against him,

drenched with my climaxes.

Finally the ride slowed and the swell of incredibly intense orgasms softened, letting me come down.

I breathed deeply, trembling against him, draped over his massive shoulders. There was zero stress left in my body. Now, *that* was a hard fucking.

We approached the stables.

"Turn around," Nyfain growled at Gyril in a voice that sent a merciless shiver rolling down my spine. Heat tingled in my core, and my animal pumped out power, wanting more action. Wanting more of him. All of him.

You need to chill the fuck out, I told my animal. *Let's all just chill the fuck out.*

He needs to fight us, prove his physical dominance, and then mate us. It's time. His dragon is getting restless, and so am I. I don't care about his stupid plans to send you away. They don't make sense, and they are not happening. His dragon won't let him. We're staying with them, and we'll fight what comes together. End of story.

I ignored her. If she had her way, a ground-bound dragon and a tabby cat, or whatever, would take on the demon king and his forces…without an army. Yes, why not? Let's all die.

Nyfain kissed me deeply, running his hands up my back, still hard within me. Fuck, he was a good kisser.

"I regret to inform you that we lost your pants along

the way," he murmured against my lips.

I glanced down quickly. "Ah, man. I liked those. Also…now I have no pants. Or underwear."

"I can lend you my skirt." He pulled back so that he could put his hands under my armpits.

"Your…*skirt*, did you say?"

He hefted me up, his cock sliding out of me. My wetness coated his length, and he tensed, holding me in the air, every muscle on his big body tense. A vein pulsed in his jaw as he turned and lowered me, dropping me the last foot to the ground. He bent then, bracing his hands on his thighs, clearly in pain. I had no idea how he hadn't blown his load in that last stretch.

"We're not far from the castle," I said with a suppressed smile, checking to make sure Gyril was still turned around and couldn't see my bare ass or out-of-control lady beard beside the hanging dagger.

"No." Nyfain stiffly pulled his leg from around the animal's back and jumped off. "I will attend to you now, and finish deeply inside of you when I can't stand it anymore."

His cock still out, he pulled his shirt from over his head and bent, holding it out for my feet.

I braced a hand on his shoulder. "What's happening?"

"Step into the neck hole. I'll stretch it to fit around

your waist."

"You're going to ruin your shirt."

"I've lost your pants. It's only fair that I now ruin my shirt. It isn't as magnanimous as the dragon letting you torture my balls, but it's a start."

I laughed and slipped in one foot, then the other, standing with my legs close together as he stretched the neck up over my knees and then started tearing it to fit over my hips. He cinched it around my waist, and the shoulder area draped down my hips.

"Huh," I said, keeping it put. "That actually worked."

"I'm bigger than you."

"Oh yeah? I didn't notice that when you were looming over me in barely contained rage all those times."

The corner of his mouth lifted in a smirk. He tucked himself into his pants. "You love my rage."

I really did—especially when he exploded into my body with it.

A gush of wetness dripped down my upper thigh. His nostrils flared, and he tensed all over again, breathing deeply.

"Stop," he pleaded.

"This is your fault, not mine," I replied.

"I was talking to the dragon." He put a hand to my hip and gently pushed me behind him before leading his stallion toward Gyril.

"Hadriel will be along shortly," he told the stable master.

"Very good, sir."

Nyfain draped an arm around me as we walked toward the castle, stopping behind a hedgerow to drop to his knees in front of me and lift my pseudo-skirt. He ran his tongue within my folds and then sucked in my clit.

I looked up at the castle looming just behind the dead lawns, three stories of windows looking down on us.

"Someone might see," I said with butterflies exploding in my middle, my fingers in his hair.

"I can feel how much that excites you. My goodness, princess. Naughty, naughty. Maybe tonight we'll join the perimeter of a party, and I'll bounce you on my cock for all to see."

He thrust two fingers into my wetness, stroking hard. His tongue swirled my clit.

"Didn't...*mmm*...a moment ago you tell someone to turn around to prevent him from seeing me?" I panted as his fingers worked, his tricky mouth winding me up once again.

"That was different." He wiggled my clit with his tongue. "You would've been standing nude on your own without the protection of my scent to mark you as mine. When I'm inside of you, it's very clear who you belong to. I protect to the death what is mine."

I tilted my head back as my animal beat a drum of pleasure at his words.

"I don't belong to anyone," I said in a throaty whisper.

"You know that you do. You also know that *I* do." He replaced his fingers with his tongue for a moment, tasting me. "I belong to you, eternally, body and soul. I am yours, completely."

He plunged his fingers back in again, curved just right, hitting the spots I needed. I tangled my fingers in his hair and rocked against his mouth, my pussy clenching around those fingers, everything tightening up. I moaned in little bursts, giving myself to the feeling. To him. Feeding him my desire and something deeper through the bond. Feeding him my acceptance of who I belonged to, at least for now. At least while we could belong to each other.

"Yes, baby girl," he whispered, feeling it, working faster. Harder. "Come for me."

I shattered, my chest heaving, my world cracking. A surge of euphoria ran through me, and I sank to my knees in front of him, meeting his eyes. He kissed me dominantly, salty sweet, reacting to my silent admission.

I might be damning myself, but I would give myself to him, body and soul, and ride it for as long as I could. Our futures might collapse, but when it all went tits up, at least I'd have the memory of him to keep me company in the darkness.

He stood with me and swung me up into his arms. I leaned against his solid chest as the afternoon waned, the sun starting its retreat toward the horizon.

"Now what?" I asked, lethargic in his arms. I didn't care whether the staff saw. I could be a tough girl tomorrow. Right now, I just wanted to bask in this big alpha's pampering.

He entered the castle and climbed the stairs to the tower, meeting a straight-backed man with an air of importance along the way. I'd never seen him before, not roaming around at night or even in the halls during the day. He wore a crisp black suit with a black waistcoat underneath, over a stiff white button-down shirt. A black tie completed the ensemble.

"Sir," the man said, his arms straight at his sides.

"Prepare the largest salon room. We'll be down shortly."

"Yes, sir." He walked away like he owned the world.

"Who was that?" I asked as Nyfain continued up the stairs.

"My valet. He's all that's left of the original valets."

"Why haven't I seen him before?"

Nyfain stopped next to the door, looking at me for a long beat, and realization dawned. "The key was in my pants."

Still, he stared down at me. I couldn't read the look in his eyes or the complex emotions coming through the bond. He turned with me and headed back the way he'd come, down the stairs to the second floor and back to his room. He set me down gently before moving away, into his bedroom. In a moment, he was back with a key in hand.

"This is the only key in this whole castle at the moment that can access that tower. I'll take you up now and let you get freshened up. You won't need to eat or bathe. I'll be taking care of that. But if you want your lady's maid to help you work out what to wear tonight…"

"For dinner?"

"Dinner and dancing, yes. It'll be a formal affair."

I swallowed. I'd never participated in anything that could be called that. I had the dresses for it now, but I didn't know if I'd hold myself the right way. Or use the right cutlery. Or dance well enough not to make a fool of myself. I never had managed to sneak in a lesson.

He smiled softly, probably feeling all that through

the bond. "It's just us, Finley. No one else will be permitted in the same room. You can be yourself with me, always. Save being someone different for when you address the villages."

"I'm very me, actually, when I address the villages."

"That is true. And it works very well." He swooped me up again, nuzzling my neck as he did so.

"I can walk," I murmured, wrapping my arm around his neck and leaning into his warmth.

"My dragon is demanding this closeness, and I want it too. So do you."

He wasn't wrong. My animal had calmed somewhat, approving of this treatment, and…honestly, it wasn't so bad. A girl could get used to being looked after like this.

"You lived up to the book scene, by the way," I said as he walked. "Including all the orgasms. That was intense."

"We're just getting started." He opened the tower door and handed me the key. "I would have had a copy made for Leala, but the blacksmith was killed, his replacement cleaned waste basins before all this, and I'm not totally sure Leala would hang on to it when she was being rammed from all angles and flogged to boot. So…"

"So here we are."

A grin worked his lips again. "So here we are. I'll be

420

up in a while. I'm going to go find your pants and that key. I don't want some creature smelling your pants and having the wherewithal to search the pockets. They take things of note to their masters, and the demons in this castle would know just what to do with it."

Cold trickled down my spine. I did not want one of those demons sneaking into my room when I was sleeping. They'd get the jump on me, and that might be all they needed.

"Right, so…dress for…"

"I'll send Leala up. She'll have the rundown." He put his hand on my arm and kissed my cheek. "Rest. Relax. Read. Put your feet up. Let me handle everything."

I nodded and he turned to go.

"Oh—" I put up my finger.

He turned back, his foot on the edge of the stairs and his hand on the banister.

"I replaced the note you left in your mother's place with one of my own. If you need inspiration tonight, or…want to try something neither of us has done, check out chapter fourteen…" I felt my face heat. "And if you're serious about a little semi-public display, that's chapter…" I bit my lip and thought, trying to stay chill but totally excited and embarrassed and naïve—and eager not to be so naïve. I wanted to try new things so that we had some firsts together, but was nervous about those things all the same. "Um…I actually don't remember. Scan the notes. It's at about three-quarters, I think. At the corner table in a busy tavern. Oh, and…I don't remember the book, but…there's a tying-up scene with a blindfold. If…that might suit you."

If a dragon could smile…

Hunger burned in his eyes.

"Also…" I shrugged. "I don't know if you care what I'm thinking and feeling, but since we communicate better in letters than face to face, I let myself ramble on about life."

His eyes softened. "I do care. Keep them coming. I assume…you read mine?"

"Yes." I ran my fingers down my stomach.

He caught the movement, and longing bled through the bond but didn't interrupt the planes of his face.

"And obviously you haven't bled yet," he said evenly.

"No. Should be any day. Sometimes stress can delay it a while."

"How long is a while?" He couldn't keep the growl from his voice, it seemed.

I ignored it. "The longest has been a week."

He tensed and closed his eyes, longing and hope warring with fear and anxiety in the bond. He half turned away, and this time I could feel his dragon sing through the bond, possessive and dominant and desperate to get at me. Desperate to mark me and claim me and mate me. They were currently in a battle for control.

"What's going on?" I asked. "Pretend you're writing a letter instead of just about to explode and ruin the whole night before it has even begun."

He sucked in a deep breath. "The idea that you might be carrying a child—my child—has sent the dragon into a possessive frenzy. Again." He leaned heavily on the banister. "It's overwhelming, to say the least. He can't get at your beast, so he is trying to shove me aside and get at you in my skin. He knows your animal will welcome it."

She would, no question.

"He can't get at my beast as in...they... The beasts bang in animal form? Does that happen?"

"It's not something people talk about. It's...a different sort of experience, having sex when one's animal is in control, as we know. More so, though, in...the other form. But yes, I've heard it happens when the animals are desperate for each other and the humans aren't acting on it. They'll force the hands of their humans. I remember a couple that absolutely hated each other. They couldn't stand the sight of each other. But their animals couldn't get enough, and they ended up having three kids together before finally getting over their differences and mating officially. Then imprinting. Their bond ended up being incredibly strong, but they only got there because their animals forced the issue."

"As our animals did."

"Yes. And continue to do."

My animal surged up out of nowhere, sublime and content one moment, and shoving me aside the next. I couldn't get my bearings fast enough to claw her back down. I couldn't even get out the gasp that I'd tried to utter.

Our voice came out breathy. "Let me stop the tea, Nyfain. Fuck me as nature intended, with no barriers. No safety nets. Mate with me. Ensure that I carry your brood."

He squeezed his eyes shut and wilted over the banister, resting his forearms on it, his body shaking. Power flooded the bond, washing into us and boosted by my animal before being fed back. It nearly stole my breath.

You cherry-flavored cumstain! I roared at her, grappling with her presence. *I told you I would not incite his dragon!*

That ought to do it, she said, preening, and drifted into the background.

You are such a cum-gargling twat, I swear, I ground out, my body trembling, half crouching and my nails digging into the wooden doorframe. How I'd gotten in that position, I didn't know. *That isn't fair to them.*

The dragon relishes in the sweet rush of power. He thrives on it. Didn't you just feel it? His need to mate is stronger than magic; I told you that. It is embedded in his very foundation. It should be able to help him push through more of the curse. He welcomes this. Let him take us and see. If the man wasn't so dense, he would encourage this and not try to keep the dragon at bay when he seeks to claim his mate!

For once and for all, he is not *going to claim us. Let it go.*

"Go...inside," Nyfain said, gripping the wood now, straightening up slowly. "Go in...your room. Lock it. He's...pushing too hard."

That's because the dragon just accessed more of that big well of power he has, my animal said with pride.

I wish I could punch you in the vagina.

"I'm sorry!" I said to Nyfain. "That wasn't me! My animal is being a real shit." I stepped into the tower room quickly and grabbed the door.

"I know. Go!"

I slammed the door, but I had to quickly open it again as Nyfain turned toward me, his eyes glowing brightly. After grabbing the key out of the lock where he'd left it with a shaking hand, I slammed the door again. Metal clinked, but I got the key in and turned it right before the handle spun. A moment afterward, something thudded against the wood, as though two palms had collided with it. They slid off in a moment.

Need coursed through the bond, hard and hot. It dribbled down my body like lava, making my nerve endings tingle as it flowed toward my core. A gush of power filled me, overwhelming me. With it came a strange sort of serenity.

My hard breathing was the only sound in the quiet room. His scent drifted from under the door.

A low, amused chuckle sparked electricity across my overly sensitive flesh. Nyfain's raspy voice had taken on a dangerous edge, filled with malice and carnal sin. Crackling with power and confidence.

"You can run, my princess," he said, and it was obviously his dragon. "You can hide, if you'd like. But I will find you. I will drag that passion out of you, kicking and screaming if I must, and claim you. You are *mine*."

Goosebumps covered my flesh, and my animal pounded me with her pleasure. My stomach flipped, and damned if my knees didn't go weak with the urge to run. To hide. To fight. And to be taken.

Fuck, what was wrong with me? These weren't the thoughts of a normal person. These were the thoughts of—

A shifter in mating lust, my animal supplied gleeful-ly.

You're dead to me. I pushed off the door with some effort.

She laughed, feeling absolutely no remorse.

Footsteps led away from the door. He was leaving me be, thank the goddess.

I moved to the window and looked out, catching my breath.

You should have let him mate us, she thought. *Claim us. The dragon would've.*

I shivered but didn't respond. She wouldn't under-stand why I wanted to honor Nyfain's wishes, not when I did want to be claimed by him. When I wanted to claim him so no other woman ever would touch him without knowing I'd been there first. He just felt so damn *right*.

But Nyfain knew the score better than anyone, and I was learning what was at stake within this curse. Primal urges were well and good to access power, but to beat the demon king, we'd need a heavy dose of logic and strategy, too. The beasts' desires were shortsighted.

Knuckles rapped on the door, thankfully pulling me out of my reverie. A shape came into view below me at the same time, Nyfain walking out beyond the garden without a stitch. He turned and looked up at my window for a full beat before changing into his animal. He puffed up his chest, tilted his head back, and roared so loudly that the windowpanes shook.

Something stirred in my middle—a memory of a golden dragon cutting through the sky, his roar pulsing within me like a command. A call to arms. A leader summoning his people.

And now...a mate calling his beloved.

My animal thrashed against my hold. Fire filled my blood, and stinging pain rolled over my skin. She stretched for the surface, expanding until my skin felt tight, itchy. Needing to come off.

"Don't you fucking dare," I said, bracing my hands against the window frame. "Do not try to force me to change."

She continued to slash at my control, desperate to get to him.

The dragon huffed, and flame spouted from his nostrils, boiling across the dead grass. Blackness curled in its wake.

In a moment he launched forward and ran, all robust muscle and sinewy grace even when ground-bound.

Tell me you wouldn't fight for that, my animal demanded. *Tell me that he isn't worth tossing everything aside for.*

I turned and crossed the room to the door. "What would I be tossing aside? I don't have anything."

I twisted the key and opened the door to find Hadriel frozen with wide eyes darting all around.

"You okay?" I asked.

"What was that?"

"That was Nyfain. Haven't you heard his roar before? I have, loads of times."

He shook his head in tiny jerks and shoved past me into the room. "Not like that. That was…" He blew out a breath. "And my stomach was finally settling down. It would be ideal if I didn't shit myself right now."

I couldn't help but giggle. "It's not like he was attacking or chasing you. That's usually when I've heard his roar before now."

Although…I guess he *was* kind of chasing me. The dragon was, at any rate.

Hadriel continued to shake his head. "I don't know. It just… Wasn't it terrifying? I thought it was terrifying."

Leala poked her head into the open door. She smiled and walked in, her eyes sparkling. "Did you hear the master?"

"See? Leala isn't scared," I told Hadriel, splashing my face at the water basin.

"Of course she isn't scared!" Hadriel yelled, sitting

in my chair and wiping his face. "She isn't scared of anything. She lets demons beat the shit out of her and smiles while they do it."

Leala rolled her eyes as she opened the wardrobe. "You're such a baby. That roar had nothing to do with you. It sounded like he was warning away enemies or something. Anyway, it had a lot more power than before, don't you think? Or am I just imagining it?"

See? my animal said.

Shut up. You're dead to me.

Her laugh grated.

Leala laid a white slip on the bed, and then my large purple robe. "What did you want to wear for dinner, milady? I was thinking maybe..." She pulled out a slinky little number.

"No, the master already saw one like that." Hadriel waved it away. "It needs to be something grander. How about red? Now, Finley, tell me." He crossed an ankle over his knee and entwined his fingers. "Are you not over the moon about today? People just, like...came back to life! I've never seen anything like it. That one guy—the one who was literally on his deathbed?—I stayed in the room with Hannon after you left. I figured he'd die, but his eyes started fluttering! And then blinking. He was confused, I could see that, but little by little, tiny things started changing. It was like watching a flower grow. It was so fucking cool."

"What's this now?" Leala asked, sitting me down and taking a hairbrush to me.

"And the rest of them. They didn't really believe they were getting the real stuff, did you see that?" Hadriel went on. "They were dubious. Sure, they drank it, because you looked so fine and you have this air of 'shut the fuck up, this is happening,' but they were dubious. And then within hours they were feeling loads better. Like a switch had been flicked, did you see that? Hah!" He put a fist up. "Holy fuckstains on the goddess's sheets, I'm seriously pumped. That's better than gardening. Because you're, like…growing people! No, that's making a baby. You're, like…harvesting people. I don't fucking know—you're helping them, anyway. You're keeping life going."

"You're starting to lose it," Leala muttered.

He stood. "I feel good. It feels good to help people. I'd rather do that than be a butler. I think I'll switch jobs."

"You'll get killed a whole lot faster for curing people than prancing around like you know what you're doing at butlering," Leala said, now washing my face.

"Not likely, since I'll be near Finley, and she has no qualms about killing demons."

"It'll also be during the day," I added.

"Yes!" He pointed at me. "It'll be during the day! So you see, Leala? Suck a ballsack."

"You first," she replied. "Now leave so I can get the miss ready."

"Yeah, yeah. See you later, Finley." He knocked on the frame of the door as he left. "Enjoy your date with the scary, somewhat unhinged dragon. Better you than me."

When he was gone, Leala tsked. "He's just remembering getting picked on by all the dragons when he was small. He'd run his mouth, and then they'd kick him around. Schoolboy stuff. Now he nearly wets himself when one of them spouts off. Though obviously…" She stood back, eyeing me. She tousled my hair. "He hasn't heard one in a long time. After the curse, the master's roar was nothing special. Equivalent to a lion shifter back in the day or something. But today…" She shivered. "He really amped it up. Did you have something to do with that?"

"No!" I said automatically. "Why?"

She shrugged, moving to the wardrobe. "Let's pick that dress so we can wow him. From the sounds of it, he has an incredible night planned for you."

CHAPTER 20

"**M**AYBE HE'S NOT going to come," I said into the hush, sitting in the corner of the tower room with a book that I couldn't concentrate on enough to read. The twilight sky behind me continued to dim.

"He'll come, miss," Leala said, putting my dress in the washroom so that he didn't see it when he came to get me. "Otherwise I would've been informed of a change of plans. He might be delayed, what with tracking down your pants."

I'd told her everything, of course. Finding the pants wouldn't have taken him but a moment. He could move fast in his dragon form, and his sense of smell would be more useful than his eyes. Forcing the dragon to shift and give Nyfain control back, though, might take a little longer.

A knock sounded at the door. Leala gave me an excited smile as I put the book down and stood. She brought over the robe, and I slipped into it, pulling it closed over the little white slip that flowed over my body, stopping at my upper thighs. No slippers adorned my feet. I was supposed to remain barefoot for reasons unknown.

My stomach fluttered as I pulled the door open. Nyfain stood before me, wearing a flowing tan shirt and dark brown pants, equally loose and easy to move in. Slippers covered his feet, and his hands were clasped in front of him, his body language subdued. The bond gave him away, though. I felt a swirl of excitement and anticipation and warmth.

"Hello, milady," he said, tilting his head. "Will you come with me?"

Leala tiptoed forward and handed him the key to the room. He took it without comment, holding it until both of us stepped out. Leala winked at me and then hurried down the stairs. Nyfain stepped around me and locked the door before sliding the key into his pocket.

I took a trembling breath, no idea why I was so nervous. He bent and scooped me up, cradling me against his chest.

"Is it the man or the dragon?" I asked, slinging my arms around his neck.

"The man. The dragon is in timeout."

"So is my animal."

"Please don't mention why. My control is tenuous at the moment."

I smiled. "Still no walking for me?"

"You have bare feet. I wouldn't dream of having you walk on the floor of this castle in bare feet."

He had a point there.

"I was worried you wouldn't show," I admitted, nuzzling my face against his cheek.

He pulled me in a bit tighter. "Sorry for the delay. I had to change the setup of the salon room to fit with one of the scene suggestions you gave me."

I smiled, embarrassed and excited again. "What'd you think about all of that?"

"I think we can knock most of those out."

"Are any of those…a first for you, or…"

He descended the stairs. Various staff members glanced at us on their way past, probably heading to their rooms to change for whatever was going on tonight.

"All of them, yes. I wasn't much into rule-breaking back in the day, and my father wasn't one for…thinking outside of the sexual box. This castle after the curse drastically opened my eyes. I was particularly interested in your notes on chapter eighteen."

I ran my lips against his jaw, thinking. "Jog my

memory."

"Our brazen heroine decides to lure her enemy and his lover into her rooms and seduce them to get information."

"Ah yeah. That setup was odd, but the threesome scene was hot."

"It was hot, yes. Particularly when the notes revealed that you have experimented along those lines."

"I've never had a threesome—Oh, you mean letting a girl go down on me?"

"Yes. That is exactly what I was getting at, yes."

I laughed as he reached the first floor and went right. It was a part of the castle that I hadn't done any wandering in. It occurred to me that for the amount of time I'd been here, I hadn't done nearly as much exploring as I should've. Then again, without access during the night hours, I didn't have much opportunity.

"It was an erotic experience." I kissed his cheek and then the scar running from the side of his lips. Unlike in the past, he didn't flinch away. "I was staying at her house for the night, and she had her own room. We got to talking, and the conversation turned sexual, as they do."

"Yes, they certainly tend to with you."

"We were sixteen, and neither of us had gone all the way, and the world around us was crazy. So when she asked if a boyfriend had gone down on me, and I said yes but it hadn't been all that great, and she asked if she could try…"

"You went with it."

"Why not?"

"Why not is right. I agree."

He entered a room with a round foyer. Seats lined the walls, facing a central desk. All were empty. No candles had been lit to brighten the dark space.

He moved through without a problem, using his animal enough to see in the dark. Or maybe his connection was constant, and he didn't have to pull and push at him to get at the power and extra talents. I would've asked, but it didn't seem wise to bring up the dragon right now.

"Then what happened?"

I chuckled. "First we kissed, and it was light and kind of teasing. She didn't jam her tongue in my mouth and root around like men tend to do. Don't get weird—*you* kiss exceptionally well. But most of the men I've ever kissed—Stop tensing. They are ancient history. I feel nothing for them."

"My reaction to you mentioning other guys is not rational. It's primal. As you have seen, it's rooted to my dragon. I can't control it, and lately I can't control him."

He stopped in front of a nondescript door at the

end of a hall filled with nondescript doors. They didn't even have numbers on them.

"Well, anyway, most guys just jam in their tongue and take over your mouth. Or they stick their tongue out and, like…try to play with yours. I don't know, it's not great. But she teased and kissed with lips and only went deep with the tongue when we started touching and shedding clothes."

"Hmm. Mmhmm. Tell me more."

I laughed as he carried me into a little chamber with a curtain across the space in front of us, like a changing room. He put me down and delicately stripped the robe from my shoulders.

"What did you do after shedding clothes?" he asked, sucking in a breath when he saw what was under the robe. "Oh, baby, this is nice. Great goddess above, I know you don't like to hear it, but you are so beautiful. So perfect."

I laid my hands on his chest and slid them down to his stomach. "I like hearing it from you. I know you see more than just my face and tits. Anyway…"

"Yes, tell me more about this experience while I fondle you." He ran his hands over my breasts and down the silky fabric, gliding them over my hips next. They went along my butt and up my back, outlining my body, touching and feeling sensually.

I closed my eyes and savored the feeling. "She kissed down my skin, and I can remember closing my eyes and my body getting hot. Her touch was so light over my flesh, and when she gently flicked my nipple and hesitantly sucked on it, I couldn't help just lying back. It felt so good. It, like...speared all the way down to my pussy."

He moaned softly, kissing down my neck now, pressing his hardness against me but not going further.

"Wait, why is it okay to hear about women touching me but not men?"

He paused in his movements. "I honestly have no idea. Maybe because I know you romantically lean toward men? And therefore women, especially in your past, aren't a threat?"

"Well, after she spent a glorious amount of time on my breasts, I was really turned on. I would've let her do almost anything. Then she started kissing down to my navel. I got a bit nervous, but I was also turned on, like I said..."

"Mhm, mhm. Go on..."

"Her fingers..." I closed my eyes, remembering. "They skimmed so lightly, and I was so hot from her touching. It drove me crazy. The nervousness fell away. She crawled between my thighs and gave me these...feathered kisses, her lips skimming my flesh. I remember I was writing

remember I was writhing and squirming and panting. And finally she got to my pussy and licked up my slit and just...like...savored it all. She took to me like you do, but lighter and more teasing. It built the anticipation, and when I thought I was going crazy, she sucked harder, and I fucking...fell apart. It was the first real orgasm anyone had ever given me. It was sensational."

"Did you return the favor?"

"I...tried. First with her nipples and then with her pussy, but it wasn't really my thing. I mean, sucking dick isn't a great thing in general, but something happens when it's someone I want to please. I did want to please her as a friend, but..."

"Your heart wasn't in it."

"Yeah. I mean, I tried, but she ended up stopping me and treating me to more of her pleasure. She wasn't getting it from me. I felt bad about it at first, but then I was on the road to another orgasm—Fuck, I was being a dude. I just took, took, took, accepting the orgasms she gave me without returning the favor because I was bad at it. Damn it, now I feel like a real asshole. No wonder she didn't want to do that with me anymore."

"That's a really bad ending to the story," he said with a slight smirk. "That's a tragic story, not an erotic romance story."

"It gets worse. About a year later, she realized I was

becoming a social pariah because of the way I dressed and my interest in hunting, and she stopped being my friend. She started throwing insults and talking shit. I didn't have many friends before her, and after that, I had hardly any."

He looked down on my face, stroking my chin. "That is a horrible story, and now I feel bad about life, and I hope you never take to writing romance novels."

I blurted out a laugh, propelling tiny droplets of spit onto his face.

"Yes, spitting in my face about sums up the ending of that story." He wiped his face, and I laughed harder.

With a little chuckle, he leaned down and kissed me lightly on the nose.

"I'm sorry about your childhood," he said softly. "That doesn't sound very fun."

"You were mister popular, right?"

"I was the prince. I had all the friends a guy could ever want, and at the same time...none. No one would share anything too personal for fear that my father might try to get it out of me. I was set apart because of my position."

"That doesn't sound any better than my situation."

"Only I didn't start off the story in one way, then take a left turn into Slit-My-Wrist-Ville."

"Oh my—" I slapped him, laughing.

He laughed with me, pulling me into a hug. "Okay, are you ready? It's time for your visit to the salon."

"You're not going to choke me with your dick?"

"I don't know, honestly. But not at first. Not until I lose control, at any rate. I'll make sure you get plenty of pleasure, so you don't end up like your ex-friend and get nothing for all your hard work."

"I wish I never told you that story." I laughed. "You are the worst!"

"I have my moments. Okay, turn—Damn it, I forgot the blindfold. Hang on." He stepped back. "Actually, close your eyes."

I did as instructed, nervousness coiling through me.

"Don't be nervous," he murmured. His hands curled around my upper arms. "Open your eyes."

Confused, I did as he asked.

His face was the picture of seriousness. "You will be at my mercy in a moment, Finley. If at any time tonight you are uncomfortable, say something. If you want me to push your boundaries, I will, but we'll need to establish a signal so I'll know if I've gone too far."

"Banana hammock."

He tilted his head. "What?"

"I'll say 'banana hammock' if you've gone too far."

His eyebrows lifted. "Right. Odd choice, but sure, fine. Please know that I will always keep your best interests at heart, and only hurt you if you want me to."

I swallowed. "Okay. Don't spank me. Or flog me. No hot candle wax. I will not call you Daddy. If you're going to tie me to the ceiling and floor, fine, but stick to tickling and not something painful."

His eyebrows dipped low. "Looks like you got an eyeful when you were sneaking out the other night, huh? Ms. Smith told me you got to see her purple dildo in action."

"Yeah. That I was surprisingly fine with. I might want to pop you in the ass with one someday."

"Oh, lucky me…" he said dryly, and I laughed.

"But the stuff with Leala and that demon was a bit much for me."

"What a fucking life, huh?" He stroked his fingers across my cheek, leaving a trail of fire in their wake. "Do you trust me, Finley? Please answer honestly. I need to plan accordingly for what comes next."

"Yes," I whispered.

"Okay. Stay here, close your eyes, and *no peeking*. I want to get the blindfold."

He came back a moment later, his scent putting me at ease. A slip of material pressed against my eyes, and I waited as it tightened. His arms came around my back and legs, and he lifted me, carrying me past that curtain and presumably into a room where something sensual that would require a modicum of trust was bound to happen.

"Don't be nervous," he whispered, setting me down gently.

I gave him what was probably a crooked smile as I tried to ignore the butterflies floating around my stomach and ribcage.

His hands touched down on my outer thighs, right below my slip. He slid them upward, lifting the silky fabric as he did. Up and over my hips, my waist, on up until he was lifting my arms with the fabric seemingly pooled at his wrists. Then it was gone.

"No panties," he groaned, and my smile brightened. I liked torturing him. "I'm not sure I'm as good as your tragic ex-friend, but I'm going to try my best."

His lips barely touched down on mine, light and teasing. Fabric whispered and air caressed my skin. Was he taking off his clothes?

"How was that?" he asked, his tone subdued as he took my hands.

"I think you should kiss the way you always kiss and leave the more erotic kissing to the ladies."

He laughed, deep and delighted, and my heart fluttered. "Note taken. Okay, I'm going to help you get into here…"

He pulled my hands gently to get me to walk forward.

"Step up," he said as my toe bumped into a barrier.

I did, and then again, and again, climbing steps.

"Okay, stay there," he commanded softly, power infusing his words. He held my hand, lifting it a little as he moved. Water sloshed, the sound like two feet stepping into a basin. It sloshed a little more, and then he was leaning into me, his tongue flicking across a nipple. "Here we go."

His hands pressed firmly on my ribs, and he lifted me into the air and then lowered me, sliding my front down his. His hard cock skimmed my right inner thigh until it caught at my apex, but he didn't allow me to stop and play. My body pushed it down between us until my feet hit warm water. It traveled up to my mid-thighs before my soles touched a warm metallic surface.

"Is this a...bathtub?" I asked.

"Of sorts. No offense, and not to impugn my own salon experience, which I wouldn't trade for the world, but I think you'll find this a little cozier than a breezy seat on a bunch of slats in a makeshift bathhouse. If it weren't for the grumpy salon worker, I might not have enjoyed myself."

I laughed at his description of the sponge bath I'd given him, then sucked in a breath as he walked me back a step. My calves met resistance, but he kept pushing until I lowered onto a seat partially covered by warm water.

"This has been cleaned, right?" I asked as he continued to lower me, my top half leaning way back.

He paused, and I tensed. His dark chuckle said he was kidding, and he kept going.

"I cleaned it myself, princess," he said as my back hit a soft cushion. The seat was heavily reclined, nearly like lying in a bathtub, but with my lower half higher so that the water cut across my body. "The surfaces are magically treated. They don't decay in the water, and the water doesn't get cold once it is poured into the bath. It'll only chill again after it is drained. These baths aren't a new addition since the demons took over. They've been in existence since before I was born. The salon was primarily a place for women to get themselves looked after—hair, nails, that sort of thing. But given the setup, which I only discovered after the curse, something more was going on here. My father would not have approved, but since it was *women's business*, he clearly never stuck his nose in. You'll see what I mean."

"Kinky?"

"I think so. I suspect there were lots of happy endings. There was probably a reason the women of the noble class were so well groomed."

"But demons didn't work here, then." The water came up just past my bust, leaving my head and neck out of the water.

"No. I'm not sure who was actually doing the…treatments at the time. I haven't been able to bring myself to ask the staff."

"So you want me to go in undercover?"

A pulse of power slithered across my flesh. I moaned and couldn't help spreading my thighs a little on the seat.

"That answers that," he murmured darkly.

"What?"

"I do not want you to go in undercover, no. I don't want anyone else servicing you but me. Not even women. I can see my reaction gives you pleasure."

"I want you to claim me."

His hands pulled back from my knees. Silence curled around us, and my animal vibrated in pleasure.

"Sorry," I said, realizing what I'd done. I'd called to the dragon.

"It's good. I've got that bastard locked down." The strain in his voice said otherwise. I couldn't help but chuckle. "But if you want to maybe…ask Leala about the situation in the salon…"

"No problem. She's not real bashful, I don't think. I mean, she's definitely professional—she's very polite and doesn't swear—but she's not reserved."

"She was a lady's maid to a noble who lived in the castle. A woman a bit older than I am now. She wasn't a blood relative, but I thought of her as a cousin. Her parents lived in the Red Lupine kingdom—a wolf kingdom. Her father was a beta, her parents both wolves, but despite the odds, her animal was a dragon. They thought she should come here to learn guidance from those with the same animal. She was welcomed, of course. Dragons always are. With her connections in the other kingdom and several vicious, well-placed challenges, she was working her way to the top tier of the noble hierarchy." Water sloshed, and waves reached farther up my chest. "Okay, I'll be washing you first and then shaving you. You are wearing the blindfold because I don't want you to see the room." Humor entered his voice. "Don't worry, I won't accidentally slice your clit off. I need you to be able to come, and working with that is the easiest way."

I sighed as his hands rubbed my neck and moved down my body, leaving suds in their wake. Soon they dipped under the water, where suds obviously wouldn't form. He should've made me stand to do this. And also used a sponge. Clearly he wasn't used to washing other people.

"How did she turn out a dragon if her parents were

wolves?" I sucked in a breath as he rubbed his thumb across my clit.

"It still shocks me how little you know about your own kind. If this curse ever ends, I worry about how many will die trying to accomplish their first shift. It'll be chaos." He worked down my legs.

"We didn't have many shifter books. I need to hunt for those in your library. I got distracted by all the fictional stories and...notes."

"Easy to do. I, myself, have been quite distracted. And was a little later than I could've been this evening because I got engrossed earlier." He kneaded my feet, and a little more tension drained out of my body. "A person's animal is almost always chosen by genetics. More often than not, if a person has two strong wolf parents, the child will be a strong wolf. If they're weak, the child's power will be weak. Same with dragons, bears, whatever. Occasionally a latent gene presents itself within a child, though. Two wolf parents turn out a bear. Or a dragon. Typically, the child will stay with the parents until they come of age, since the first few years as a shifter are all about learning one's animal— how to shift and share space. After that, most often the child will be grouped with similar animals so they can learn more about that animal. Dragons aren't much for packs, so a dragon would not understand the pack mentality of wolves. And vice versa. So usually dragons are sent here, since this…used to be the largest collection of dragons in the world."

"Do shifters tend to mate with like animals?"

He washed water onto my exposed areas, probably getting rid of the suds. His palms touched down on my knees, and he gently pushed them apart. Nervousness swirled in my belly.

"Oh, Finley…seeing you so vulnerable and nervous, trusting me completely to take care of you… You'll be my undoing in this life."

His body lay on mine, his hard cock rubbing against my clit. I moaned softly as his lips touched mine. His kiss was soft and sensual, his tongue lightly skimming across my bottom lip but not darting in when I opened my mouth to him. Instead, he continued to use his lips, sucking a little, nibbling, teasing. He'd taken the note.

"Why are you smiling?" he murmured.

"You're a quick study."

"For the first time in my life, I'm listening to the teacher." He backed off, his hands flowing down over my body and back to my legs. His forearm came across my thigh, and my butt rose a little on reflex. The water line now cut across my pussy, tickling.

"Oh wow," I said, wiggling just a little, wanting to reach down and stroke. I resisted, though, knowing he'd get to it. Wanting him to remain in control.

He applied something cool to my mound and beside my folds, probably shaving salve.

"For the more powerful shifters, yes, they absolutely mate with their animals in mind," he said. "They seek out shifters who have the same animal and a similar power level. The goal is to produce the most powerful shifter possible."

"But if power is the most important factor, then it shouldn't matter if the offspring's a wolf, a dragon, or whatever."

"You're forgetting that often beasts are sent to be with like beasts. So if a dragon and a wolf mated and had a wolf offspring, the wolves would get a powerful shifter instead of the dragons. Not to mention the parents might have to send their offspring away."

"Ah. Gotcha. So it comes down to shoring up strength within the kingdom."

"Yes, princess. Now you have it."

Cool metal touched down on my upper thigh, right beside my folds. It scraped across in little brush strokes, shearing me like a sheep.

"Why are you embarrassed?" he asked in a subdued voice, and the mood in the room changed dramatically. Tingles crawled up my body, and I involuntarily parted my knees just a bit more.

"I've let things grow a little wild since my ex. And before that, it was just a trim job. I didn't realize…"

"I'm no ladies' man, but only a fool would complain. I'm only doing this because you asked for it."

He was absolutely a ladies' man, but he didn't need to charm or cajole for it. He just had to show up. His stellar body, his large frame, his power and strength, his severe attractiveness—all he had to do was walk into a room, and every woman there would take notice. He could probably insult a woman, and she'd willingly come to his bed. I was guilty of it, surely. I had definitely tried to push back, but I couldn't deny I was all too happy to get this delicious alpha between my thighs. Damn my animal for rubbing off on me.

The metal continued to glide, not touching anything distinctly pleasureful but sending shivers racing across my flesh all the same. His diligence, focus, and clear attention to detail were obvious as he went back over certain areas, heightening my anticipation for his touch, the sensations of the moment. My body quickly keyed up, all my attention on the feel of that blade and his fingers as they pulled the skin taut or braced against my inner thigh. In a strange way, this was more sensual and erotic than anything I'd yet experienced.

"I don't think you give yourself enough credit," I murmured huskily.

A breath fell against my aching, sensitive flesh, his huffed laughter. He paused, clearly noticing my body's response.

His breath pushed air at my pussy in a steady stream now, caressing. Tickling. I whimpered and arched back, the non-touch so tantalizing I could barely stand it. He kept at it, driving me crazy. I clenched the muscles in my pussy rhythmically, contracting my hips, responding to that non-touch. Anticipation and desperation to be touched wound me up to impossible heights. I whimpered again as I tensed. My nipples tightened to hard buds.

The breath stopped, and then a hot tongue flicked my clit.

"Oh fuck berries—" I clenched as an orgasm hit me, jarring my body into shaking on the seat. I groaned, the release only tiny, shallow, my entire person now hyper-focused on his proximity and the quest to be fully sated.

"And now I fully understand the virtues of light teasing." He chuckled darkly. "This will be an excellent tool in my arsenal. I'll make you beg and plead to come."

"I'm not proud. I'll beg to come any day."

"Self-serving little wench," he said with a laugh. "But you are lying. We haven't played dominance games yet. Our animals are desperate for each other because we've held back from claiming each other. If we decided to do so, our beasts would do battle. To claim and mate a female, a male must overcome her by sheer force. I doubt it makes sense to you now—you're not the type of woman to think fondly of someone over-powering you—but I've only ever heard it's the most erotic experience for both people. The male feels powerful, which we like, and the female feels that she has chosen a strong, sure mate to protect her and her brood. Win-win. Or so I've heard."

"But what about will? I thought you said that a man's domain was physical dominance, and a female's was will."

He pulled back and laughed.

"That wasn't a joke. I'm serious," I said, a little miffed. "I stopped you the other day. I even hit you with my power…somehow. You're more powerful than me physically, but I can shrug off your commands. You can't shrug off mine so easily."

The metal touched down again, on the other side now, working steadily.

"Yes, you're exactly right, princess. And trust you to think of that when I'm talking about dominance. You're an alpha—you won't easily relinquish power."

"Right, but…about my question."

"Honestly, I don't know. I've only heard about this

from men, and none of them have ever brought up their woman's will. Either they claimed women who didn't have a strong enough will to fight back, which wouldn't be something they'd want to admit, or women pretend they don't have that weapon so their men can win and feel mighty. My mother used to say that sometimes it felt like a woman's entire job as wife was to protect her mate's ego. This is probably direct proof."

He chuckled as he worked down the other side.

"You'd like me to protect your ego when you claim me, then?"

The metal pulled away, and his other hand grabbed my thigh, squeezing firmly but not enough to hurt.

"Sorry," I whispered, grimacing. "That was me, not my animal, but I... That thought just got away from me. Sorry!"

"For now, so we don't ruin the moment, we'll just pretend that's a possibility, shall we?" he rasped.

"Yes."

"The honest answer is...probably. I'm not worried about my ego—these last sixteen years have completely shredded it. But if you use your will, I don't think I will get close enough to fuck you. What happened earlier today, when you shoved me back with it..." He splashed water around my groin and lifted my butt a little higher. He started on the underside, and now his touch was right about where I wanted it. On the outside, but I needed it in.

I expelled the breath out of my lungs and spread my legs a little wider, imploring him to take a break and push a couple of digits into my needy cunt.

"Do you like that?" he whispered.

"Yes," I breathed.

The razor kept going, slowly and methodically. My inner muscles were back to working, trying to heighten the sensations in my body.

"Your animal is still greatly hindered, not suppressed but not far from it, and yet you unleashed enough strength of will that it knocked me back. I'm not the biggest dragon, but I'm bigger than most. I was the strongest, the most powerful, before the curse. And I felt that blast like a brick wall. With all my strength and power, I probably could've stopped myself from taking a step back, but it would've been tough. Whatever your animal is, she packs a lot of power. You're still growing into it, too. When that power is finally unleashed, you'll be mighty. Mark my words, princess. I felt it in the woods when I kidnapped you the first time, and it's only grown."

"You told me that I could've been great. As though you grabbing me would destroy that."

"Yes. But I can't really explain, or I'd die. I've

changed my opinion, though. You *will* be great one day."

But he still believed I'd have to leave him to do it.

"Now," he said, pushing past a potentially bleak moment, "how much am I shaving off? A lot, a little?"

"All," I said.

His hand touched the outside of my thigh and stroked down softly, supportive. He kissed the middle inside of my thigh delicately, and tears crowded my eyes. I heaved a shuddering breath.

"It's going to be okay," he whispered, planting another soft kiss. "Everything is going to be okay. Please believe me."

But it wouldn't, not without him.

"Let's just pretend we're in an alternate reality," he went on, wiping the salve across my skin. "A reality where we find ourselves stranded in this strange castle for a night, with just each other. This night is the only one that exists. There was no yesterday, and there is no tomorrow. There is only this moment. I, for one, don't want to waste it. How about you?"

"Okay."

He ran his hand down the outside of my leg again. "Prepare to be amazed."

CHAPTER 21

I LAUGHED SOFTLY as I struggled to get myself back under control. He continued working that razor the whole time, slowly and methodically.

"So, you never said, what did you think of that latest book I sent up to you?" he asked. "The epic fantasy. Did you hate it?"

I pressed on the cloth covering my eyes to soak up the dampness of my stray tears. "I liked but didn't love it."

"Interesting. Tell me more."

"Well for one, the hero. Really, guy? You're amazing at everything? He stumbled into the king's guard—literally, because he'd been drinking at a pub—and got a job, because *of course* a drunk jerk got a job offer, and then he is suddenly the best at it. He knows it all because…logic! His only weakness? A woman. That's it.

He's a Mary Sue, guy style. A Gary Sue. He's that guy who saunters into a room, loudly bragging about how great he is, and then mansplains your job to you."

"Yes...I see your point, though I *did* enjoy putting myself in his shoes. The young, misunderstood, hot-headed new guy who could have had it all but for the woman of his dreams."

"Oh, goddess help me. I am going to pinch you if you blame his faults on a woman. Guys always act like sacrificing anything for a woman is a noble gesture. That's bullshit. Women are *always* sacrificing themselves for men and children. It's literally expected of us. What does your big hero do once he gets the woman? He goes back to exactly what he was doing before, only now he has someone else taking care of his personal life. He detoured to trap her, then resumed his dreams and aspirations." I huffed out a breath. "In the next book, she'll probably die to give him a hero's vengeance journey. She'll be nothing more than a plot device."

"I think I've struck a nerve."

"Yes. Yes, you have. I've spent my life thus far rebelling from all of that, and look what it's gotten me."

"Kidnapped into a weird fetish castle, being wooed by a man with a razor trimming your lady beard!"

I broke down laughing. "Yes. All of that, yes."

"I hear you." He chuckled and washed water over

me. "Let's backtrack. Were there any books in that last batch that you *did* like?"

"Yes. The one with the pirates. That one was exciting."

"Yes, I liked it too. Not many heroes to speak of. Kind of all bad men."

"Just on the wrong side of the law. They treated the female hostages well."

"They didn't push them against a tree and finger-fuck them to a near-climax, true."

"Yes, and—"

My words dried up as his lips skimmed my inner thigh, this time in raw lust. He sucked and licked until he reached my apex. Once there, he licked up my folds and then to the sides. He kissed the newly shaved area, running his lips over the top and then down to my clit, sucking a little.

Heat pooled hot in my core. He'd distracted me with talk of books, and now the need for him rushed back in scorching deliciousness.

"Shall we move on to the next thing?" he murmured against my skin.

"No, I'm good right here."

"Let's do the next thing." He ran his big hand up my leg, over my hip, up my stomach, and down the side, wrapping it around my ribs. His other hand joined on the other side, helping me sit forward.

After standing me in the water against him, taking a moment to nibble my earlobe and then my lips, he helped me out of the bath. The blindfold prevented me from seeing anything, but soft towels that smelled like fresh afternoon wrapped around me, drying the water.

"Just over here."

He led me by the hand across the smooth, slightly warmed floors, as though there were a smoldering fire under the tiles. He lifted me, setting me down on a wide bit of leather that hooked on my butt cheeks. Another strap came around to hold me in place. One of my wrists was pulled over my head, tugged up and to the side by a leather strap. Then the same was done to the other.

A thrill went through me as Nyfain gripped my ankle. A slip of leather went over my foot and ran up the back of my leg until it tightened on my lower thigh. The other leg was secured, too, and the ropes spread them wide. I was now trapped and suspended in the air by my ass and limbs.

He held up my head before securing another wide strap under it, helping me support it. In a moment, he stepped away. A small jerk, and suddenly I was lightly turning in the air, my body spread wide and on display for him. Even if I could manage to get my feet out of those straps, I was secured in the others.

"This is a modified sex swing, if you were wondering," he said, and something rolled across the floor. "Modified because various elements were added to restrain someone. We had three of them in the salon before the demons even moved in. The ladies of the castle have always been into a little kinky fuckery, it seems."

His hand touched down on my knee and slid down my inner thigh.

"I'd always wondered what it would be like to have a woman trapped in it, completely at my mercy." His hand roamed over my newly shaved pussy, his thumb running across my clit. His fingers dragged down the side, and then his hand turned, fitting two fingers into my wetness. "Mmm, baby. You're already so wet."

He pulled his fingers out, and his two hands gripped my ass. His hot mouth fit over my clit and sucked in pulses. I moaned his name, arching, as he ran his tongue down my slippery folds and pressed it into my opening. His soft growl sent shivers of desire racing across my overheated flesh. He dipped lower still, tickling my asshole before prodding it.

"I've always wondered what it would be like to pump my dick into a woman's ass," he whispered, moving back up to my clit. His thumb circled my asshole before popping in. Teamed with his mouth sucking on my clit, it was a strange but erotic sensation.

"This evening I'll find out," he said darkly, pulling away.

I was breathing hard, incredibly tight in some places and pliant in others, waiting for his next touch. Excited to be used for his sexual pleasure, like he'd let me use him in the woods.

"I said I would never use the demon's toys," he murmured, kissing my inner thigh. "But if I use it on you...that's not exactly breaking my promise, is it?"

A light buzzing filled the space, and then a cold, vibrating thing was set on my clit. I jumped with an "oh!" that quickly turned into a desperate moan. It was like when I massaged my clit, but so, *so* much better. I whimpered as it set my blood to boiling with delicious pleasure, working me toward orgasm in record time.

"Do you like that, princess?" he asked quietly, holding it there as I squirmed, now pumping my hips.

"Yes, Nyfain. Yes, very much *yes!*" I climaxed, jolting, pulling my knees wider and back. "Put your hard cock into me, Nyfain, please."

"Hmm. Tempting, but not yet, princess." He pulled the thing away. My clit tingled in its absence, and my body floated in bliss.

That vibration sound cut off, and a deeper one

started. Another hard, vibrating surface rolled over my clit, this toy larger than the first. It slid down to my pussy before pushing inside. The size didn't have anything on his cock, but the vibration was fucking amazing, rubbing against the right spots. He thrust it into me and pulled out, speeding up, fucking me with it.

"That's right, baby girl," he cooed, pumping it into me as I rocked my hips. "Come for me again. You'll need to be coming a lot tonight so that I can say I'm as good as one of your book heroes."

He flicked my clit with his tongue, working the vibration inside of me. I arched, moaning like a banshee, nearly there already, these vibrating things pure gold.

"Faster," I groaned, tilting up so it continued to hit me in the right spot. "Faster."

His tongue licked my clit. The vibrating thing sped up, rubbing gloriously. I hit a peak and stalled for two seconds, my body too tight. The need to come so strong it was driving me insane.

"Yes!" I shouted out as the orgasm tore me apart. My groan was long and low as he pulled the vibrating thing out and replaced it with his tongue.

He pulled away, leaving my pleasantly aching pussy open to the chill of the air. He kissed my thigh, and then his hand wrapped around my breast, feeling its fullness.

"Have I told you how perfect you are, Finley?" he

asked softly, his fingers replaced with his kisses. "You're an absolute vision. I can't believe I am lucky enough to get to experience you like this. To work the everlass with you and spend my days in your company."

His lips worked down to my belly and his hand followed, sliding over gently. He sighed softly, and then his touch pulled away.

"Ready for more?" he asked, at my head now. His lips touched mine and then applied pressure. His hand cupped my head, and he opened my mouth with his lips, sliding in his tongue. His taste drove me wild, spicy and exotic and delicious, better than any food or drink I'd ever tasted. Warmth filtered through the bond, his feelings expanding the longer we kissed, until I was drowning in his emotion for me.

When he backed off, still touching my lips, I said, "Whatever comes, I'm glad I have this time with you."

"Me too, princess," he whispered, kissing me again.

He pulled back, and I felt the smooth head of his cock brush across my lips. When I opened my mouth, he pushed it in, cupping my cheek as he did so.

"That's right, baby, suck my cock," he said huskily, and his hand slid down to my neck. "Take it all."

He pushed it farther in, hitting the back of my throat and making me gag.

"That's right," he said, pulling it out as I sucked and

then pushing it back in deeper. "Choke on it."

His dirty talk revved me up. I hollowed my cheeks as I sucked, my empty pussy open to the air, my hands and legs trapped, completely at his mercy and loving every second of it.

He pulled his dick out and moved, adjusting the strap under my head until it was on my neck. Knowing what he wanted, I tilted my head back. His growl of pleasure quickly turned into a groan as he pushed his cock in deep. He pulled out and pushed in farther, almost all the way. Another go, and I accepted all of him, his balls bumping my face. He pulled the strap near my hips, bringing me even closer, and then I felt the first vibrating instrument again, turned on and placed on my clit.

I moaned around the cock fucking my face, pushing all the way in without mercy. My eyes watered, and my throat constricted, my gag reflex active and squeezing his dick. The vibration lit my body aflame, and his harsh treatment of my mouth with his cock built me higher. I groaned and pulled against the bonds, liking the struggle. Liking the violence in our fucking. *Loving* being bound for him to use. My animal purred in delight.

He pulled his dick out, and spit dripped down my cheek. He left it like that, left my head dangling. He pulled away the vibration, and I could feel the breeze as he moved to the other side of me.

He grabbed my hips and slammed his cock home. My gasp turned into a moan as he used the swing in time with his thrusts, pulling me toward him as he pounded into me. The rhythmic slapping echoed through the room. The vibration touched down on my clit again, spiraling my pleasure higher.

And then it changed location.

It bumped up against my asshole as he ruthlessly pummeled into my cunt. He pushed it in, the feeling a strange violation that I didn't *not* like. A moment later, I was a hundred percent for it, the sensation unlike anything I'd felt before.

"Oh fuck, I can feel that through your ass," he said in a heady groan. "I am rethinking my stance on these demon toys."

"The demon toys are a go, yes," I said. "They are a definite go."

"Can you handle more?" He wiggled the vibrator, meaning in my ass.

Knowing what he was trying to gear me up for—wanting it—I groaned out an assent.

"Good girl," he said, the vibration lifting. He stalled in his thrusting for a moment. "Just going to keep things hygienic for you…"

I didn't know what he meant until the first vibration resumed massaging my clit. Clearly he'd wiped it off.

"Thanks," I said with a grin.

He chuckled as the second vibrator clicked on. The slick, blunt tip hit my ass, his cock still pushed all the way into my pussy. He pushed the vibrator in slowly as the clit vibrator worked me higher. The larger vibrator hit a barrier, and I tried to relax like the heroines in the stories. He started moving his dick slowly, backing out the vibrator before pushing it in again. He must've put lubricant on it, because the next time it hit that barrier, it slipped past.

"Hmm," I said, uncomfortably full at the moment, needing to get used to this second assault to my senses.

He read me easily, leaving it in that position while he slowly worked his dick in my pussy. As my body reacted to his cock and the clit vibrator, he started pushing the big vibrator in a little more. Then more, until it was all the way in.

The fullness was indescribable, and the vibration made everything that much more fucking awesome.

I used my knees to push harder into Nyfain. He took the hint again, putting down the clit vibrator and grabbing my hip. He yanked me back and slammed into me, keeping hold of the second vibrator. Again. Again, and then he started moving the vibrator, too, working it in my ass in time with his thrusts into my pussy. I now knew what that woman felt like taking two cocks. I understood her moans of pleasure. The sensations quadrupled by the feeling of being stretched and full. The vibration, his thrusts, the friction...

"Yes," I breathed, my nipples hard. "Oh goddess yes," I said, taken outside of my body. Pummeled. Fucked hard in both holes. On the verge. "*Yes!*"

I came violently, shaking and pulling my head up, everything going tight. The pleasure vibrated through me. I groaned long and low, and he stopped moving but kept his cock and the vibrator buried deeply, dragging out the orgasm.

"Oh fuck yes," I said, dropping my head back again. "Again. Fuck me in the ass, Nyfain."

"You're so goddess-damned sexy," he said, pulling the vibrator from me quickly, leaving an empty feeling behind. His cock pulled out a moment later, and my stomach fluttered with the knowledge of what was coming. Another of our firsts together.

"Yes, Nyfain," I said, desire soaking me. "Fuck me in the ass."

He swore under his breath, intense lust lighting up the bond. From both of us.

His cock prodded my ass. He pushed in slow, bigger than the vibrator. When he met resistance, the smaller vibrator clicked on again, applied to my clit. He pulled out and then pushed forward, working me, easing past the barrier and deeper. Deeper still.

"Oh fuck," I breathed out as he seated himself all the way in, uncomfortably but gloriously full. He wrapped his hand around my thigh as he pulled out, and then pulled me to him as he worked back in. The pleasure came slower, but the vibration on my clit patched the difference, keeping me steady. When he got moving, new sensations wrapped around me. Deeper, naughtier. He pumped into my ass, and I moved my hands until my fingers were curled around the straps, holding on for dear life. His grunts set me on fire. My animal soaked in the feelings, loving this. The vibrator sent me over the edge.

"Holy fuck, Nyfain!" I cried out, shaking with an orgasm.

He kept going, though, not there yet, sending me over the edge and then pulling me up so I could go higher and higher yet. Nothing else existed but the feeling of his body.

When he pulled out, likely cleaned off, and thrust back into my pussy, it was like the final piece clicked into place. I didn't want to do any of this with anyone else ever again. It was his touch I wanted. His heart connected with mine.

He put the vibrator down and grabbed my hips again, his thrusts reverent, the feelings through the bond deep and soulful.

"Come with me this time, baby," he said, his fingers massaging my clit now. I knew without asking that he wanted this final time to be just us. No vibrators.

I wanted no impediments between us either.

"Take me out of this thing first," I said. "Take off the blindfold. I want to see you."

He didn't argue or hesitate. He stopped, unstrapped me, and lifted me from the swing. He pulled off my blindfold and smiled at me, wiping the moisture from under my eyes from where I'd teared up choking on his cock. I let my gaze travel his handsome face for a moment before settling on his beautiful eyes. He bent to kiss my lips, and I wrapped my arms around his neck. We sank to the heated floor, he on his butt and me on top of him, wrapped in each other's arms.

I rose a little so he could line us up and sat down again, impaling myself on him. I moved my lips to his ear and murmured the thing I knew his dragon wanted to hear. That thing my animal had said would somehow make him stronger.

"Come inside of me, Nyfain. Brand me as yours."

He snarled, his arms constricting. He gripped my shoulders with one hand and my hair with the other, holding me tight as he thrust up into me. Rolling me onto my back, the floor nice and warm, he pumped in deeper and trapped me under his big body. There he rammed into me like a man possessed, his primal side taking over and wanting to do exactly what I'd suggested.

Make it more explicit, my animal prodded, right near the surface. *Push him harder. Reach his primal side. Incense his dragon.*

"Mate me, Nyfain," I said through pants, clutching his back, digging my nails into his scars. Going a little filthier, shifter-style. "Breed me."

"Oh fuck," he groaned, slamming into me, needy and possessive. His grip was tight. His body imposing. He slammed his cock home over and over, the sensations brutal and dominant and unbelievably good. So intense. So consuming.

"Yes, oh—yes, yes…" I couldn't stop saying it. I couldn't get anything else out. Just "yes," over and over, as I relished in the onslaught. As his power slithered over my skin and pounded through my blood. "Yes, yes—"

The world dropped away. Ceased to exist. His touch scored me. His cock branded me.

He bent and bit into my neck, *hard.*

I cried out as a thrill arrested me. As the delicious

pain brought me again to the verge.

"I'm going to come, I'm going to come," I uttered.

"Not yet," he replied, his power blistering through me.

I whimpered as he kept going, his teeth on my shoulder, pressing. My nails dug into his back. My animal fought for control, probably to shove him over the edge, but I bore down and held on, not wanting to push it, to force him to claim me through trickery.

Still he battered into my slick sex with hard, dominating thrusts. His teeth scraped. I shivered, pushed higher still as I held back. Fighting the pleasure. Fighting to keep my soul from fracturing, worried I'd never be able to put the pieces back together.

"Come with me," he commanded, and everything shattered. His roar of climax drowned out my cries of pleasure. He shuddered against me, emptying himself inside of me. I shook under him, holding him tight. My eyes squeezed shut. Waves and waves of bliss crashed over me until I was nothing more than a shaking, whimpering pile of bones and sinew. He'd wrung every last ounce of tension out of me.

In the aftermath, we lay on the floor breathing hard. He kissed me and then rested his forehead to mine.

"There are no words," he finally said. "No words. That was incredible."

"More than incredible," I whispered. "Life changing."

His lips felt like forever, even though they were really just for now. I tightened my arms around his neck and let a few tears fall, my heart ragged and bloody.

"None of that," he said softly, sitting up and pulling me with him. He got me settled in his lap. "And yes, life changing. Let's get changed for dinner. Your night isn't over yet."

"YOU LOOK FABULOUS, milady," Leala said as she stepped back and surveyed her handiwork. Her eyes glittered. "You're glowing."

Was it any wonder after the sex I'd just had?

After Nyfain dressed me and carried me back to my room, I'd given myself a sponge bath to freshen up. Leala had come up to help me prepare—fixing my hair in relaxed curls and applying a dusting of makeup to accentuate my features. Finally I slipped into the dress, a deep crimson flowing number with a heart-shaped neckline allowing for ample cleavage. It cinched down my waist and slid over my hips, parting at each thigh in a slit down to the ground. A shimmer worked through the fabric, and the mesh overlay gave it a whimsical feel. If he planned on dancing, it would float on the breeze as he spun me around the floor.

I stood in front of the mirror in the washroom and barely recognized myself. I'd never dressed in anything so fine, and nor had my hair and makeup been done to such perfection. Leala was a master, and while it was still weird to have someone waiting on me, I couldn't deny she did it exceptionally well.

"Ready, milady?" Leala asked, holding the key to the tower.

Nyfain had asked me to meet him on the second-floor landing. Apparently it would be grander that way.

"Are the demons not out tonight?" I asked as we exited the tower and she locked the door behind us.

"They are. Same as always. Tonight, though, they have less power than usual. I'm honestly not sure why."

Their having less power for whatever reason must've been why no creatures came through the portal. Or maybe the portal wasn't working without the right amount of power? It was something to research. All knowledge was essential when it came to our enemy.

She gave me some distance as I walked down the stairs, my dress spreading out and trailing along behind me. When I was on the second flight, I saw him down below, turned to the side and with one hand in his pocket.

The breath left me, and I slowed.

A perfectly fitted suit molded to his large span of

shoulders and elegantly pulled in at the waist. His hair was styled to look artfully messy, long on top and short on the sides. A livery collar lay across his shoulders and draped across his upper chest, the golden emblem of the kingdom repeated in two-inch round gold pieces connected by little golden clasps. Various gems sparkled within them, diamonds and rubies and sapphires.

On someone else it would have been a vulgar display of wealth, but on him it looked immaculate. His poise, his air of ruthless confidence, and the way he held his shoulders displayed exactly what it was—a birthright.

The crowned prince of Wyvern kingdom waited to dine with me.

Suddenly I felt horribly, terribly out of place.

CHAPTER 22

I PAUSED HALFWAY down the stairs and ran my fingers across my bare chest.

"What is it, milady?" Leala whispered, coming to stand just a little behind me.

"I should've picked out a nicer dress. Or…maybe more makeup. I don't have any jewels or anything. Should I have worn the dagger? Or maybe the sword?"

Except he looked up then, and the bond filled with such warm softness that I started forward without consciously deciding to. I met him at the bottom, placing my palm in his proffered hand.

"Goddess give me strength, Finley," he said on a release of breath, his golden eyes taking me in. "You are an absolute vision. Ever the princess locked in her tower." He bent to kiss me delicately on the corner of the lips so as not to upset my lipstick.

"You clean up very well," I said, tracing the royal livery collar.

"I haven't done it in sixteen years. It feels…odd. Like I am trying to step into a past life."

He held out his hand for the key to the tower. Leala supplied it immediately, curtsied, and headed back up the stairs.

"I have pockets," he said by way of explanation, dropping the key into his pants pocket.

"Wouldn't it be nice to not have to worry about locking doors?"

"I'm just glad there's one place in the castle they can't access through the hidden passageways. There's no point in locking any other room. You at least have a semblance of safety."

He walked me down the next flight of stairs to the ground floor. No one loitered in the large foyer or meandered through the halls. It was too early for the parties by an hour or so, but usually there were a few weirdos bustling about as night descended. Not so now. I wondered if he'd cleared the way for me. If so, I hoped it didn't have anything to do with him not wanting others to see him taking a common girl to a nice dinner.

The hall arched above us, and two staff members dressed in tuxedoes with white bow ties waited beside a grand double door up ahead. A deep purple rug ran underfoot, and gold etching adorned the walls. The setup screamed *royal*.

They waited until we got closer before reaching for the handles and pulling the doors open almost in sync.

"It's been a while since I allowed myself to notice the staffing...errors," he murmured as we entered a grand room with large oil paintings on the walls and a table that could seat thirty or more. Flower bouquets dotted the surface, along with glowing candelabra. Two places were set at one end, one at the head of the table and the other to its right.

"What do you mean?" I asked as he led me to the place settings.

"Servants here used to go through rigorous training. Perfection was expected and demanded. If a servant couldn't fulfill the requirements, they were let go or moved to a less strenuous position. All of that has changed, obviously. Most of the current servants haven't had any training for their positions at all."

"And they also try to fulfill their duties badly so they don't get noticed by the demons."

"That as well, yes. When I dress like this, with you like that, using the finer areas of the castle...these things stand out. It's...humbling. Frustrating."

It was sadness, though, that radiated through the bond. Probably sorrow for what had been lost. For a glory he clearly thought he'd never regain.

He stopped by the seat at the head of the table. A guy in the same fancy dress as the others strutted forward. His confidence was somewhat undermined by the way his shirt didn't quite button over his bulging belly. The arms were too short, and white socks shone under the black trouser legs that didn't reach his ankles.

He pulled out the finely crafted head chair and waited patiently.

So did I.

Nyfain pulled his arm forward, moving me closer to it.

"Oh," I said in confusion.

He took a step back.

I put my hand to my chest. "Me?"

"Yes, princess," Nyfain said softly, his eyes deep and open. "You."

When he said "princess" this time, it didn't sound condescending. It sounded like a title.

Goosebumps stood out on my arms as I stepped forward, taking the seat and then waiting for Nyfain to sit beside me.

"Shouldn't royalty or the person with the highest social standing take the head of the table?" I asked. I couldn't help it.

"Yes. In this case, it is the person who will make the

most difference in this kingdom. When I went off in search of your pants, I met a few people traveling to the nearest everlass field. They were in awe of your knowledge and determination to heal. They've taken your deal, by the way. The higher classes will work with the poor to see that the sickest members are treated first, regardless of class. The woman that is typically in charge of healing the village met with Mary…"

"Anne. Maryanne."

"Right. They are creating a network of healers and trying to educate as many people as possible so that the entirety of the village can help. Much like in your village."

"It's the best way."

"Yes." His mouth twitched. "And I can only imagine you offered plenty of…encouragement to push the people in your village to work together, as well."

I opened my mouth to refute the statement, then reconsidered. Could he be right? It was highly likely. I'd been too young to care about social norms and polite conversation, too worried about my mother after losing my nana. I had wanted the death to stop. All of us had. It hadn't taken much to convince everyone to acknowledge that medicine wasn't something only gifted to the privileged, not that we'd had many of those in my village. I'd just made them see reason.

Wine was poured in the super-pretty crystal glasses. I reached for the water.

I was sure I wasn't pregnant. Mostly sure. Mostly hoping I wasn't, at any rate. I'd taken the tea each night since my argument with Nyfain, and the timing was probably off. Still…better safe than sorry until I knew for sure, if only to keep him from wigging out.

The first course was brought out by Mr. Belly and his helper, the guy who taught watercolors. I wrestled with a smile.

"What?" Nyfain asked as the fancy gold-rimmed bowls were set in front of us.

I waited until the staff had moved away before I told him about Hadriel's watercolor penises.

He huffed out a laugh, picking up the soup spoon and sliding it sideways across the lip of the bowl before slowly bringing it to his lips. Talk about refined. Suddenly I wasn't so sure this meal was a great idea. I could pull off a fancy dress with some help from Leala, but I wasn't so sure I could pull off a fancy meal.

I gave it a go anyway, totally copying him. He paused after a moment, thoughtful, and dipped the spoon how we would've at my house.

My stomach pinched, and I set down the spoon.

He followed suit.

"What are you doing?" I asked him, my hand now

hovering over the silverware resting in the bowl. Crap, maybe I should've put it beside the bowl.

"Following your lead."

Only he hadn't looked.

"Why? What do you mean?"

"Finley...I can feel your nervousness and embarrassment. I know this isn't normally your scene. There's no one here but me, though. And a few servants who have no fucking clue what they are doing. Please be yourself."

"It's just..." I tapped the handle of the spoon. "I..."

"Look." He picked up the spoon again. "I think we can both agree that I don't spend much time acting in a way befitting someone of my rank. Even when I try, my dragon makes shit of it. I'm swearing at the table. Surely this is enough to make you feel comfortable eating a meal in my presence? I'll save the polite eating for when I'm trying to tease moans out of you, how is that?"

A flash of lust slithered across my flesh. "Okay."

We resumed eating, and although I didn't dwell on all the things I was surely doing wrong, I did pay more attention to how I went about it. I'd be damned if I'd drip food all over my fancy dress.

"This is one of our more casual dining areas, anyway," he said, looking around. "It's as small as we have."

"No quiet family dinners, then?"

"Not for our immediate family, no. My dad and mom…didn't occupy the same space if they didn't have to."

"I get why your mom felt that way, but didn't your dad like your mom?"

His smile had no humor. "She might've technically been a noble, but she was from a mountain village in a wolf's kingdom. She wasn't much better than a commoner in his eyes. They didn't celebrate wealth and finery like he did. They didn't have a slew of servants. They were—are—warriors. All of them. She came here like a fish out of water. She had to be taught how to carry on polite conversation, how to eat at a fine table like this, how to hold herself…"

"But…" I frowned at him, finishing my soup and hoping for more. This staff might not be well trained, but the cook certainly knew his way around a soup. It had been delicious. "Then why marry her?"

"To get a son like me. Mostly." Nyfain dabbed his mouth and dropped his napkin back into his lap. "My mother's line is fierce and powerful. He wanted her brood."

"And he got it. He got the warrior."

"Well…" Nyfain leaned back as Mr. Belly collected his bowl and Liron—I seemed to recall that was his name—collected mine. "He did and he didn't. He got a fighter, yes. A son with maximum power. But he didn't expect a son that preferred gardening and singing. I was more sensitive than he liked. I expressed my ruthless fighter side only when necessary. The other times...I didn't see the point in being an asshole just to seem powerful at all times. I *was* powerful. I didn't feel like I needed to constantly prove it."

"That's called confidence."

"My father didn't agree. He blamed my mother for ruining me."

"Ruining you? Good gracious." I watched as a plate of fish swimming in a buttery yellow sauce was placed in front of me. "That's a bit extreme."

"He essentially wanted me to be a tyrant. Like him. My mother was never going to let that happen, though, for which I am thankful. But when I was of age and proving to be just as powerful as he'd hoped, he took me in hand. That was when the beatings really amped up. He was going to make a man of me if it was the last thing he did."

"By beating you?"

"By making me tough. And yes, the way he thought I would be tough was to get beatings."

"And did it work?" I whispered, laying down my fork. My plate was clean. Hannon needed to take some lessons from the cooks in this place. Also, I needed to eat downstairs for dinner more often. The meals sent up to my room weren't nearly this good.

"I was already tough. He just made me angrier at him. By eighteen, I'd had enough. I turned the tables and made sure it was the last beating he'd ever give me. I scared the whole castle that day. They thought I'd kill him and anyone who tried to get in my way. Soon after that, at my mother's behest, I started looking for a way out of this place."

"Why not go to her village? Why not meet people like you'd been raised?"

The next course came, rabbit with carrots and potatoes atop a mouth-watering sauce that I would probably dream about.

"I thought about it. Nearly did. But…as a prince, I would've had to visit with royalty in the Flamma Kingdom before being allowed to travel to my mother's village. Once there, I never would've been able to relax. The wolves would've been nervous about the dragons rising up and going for the crown. And they weren't wrong. My dad would've thought about it. Maybe even tried to goad me into it. I decided to remove myself from the whole scene. Faeries couldn't give two shits about shifter royalty. They are much too arrogant. With them, I felt halfway normal."

"What made you decide to propose?" A surge of

jealousy stole over my heart. I cleared my throat and wiped my mouth in careful little dabs like he had.

He reached across the table and took my hand. "What it came down to was that she was willing to have me. It wasn't a great love story. We each had something to offer the other, and we got on pretty well. It was enough to get me out of my kingdom and escape my father, which was the overall goal. Had I known—"

"There's no sense in dwelling on that," I said, entwining my fingers with his. "You obviously know it wasn't your fault. The king sounds like... There really aren't words for him."

"He was just like my grandfather. My father tried to train me the same way he'd been trained."

"It must be right because that's how it has always been done," I said.

"Just so." He ran his thumb across the top of my hand as our dishes were cleared.

Dessert came, a chocolate mousse. I didn't know how I was going to fit it all in my belly, but I was definitely going to try.

"Would you have missed home, do you think? If you'd..." I couldn't even say it. I could not even ask about almost marrying someone else. Goddess save me, I was not usually a jealous person, especially not about something that had never come to pass.

He's ours, my animal said, resting comfortably just below the surface, basking in his presence. *You're finally starting to realize it. No one else better lay a hand on him, or we'll lop that hand off.*

I rolled my eyes.

"What's the matter?" Nyfain asked.

"Just…" I made a circle toward my chest. "My animal. She's being…"

Right. I'm being right. Admit it.

"Overbearing," I finished.

"I know what that is like, yes." He took a dainty bite of his dessert, and I just couldn't play along. I scooped mine up like I was famished. Holy crow, this dessert was fabulous. "Seriously, I used to think Hannon was a good cook. Why don't I get meals like this sent upstairs? I feel cheated."

Nyfain laughed. "Cook is one of the few who didn't get the axe. I'm not sure why, to be honest. And yes, I would've missed home. I miss it now, while living this half-life. I would've missed my friends and, of course, my mother. Missed the feel of the air and smell of the wood. I had a good childhood, for the most part. I loved hunting and fishing and running on these lands, and I always hoped to do the same with a child of my own—"

He sucked in an intense breath and grabbed the edge of the table with both hands. His eyes squeezed shut. Power pounded through the room, and the servants—standing off to the sides and waiting for us to finish our desserts—pushed back against the wall and then started slipping away. Still the power built, crashing around us now, calling to my animal. It flowed through the bond and filled us both to the point of bursting, stretching our skin and still pumping higher.

Nyfain pushed back from the table and stood on wobbly legs, slightly bent over.

"What can I do?" I asked, standing with him. "Get out of here?"

"You haven't sipped your wine."

I looked to my full glass. His was mostly empty.

"I don't like wine," I lied, now realizing what this was about. He'd clued into *why* I wasn't drinking the wine, the idea probably sparking because he'd mentioned a child of his own, and his dragon was freaking the fuck out.

"You're lying," he growled, straightening up slowly in jerky movements. His eyes glowed brightly.

In a fast, violent movement, he swiped his arm across the table. Plates and glasses flew to the side and crashed onto the floor. A candelabrum clunked down, spilling wax and dousing the flames. Shadow draped across Nyfain's severe but handsome features, his cheekbones sharper and the wells of his eyes appearing deeper. His scars cut across his skin in a cruel pattern.

Lust raged through the bond. Devotion. Longing.

He grabbed me around the hips and hauled me to him, crushing me against his hard body. He claimed my lips and stole my breath with a scorching kiss.

"I need you," he said against my lips, grabbing my butt and pulling me closer. "I need to pound my cock into you, over and over. I need to fill you with my release and mark you as mine."

I moaned softly. I couldn't help it.

He spun me around. One large palm pushed me forward over the table, food stains marring the pristine white cloth. His other hand hauled up the bottom of my dress, and I knew he was going to take me right here. Rational thought had clearly fled. His primal urges to mate had taken over, and they were pulling power up from his depths.

Is it Nyfain or the dragon? I asked my animal as I shoved back against him, sending a bolt of thunderous power his way. It slammed into his body and threw him back into his chair. He slid for a few feet before he rose slowly, swiping his hand across his lips, looking at me through his lashes.

A thrill of fear arrested me. He was an intimidating bastard. I knew he wouldn't hurt me, though. The fight was on.

Nyfain, I think, she answered. *I can feel his dragon. He seems gleeful but not in control. He's right near the surface, though. He's riding the man hard. He wants to stamp his scent on you, and if the man won't claim you, then he wants it done with his seed. And probably bites or marks. Fight him. Make him prove himself. It'll be so worth it, trust me. It'll make him more powerful, too. It'll draw out that primal power. Hopefully. Regardless, it'll be a damn good lay.*

Menace radiated from the man. Power, too. It shoved at me. Caressed me. Cocooned me.

Fuck, that feels good, my animal purred.

I had to agree.

"Fight all you want, princess," he said in a low, rough tone that sizzled across my flesh. "In the end, I will bend you over that table and fuck you."

I took a step toward him. "I'm not going to take it easy on you like those men you heard about. You'll have to get through my will, and I don't fuck around."

"Damn right you don't. You're *mine.*"

A swell of power slammed into me, pushing me back against the table. Another surge pumped through my body, but this time it sucked energy away rather than bestowing it upon me.

What the fuck is happening? I asked my animal as Nyfain rushed me, arms extended to grab.

Some sort of fuckery, that's what. His dragon is being tricky. Damn experienced bastard. I've got that mother-fucker, though. Let me work around this.

He grabbed my upper arms and spun me around. I groaned as his front pushed against my back, trapping me to the table. I could feel his hard cock just above my butt. His teeth skimmed my shoulder as I shuddered in delicious bliss, lowering my head. He latched down low on my neck, his teeth breaking the surface.

Fire roared through my blood, turning my bones molten, so hot I thought I might crumble to ash right there. His hold on my body peeled away, leaving pulsing power in its wake. I shrugged off his hands and threw back my head, bashing it into his face. His head jerked back, his body following. I added a slap of my will, knocking him farther still.

Not leaving him time to get settled, I turned and punched him in the throat, then tried to knee him in the crotch.

He caught my knee in his thighs and used my insta-bility to push me back. He lifted me by the ass and set me down on the table, crushing me into the hard surface with his weight. His mouth sought mine, his kiss bruising and wild. Only one knee was between mine, though, and we wouldn't get anywhere that way.

His power pushed through the bond again, so incredibly intense that it grabbed me and pulled me under. It blanketed me in his smell. His protectiveness and his possessiveness. The fight nearly went out of me right then and there as I moaned under him.

Not yet! Fight back! my animal shouted, yanking power from his dragon and storing it, trying to make sure he wasn't too strong for us.

I just want to fuck him, already.

It'll be better if you hold out. Rile him up a little more. Trust me. I can feel his dragon about ready to explode.

I bent and grabbed the side of his neck, chomping down before ripping my head to the side. Blood dribbled over my lips and down my chin. The taste of it shocked into the very center of me. Lava erupted in my middle, shooting heat through my ribcage and down my spine.

He roared, the sound vibrating with anger and frustration and raw hunger.

Yes, my animal said, pulling still more power. More and more, feeding it into the lava in my middle. *I could shift with this. I can feel the transformation calling me.*

Don't you dare.

I'm not a fucking idiot. I don't want to come out all fucked up. But I could. We can take more power, though.

She was right. We could.

That glowing pit of lava took all the power I had to give and then fed it around my body. I exploded it at Nyfain, forcing him to physically back off.

He snarled and grabbed my neck with one hand. I lifted my right arm and swung it across my body, catching his arm with it and forcing it aside. I ripped back the other way, leading with my elbow, and clocked him right in the face. His head jerked that way, his body ripping to the side, and my throat was released from his hold. I finished the turn and slammed my other elbow into him. My will smashed into him too, shoving him across the end of the table, dragging my place setting and everything else that had been left on the table onto the floor with him. Red wine spilled across his front, ruining his shirt.

I darted in and gave him a kick, because I wasn't really sure what else to do. I didn't want to get too close or he'd pull me to the ground, and I doubted that was a fight I could win. He had size and strength and gravity on his side.

His hand darted out and grabbed my ankle. His power built. My animal still pulled at it, still siphoned it away from him and stored it. But she was starting to get excitedly nervous—I could feel her anticipation. Whatever she was expecting was coming soon.

Not that I had a moment to wait and wonder.

I tried to pull out of his hold. His damn hand was too fucking strong. He latched on, his body like a big, immovable weight.

I shoved at him with my will, pounding him with it, but then heard a pained grunt. A shock of real fear ignited in my middle, and I pulled back. Kicking and biting were one thing, but I didn't want to do any real damage, which was exactly the reason he hadn't squeezed when his hand was around my neck. But at least now I knew I could do more if the situation ever arose with someone else.

He pulled back on my ankle, and I stumbled into the table, clawing at it to stay upright. Getting to his knees, he grabbed my other ankle. He pushed to his feet and reached for my hips. I turned to punch, but he caught my hand and forced it behind my back. I twisted to get it out, shoving with my will.

He roared, the dragon's voice ripping through the man's throat. His power rose all around us, filling the room, shoving at the doors, shaking the windows along the far wall. It crashed down on me and swept me away, splintering my desire to resist, driving my need for him so deeply into my very center that it threatened to tear me apart. All I could do was tremble before him, his for the taking.

And take me he did.

He spun me around and pushed me forward, pulling my dress up to my hips and tearing away my panties. I thrust out my butt, desperate for him to be inside of me. That same desperation was driving him, and he didn't waste time with fingers or tongues. In a moment, he had his pants down and his cock thrust into me with another swell of power. I cried out, impaled with liquid heat so delicious my knees gave out. I lay with my front on the table and him behind, leaning over me, ramming into my slick heat.

Power continued to build in the room. It blossomed in sparks within me, mirrored by him. Back and forth it rolled between us, until it was one solid force. His cock slammed into me. His hips pounded against my ass. I whimpered from the onslaught, not even able to push back against him, just taking it. Fucking loving it. This was the fighter. The battle-hardened hero. The man who stalked the woods for his enemies. And I'd given him a helluva fight. He'd earned the right to this fuck.

I held on for dear life, the pleasure so intense there wasn't a name for it. My nails scraped against the wood, and I arched back, wanting to be closer to him. Wanting him to finish this. To finally claim me. I could feel his intense desire to do it. I could feel his dragon riding him, trying to steal control so he could do it himself. And yet still Nyfain held back.

His arms came around me, hugging me tight, his lips on my neck. Sweet words of devotion rode his breath. Power continued to swell, infused with the delicious sensations of his body against mine, within me. It built and built until I couldn't stand it anymore. I couldn't take the delicious burn of pleasure.

His teeth slid against my neck and then down to my shoulder. They grated along my skin, pressing, though not hard enough to break skin.

"Nyfain," I begged. I twisted against his hold, wanting to get at him. Wanting to do it myself. He'd said he was trapped in his feelings for me. Great—I'd make that shit permanent. I didn't know how to claim, but I was confident my animal and I could figure it out.

He held me fast, his strength wrapped around me, his arms immovable. He knew what I was trying to do. He knew he was literally the only one of the four of us still holding out.

"Come for me, baby girl," he growled.

The orgasm stole my breath. I was locked in a silent scream as wave after intense wave shook me to my foundation. I shuddered against him, turning my head and closing my eyes. He pressed his cheek to mine as he made the final thrusts to finish out his climax deeply inside of me. I shivered as intense emotion welled up between us. He leaned over and cupped my cheek, twisting my face just enough to kiss me languidly.

We breathed heavily in the aftermath. My body turned liquid, slinking down against the table. Still inside of me, he leaned over it with me, his arms now braced on either side of my body.

"I'm afraid we might've scared away the servants. Now we'll never get our cheese plate," he murmured.

I laughed as he pulled back and helped me up. He grabbed a napkin to clean us up before pulling me into a tight hug.

"I lost control there for a moment," he said, burying his face into my neck.

"Which part?"

"The part where I initially tried to bend you over the dinner table to fuck you, and then fought you to do just that, and then pummeled you with my cock."

"Several moments, then."

"Right yes, okay. Several moments. Fuck, I'm winded. You gave me hell, princess. Now I understand what the guys were talking about. My dragon's extreme, primal need to mate pulled out that little will-splintering thing. That was incredibly handy."

"Can you do it again?"

"No. I think the sole purpose of that little feature is to dominate my intended and mate. Fuck me, my dragon is after me again. He's intolerable. Your animal depleted me to the point of danger, forcing us to build more and more power. At the brink, we exploded, ripping the power back and using it on you. Clearly it's all a dance with the beasts. A very delicious, erotic dance that I enjoyed very much."

"She basically helped you dominate me." Something she had not mentioned, and I had not been able to feel.

"Yeah. Thank her for me." He touched the ragged wound on his neck, then looked down at his ruined suit.

"I can fix up that...ah...bite for you," I muttered, a bit embarrassed.

"No, thanks." When his eyes came up again, they were full of pride. "It's not a typical mark, but it is a mark, and I want it to scar. I want everyone to see that you fought me and left something permanent on my flesh. You are incredible." He smiled as bruises started to color his face from my fists or head or elbows. "That was exciting. There is not a woman in this world who would've given me that sort of fight and then gladly taken the onslaught afterward." He pulled me closer and kissed me. "You're incredibly powerful, baby. You'll be a shining star in an otherwise dull sky."

"Except for the golden dragon."

He didn't comment. I knew full well it was because he didn't think he'd make it. He thought he'd die in this half-life as his world fell down around him.

I was not going to let that happen. A long time ago I'd set out to cure the demon sickness, to save this kingdom from demon magic. I would save Nyfain, too. I just had to figure out how. There was a way. I had a huge library at my disposal. All I had to do was gather information and put the pieces of the puzzle together.

Not now, though. Now, we were living for the moment. It had been a perfect evening so far. I wanted to keep it going.

So I let him take my hand in silence and lead me from the room.

"I'd planned to take a turn around the ballroom. Thoughts?"

"My legs are wobbly, and…"

"Hit me with it. What else are you thinking?"

"Leala said the demons are low in power tonight. I think it's a perfect night to harvest the everlass. Whatever suppresses the demons might make the everlass more powerful. I mean…it's worth a try. I'd like to get the recovery time down a bit."

He laughed softly and entwined our fingers, bringing me down the hallway and toward one of the rear exits. Loud music and raucous laughter vibrated through the castle, suggesting the parties had broken out after all, but I didn't have any desire to play voyeur or put on a public display tonight. No more public than in a dining room where staff might've been watching, at any rate.

The night was mild, but the stars were vibrant pricks of light above us. Nyfain carried the tray for me, and once we were in the field, he helped me pick the leaves. Afterward, he took my hand and led me through the field again. We walked side by side through the plants, in different rows but close enough to touch, the moonlight seeping in around us. The moment was perfect and sublime, and heat constricted in my chest as I looked over at the handsome dragon.

"Why is gardening and healing considered a woman's activity?" I asked softly as we stopped in the field, still holding hands. "Why did only women do it?"

He turned and faced me. "I honestly have no idea. It isn't like that in other kingdoms. Maybe my father, or his father, or his father's father, was just bad at it and they decided that was because they had a dick."

I laughed. "Maybe so. Why do only kings make the rules? Why no queens?"

"Tradition. When I was young, I pledged to change the rules so any daughter of mine would be just as entitled to the throne."

"Why haven't you?"

"I'm not a crowned king, and at this point, I doubt I ever will be."

I sighed. "Have a little hope. This kingdom has been through hell, and we've managed. We'll continue to manage until we find a way out, and then we'll figure out how to kick the demon king's ass. We got this."

He leaned over and kissed me. "Okay."

I nodded. "Okay. Now, let's go take that bath and relax. I'm full and tired, and I just want to feel you near me. I don't need all the weird theatrics of this crazy castle."

"As you command," he whispered.

We walked back in silence, hand in hand, my chest filled with a strange, aching need for him. Even now, after tonight, after all the sex, I still craved him. All that raw, unfiltered masculinity should've stopped affecting me by now. I should be used to it and able to shut out the need. Instead, he pulled at me like never before. Like a fisherman reeling in a catch. Whereas before I would've tried to find that hook and yank it out, now I wanted it. I wanted him to seal the deal.

I was falling for him. Hard. This was a hook I didn't think I'd be able to pry out.

CHAPTER 23

"FINLEY, HOW ABOUT this?" I looked up from the roses I was tending and wiped my forearm across my forehead. Nearly a week had passed since my dinner with Nyfain. Nearly a week of helping the villages with everlass, tending the queen's garden, and spending as much time as possible with him. It was never enough. I just kept craving more of his touch, more of his smell, more of *him*. Didn't matter if he was teasing or brooding or sensuous. I loved it all.

We'd developed a sort of schedule around each other. In the mornings I'd tend to the queen's garden—planting herbs, weeding, and pruning the rosebushes. When he woke up, he'd meet me there, and we'd share a meal before traveling to the everlass field. Sometimes we'd talk while we worked, but usually he sang to the everlass. Then we'd create the nulling elixir starter, dry or pick leaves if they were badly needed, and work together in peaceful camaraderie. It was my favorite time of the day.

We'd have lessons in the evening, dancing or sparring, then we'd put our clothes back on from our almost always furious lovemaking and share another meal, maybe hit the library or just read together, and off he'd go into the Forbidden Wood.

I'd changed up what I was reading, doing more research into shifters. Annoyingly, while there was plenty of history, few of the books focused on the day-to-day realities of being a shifter. At least I was learning about the first shift, the need for the animal to get out and run, and ways to work with demanding animals. So far none of the approaches had tamed my beast, but I kept up hope.

Hadriel crouched near two even rows of herbs, looking at the base of some thyme. "This should take root, huh?"

Gyril and Jawson, still helping with the garden and happy to do so, looked over.

"All you're doing is putting a plant in the ground," Jawson drawled. "Do you need approval on every little thing?"

"He probably asks how his farts work out," Gyril muttered, and Jawson shook with laughter.

"It's good, Hadriel, just—" I paused as a gush of wetness filled my panties. Nyfain and I had been having an obscene amount of sex, to the point where I was sore most days, but he'd been too tired last night. This morning, he'd been asleep. This wasn't some aftereffect of sex.

Which meant…

My chest constricted, and I hurried out of the garden and through the sliding glass door to the queen's room. Usually I didn't like to cross the threshold, leaving this space to him and his memories, but right now…

"Finley?" Hadriel called out as I pushed into the cool space and hurried to the washroom. I pulled down my trousers and then my underwear.

My heart sank at the sight of the red stain.

My period. It was over a week late, but it had come anyway.

I couldn't say it wasn't a total surprise. My breasts had been a bit more tender these last couple of days and the bloat had settled in. You could only blame the excellent chocolate mousse for so long.

Even so, I wilted where I sat, a deep, profound sadness dragging me down. It was stupid, wanting a baby with all that was going on. Beyond stupid. I knew that.

Even if we weren't living in such a fucked-up world,

our kingdom on the verge of extinction, there was the rank difference between Nyfain and me. He'd worn a golden collar to our dinner, depicting his rank and status. I'd worn clothes that he'd had made for me. He was a dragon, and my animal purred. True mates shifted into the same animal. All the books I'd read had made that same point.

But the daydream had been a pleasant fiction, I couldn't deny it. Lying with him, his hand gently resting on my belly, had brought a strange sort of peace over all of us. Nyfain, me, and our animals. And, for that short time, I'd allowed myself to wonder if I actually *was* his true mate. Common or no, purring animal or no, I'd wondered if maybe the fates had aligned in my favor and I could finally have my prince. And if we were destined to be together, surely that must mean we could break the curse together somehow. I mean, I'd found a cure for the demon poison—why not take the next step?

But here we were. Eventually everyone woke up from their dreams, however pleasant.

"Finley, love, what's going on?" Hadriel ventured in with raised eyebrows and a plain gray shirt. He was tired of having his butler outfits laundered after gardening because Cecil, the seamster with the attitude problem, had to do it, and it was nothing but abuse when he went to pick everything up.

"Nothing, I'm fine. I'll just—"

"Oh." Hadriel braced his fists on his hips and wandered closer, looking at my underwear.

"Ew, get out!" I tried to pull down my shirt. "I do not need you in here when I'm sitting on the toilet!"

"Honey dove, I have seen it all. I'm already scarred for life. I'm not worried about a little blood here and there. Now…how are we feeling?"

He pulled over a chair that a lady's maid had likely used to wash the queen and sat in front of me.

"Relieved? Sad?" he asked, peering deeply into my eyes.

Intense sadness welled up, not just from me, but from my animal. I shoved it away. I wouldn't have felt anything right now if not for the dragon's raw, primal need to jump me whenever anything reminded him that I was late. Or the soft look in Nyfain's eyes when he gazed at me with his hand on my belly. Or the kisses he feathered across my navel. I'd allowed myself to delve too deeply into the fantasy, and now it was time to get my head out of the clouds.

"I'm good," I said, looking around. "But I need…"

"Say no more." Hadriel stood and raised his hand. "I'll run and get Leala. She'll handle the details." He peered at me intensely for another long beat.

I lifted my eyebrows.

"Right. Just…" His salute turned into a raised finger. "Just getting the lay of the land. So you…aren't relieved, as such…"

"Hadriel, get out. Seriously. It's just a period. I have many."

"Right. It's just that, you know, you hated the guy when you first came, but now you seem pretty fond of him, and he's almost palatable now—" He lifted both hands, clearly reading the murder in my expression. "I'll just go get Leala. Sit tight. There are rags coming, my love."

An hour later, I hacked at the roses like a woman possessed. Slashes of red covered my arms, and a few gashes lined my face, but I refused to yield. The work was a distraction from thinking about Nyfain. Because I'd have to tell him the news.

Not that it should matter. He'd been living a pleasant fantasy, too. If I'd actually been pregnant, he would've lost it. He would've been pissed about the timing, about my fragility in the face of what he wanted for me, about having a child when locked in a curse…

Still, fantasy or no, I would have to be the bearer of bad news.

Part of me feared he'd only allowed me so close so he could watch over things. If maybe his desire for a child, an heir, had overshadowed the person actually carrying the child. I wondered if, when he found out I wasn't pregnant, he'd want things to go back to the way they were, where we fought our attraction and mostly kept to ourselves.

The fear of it hurt the worst, because it wasn't a baby daddy or a prince I craved. It was Nyfain the man. The brooding asshole whose mood could turn in a moment. Who could silence a room just by walking in and scare the house staff with a look. Who went out of his way to make things easier for me. Who backed my decisions, allowed me to be who I was, and would give his life to save mine. The fighter, the protector, the reader, the lover.

Shit.

I was so fucked. This whole situation had gotten so fucked.

"Finley."

His rough voice washed over me. Terror of what came next fought with the pleasure of his presence.

The insane thought of not telling him rolled through my head for the umpteenth time since I'd found out.

Pulling the pruning shears out of the bush, I wiped my cheek with the back of my arm. I'd probably just wiped blood on my face, too.

Time to face the music.

The dragon will just want to try again, my animal said.

No. It wasn't a good idea then, and it isn't a good idea now. His dragon might be dreamy, but I don't want to play these games. He probably won't want me after this, anyway. I'm a common girl. Enough said.

Goddess on a spit, when did you get so unbearably chatty?

I rolled my eyes and turned, finding Nyfain on the patio in his worn jeans and white T-shirt. His hands dangled at his sides. Usually he'd venture into the garden and ask about the day's labors. We'd then leave out the side where the guys had painstakingly beat a hole in the brick wall. It was correctly thought that they (we) shouldn't be traipsing through the queen's chambers every day. Today, though, he remained on the patio.

The other men had all noticed the change. Gyril gave me a sideways look but stayed bent over his shovel. Jawson curled his lips, making a show of being focused on planting bright and cheerful flowers that did not fit the current mood. Hadriel stared at me with a flat expression, his back to Nyfain.

"What's up?" I asked, staying put.

"I'd like to speak with you."

I scowled at Hadriel.

He extended his hands in front of him, putting up his palms. He mouthed, "I only told Leala."

Leala had needed to get the supplies, though, and women in the castle didn't have periods. Not since the curse. They were all frozen in time. The need for such items would be noticed, and everyone would understand they were for me. Rumors would spread, and Nyfain's valet would naturally hear them. He'd know what they meant.

I didn't have to be the bearer of bad news after all. I'd just have to deal with the fallout.

"Yeah, sure." I took a moment to tuck my tools into their canvas pockets in the gardening bucket before crossing the dirt with a straight back. He waited for me to pass him, and I couldn't help inhaling his intoxicating scent. Why did it have to be the best damn smell that had ever come across my nose? It wasn't fair.

I reached for the sliding glass door, but Nyfain got there first and slid it open for me. He waited for me to go inside before following me and letting the door shut behind us. He didn't stop when I did, though, instead walking on to the center of the room.

Stopping in front of the enchanted rosebush coming up out of the floor, he said, "Look at this," his voice rough.

My stomach flipped, and unease rolled through me.

It felt like fear drove holes through my center.

I stopped opposite him and stared down without seeing.

"What do you see?" he prodded.

I shook my head, willing myself to focus, but it felt like waiting for a guilty verdict. I couldn't. I just couldn't.

"Finley, *look*," he barked, power riding his command.

I stepped back and wiped my forehead with my forearm, pushing back on his command. If he kept it up, I'd give him one of my own, and we both know mine landed a helluva lot harder.

"Please," he said softly. "Look at the rosebush."

Gritting my teeth, hating all the unsaid words hovering between us, I did as he said.

"What do you see?" he repeated.

"The enchanted rosebush, Nyfain, I don't know. What am I supposed to see?"

He pointed at the trunk, sparkling with color. Then a branch that supported five full blooms with little specks of pixie light floating around them.

"This is your village, I now realize." He kept pointing. "For a long time, it was the only branch with any blooms. The rest had wilting flowers or outright dead. But this..." He pointed to a different branch. The wilting roses were magically lifting back into full blooms. The branch was turning from a cracked, weather-beaten brown into a vibrant, new-growth green. "This is the village we recently helped. This..." He pointed at the base, where the stem was changing color. "This is the castle, I think. I'm not sure what it means, since we don't get sick, but it looks like life is resurging here, too. Your everlass elixir is changing the fate of the kingdom. It's showing in the rosebush."

I stared at it in wonder.

"This is great news, obviously," Nyfain said, his voice subdued, "but now we enter the race."

"What race? What do you mean?"

"The demon king monitors the progress of his efforts. We're going to need to heal as many as we can, as fast as we can, before he shows up and attempts to find a way to stop us."

"But..." I stared at him, not comprehending. "Do you really think he cares? We were worried about Jedrek, and nothing seems to have come of that. And now this... He hasn't been here in how long?"

"When the curse was fresh, he used to show up for progress updates every few months. While he was here, he'd do whatever he could to make it harder for us. He'd kill anyone who angered him. He'd battle wills with me when I tried to stop it. Then, as we began to deteriorate, it was twice a year. Then once a year. We haven't seen him in over three years, I think. The kingdom is fading, and he's happy to let it. But now, suddenly…"

He looked at the rosebush.

Anger rose, an easier emotion than the fear and uncertainty and now dread firing within me. "You're using the threat of the demon king to hurry me up? Because you assume you'll lose your healer when he comes, right? I better get it all done before you sacrifice me to your cause."

A line formed between his eyebrows.

I heaved a sigh. "I'm sick of hearing that he might show up. *Might* being the operative word. I'm sick of you hinting or outright saying that I'll need to make a deal with him—meaning I'll obviously need to leave. I'm sick of letting demons rule my life. Just sick to hell of it. Let him come. Fuck him. In the meantime, yeah, I'll heal everyone I can. That was always the end game. I don't need a rose and a curse and the threat of the demon king to do it as quickly as possible. I'll do it to save lives."

I turned to go.

"Finley, wait."

"Nah." I pushed out through the sliding glass door.

"What's happening?" Hadriel asked. The others

looked up too, then quickly looked away. From the way Hadriel's mouth snapped shut, I presumed Nyfain had followed me out.

"Finley, stop," he commanded.

I pushed through the urge to do just that, shaking off his power. I'd come a long way since I was first dragged to this castle.

Past the garden wall, I felt his hand wrap around my upper arm. He swung me around, his expression terrifying to behold. If you weren't past caring about his scariness, obviously.

"Finley, would you wait?" he said in a low voice, his eyes roaming my face. "I didn't mean... You wouldn't be sacrificed to the demon king. It'll be your choice. You'll see what he's like when he comes. I want—"

"What's best for me, I know." I yanked my arm to break free of his grasp.

He didn't let go. Instead, he shook his head, and frustration filled the bond. His lips tightened and his arm jerked a little, as though he were about to fling me away like he was so good at doing. I readied for the emotional blow, hardening myself.

"Damn it, Finley. We can't both be this stubborn." He grabbed my other arm, bending to peer down into my eyes. "Why are you afraid?"

I'd forgotten that emotion was squeezed into everything. It was embarrassing to admit I was worried he'd disown me now, so I figured playing dumb was my best bet. "What?"

"Your sadness woke me up this morning. I wondered what happened. The rest of your emotions helped me piece it together. The only one I don't understand is the fear. Did you think I'd hurt you when I found out you weren't with child?"

"What?"

He breathed deeply through his nose, fire erupting in his eyes. "Fuck this dragon," he muttered, bending his head a little and squeezing his eyes shut.

Another trickle of fear wormed through me as I watched him wrestle with his dragon's obvious desire to try again. A pang of longing followed by unease rushed in. Suddenly, I just needed space from him, from *this*.

"I'm not afraid of you, Nyfain. Give me a break." I pulled back, but his grip made it clear that I wasn't going anywhere. It was anyone's guess why I didn't push the issue with my will.

"Back off for a fucking minute. Can't you see she's hurting?" he snarled, snapping his eyes open and refocusing on me.

I stilled in his grasp.

"Finley, I can feel your emotions through the bond. I just don't understand what they mean. Why fear?"

Heat prickled my traitorous eyes.

Just tell him, my animal implored me. *You hate when he doesn't explain why he's being an ass, so explain yourself. Because right now, you're being an ass.*

"Is there any way to separate from our animals?" I grumbled.

His lips tweaked up at the corners, but his eyes were so full of concern.

"It's nothing," I said, trying to get away. "Look, we had a good time, but I understand it's over now. So that's fine. Let's go back to normal."

"And what is normal?" he growled.

"We'll heal the land, the demon king will come, and you'll be rid of me. The whole kidnapping issue will be behind you, and the desperate need to fuck will be a long-lost memory. You'll find your soul mate and live happily ever after. Done and dusted."

That was a lot of shit coming out of your mouth, my animal said in disgust.

He gritted his teeth, his eyes sparking. "What do you know about my soul mate?"

"I know that she'll be able to eat at the table with you and not be embarrassed." I raised my chin. "She'll have that dowry your kind are into. A title. Probably huge tracts of land..."

"My mother didn't know how to eat at a fine table.

She was taught, and she only did it when she had to. We rarely ate that way together. I'd much rather sit in front of a fire with you, eating off a tray. Those are some of my favorite meals. As for the dowry, these aren't normal times. And, if you ask me, your dowry is more robust than anyone who has come before you."

A response like that deserved more than one word, but it was all I had in my arsenal. "What?"

"You are literally healing the kingdom, and you are doing it for free. If you'd put a price tag on that, you would be rolling in coin. I, on behalf of the villages, would owe you a fortune."

I shifted my weight, popping out a hip, not really sure where to go from here. Not really sure what any of this meant.

"Look, neither of us knows what the future holds," he continued. "Let's just leave it a question mark. For now, let's carry on the way we have been, okay? We'll keep lighting up that enchanted rosebush with new blooms. You know, someone I'm quite smitten with, who is currently out of commission for vigorous fucking, told me to have hope."

Tears pooled in my stupid eyes, and I offered him a watery smile. "Sounds good," I managed.

"So that was it, then," he said softly, tracing my chin with his thumb. "You worried I wouldn't want you anymore."

I wiped my suddenly tear-stained cheeks, not commenting. I wasn't fond of sounding like a sad sack.

He clucked his tongue, his eyes so incredibly deep and soft. He pulled me into a tight hug.

"You're the stupidest smart girl I've ever met. I'm incapable of pretending, Finley. I might be able to hold back, but I don't play false. There was something incredibly primal and erotic about trying for a baby— Fuck it." He tightened up around me, burying his face into the crook of my neck, then breathed in my scent, shaking. "I'm not going to be able to mention that anymore, actually. My fucking dragon has been trying to rip control away from me since I woke up this morning and realized what happened."

"I just...didn't know if I'd be as interesting without that primal need pulling at you. This last week has been great, but I didn't know how much of that was real and how much was...your dragon, basically."

"All of it was real, and half of it was my bloody dragon riding me. The fucking bastard is getting out of control."

"Why all of a sudden?"

He tensed. "Because he senses what the future...might hold, and he has clearly forgotten what we're up against. There is not a magnanimous bone in his big, scaly body. Anyway, it doesn't matter. We're not worried about the future. We're focusing on the present." He leaned down to kiss me, and then his voice reduced to a whisper. "Why didn't you come to me this morning?"

"I woke up with you. What do you mean?"

"When you found out. When you felt the loss and sadness. Why didn't you come to me for comfort?"

I stared up into his golden, sunburst eyes, so beautiful. So expressive. I didn't know what to say. That had been the furthest thing from my mind, and not just because I feared how he'd take it. I'd never had anyone to go to for comfort. That wasn't something my life had ever afforded. I dealt with things blow by blow, and I trucked on. That was all I'd ever known.

He clearly read the confusion and stroked his fingertips down my cheeks. "We may not officially be mates, but let me fill that role for you. When you need help or comfort, or a punching bag, come to me. I'll never turn you away. Okay? We're in this together."

My emotions betrayed me again and tears leaked from my eyes. I ran my hand down his chest. "I'm not out of commission for vigorous fucking if you don't mind a midmorning bath…"

He scooped me up into his arms. "The villages can wait an hour."

WHILE THEY DID wait an hour that day, they *could* wait. Their time of sickness had come to an end. We worked long days, training people to care for the everlass and make the nulling elixir, teaching them who to treat with the crowded elixir.

More time passed.

In the beginning, I was the only one making the crowded elixir. A few other experienced healers and plant workers tried it and killed their patients. But a few unlikely villagers proved surprisingly adept at it, one of them Dash. He tried it on three people behind Hannon's back and cured them. All of his learning from me, plus a natural propensity for gardening, had allowed him to shine despite his age. I hated putting the burden on his shoulders, but there were so few who could make the crowded elixir that we had no choice. He was happy for that fact.

Two months went by. When Nyfain tried to do too much, working day and night, I forced him to go to bed and sleep. I certainly didn't need him as protection. After a couple of weeks, I was receiving big smiles whenever I entered a village, followed by stories of how the elixir had cured a sister, father, aunt, or grandfather. Children ran through the Forbidden Wood in the daytime to the nearest everlass fields, pruning and tending, as I'd taught them. Singing songs and *helping*.

The demon-be-gone elixir was also in high demand. In some villages, everyone who went out after a certain time was mandated to take it. If they wanted to get it on with a demon, so be it, but they'd do it with a clear head.

Alcohol sales went through the roof.

Nyfain and I basically shared the tower room. I'd fall into the covers in a heap, only to wake up when he slid in beside me in the wee hours of the morning. His big arm would pull me into his warm, strong body, smelling fresh and clean from a hasty washup. I'd snuggle in close, curling into him, and inevitably feel his hard length pulsing against my bare flesh. The slightest wiggle of acceptance, and he'd thread his large cock deep into my suddenly wet depths.

Most nights, I gave that wiggle.

Occasionally, when he'd had a tougher night than usual and his dragon was closer to the surface, his teeth would scrape my neck or shoulder. Sometimes they'd even dig in, nearly drawing blood, and a new sort of feeling would tingle across my heated flesh. Like little prickles digging down, sending a strange sort of electric pulse through my body. It was always over too soon, and shortly thereafter we'd come together in a tangle of limbs.

When I woke up for the day, only a scant few hours

later, more often than not we'd have another session.

Even after a couple months, I still could not get enough of him. Each lovemaking session was better than the last. Each conversation felt like it could go on forever. Our animals were still major assholes, though, always pushing for more. They wanted to seal the deal.

Nyfain's dragon was worse than ever. Worse than my animal. He seemed to feel a threat coming. He wanted us protected, and claiming, mating, imprinting, and knocking me up were all on his list. We'd had a few good battles leading to explosive sex. Nyfain was always able to regain control right before the pivotal moment, though, much to the dragon's increased dismay.

He was right to worry.

All good things would come to an end, and the demon king had noticed our efforts.

CHAPTER 24

I WOKE BEFORE dawn, shivering from the cold. My blankets were still wrapped around me, but the furnace that was Nyfain was absent.

I frowned, glancing at the somewhat lightening sky, black shifting to a bruised purple. He definitely should've been back from his rounds by now.

A deep, soul-crushing misery radiated through the bond. Pain, but not of the physical variety. This was of the heart.

I threw back the covers and lit a candle, intending to go to my wardrobe and dress, but before I made it more than a couple of steps, a light knock sounded at the door. I paused, listening.

"It's just me, milady," Leala said in a somber voice, not usual for her.

With shaking hands, I turned over the lock and

pulled open the door. She held hangers in both hands, additional clothes for me. Her expression was tight with worry.

"Good morning, milady," she said, waiting for me to get out of the way and let her in as normal.

"What's happened? What's going on?"

She set the clothes on the bed and pulled open the wardrobe before starting to rearrange everything.

"We have a new visitor in the castle," she said in clipped tones. "The demon king has come for an inspection, as he does. The master ran into him last night in the wood."

Cold dripped down my spine. Suddenly, the emotions through the bond made a lot more sense.

I raised my chin. We couldn't both go to pieces.

"And what usually happens when he comes?" I asked as she put the new clothes away, leaving out a dress. "And what is this?"

"The master thought it would be best if you tried to blend in with the servants. At least at first. You'll be subject to more ill treatment from the demon minions, but at least you won't have the eyes of the demon king on you."

I contemplated that for a moment. Getting one's bearings was certainly a good strategy in response to a new threat. But with some things, like hunting wild boar, you could have your bearings and still the fuckers managed to blindside you. I had a feeling the demon king would be very like a wild boar: cunning, ruthless, and dangerous.

"Give me Nyfain's old clothes."

Unlike many, I'd never shied away from hunting wild boar, bastards though they were.

She turned around slowly, alarm on her face.

"Nyfain's old clothes, Leala. The more ill-fitting, the better. I'll do my own hair, too. I want to feel like myself, and I was always a hot mess before Nyfain polished me up. I'll wear the dagger, too. The fine one. It works better."

"I really don't advise you to start any trouble with him, milady. He isn't like the normal demons here. He is much more powerful."

"I'm not the one starting trouble. I'm not the one who showed up uninvited and lorded over someone else's kingdom, causing death and ruin. Fuck that guy. If he wants to come after me, then he gets what he gets. I've never backed down from anyone in my life. I do not intend to start now."

AFTER BREAKFAST, I made my way to the queen's garden as the sun crested the horizon. I took my usual route around the grounds, noticing a distinct lack of bird calls. The Forbidden Wood waited in the distance, still and dark and full of monsters.

Nearly at the garden wall, I noticed a shape standing off to the side. A male, judging by the width of his shoulders and slim hips. He stood straight and stoic, his build wiry and height on the shorter side, compared to my six feet, anyway. It didn't take long for his gaze to swing my way, rooting to me and watching me advance.

I'd never seen him before, but his funky smell gave him away. A demon, quite strong in power. I guessed these bastards weren't fully contained by the night.

Kill him, my animal snarled.

It would be a fine hello.

He wore a black button-up shirt with the arms buttoned tightly at the wrists and around the neck. His black slacks were pleated beneath the black belt. His black shoes had been polished up to a mirror shine, and his bleach-blond hair in a bowl cut just confused me.

He angled his body so that he was directly facing me now, waiting for me to draw near. As I did, he sidestepped so that he was standing directly in my way.

"What are you doing out here, wandering the grounds?" he asked in a highish voice with a strange lilt.

"Looking for you, actually. I was hoping for some fashion advice. My goal is to confuse everyone while also making them pity me. This is my start..." I flowed my hand down my front. "And I can only assume you'll be my finish. Nice pleats."

"You smell...off."

"You look ridiculous."

His eyebrows dipped. "Is this your pathetic means of rebelling?" Claws elongated from his fingers, shiny black things. I got the feeling he meant it as a threat.

My animal took it as an invitation.

I drifted my hand toward my dagger, careful to keep her far enough down that my eyes wouldn't glow. I wanted his death to be a surprise.

"Rebelling?" I said nonchalantly. "Kind of like what you're doing with that hair? The demon king must have a sense of humor."

"Your kind are to remain in the castle until the king can assess who is left."

Who is left...

My animal tried to rise to the surface on my sudden blaze of fury, but I held her down. He hadn't made a move on me yet. I would kill in self-defense, and only then. For now...

"Why does he care?" I asked, flexing the hand near my dagger.

The demon tilted his head. "My patience is wearing thin, girl. His prolonged absence does not mean he has become any more merciful. Take note, or become one less member of this castle."

That was definitely a threat.

Kill him! my animal roared. She struggled against my hold.

Not until he attacks!

"Be a lamb and let him know that I'm in the garden, would you? I couldn't be bothered to send a note."

I walked past him at an angle, giving off an air of arrogance carefully calculated to incite him. My distance away accounted for my height, and therefore my arm span, putting him at a disadvantage. The second my shoulder was even with his, he struck out, just as I'd known he would.

He was fast, but I'd been training with Nyfain for months. This demon didn't have anything on the dragon prince.

I stepped to the side at an angle, grabbing for his reaching hand, and yanked him to me. Wrapping my arms around his neck in a sideways hug, I grabbed his chin and near his temple, and wrenched at an angle. His neck cracked, and his arms went limp.

"Yeah. I became a master at neck snapping, fucker. Now what?"

Pulling my animal closer to the surface so I could use her strength, I draped the dead demon over my shoulder and jogged toward the wood not infested by demons.

I'd read just about every book on shifters in the library by this point, and had pieced together some very interesting takeaways. Once a person could properly shift and establish a working bond with their animal, they always had access to the animal's primal attributes. They'd always be strong and agile, have a great sense of smell, and see in the dark (in a black, white, and yellow color spectrum). That was why Nyfain didn't have to pull and push as much with his dragon. He could use some of the dragon's abilities without asking.

I still hadn't shifted, though. The books referred to me as a "restrained shifter"—a person who could feel their animal, even establish a sort of working relationship with them, but still could not shift. Some people, for whatever reason, were never able to shift, although it was rare as a natural occurrence.

Of course, it was even less common for a shifter to be utterly suppressed…which cast a stark light on the kingdom's situation. Most of the people around us couldn't even feel their animals, let alone speak with them.

It was possible for a strong alpha to pull a suppressed animal from a person. Once that animal was pulled free, it should remain accessible. That didn't mean the person could shift, especially if it was a genetic issue, but they could try. Often, it worked.

Nyfain and I could pull animals from the shifters around us, and often did by accident when we riled each other up. But we couldn't get their animals to stay. The magic of the curse punched them back into suppression.

Another interesting tidbit—the demon king was known for his ability to suppress shifters' animals. Yes, I'd read up on him, too. It was amazing the things a person could learn in a well-stocked library. The demon king was a wily cunt, apparently.

By himself, he had a certain level of power, like anyone. Quite a lot, obviously, since he was a king, but not unstoppable. His true power, though, came from making deals. When he made a deal, he could combine his and the other party's power to bring that deal to fruition. It was why he was able to trap an entire kingdom—he used his power plus that of the mad king, who had a lot of power in his own right, to lay down the deal, or curse, in this case.

Being a wily cunt, the demon king excelled at trickery within those deals. The mad king likely asked for one thing, but through the negotiation period, the demon king twisted the terms, worked on the king's confusion and apparent health issues, and created a final deal that worked heavily in his favor. The mad king had been outmaneuvered. Horribly.

I got the impression that was a demon king's claim to fame. They might not be the most powerful king in the world, but they were often the most cunning. We were up against a strategist.

I suddenly wondered what happened to the kingdoms that had disappeared over time. Was it just the natural evolution of their kingdoms, or had they been trapped in the same way we were? Were some of them still out there, struggling to hang on?

In our case, and in the case of any shifters, here was the kicker. Breaking the curse wouldn't automatically un-suppress all the animals. Once the curse was broken, the alpha would have to visit each person and pull their animal free. And while that wasn't the end of the world, things got dire when the demon king planned to invade the second the curse was lifted. There would be no time to free the animals before war was upon the kingdom.

Definitely a wily cunt. It would not only take courage to take him on, but a damn good long-term plan.

When I was good and deep in the wood, I just chucked the body. I doubted they'd comb the wood that wasn't already festering with their magic. And if they caught his scent and followed it here? Well...he started it.

The guys didn't turn up in the garden as they usually did. When the morning started to wane, I felt a blast of panic through the bond. Nyfain was not having a very good day. Not long afterward, I heard the sliding glass door open behind me. Relief washed through the bond, and then I was in Nyfain's arms, squeezed within an inch of my life. He breathed me in, and then tensed.

"Why do you smell like a demon, Finley?" he asked slowly.

Possessiveness rang through his tone. I grinned, closing my eyes within his embrace.

"I hugged one, that's why. Well...I danced with him first, *then* I hugged him. Then we went for a walk in the woods. Oh, and I adjusted his neck. He had an awful kink in it. Or at least he did when I was finished."

He pulled me away and searched my eyes. His snort of annoyance dusted my face before he pulled me in closely again.

"Don't antagonize them, princess. They'll kill you for it."

"I didn't antagonize him. I killed him. Well...yes, okay, I did antagonize him first, but you should've seen his whole setup."

He blew out a breath and kissed my forehead. "I see you decided to stand out rather than fit in."

"I decided to be me, and I'm weird. Ask anyone from my village. It's one thing to play dress-up while roaming the castle and working in the villages, but it's another when I need to think on my feet and stay alive. I can't focus when I have you for protection. I need to remember what it's like to stand on my own."

He looked down at me as he ran his thumb along my jaw. "For some fucking reason, the dragon approves of that speech."

"And you don't."

"No. It is my job to protect you. It's my entire duty as your—"

He cut off.

I patted his chest. "Exactly. You're not my mate, and you haven't claimed me. I've given you plenty of opportunities, but you've held back because you were preparing for this moment. So let me have my moment."

I turned back to the garden. In a moment, he followed me to the rosebushes.

"What are you doing?" I asked, startled.

"Helping you. We need to stay away from the everlass while the demon king is here. If he knows how we're making the elixir, he'll torch all the fields."

"What does he get out of controlling our kingdom, anyway?"

"When I die, he'll have access to our gold reserves, our gold mine, and the extensive crown jewels. He'll be able to take what he wants. People, too, I guess. It's been said that he makes prizes of the people who got the short end of the stick on one of his deals."

"What did the mad king give him to lay the curse?"

"Coin, I think. He was a damned fool. He paid the demon king to essentially set us up. My father was proud, though. We were a wealthy kingdom with desirable commodities to trade. In my father's heyday, he was heralded as a shrewd trader. He would always walk away with the better end of any deal. I'm sure he brought that arrogance into his negotiations with the demon king. He was clearly thinking like a man in his prime, when in fact he was a man teetering on the edge. He was already unhinged, but then I'd severely disappointed him, and his wife died. Given his health, he probably realized his ability to produce a new heir was fleeting. Without an heir, he feared losing control of his kingdom. Of his status and his legacy. It clearly made him desperate. He was not in his right mind, and not just because of the possible brain fever. The demon king obviously preyed upon that."

"But he can't kill you until the curse is lifted."

"Correct. He can't. Others can. His beasts could, if they were able. But he personally cannot."

"And you realize the shifters' animals won't automatically be unsuppressed once the curse is lifted?"

"Give a smart woman a library and then stand back," he said softly, and pride glowed through the bond. "I do know that, yes. And I knew you'd figure it out when I saw that book in your room. I can't say more. I'm toeing the line as it is. With your help, I've been able to access more power, but it won't be enough to save me from the full brunt of the magical gag."

That was why the demon king would try to kill him immediately. If he managed it before Nyfain helped the other shifters, their animals would stay suppressed, and our people wouldn't be able to fight back when he swooped in to steal our riches.

I let out a breath and refused to let my confidence wobble. I refused to let the prickle of tears in my eyes manifest. The future did look bleak, but it always had, hadn't it? The sickness had been bleak, but I'd set out to cure my father, and ended up curing the kingdom. My will was strong. It was stronger than anything the demon king could throw at me. I would see this kingdom saved—I just had to figure out how.

"Well, fuck." I stood back and looked at my handiwork. The last of the roses had been restored to loveliness. It was a mistake to call them docile, though. Or tamed. As pretty as they were, those barbs could still draw blood.

"So if we can't work the everlass, or cure people, or

fight...what do we do?" I asked.

"Take a day off, I guess. None of his creatures will be in the wood while he is here."

"In that case, which would you rather do? Dance or read?"

"You shouldn't be seen with me, Finley."

"Nyfain, give me a break. He's going to smell you on me. He's going to hear about me from the demons in the castle. I'm sure the demons in the villages have heard about me, too. How long do you suspect I'll remain a mystery? I'm wearing your clothes, for fuck's sake."

He was silent for a moment. "Well, in that case, dance and then read?"

IN THE LATE afternoon, Nyfain and I lay on the lounger in the library. I was between his legs and curled up on his chest with a book, and he had his arms wrapped around me, reading with his cheek pressed to my head. It had actually been an incredibly lovely, restful day. For the first time since I'd come to the castle, we didn't need to worry about doing nothing at all. We'd danced, I'd listened to him play the piano and sing, and for the last couple hours we'd cuddled and read.

Unfortunately, he couldn't totally relax. His dragon was apparently going absolutely crazy. The threat to his territory, and to *me*, had riled him up something awful. The only thing that seemed to soothe him was my presence and touch. I was happy to provide it.

"What do you think, should we go find something to eat?" Nyfain asked, dropping his book to his chest while he wrapped his other hand around me.

I held up a finger. I was almost done with the chapter.

He waited patiently and softly kissed my head.

When I finished, I looked up at him and smiled. "Go and get it, or have Leala or Urien bring it to us?"

Urien was his valet. He was mostly a ghost until he was needed. I literally never saw him until the second Nyfain had a need. It was eerie. He was hiding from the demons, of course, trying to stay alive. It must've been a long sixteen years for him, more so than anyone else.

"I'll need to show my face around the castle, but I can do that tomorrow. We can have it brought to the tower."

"Who do you need to show your face to, your people or the demons?"

"The demons. They get haughty and destructive if I don't put them in their place. It helps my people." He murmured, "What's left of them."

I tilted my face up so he could kiss my lips.

"Come out, come out, wherever you are," we heard.

The voice was flat and bland, even in its attempt to be musical.

Nyfain tensed, and power created a vicious cloud of intent around us. His fingers dug into me for a second, but then he rose beneath me, getting me to sit up.

"You stay here," he whispered, standing and pulling his leg from the other side of the lounger. "Don't speak."

He kept his book in hand and exited from around the tapestry. I scooted up so I could see, looking between the tapestry and the plant, all but a bit of me hidden.

A...man-thing waited just inside the double doors of the library. Two horns lightly curved into the sky from his forehead, about one foot tall. Their color gradually changed from sky-blue to an indigo that matched his skin. His ears stuck out a bit to the sides, changing from the blue of his face to a chartreuse at the painted tips. His thin face ended in a pointy chin, and his nose took up a bit too much real estate. His long hair draped down his shoulders, over the high-collared black duster he wore. He had on a black button-up underneath, tucked into pleated pants, just like the guy acting as fertilizer in the woods.

"Ah. There you are," he said, turning toward an approaching Nyfain.

Nyfain cut through the library like a predator sizing up his prey. His sleek, graceful movements screamed his fighting prowess, and his height and broad shoulders absolutely dwarfed the much smaller demon. Despite wearing a worn-in white T-shirt and old jeans, he radiated power, prestige, and authority. It was clear who owned this library and the soil beneath it, regardless of who currently managed it.

"Nyfain." The creature clasped his fingers in front of his body. "I've missed you today. I haven't seen you skulking around, trying to intimidate my people with your presence."

"There'll be plenty of time tomorrow," Nyfain said, his deep, rough voice crackling with menace.

"So there will." The man-thing leaned forward just a bit, but I could tell it was for show. It was all too evident that he didn't want to close the distance separating them. "What is that horrible smell draping you, Nyfain?"

Fear and frustration rolled through the bond. Followed by rage. That smell was obviously me. What a dick.

"And...look at this..." The man-thing must've forgotten himself, because he reached forward to pluck something off Nyfain's chest. Possibly one of my hairs.

Nyfain snatched the man-thing's wrist out of the air

and wrenched it wide, bending him to the side as if he were nothing. The man-thing tensed, and the air crackled with electricity and magic, sputtering and spitting between them. Pain rolled through the bond, and my animal roiled within me, desperate to help Nyfain. She shoved power to his dragon, drawing and readying more, and the pain lessened.

The two men held each other's gazes.

"If you kill me, the deal is forfeit and your kingdom will die with me," the man-thing gritted out, clearly under pressure.

I pushed a little closer to the plant. This was the demon king!

Nyfain just stared for one more beat before releasing the demon king's wrist. The last of the pain cut off.

"You know better than to touch me, Dolion," Nyfain said, and the violence in his tone made my small hairs stand on end. He was a scary fucking bastard when he wanted to be. I doubted Dolion had known what he was getting himself into, tying a chain around that big dragon's ankle.

"Where is she?" Dolion asked, adjusting his duster. Although he was trying to pretend otherwise, their little standoff had rattled him.

Nyfain didn't answer.

"I can make you tell me," Dolion said, electricity

crackling again.

Agony throbbed through the bond, but if I hadn't felt it myself, I would've never known Nyfain was under strain. He stood straight and tall, his shoulders squared and his arms loose, ready to grapple or just walk away. There was no telling.

His pain intensified, blasting through the bond. His fists clenched, pushing back. Refusing to yield. At this rate, he'd black out. Clearly he'd rather do that than give me away, as if a standoff today would somehow protect me tomorrow.

I rose from the lounger and walked around the tapestry as though I didn't have the first idea what was going on. I held my book with my thumb stuck within the pages to hold my place.

"Oh, hello," I said, closing the distance. Nyfain's physical pain lessened somewhat, but his emotional pain more than compensated for it. I ignored it. He was the one who'd always encouraged me to hitch a ride out of here with the demon king. It was time to face the music. "I didn't realize the circus was in town. Which clown are you supposed to be?"

Dolion took me in, his gaze lingering on my face, drifting over my body, and my clothes.

"My goodness, Nyfain. You certainly found yourself a pretty one. I'd have her draped all over me as well—"

Nyfain moved so fast that Dolion and I both jumped. He wrapped his fingers around the demon king's throat and bared his teeth, his rage blistering through the bond. He squeezed and lifted, forcing Dolion to grab his wrist and hold on for dear life.

"Whoopsie." I placed my hand on Nyfain's forearm. "Dolion, is it?" I patted Nyfain. "You shouldn't rile up a dragon. Now you know. Nyfain, put him down before he pisses himself all over the floor."

Nyfain shook, pain blasting through him from the magical hold the demon king had on him. He opened his hand and let the bastard fall to the floor.

Dolion picked himself up and snapped down his duster, angry and probably embarrassed. "For a *dragon* who usually claims to love his servants, you're not too worried about seeing a few go tonight, are you?"

"You kill his, I'll kill yours," I said without thinking.

His red-tinged eyes flicked my way.

"You really are hard to look at," I said, squinting at him. "Can't you change form? It would really help everyone else out if you would. I'm not kidding."

"And what a mouth she has on her," Dolion said.

I held up a finger. "Don't make a face-fucking joke. I can already see the bruises forming from the last little slip of the tongue."

His eyes narrowed slightly. "Hmm. Maybe you

won't be so bold when you don't have your bodyguard to protect you."

I shrugged. "Maybe. Maybe not."

"I've heard Nyfain has kept you to himself these last months. Locked in a tower? How cliché."

"Certainly not as cliché as that stupid duster you're wearing. It does not help the situation with those pleats in the least."

"Be careful, little girl…" His eyes flicked to Nyfain, then back to me. "I am not one to be trifled with. You will walk the castle tonight, without your dragon by your side. You will wear something slinky and revealing."

Nyfain tensed up, and I could tell he was holding his breath, trying not to explode.

Dolion continued, "And when the time inevitably comes for you to succumb to the erotic magic circling you, you will moan with pleasure like a whore."

I laughed. "You had me, and then you lost me. Moan with pleasure like a whore? Do you honestly think sex workers feel any sort of pleasure from deadbeat Johns rutting at them like some pig? No, they are bored as fuck and just waiting for him to finish. Probably like all the people you bang. Get your insults straight, you slack-jawed cumgoblin. But sure, I'll show up tonight without Nyfain. I'll choose my own outfit, but I'll show up. How about a little wager? I hear you're into that sort of thing."

Nothing in his expression changed, but his eyes lit up. He *did* love a wager.

"If any of your minions touch me without consent," I said, "I get to kill them. No questions asked, no risk of punishment."

"What if you can't kill them?"

"Right, fine. If any of your minions touch me without consent, I get to *try* to kill them. No questions asked, no risk of punishment."

"You can try to kill them. For tonight only."

"As part of our wager, yes, for tonight only. Which is not to say I won't continue to target them as an ongoing joy of my life."

He studied me again. "And what do I get?"

"What do you want?"

Nyfain stiffened.

"Compliance from the dragon," Dolion replied.

"Yeah, right. Like I have that sort of power. Not to mention it's much too broad. Try again."

I'd been burned a time or two in my life, and when a girl with nothing gets burned, the lesson sinks in deep.

Dolion's lips curled at the corners. Sharp teeth peeked out. "The dragon doesn't physically touch me during my stay."

Wow, he was wary of Nyfain, that was for sure. Imagine if Nyfain had been allowed to assume a throne on his own terms? He would've easily dominated the demon king—and his own father. His father had to have known it, which was why he'd gone to extreme measures to ensure he had an heir and not a rival. Now here Nyfain sat on a throne of ruin. What a shitty thing his father had done to him.

"Are you thick?" I spat. "Do you only do deals with mad kings? I don't have any sort of power over the dragon. None. Zero."

"But I think you do. He hasn't spoken once since you walked up. He is deferring to you, which means he greatly respects you and honors your place at his side. Dragons are incredibly loyal."

"You're going to stand in a ruined kingdom and claim the guy who got us into this mess was loyal? You're a fucking idiot, and you're wasting my time."

I moved to walk around him and toward the door.

The mad king might've thought he was good at bartering, but he was the same sort of shrewd and cunning as the demon king. They spoke the same language. That sort of competition was not about playing the game—it was about playing the man.

Enter me. I was a shit barterer. Absolute crap. I didn't like to cheat people. It wasn't a game to me. I wanted everyone to walk away feeling like they got a fair trade. It was why I'd gotten the short end of the stick a few too many times. I was also common. I had no wealth, no power, no social standing, and no knowledge of how people who did have those things got by. People like me were staff to people like the demon king. Or prisoners. He and I might as well speak different languages. He didn't know what rules people like me lived by, so he had no basis for sizing me up.

That was my biggest asset. My only asset, actually. It was important that I stayed an anomaly. The second he learned my quirks, I'd be outmatched.

"How about this." He held out a hand to stop me. "During my stay, you interject if the dragon comes for me."

"I'll give you one day, same as you're giving me," I replied. "And I'll only promise to do what I can. I can't work miracles."

"Ah, but I am giving you more than a promise. If you cannot guarantee compliance, then I should get longer."

"Three days, then. No more."

His grin said he had gotten exactly what he wanted. A shiver crawled over my skin.

"Done," he said, and an invisible magical line snapped taut between us.

"I'll be downstairs when it gets dark," I said, continuing to walk from the room.

Nyfain met me in the hall. "I'm not sure if that was incredibly smart or incredibly stupid."

"Why smart? Because I can think of a lot of reasons for the stupid one."

"He wanted to see how much I'd defer to you, but you flipped the script. You've clearly intrigued him. He wants a real show of your power. He'll set his people on you tonight."

"I figured. It'll give me something to do. Their magic doesn't work on me."

"And it won't work on anyone else, either. We'll give everyone the demon-be-gone draught tonight."

I nodded.

"He was right, though," Nyfain said softly.

"About what?"

"About you being able to influence my actions. I'd defer to your judgment because I respect and honor your place by my side."

I reached out in a rush of emotion and grasped his hand. "That's incredibly sweet of you to say. It's also incredibly incorrect. When your dragon is riding you hard, you don't defer to anyone. You're vicious and wild, and this kingdom is in good hands with you. I can see that. All we need to do is set you loose. That'll have to be my job. Somehow."

And it would start with playing a dangerous game that might destroy me forever.

CHAPTER 25

A N HOUR AFTER the sun went down, I walked down the stairs wearing a slinky little black number that plunged down my neckline and showed off most of my back. The bottom fell to my knees with slits up both sides. It was lovely and fit me perfectly. My dagger was out of place hanging at my hip, and the throwing knives around my thighs only added to the look.

Leala had done my hair in an overstated updo and applied extra makeup. The goal was to look vain and extravagant and foolish. To encourage the demons to underestimate me. Besides, swinging wildly out of character would keep them from guessing my real personality.

Maybe I was foolish to think I could go toe to toe with the demon king, but I had to at least give it a shot. Otherwise I'd be under his thumb like everyone else, and the kingdom would definitely be doomed.

All was quiet on the third-floor landing. Not a soul stirred. On the second-floor landing, I heard shouts and laughter. A man ran by the foot of the stairs on the first floor, leather straps crisscrossing his body, studs lining the straps. A demon woman followed, cackling madly, shiny pinkish scales covering her body and her tail whipping out behind her.

Usually the demons wore their human masks around the castle. For the most part, anyway. Apparently they were letting it all hang out tonight.

"Need an escort?"

I turned to see the demon king sauntering up behind me. The duster and pleats had been replaced with a tuxedo and a black bow tie. His reddish eyes and slick smile set me on edge.

"Actually, no. I doubt your people will approach if you are hovering around like a ghoul."

"My goodness. So prickly. Do you ever drop the tough-girl act?"

Tough-girl act? my animal thought. *Give me time, ass clown. I'll show you how much of our personality is an act.*

I kept from smirking. Dolion would definitely die one day, and it would be my blade sticking out of his neck.

I shrugged. "It's your circus. I'm just trying to fit in."

He stuck out a hand, indicating we should take the stairs to the first floor. "You dressed the part."

"Of a tough girl? Hardly."

"The dagger, the throwing stars…"

"You're out of touch, love," I said, borrowing from Hadriel's playbook. "Shifter ladies like to accessorize. We do it with fine daggers and perfectly balanced throwing knives. I *do* need a new belt for the sheath, though."

"Shifters, yes. Nothing but animals growling and spitting at each other. It never sat right with me that they should have so many kingdoms, such an abundant population, and so many seats on the council." He smiled at me, and I kept my face perfectly blank.

Council? That only vaguely rang a bell. I was sure it was mentioned somewhere, in one of the many books I had poured over lately, but it hadn't been touched on enough to stick.

Yet another thing to add to my continual research list.

"But that's enough of politics," he said. "One of those seats has been given up, and it will remain vacant. I can see you like that dragon—he's quite striking, I must admit, except for the scars—but you'd do well not to get too attached. Consider it a hint from a friend."

"Oh, we're friends now? Fantastic. Except friends don't threaten each other, bub."

His brow furrowed. He'd probably never been called "bub" before.

He walked me to a grand ballroom. The doors had been thrown wide and candlelight spilled out into the corridor. Raucous laughter reverberated around me, and I was starting to clue in to the fact that these nights produced no other type of laughter.

He stopped by the door, his smile sly and eyes twinkling. He thought he was about to throw me to the wolves.

"Enjoy yourself," he said, and walked away.

The scene in the ballroom stopped me for a moment. It reminded me of the first night in the castle, when I'd walked into what was essentially one big orgy. Except this time, the demons were in their true forms. Scaled beasts hunched between creamy thighs. Demons thrusting with their tail curled around the ankle of the receiver. One demon looked very like a minotaur.

"Super," I said, forcing myself forward.

Their demon magic hit me immediately, but it wasn't all sexual. I felt rage and sorrow, too, suggesting these demons fed off a whole range of emotions. They all hit me at once, a clusterfuck cocktail.

"Double super." I sauntered right into the middle, because what the hell else was I supposed to do? It wasn't like I was here to watch, and I definitely wouldn't partake. My goal was to kill any demon that gave me the opportunity.

"Hmm, come to join the fun, my sweet?" A demon scuttled closer, its head reaching to about the level of my breast. Its forked tongue flicked out, possibly sampling the air like a snake. Or maybe it was just gross. Its hard brow ridge arched over shiny black eyes that showed no whites. Small spikes rose along its arms, and the rest of its nude body was covered in leathery skin. Two batlike wings were scrunched up behind it.

"My sweet? What are you, a storybook villain?"

I made sure I didn't face it directly. I wanted my shoulder to be the closest point of contact for it, because that meant it was the body part most likely to be touched.

Another demon walked out of the fray, directly toward me. This one was about my height and covered in greenish scales. No horns marked its face. No nose, either. Its bald head had bony ridges, and its absolutely massive dick stuck out much too far.

"You," he said to the leathery demon at my side. "Go."

The leathery demon scampered away with a strange

sort of squeal. The newcomer stalked toward me, and I could tell he had something in mind. Some sort of action.

Watch, folks, as this big fucker gets handsy and loses the thing on his body with the farthest reach.

Please stop talking to imaginary people, my animal thought. *People are going to have proof that you're batshit crazy.*

I huffed out a laugh.

"You have humor, animal?" Dong Song said, stopping in front of me.

"That's not very nice," I told him. "Do you know what else isn't very nice? Me calling you an ugly cunt. But I really want to."

"You are meant to come with me." He gestured me onward. "Come."

"No thanks."

He waited for a moment. "Come!" he demanded.

"Does that ever work? Offering no foreplay and then shouting at women to come?"

In a flash of anger, he reached out to grab me. It took everything I had to stop from slapping his hand away and stabbing him right then and there. I had to wait for him to go for me, though. I didn't want the demon king to get one up on me because of a technicality.

I didn't have to wait long.

He grabbed me around the throat, something Nyfain and I had worked on a lot. It was one of his moves, after all, and he wanted me to be able to fight back in the best way possible.

I didn't use any of those moves now, though. I just smiled, then wheezed out a laugh as the demon tried to jerk me in the direction he wished I would go. I stuck my dagger in his gut with one hand, grabbed his dong with the other, and then pulled out the dagger and sliced downward.

Incredibly, he didn't start screaming.

"Come!" he said again, attempting to twist and pull me along. His brow pinched when the movement didn't work out so well. He looked down in confusion.

With a dagger this sharp, it would take a moment for the pain to get to his brain, but this was ridiculous.

"Bud, I am literally holding your severed dick in my hand. Why the fuck aren't you freaking out right now?" I asked, aghast, then dropped his dick, because great goddess it was gross.

His eyes widened, and he belted out a high-pitched wail. He reached for his dick. He clearly wasn't as concerned about the gooey deep red blood gushing out of his stomach.

"Oh, good. Phew." I nodded at him. "That's the reaction I was expecting. If you'd done that in the beginning, I would've made a quip about only coming for one man—Oh, never mind."

I stepped on a diagonal and stabbed him in the kidney.

"Night, night." I continued on, really not sure what to do about my bloody blade.

A woman off to the side lay on a blanket, propped up on pillows with her legs spread wide. A purple-scaled man-thing licked up her flesh and sucked a nipple into his broad, flat lips. He continued to crawl up her body before sitting back and wrapping his clawed fingers around his knobby, curved dick, like a road through a mountain pass. In the middle it kinda ballooned up, thicker there than at the base. I'd seen a lot of ugly dicks around here, but that one had to take the cake.

"Oh no, no, don't let him put that thing in you," I whispered, transfixed, like watching a disaster in progress.

He threaded it into her clearly slick depths. She moaned, rubbing her hands along his bent back, tracing the pointed edges of the fin along his spine. It was good defense to keep someone from hugging him from behind. He thrust, slipping in that thick bit, and she shrieked in pain turned pleasure. He shoved against her, pushing in as deeply as he could go, before pulling back about halfway and lightly thrusting back and forth, as if he were working her G-spot with the thick bit.

I stared with a grimace as she swung her hips up against him, clearly getting the friction she needed as he kept rubbing his dick in the exact right spot. She spread her legs wider, leaned back hard, and pumped her hips before slapping her hands on the ground. She came in an actual scream, writhing like she was possessed.

"Right, well…fuck. I guess I stand corrected," I muttered, finally tearing my eyes away. "Gross dick for the win."

It took all of one moment for me to realize that distraction had put me at a severe disadvantage. A wall of seven demons had noticed me killing one of their own, and they'd lined up to face me, anger clear on their faces.

Ah. I wasn't here to see the sex. I was here to battle. The sex was just a distraction. A very thorough distraction.

"You will pay for what you have done," said the female demon in the middle in barely contained rage. Good goddess, she had a great set of blue-scaled knockers.

They started forward, forming a vee. I reviewed the parameters. I could kill if they touched me without consent. *Touched* me without consent. I had to wait for them to make contact.

Although…the demon king had agreed I could try to *kill* them if they touched me. He'd said nothing about beating on them until they got a shot in, then using that non-consensual touch to shift into kill mode. It was important to always look for those little loopholes.

"Milady, should we help?" someone asked from the side. I didn't dare turn to look in case there was some sort of fuckery going on.

"No!" I commanded, and a shock of power filled the room. Gasps rose. I'd pulled out the shifters' animals. Lot of good that would do any of us. "Leave me to it. The deal was for me to get involved, not you. You will be punished just to spite me."

My animal throbbed in my middle as the first demon reached me. Power pumped through my veins. Strength filled me. My senses went on high alert.

The dragon is on standby, my animal said. *He'll feed us as much power as we can handle.*

I'm surprised he isn't rushing in here to fight by our side.

He's confident we can handle it. The man is not so calm.

The demon hovered right in front of me, as though waiting for something. I assumed it was a knife in the gut. Instead, I punched her in the nose, stepped down the line, and slammed my foot in the second demon's balls. At the third, I slashed my dagger shallowly across her boob, accidentally slicing off her nipple.

"Ah shit, sorry! That's a low blow. I didn't mean for woman-on-woman crime. Also, I do not want to be touched!" I figured I better get that out there. "I do not consent to touching!"

Nipple-less hissed at me, showing fangs, before slicing down my arm with claws.

"You're out!" I took my dagger in two hands and sliced across her throat. At the end, I jabbed downward, sticking the blade into the base of her neck.

Another clawed hand grabbed my arm, and yet another swung at my face. I pulled back just enough for two claws to graze my cheek. The rest of the demons crowded in, quickly surrounding me.

In the past, this might have been cause for alarm. Now, however...

I used my will to push the ones who hadn't touched me yet. They bumped back, probably confused, and I made short work of the two handsy bastards. I sliced across the wrist that held me, then bent and stabbed the second one in the side. I yanked my blade sideways, gutting him. Back to the first, I sent stabbing knives of pain with my will, just to see whether it did anything.

Her leathery skin slashed open in multiple places, and her insides fell out of her stomach.

"Oh shit," I breathed.

Oh shit, my animal mimicked. *That's handy.*

It *was* handy. And I wasn't terribly winded from doing it. I hadn't read about that trick in any of the shifter books, though.

I released my will and turned. Four demons immediately crashed into me.

"That counts!" I yelled, shoving them back and bringing out the throwing knives. I loved those things. I wasn't a master by any means, but I could get the pointy end in the soft parts of dummies.

I threw two in quick succession, hitting center mass. One day I hoped to pull off trick shots, like hitting them in the eyeballs.

What was wrong with me?

I stabbed another demon and turned his body to block the one approaching behind him. I peppered my demon shield with the dagger, then ripped him away and got the one behind him in the peeper. I might not be able to hit a small target with a knife yet, but I could certainly manage it with a jab.

Something was definitely wrong with the pride I took in that fact.

Nothing is wrong with you, my animal thought. *That*

is how normal people think.

Coming from her, that didn't inspire confidence.

Two left, one having just pulled the knife from his center. I took it back and stabbed him in the throat before whirling around and throwing the projectile toward the other one, gaping down at the knife sticking out of her midsection. It sailed safely by. I'd missed.

"Dang it," I said, hopping forward and stabbing with my dagger instead. I got her that time.

In what felt like a moment, it was all over. I stood in the middle of a cluster of dead or dying demons.

The music had stopped. The deep bass from the demon machines had dried up. All eyes were on me, some wide, some over smiles, and some narrowed.

I focused on those narrowed eyes, demons all. Anger kindled there. The desire to do something. But they held back. They hadn't been given the green light to try me.

I wondered how long that would last.

A slow clap echoed through the space.

I turned to find the demon king leaning against the doorframe. He straightened up.

"Well done. I didn't think you could handle so many."

"I'll be honest, I was hoping for a glass of wine before we got to the nitty-gritty. Would you have let them kill me?" I asked, walking toward him. I figured this was my go-ahead to leave the room.

"Certainly. It would've dealt a terrible blow to the dragon, and better yet, it would've been his fault."

"His fault?"

"For letting you make that deal, and for not being here when you needed him. Maybe not all dragons are loyal, young Finley, but that one certainly is. It will be his undoing."

"Your mouth will be yours."

I wasn't lying. He'd basically just told me his favored method of preying on Nyfain. I'd already had a pretty good idea, of course, but this was from the horse's mouth, as it were.

It also demonstrated his arrogance. He didn't think it mattered if I knew about his little tests.

"So what's my next trial?" I asked, grabbing the knives from the bodies around me. "Apparently you are under the impression I shouldn't be enjoying myself tonight."

"Not at all true. You are enjoying yourself, are you not?"

He had me there.

"There's an odd thing in the air tonight, it seems," he went on, leading me out and up to the second floor. From there, we ventured deeper into the castle. "The people of the castle are not taking to my minions as normal. They act like they are forced to be in our company."

"I would imagine that is true, right?"

"An issue only until our magic affects them. But the magic of my minions isn't affecting them tonight. Orgasms are faked, females are dry, and the males can't seem to get it up."

"Huh. Well, you're all gross, so there's that. And clearly terrible lovers. The things you learn when your magic is on the fritz, huh?"

We stopped in front of a closed door, and he turned to me, his eyes a dirty red that spoke of blood and death. I hadn't realized they changed colors based on his moods. That would be handy. For instance, right now he was clearly very angry. A fact that wiggled my bowels a little despite myself.

"In sixteen years, we have warped the minds of these miserable shifters. We have bled them, poisoned them, tortured them, and slowly killed them. We've stripped them of their honor and forced them into depressed, shame-riddled lives until their miserable early demises. I have enjoyed watching the dragon slide into a dark pit. A few more years, and he would've begged me to end his life. He would've begged me for any way out possible." His smile was cold. "And then suddenly a woman appears in his life, and he perks up. He wants to live again. He heals the kingdom and somehow deadens the effects of my demons. Quite the coincidence."

I kept my mouth shut. This guy had gotten bad information. Nyfain hadn't healed anything. Nor had he figured out how to deaden the effects of the demons. He also never would've begged this asshole for anything. He might've wanted to die, but he would've trucked on even after there was nothing left to truck on to. Or for. I knew that in my bones. He wasn't like his father. Whenever he devoted himself to something, he gave it his all.

Dolion stared at me, looking for a reaction.

I gave him one.

"I must admit...I am *quite* the lay. I'm not kidding. My vagina brings men back to life."

His eyes narrowed. He didn't comment for a moment, and I didn't rush him. I didn't want to say the wrong thing and give too much away.

"You'll dine with me tomorrow evening," he finally said. "Bring the dragon. Dress nicely. We have...things to discuss."

His tone sent a shiver down my spine.

He walked away, and all I wanted to do was throw a knife at his back. He'd preyed on the mad king, thereby cornering Nyfain and our whole kingdom into an impossible situation. A situation that might eventually result in mass murder or servitude. All for what? Gold and one less shifter seat on some council? How could a guy like that sleep? How had no one torn him down?

Fire raging through me, I pulled open the door. The demon lust magic was so heavy it felt like walking through a curtain. It turned my stomach, and my eyes started to water. A smaller orgy was taking place in this room, but most of the participants were humanoid.

"Finley." Hadriel pushed out through the center of the crowd. He wore green lipstick and a bright pink wig that bobbed with each step. A little maid's dress partially covered his body, but the hem only reached to his upper thighs, and his dick waggled out of the bottom. He clearly was not wearing underwear.

"What…" I wasn't sure what to say.

"Yeah, this…" He waved it away as he got closer. "That fucker Cecil heard that I wanted a proper maid's outfit, just in case…you know…we have to travel. But he chose to make me one for a party instead. He is getting on my last nerve. Anyway, first, I am steaming that I have to be here after taking that draught. Do you know how fucking terrible it is getting it on with…creatures? It's fucking terrible. This is an all-time low for me, Finley, and it is all your fault. I'm going to have nightmares. Some of them have, like...knobby dicks! But I need to play along with the demons, so I think—I'll just stick it in a vagina, right? It's wet and warm and I'll just look at a stacked guy across the way to keep it up." He stared at me with wild eyes. "The demon's vagina had fucking teeth, Finley!" he yelled. "It scraped my pecker. I was already wary of the mighty vagina, but now I'm just fucking terrified. I'm sober, for fuck's sake! You need to talk to the master. We at least need alcohol if we're going to keep up this tomfoolery. It's a fucking nightmare."

"Cheers!" I tried desperately not to laugh when he glowered at me. It really wasn't funny. It wasn't! But his rendition of events...

"Not cool, love," he said to me in a dark tone.

That made me laugh harder. "Sorry, sorry." I waved my hand. "Sorry. Anyway, Dolion—"

"Don't tell me you call him by his first name," he said, horrified.

I paused. "Um...I think I did. Why? What am I supposed to call him?"

"He's a *king.* You call him 'your majesty.'"

I hadn't thought of that. Not that it would've mattered. Had I known, the mistake would've been on purpose.

"Anyway, he mentioned that Nyfain cured the

kingdom and stopped the demon magic because of me."
I stared at him for a moment, making sure he wouldn't
blurt out who'd actually done those things. "It's not
likely Dolion will make you all party like this again. The
demon king mentioned fake orgasms and flaccid
penises."

Hadriel aggressively pointed down at his dick. "It'll
probably never get hard again out of fear. Forget
blowjobs. Fucking *teeth*, Finley!"

"Right, yes," I said through laughter, thinking of my
first lay with Nyfain. "Yes, exactly. So hopefully tomorrow he'll settle for tormenting Nyfain and me."

"Why?"

I told him about the invite to dinner.

"Ah, fuck." He blew out a breath and directed me
toward the side of the room. A woman was bent over a
small table with her chin braced on her hands in an
expression of utter boredom. A demon who looked like
a skinny man with clearly defined ribs pumped away at
her, frustration on his face.

"Sheila, darling, I need this spot." He waved her
away.

She straightened up. The demon bent his legs, still
pumping away. She rolled her eyes.

"I mean, I don't mind banging demons when they
are in this form," she said, "but I used to think they

were amazing. Take away their magic, and you realize they might not even know what a clit is, and if they do, they certainly don't know where it's located. I'm bored to tears."

"Then stop, Sheila. The master said we didn't have to fuck anyone we didn't want to. I think he hoped we wouldn't get intimate with them at all."

She looked down his front before pushing the demon behind her away. "How about you? You're good with that thing even though you don't like women." She lowered to her knees and tilted up her face at him. "Why don't I suck you to get you hard, and you can take me on this table? I won't tell anyone."

"First, you'd tell everyone. Remember when you pegged Bronson, and he shat all over? The whole castle knows. He's a laughingstock. Second, get your fucking mouth away from my dick. Third, I don't see what the big whoop of pleasuring a woman is. A reach-around is a reach-around. Instead of tugging, you just wiggle your fingers." He glanced at the demon, who was currently stroking his cock in aggravation. "I don't see you taking notes. She just said you were shit at fucking. Don't you want to take notes from someone who doesn't like girls but is still better at fucking them than you are? That's an ego blow, my boy. A serious ego blow. Anyway..." He pushed Sheila's face so he could get at the chair against the wall. "I've got business, and my dick hurts. Get out of here. Also, about that pegging venture that literally turned to shit, unless you are into a dom/sub thing, it makes no sense to strap on a dildo and have a man blow it. Especially a man who is not a sub. That's just dumb, Sheila. You're making very poor decisions these days, and that's saying a lot coming from a guy who tried to fuck a vagina with teeth."

She got up, annoyed. "You're just mad that—"

She did a double take when she saw me. Her face turned red.

"Milady, I'm so sorry…" She put her hands out and curtsied.

"Are you grabbing the hem of a fake dress?" Hadriel asked. "Want to borrow my maid outfit? It would look more professional than curtsying after she just heard all of that."

"I'm sorry, milady. The master told us to be here…" She stepped away, clearly not sure where to put her hands.

"It's fine," I said. "I've seen weirder, trust me. I was down in the grand ballroom a moment ago."

They both said "ugh" at the same time.

"Were they enjoying themselves?" Hadriel asked.

This felt like kissing and telling, even though it wasn't me doing it. "I saw one woman who was. The knobby demon dick apparently hits all the right spots…"

"No." Sheila put up her hands. "No, too much for me. I have my limits."

"Who would've thought we had limits, right, Sheila?" Hadriel called as she walked away. "She knows what I mean," he mumbled.

The demon had stayed where he was, eyeing me. He pointed at the table.

"Bend over. I'll fuck you," he said.

"I hear you're not very good at it."

He grabbed my shoulder to shove me forward. Apparently he hadn't gotten the note.

I whipped out my dagger, stabbed him in the neck, and then shoved him back. His legs gave out, and he fell, convulsing against the floor.

"Oh, *fuck*!" Hadriel jumped up on top of the chair as though he'd just seen a mouse. "What the… Fuck, Finley." He braced his hand against his chest. "You scared me. That all happened too fast."

Conversations dried up, and movement slowed. I wiped my blade on the demon's socks, which he was still wearing, before putting it away. The seat was clear of gross things, so I gingerly sat.

"What's up?" I asked Hadriel, who was still crouching on the chair.

He let out a breath and slowly stepped down before sitting. I was sure his ass crack was touching upholstery. It made me rethink my current seat.

"Listen…" Hadriel leaned over the table and lowered his voice. "I'm sure by now you know that demons and shifters are like oil and water. We aren't much alike. The demon king thinks he's got us all figured out. Including the master. You need to make sure you give him some surprises. Now, let's talk about the end game and find a way to it. There's a reason they won't let me play chess anymore, and it isn't because I got drunk that one time and tried to shove a queen up Cecil's ass. He was cheating, though. He deserved it. No, the reason no one will play with me is because I am excellent at it. It was my mom's favorite game, she taught me well, and I've been a die-hard ever since. I'm good at strategy. I'm also incredibly good at puzzles, as you know. So hit me. What is your plan?"

LATER THAT NIGHT, I staggered up to the tower. My stomach was twisting and my knees were weak. I'd spent too long in that room with all the sexy demon magic. I should've taken the draught so it didn't affect me. As it was, it had gotten bad enough that I needed to leave so I could purge my stomach.

Halfway up the third flight of stairs, I stalled against

the railing, struggling to keep the bile from evacuating. I heard footsteps and recognized Nyfain's delicious smell before his strong arms wrapped around me and pulled me in close.

"What's the matter?" he asked, carrying me the rest of the way. "Are you okay?"

I breathed deeply and leaned my face against his neck. "Demon lust magic. It's..." I pushed my fingers to my lips and struggled to get out of his grasp. "Going to vomit."

He hurried me into the washroom and bent me over the basin in the corner, thankfully empty and clean. My stomach convulsed and my back arched as I purged. My disheveled hair was gently scooped up from around my face, held back behind my head. Nyfain knelt next to me and rubbed my back with his free hand.

My stomach heaved again, and I gripped the edges of the basin as sweat covered my forehead. Comfort and support radiated through my bond with him. After the third time, I sagged and moved my face to rest on my arm, breathing fast and shallow.

"Water?" Nyfain whispered. He smoothed my hair to the side.

"Yes, please."

A moment later he handed me a glass and sat beside me, pulling me against him.

"Had a great time, huh?" he asked, stroking my shoulder with his thumb. I didn't miss the anxiety in his tone.

"I can't stand that lust magic." I shuddered. "The whole room was stuffed with it."

I put the glass on the floor and breathed in his scent, closing my eyes. The waves of nausea subsided.

"Have you been up here all night?" I asked weakly.

He lifted me up and took me to bed, stripping me of my weapons and clothes. I still needed to retrieve that one throwing knife from the grand ballroom, but I'd collected everything else. He tucked me into bed and a moment later joined me, wrapping his arm around me and pulling me close.

"No. I was outside for a while, on hand in case you needed me. It seems you didn't, though. You handled a group of seven pretty powerful demons at one time on your own."

"How'd you know?"

"Everyone was sober tonight. I heard the full account." Pride rang through the bond.

I curled into him, my talk with Hadriel still fresh on my mind. "Dolion wants to meet us for dinner tomorrow. He wants to chat."

"I heard that, too."

I nodded and curled my lips under. A tear streaked

across my face.

The way forward was clear, but I didn't know if I had the strength to start the journey.

CHAPTER 26

I WORE MY fine shirt and trousers because I didn't know how dinner was going to go down. I wanted to be prepared to fight if I had to. Nyfain had dressed in a suit, but when he saw me, he turned around and came back in a button-up shirt and slacks. He was very conscious about dressing to match me. Clearly it was something nobles did.

We walked down the stairs and quiet corridor in silence, hand in hand. His demeanor was stoic and the bond was on fire with all his raging emotions. His dragon was clearly riding him hard. I didn't ask about what. I assumed I probably knew.

No one walked on the stairs. Not a soul, not even demons, dotted the corridors. Dolion had cleared the way for us. That couldn't be good news.

Nyfain's staff waited with grim expressions in front

of the room where Nyfain and I had dined a few times before, the first of which had been our date. I really didn't need those memories tarnished, but...what choice was there?

This time, the table was set for four guests, one at either end, plus the seat beside each head of table position. But who was the fourth?

I lifted my eyebrows at Nyfain as he led me to the right, the place we'd always sat before. He jerked his head from side to side. He didn't know. It would be a surprise. Lovely.

He pulled back the seat at the head of the table for me and took the place beside it. Even here, when his enemy would be present, his rock-solid confidence held true. He didn't need to take the head of the table to ensure others realized he was alpha. He could sit in the corner on a dunce chair and still draw every eye in the room. He radiated his status and position just by being present.

A demon with horns curling from her head and glittering black scales made her way down to us. She wore the classic black button-up shirt and black trousers with pleats. Her hair was black as well.

"Dragon." She jabbed a finger in the air at Nyfain. "You sit at the end."

He leaned back and to the side in the chair with a

little grin, like a rich playboy with no respect for authority. He didn't comment.

She visibly bristled. Prickly power curled through the air, scraping along my skin.

Nyfain laughed and held out his hand to me. I filled his palm with mine.

"She is attempting to scare us into complying," he told me conversationally. "But she lacks the power to compel us. Just like her master. They sneak in through back doors and corrode kingdoms while the residents are sleeping, pillaging all they can in the shadows. Like cowards. His stolen riches are the only reason the other leaders suffer his presence at their tables."

"Big words from a prince sitting on a crumbling throne." Dolion sauntered in wearing a tuxedo. His powder-blue skin looked sallow in the candlelight.

"You took advantage of an ailing and grieving man." Nyfain didn't turn to face him. Nor did he pay attention to the demon woman gesturing for him to stand in the presence of her king. "I merely got sucked into it."

"That is true, of course. It doesn't change your predicament."

"No, it doesn't. Regardless, my crumbling throne doesn't negate your cowardice. How you have retained power this long is beyond me. Surely the other kingdoms are tired of your maneuverings."

"There could be worse on the throne than me." Dolion stared at me sitting at the head of the table. "You're not hiding your affection for the girl?"

"Obviously."

His eyes narrowed. He was clearly wondering if it was a trick. It wasn't. Nyfain couldn't be bothered with his presence. It was as though a fly were buzzing around the table. Even hindered by the curse, Nyfain's power was clearly a match for that of the demon king. His arrogance trumped Dolion's tenfold. This kingdom had been at the top once, and Nyfain's disregard for Dolion showed it.

"Well, then. Shall we start?" The demon king moved to his seat. The woman held the chair for him before pouring his wine, then walked down the table to pour ours.

Glancing at me, Nyfain minutely shook his head. *Don't drink it.*

"I have a few questions," Dolion said.

"And you will get no answers," Nyfain replied.

"You know, dragon, that I am aware of the status of things."

"I do. What I don't know is…what is the point of this dinner? Let's fast-forward to that, yes? Your company is tiresome."

Through all the décor on the table, I could just see Dolion tilting his head. Likely in anger, though I couldn't see his eyes to make sure.

"What is the point of sitting all the way at that end?" I asked Nyfain. "We have to basically shout down to him. I can't even see him."

"It's symbolic. He wants you to know his status. This setup shows his ignorance of how these things are done, however. What he should have done is place us to his side."

"You seem a lot less worried about your kingdom than you did on my last few visits," Dolion said as a basket of bread came out. Nyfain didn't reach for it, so I didn't either. Clearly we wouldn't actually be eating.

"I have other things on my mind. My chief concern is holding my dragon at bay so he doesn't kill you where you sit."

"And kill the kingdom with me."

"Exactly, yes. We all know the score. Just to be clear, though, while I might graciously defer to Finley when I see the need, my dragon will not. Nothing will stand in his way if he decides to tear your head off. Not the curse, not you, and not her."

"And what, pray tell, has you so worked up?"

"Don't play dumb, Dolion. You're already stupid enough."

A shock of power rolled through the room. Dolion was losing his temper. "Have it your way, dragon. You have forced my hand."

"I sincerely doubt that."

Uneasiness rolled through the bond. Whatever trick Dolion had up his sleeve, it would clearly come now. Nyfain's hand tightened on mine.

His dragon is losing his shit, my animal said, crouched just below the surface. She didn't like the atmosphere in the room. I couldn't say I blamed her.

The demon attendant opened one of the double doors. A moment later, in walked a blast from my past. Jedrek, dressed in an older suit, with black hair slicked back and a smug expression.

My heart sank. He'd finally gotten his audience with the demon king, and now he'd come to collect. I should've had Nyfain kill him after all. The only reason he hadn't was because I worried how it would look for him. Damn it.

Nyfain gripped the table edge, his knuckles turning white. He was undoubtedly thinking the same thing I was, though I doubt he was blaming me as he should.

"Well played, sir," I said under my breath as though speaking to Dolion.

"I believe you know this man, Finley, correct?" Dolion asked.

"You know I do."

Jedrek's gaze slid to Nyfain, and the blood drained out of his face. His step lost its strut, and his spine began to bow. If he were a puppy, he would've piddled himself. He still might. For all his bravado, he recognized when someone was higher on the food chain.

"I paid him a visit and told him to never look at you again," Nyfain whispered, his lips hardly moving. I tried to hold back my surprise. I didn't realize he'd done that. "I scared him to within an inch of his life. Clearly he thinks Dolion will protect him from me. I should've just killed him."

"What's he doing here?" I asked Dolion.

"Well, now, that is a funny story," he replied. "He says he made a deal with the demons in his village, who had planned to bring him to the castle to meet their superiors. I couldn't validate that story, of course, because those demons have since disappeared."

The silence stretched.

"You'll have to send up a signal when you're tired of hearing yourself talk and want some input. I can't actually see your face," I called down.

Another burst of power bore down on me—incredibly unpleasant, bordering on painful. A gush of power washed into me from Nyfain or his dragon, reducing the effect somewhat. He'd clearly dealt with this many times before.

"He approached the demons who moved into the village, and they were able to get a message to us," Dolion said. "When I learned he was from the same village as you, the newest thorn in my side, I sent for him immediately. He had a lot to say about you. It seems he was not exaggerating about your beauty. I've seldom seen your equal. He wishes for me to arrange a love marriage between you two, using magic to coerce your feelings if need be. In return, he has offered your firstborn."

I suddenly felt dizzy. Nyfain's expression was one of pure confusion.

"What?" I blurted, hardly able to wrap my head around any of it.

Dolion chuckled. "Pedantic notion, yes. First, I cannot make you want to marry him with magic. I do not make love potions. I won't even get into the ridiculousness of offering a firstborn to a demon king. What would I do with it? Second, I'd much rather have a beauty such as you decorating my court. A gilded cage would suit you nicely. Loaning you out to whomever I pleased would be just the thing."

Nyfain's entire body tensed up. He gritted his teeth and squeezed his eyes shut, turning his head toward me a little and refusing to breathe. He was struggling against the urge to run down there and snap off Dolion's head. I knew that because I was fighting the same urge.

"I had planned to just kill him," Dolion went on, "but I have thought of a better solution. I cannot make you love him, but I *can* force your hand into marriage and all that comes with it."

I breathed evenly, sitting very still. I hadn't accounted for this in my scheming with Hadriel. This was not part of my plan.

"And how will you do that?" I asked in (I hoped) a bored tone.

"A trade, of course. You will marry him, bear his children—I have attendants to hold you down and force your compliance if necessary…"

Rage filled the bond a moment before Nyfain roared. He launched up, and his chair went tumbling backward. He grabbed the edge of the long table and strained for a moment before throwing it up and flipping it over. It went skidding across the floor on its top. The candles snuffed out, leaving only the flickering sconces on the walls. He rushed down the empty space where the table had been, hellbent on reaching Dolion, whose eyes had gone wide.

"No, Nyfain!" I yelled, jumping up and swatting him with my will. I had to hold up my end of my deal with Dolion, or he'd be able to hold me accountable for all the demons I'd killed last night. Not to mention that if Nyfain managed to kill the demon king, apparently it would mean he'd kill himself and the rest of us all in the process.

My will knocked Nyfain to the side, directly into Jedrek. The two of them rolled, Jedrek screaming. When they stopped moving, Nyfain picked himself up and lunged for Dolion.

"No, Nyfain! Please, no!" I pushed him away with will again, feeling his power growing. My animal siphoned from it and stored it, then grabbed more and stored that, too. On and on, not letting him build. She knew we couldn't let him get his hands on Dolion.

Make sure you don't give that back to them, I told her, just to make sure.

I know, she said, seeming out of breath.

I caught him up with my will and threw him at the door. I needed time to talk to him alone.

With a finger in the air at Dolion, I said, "Give me a minute to send him away."

"Of course," he said, struggling for composure and attempting to look like he wasn't. "Take half the time you need."

"Don't try to be clever. It just makes people feel sorry for you."

I shut the door behind me and pushed Nyfain down the hall and into an empty room. There was no stench of demons, so I closed the door. He pushed to standing, rage still flowing freely through the bond.

"Nyfain, no." I put a hand to his chest. My aching sadness was surely leaking through the bond. Tears coated my cheeks. "You knew it was always going to come to a deal. I see why that is now. I see why it has to."

His chest heaved. Rage still pounded in the bond. His gaze dropped slowly to mine.

I pulled him to the window at the other side of the room so I could see his face.

"Let me go," I said, my voice cracking. "Now is the time you've been preparing for. Let me go."

Agony mixed with the rage. Desperation. His eyes turned glassy.

"No," he said softly. "I won't. Not like this."

"Trust in me. I *will* be great one day, remember? You have to let me go. Right now."

Tears filled his eyes, the first time I had ever seen him cry. Helplessness colored the bond. Anguish.

"No, Finley, please," he whispered, and a tear overflowed and trailed down his cheek. He made no move to wipe it away.

I put my hand over his heart. "I am yours, remember? Heart, body, and soul. I will fight to keep it that way. But now I must go to war. I must, because you cannot. This curse is the only thing keeping you alive. It's the only thing keeping this kingdom alive. If it ended now, he would bring in all his forces and kill you before you could get to another kingdom and beg for an alliance. I've studied up on him. He will not let you live, Nyfain. No demon would. Not with all the bounty in this kingdom. This kingdom is a prize, and he wants nothing more than to collect."

"This one time, I hate how much you read."

"Knowledge is power, but sometimes a heart must break to wield it. We have to even the odds somehow. I am the only one who can break out of here and do it. Let me do my part. Even if he only bothers with me because of my looks or because I'm important to you."

Another tear rolled down his face. A dozen rolled down mine. My knees were weak, and I wasn't sure how much strength I had left to do this, especially with Jedrek in the mix. Clearly he'd been brought in to torment me. Dolion had found my weakness, and he would exploit it. He wanted to see me squirm.

So be it. I'd handle the torment, as Nyfain had done all these long years. But I'd have to walk away from my prince to do it. It was the only way.

I could feel his heart breaking. Mine broke right

alongside it.

"Let me fly free, Nyfain," I whispered. "Let me fly free. I will come back to you."

He shook his head and then bowed it, his chest heaving. He clutched my upper arms, like a drowning man hanging on to a life raft. "I don't think I can."

"You have to. Now is the time for strength and duty. Be the prince you must be. I'll be the scrappy little commoner I must be. This is how it has to play out. You know that."

He took a deep, shuddering breath, his hands shaking as he gripped my shoulders. Slowly, he peeled his fingers away and dropped his arms at his sides.

"Go," he said, utter despair in the bond. "Go now before I lose control of him."

The dragon had never wanted this. He would not stand for it. He'd eat all the villagers before he would let his chosen mate run into danger without him. But he was trapped in the man's flesh, and for now, he'd need to stay that way.

I turned and ran, and to my amazement, my animal didn't fight me for control.

You are the brain, I am the brawn, she said as I closed the door on him and dried my face. There was nothing I could do about my heart or the fear festering within me. Those I'd just have to live with. *All those shifter books you read spoke of trust and a partnership. We won't survive if we don't have each other's backs. Also, I don't really want to die, and if we stayed here, that would certainly happen.*

Lovely speech until you got to the real reason.

Yeah. I thought so.

I walked back into the room. My attempt to swing the doors closed didn't go so well—only one still operated, and the other had to be propped up. Close enough.

Jedrek stood to the side, all the bravado and arrogance from the village dried up into a puddle of man. Even still, I stalked up to him and punched him square in the face. He staggered back and fell on his butt.

"You fucking idiot," I spat. "You've really gotten yourself into the stink now."

"Yes, he has." Dolion sat in a chair with no table in front of him.

I grabbed another and sat opposite him. "You want to make a deal? Fine. Let's make a deal. You need me to keep Nyfain in line. That's evident. I care about this kingdom. I will mate that turd Jedrek if it makes you happy, in exchange for you lifting the demon magic from the land *and* ceasing your suppression of the shifters' magic."

"That's two things. You'd just be giving me the one.

Unless you plan to have his brood?"

"That's the deal!" Jedrek said.

The demon attendant walked over and issued him a swift kick across the face. He slumped to the floor. If he thought we'd be happily mated in a house with a white picket fence, he was sorely mistaken. To get his dream, he'd have to live in a nightmare. Hindsight, as they said.

"I suppose you want me to go with you to the demon kingdom, right? Or do you plan to somehow control me remotely?" I quirked an eyebrow. "That's two things."

"You will go to the demon kingdom, yes. But I don't need your consent to take you."

"Nyfain won't let you kidnap me."

"He will if we leave tomorrow. Which is still within my three-day window. You'll have to hold him off, or I will have to torture you for killing my demons."

I could've argued that the deal was me *trying* to hold Nyfain off, but the point was moot. For Hadriel's and my plan to work, I would have to go with him regardless. It was better if Dolion thought he was smarter than me—if he thought he had the upper hand, both for this deal and for the long run.

Feigning frustration and defeat, I made a show of rallying and played my next hand.

"Fine. Get rid of the demon magic poisoning this

kingdom so our people can be healthy again. The patch Nyfain's using doesn't last. I don't want my father to die."

Dolion's eyes sparkled. I leaned forward just a bit, playing up my earnestness. I needed him to think I wanted this concession more so he'd give me the other. We could cure the sickness. What we needed was shifters who could actually shift.

"You'll marry Jedrek, and I will release the magic suppressing the shifters," he said, playing into my hands. "Or else I will just kidnap you now and use you however I see fit."

"We both know I am not the type of woman to hang out in a gilded cage and be loaned out to people. My personality doesn't match my face. I'd burn any bridges you hoped to create if you loaned me out. You need this deal just as much as this kingdom does. And you will release the suppression magic the second the deal takes effect, which is the moment we leave. We won't be waiting for my marriage to Jedrek for you to hold up your end of the bargain."

"My goodness. You have thought of everything, haven't you?"

His eyes twinkled. He was mocking me.

My stomach flipped. *Goddess, please look down on me.* Hopefully I wasn't making a huge mistake.

"It is a wonder you are so willing to be whisked away from your kingdom and your love."

"I'm willing to sacrifice myself for my family, actually. Having to go to your kingdom is just salt in the wound."

Dolion snorted. "Jedrek informed me the extent you'll go to in order to protect your family. It's commendable. Maybe I shouldn't kill them."

"Maybe I shouldn't kill you. There is no curse protecting you from me. I can kill you from across the room."

I wasn't sure that was true, but he didn't have to know that.

He stared at me for a very long moment. I stared right back.

"Deal," he finally said, and the air between us went taut with magic. His smile was sinister, and my blood ran cold. "Go say your goodbyes, but don't bother packing. If you won't accept my gilded cage, you'll find a new home in the dungeons. All this finery will be a distant memory. Safety, comfort—things of the past. Now you belong to me."

I FOUND NYFAIN in the tower in complete darkness, staring out the window with his hands in his pockets. I closed and locked the door behind me, my heart aching.

"It's done, then?" he asked in a rough voice without turning around.

"The deal is made, yes. I'll be leaving with him tomorrow."

He let out a breath and bent, the strength going out of him. "What are the terms?"

"He'll release the suppression magic whenever we leave. Then, at his discretion, I'll marry Jedrek."

He tensed, his arm muscles popping.

"It's not as bad as it sounds," I added. "I read about the demons' marriage customs. There's no claiming. No marking. They do have magic to tie the couple together, but it can be broken. And if a demon isn't on hand to break the magic, death can. It's not forever, and consummation isn't a requirement."

"He won't have you marry Jedrek," Nyfain said, still not turning.

"But...the deal..."

"The moment you married Jedrek, the deal would be complete, and Dolion would lose control over you. You'd be free to make trouble at will. Instead, he'll hold that portion of the deal over your head, forcing you to keep Jedrek alive. If Jedrek dies before you can marry, the deal will be forfeit. He'll still have you locked in his castle, and he can resume the suppression magic here. He's forcing you to become caregiver to the man you hate. He's torturing you, essentially. It's what he does."

I nodded with my lips downturned. "Well played, demon king. I did not see that one coming. There's just one thing he missed, though."

"What is that?" Nyfain asked softly.

"I would much rather keep Jedrek alive than marry him. All those times he said I wasn't as good of a hunter or fighter, or that I should know my place, or that I ought to leave the hard work to the men... Well, that fucker is going to eat his words. I'm going to tear his ego right out from under him and beat him with it. He'll wish he never crawled out screaming from his mother's womb. Perfect vengeance, if you ask me. I'm so glad you left him alive."

Nyfain turned from the window slowly. Incredulity washed through the bond, followed by a wash of smug pride from his dragon.

"What?" I asked. "That's only fair, right? Being forced to marry is demoralizing, but keeping someone alive is hero fodder. The demon king is forcing me to be a hero while also exacting my vengeance on a man I hate. I mean...if I have to live a nightmare, it's the best nightmare I could've hoped for. Plus, it'll give me something to focus on when things get bad, which they likely will." I tilted my head. "Unless I'm missing something?"

He stood blinking at me. "I've never, in all my life, met someone like you, Finley."

"Right." I frowned. "But…am I missing something, or…"

He crossed the room to me, bracing his hands on either side of my face and looking down into my eyes. "No, you're not missing anything." He kissed me tenderly. "I knew you were exceptional, but I didn't know…the extent of it. If you had been in my shoes growing up, this kingdom would be a much different place. It would've been in better hands."

I slid my hands up his chest and hooked them around his neck. "Don't sell yourself short. The person you trusted most sent you away for a reason. What befell this kingdom was the mad king's doing. I would've been just as powerless as you were."

He sighed as he wrapped me in his arms, stroking my back.

"I want to speak to you about something," he murmured before walking me toward the window, where the moonlight shone down on us. "I didn't claim you all this time because I was worried the demon king wouldn't be able to stomach you if my scent was mixed with yours. And likely he wouldn't have. You've seen our interactions."

"Your scent was on me, though. *In* me."

"That is short term, and he knows it. But the deal has been made now. You've earned your next cage to break out of."

Butterflies filled my stomach, and hope simmered low. "What are you saying?"

"I can't go with you and physically protect you. The only protection I can offer is as a mate. If you carry a powerful alpha dragon's scent, Jedrek won't want to touch you. Even if you're vulnerable—sick or sleeping—his primal senses will recoil from my scent on you. Other creatures, all but the most powerful, will also be repelled. It'll thin out your adversaries. Not to mention Dolion won't want to put you in that gilded cage, even if he could use me or your family as a means to get you in it. No one—not even other kings—will want to get intimate with that smell lingering around you. It'll make you unattractive to them. I am sitting on a throne of ruin now, but I am still a powerful alpha. If we mate now, today, it'll give you a little space, intimately. Other creatures might pick on you physically, but they won't want to…" His jaw clenched, and he gripped my arms hard. He clearly had to force the words out. "They won't want to force you intimately. Not even Dolion."

That's a yes from me, my animal said immediately.

He held up a finger. "But that protection comes at a very steep cost. To you. When you inevitably get free,

596

which you will, it'll be damn hard to—" He cut off and turned his face away for a moment. He took a deep breath. "It'll be hard for you to find a new mate. You'd likely have to find a dragon more alpha than me who sees my claim as a challenge. Or a faerie. Maybe a bear, though they are not much better than dogs."

I lifted my eyebrows and cracked a smile, mostly because he was entirely serious, and his arrogance in this time and place was at once hilarious and endearing.

He shook his head. "Much of my power is still suppressed, but that won't show in my scent. I am a very powerful alpha, Finley. Or was. It won't be easy to find someone who's more so. And it might make it more difficult for you to find a new place to live. People could hesitate to take you in, not wanting the smell of another alpha around even if the physical alpha wasn't there in person. It will be like shackling a weight to your leg and going for a swim. The cost of that short-term protection might be too high."

I think you should slap him, my animal said. She didn't give an explanation.

She didn't have to. What sort of absolute fool would think I could find someone else like him in this lifetime? That I would want to? I didn't care about securing his protection. I wanted his mark. I wanted to carry him with me into the next phase of my life so I'd have just a little bit of comfort when walking through hell.

I smacked my palm against his cheek then grabbed him by the back of the neck desperately, needing his body on me.

Like a dam bursting, suddenly he was all action—crushing a bruising kiss to my lips, pushing me back toward the bed, ripping at my clothes as I worked to shed his. With desperate, hurried movements, we stripped each other bare and fell onto the mattress. He ran his hand up the side of my thigh, over my hip, and palmed my breast, gliding his thumb across the hard peak.

I moaned into his mouth, pulling at his shoulders to get him closer. He settled his body on mine, his cock against my swollen, wet pussy, aching with need. His tongue swept through my mouth and then tangled with mine, his taste driving me wild.

I hooked my legs around his hips, groaning as his weight pushed against me. He dragged the tip of his cock down my wet folds, bracing himself at my opening. His kiss was deep and powerful, emotional.

He thrust into me, sheathing himself fully, and paused there for a moment, pushing his forehead against mine, breathing heavily, before pressing his hips onto mine. He pushed my hands above my head and entwined our fingers.

"I've wanted to do this since you stood up to me in the Royal Wood."

He kissed me dominantly, dragged out his cock, and thrust it back in. I whimpered as he did it again, ramming into me. My eyes fluttered as I took in the sensations, gave myself to him body and soul.

The bed shook with his strong, powerful movements, stealing my focus until all I knew was his contact, his cock sliding in deep.

Magic rose around us. Power. It slithered across my skin and dragged a moan from my lips. Strummed my body.

Goosebumps covered my heated flesh, and my pussy clenched around him, pleasure building.

His kisses became fervent. He dragged his cock back and then slammed it home, knocking the bed against the wall. I cried out from the exquisite pleasure as more power built. I could feel his dragon doing the mental equivalent of pacing. Ready to finally dominate and mark his female.

My animal purred her delight, pumping more power into the bond. Tantalizing them. Teasing them.

Nyfain dragged his cock back, his lips pressed to mine, his power thrumming around us, and rammed it in. Slowly. Methodically. Again. Again. The only thing that existed was his touch against my fevered flesh.

The buildup was excruciating. I whimpered beneath him, clawing at him. Wanting it faster. More violent. Anything to stop this torturous build.

His hips moved in sure, powerful thrusts. They slapped off my skin. His cock drove in deep.

"Nyfain, no," I said, not sure what I was responding to.

The magic around us increased. The pressure bore down.

"No, Nyfain, please. No—" I gritted my teeth against the tightness in my body. My hard nipples rubbed against his chest. The pressure ground down on top of us, overbearing and delicious.

"Nyfain."

"This is why shifters fight before a claiming," he said in a rough voice, not stopping in his pleasurable assault. "It's easier to take when you have adrenaline to buffer you. Not for us, princess. We're going to experience it in its raw form. We're going to ride this until we are hoarse from coming."

His hips slammed in again, and lava spread through me, blistering in its heat. Magic vibrated through the air, singing in my blood, scraping against my bones. His kiss took me away as his cock branded my body. I swung my hips up to meet his. I squeezed his waist with my legs. I shook my head from side to side, the pressure getting to be too much.

"Nyfain—"

And still the magic rose. It drove down through me. It spread fire across my skin.

His teeth dragged against my neck.

"Oh!" The rush of climax tore over me, my tight depths gripping him. He groaned, shuddering, coming inside me but not stopping.

He sucked at my neck, not breaking stride. Not speeding up, either. The light pain shivered across my sensitive skin, and another rush of sweet bliss washed over me. He lightly bit, and it happened again, the magic sending delicious pinpricks across my skin.

"Finley," he said softly, dragging his teeth lower, his hips swinging down. This time, they didn't stop when they hit me but instead pushed down harder, grinding his cock into me. "Finley," he whispered again, his control clearly starting to ebb. Our animals threw power back and forth at each other, jubilant, wanting this more than anything.

"Yes, Nyfain," I said, gripping his hands tightly, feeling a monumental moment approaching. "Yes, please!"

He rammed into me, grinding, and then pulled back and did it again. His movements came faster. His grunts of pleasure increased in volume. The bed rammed against the wall now.

He let go of my hands and braced his hands on my shoulders, pulling down as he thrust up, slamming into me. I cried out, taking so much of him, wanting more.

"Deeper," I said, panting, my eyes fluttering, my mind lost to the sensation.

He pulled back, grabbed me by my hips, and flipped me. He yanked my ass up and slammed his cock into my cunt. I cried out. He drove down deep and snaked his fist into my hair. One hand gripping my hip, the fingers of his other hand curled in my hair, he rammed into me, the sounds of slick sex filling the air.

He pulled me up by my hair and wrapped his other hand around my throat, trapping me to his body, putting me at his mercy. He thrust up between my legs, his lips on my neck, then his teeth.

I shook within his grasp as another orgasm took me. He shuddered, feeling the squeeze of my pussy and coming with me. Still he kept going, sucking at my neck again, prolonging it, building more power.

The animals worked at it with glee, challenging each other, daring each other, pulling from each other but only to wash more magic through the bond.

I meant to tell him to do it already, that I couldn't handle the pressure crushing us. I couldn't handle the power ripping at my flesh. But my words came out unintelligible. Nothing more than whimpers of pleasure so sharp it could cut.

He swung up in mighty thrusts now, our combined releases dripping out and around our efforts. His onslaught took me to a place I hadn't been before, drifting in a fog of pleasure, cut off from anything tangible. Sensation vibrated across every inch of my body. It filled in all the cracks and dripped down.

"Finley," he said again, so softly I barely heard him.

His teeth clamped down at the base of my throat, where it met my shoulder, breaking skin. Magic delved down into my body and then exploded outward. It seared over my flesh, the orgasm crashing through me.

I screamed with the violent release of it, convulsing within his grasp, half trying to get away. He held me tightly, his hands gripping my hair and my throat, his teeth cutting into my skin. He kept me there, pumping into me, as a strange sensation settled over me. It tingled and then comforted, pulsing hot before seeping down into my being.

His mark. His claim.

He shuddered again, emptying himself inside of me, groaning. He pulled his teeth away, still shaking. His tongue glided over his bite, and I was coming again, that spot so incredibly sensitive and deliciously erotic.

He chuckled darkly.

"*Mine,*" he said with a growl.

I knew from the shifter books that this mark would be permanent. Like a scar, only it would never heal. His teeth would appear in my skin for the rest of my days unless another mate re-marked me. His scent would be forever, though.

We settled down into the bed, and he gathered me up close.

"What about me marking you?" I asked as my lids drooped.

He trailed his fingertips across my shoulder. "I won't risk us imprinting. It'll be hard enough for you with an alpha's mark."

"That's probably less embarrassing for me, since I don't actually know how to do it."

"With the strength of your will, I doubt it would take you long to figure it out. But it's for the best you don't. There's no need for worry. You're the only one I've been with since the curse. The only one I have ever loved in my life. There will never be another, even though I'd be tempted to try just to drag you back here so you can re-stake your claim."

Tears filled my eyes at his admission. A lump lodged in my throat as I pushed away so I could look into his eyes.

He'd just said he loved me!

He smiled and kissed me softly.

I opened my mouth to say it back, but he leaned down and ran his tongue over his fresh mark. A rush of pleasure turned the words into a moan. He rolled on top of me and slid inside, covering my mouth with his, and then I understood. Hearing it back would be too painful. He was letting me go—it would probably be easier for him to pretend I didn't want to stay.

I wrapped my arms around his neck and cried as he made love to me again, sweet and sensual. I had until tomorrow. I needed to make the most of him tonight.

CHAPTER 27

THE JOURNEY WAS a miserable one. I was carried over the bony shoulder of the demon king himself, moved via teleportation. Jedrek yelled and hollered behind me, carried in a similar way by a powerful demon.

He'd essentially sold himself to the demon king in order to mate me. Our marriage bed would be in the dungeon—not that we'd ever marry if Nyfain had it right. Either way, Dolion had made it very clear I would hate my existence down there, bereft of the finery he'd thought I'd grown accustomed to.

I could survive that, no problem. I didn't know if I could survive leaving Nyfain, though. It felt like my heart had cracked in half. I only had half a heartbeat.

My animal had lost the feeling of the only other animal she'd ever known.

And me… I hadn't even gotten to tell Nyfain that I loved him.

Finally, we boarded a large boat, traveling across murky waters in the dead of night. I had no idea where we were. I only knew we were going to the demon kingdom.

Jedrek sat beside me, his face mottled with purple and blues. He hadn't spoken since we'd been thrown down into the bottom of the boat. He'd gone hoarse from screaming.

I pulled a folded-up piece of parchment out of my pocket. My hands shook as I looked down at it.

In the time I'd been granted before we'd left, I'd given some very teary goodbyes to my family, and hugged Leala within an inch of her life (something she reminded me wasn't proper as she cried). Hadriel…

Well, he hadn't taken it so well. He knew I had to go—he'd helped plan it, after all—and he knew he couldn't go with me, even with his maid costume, but he didn't want to accept it. I reminded him that he had the most important job of all, which was to watch over Nyfain and make sure he kept up with his duty. Make sure he wasn't lost to the darkness.

Hadriel was not enthused about the very real possibility of shitting himself sometime in the near future.

Every other remaining second I spent with Nyfain.

Demons had needed to pry me out of his hands in the end. I'd had to keep him at bay with my will.

I only had two things to remember him by—besides his old clothes, of course, which I was wearing.

One was the sword he'd given me. His mother's sword. The demon king must've heard from somewhere that I was absolute shit with it. He'd grinned when he told me to bring it. Lesser creatures would strive to steal it from me because of its value, he'd said. Given I didn't know how to use it, I'd likely get a beating as it was taken. He thought that was hilarious.

I'd thanked him. I'd make sure to shove it deep into his flesh when it was time to kill him.

The second thing I had from Nyfain was this letter he'd given me right before I left.

I broke the seal and opened it.

Dear Finley,

I have always assumed this day would come. I did not assume it would be this difficult to bear. I have had a lot of terrible blows in my life, but only my mother's death can compare to this. I would remain in this curse forever if you could stay by my side, but you deserve better.

Dolion stripped away my magical gag, likely to cause you pain. You deserve to know the truth, however.

You are my true mate.

I wondered when I first saw you at fourteen. I knew for sure when I smelled you in the everlass field a couple of years later, after your animal would've normally surfaced. A shifter's scent has settled by then. My dragon and I both knew without a doubt.

I waited until you were eighteen to get a glimpse, however. Since then, I have mostly kept my distance, just checking on you now and again. I intended to wait until you were twenty-five, at full power, to meet you officially, but the kingdom was dying. Fate pushed my hand.

I enchanted the birch to alert me when you were at the everlass field, and my valet kept watch to track your movements. He is only able to shift because he is a small animal, and even then, it takes a boost of my power for him to manage it. He's the owl you threw rocks at. Don't worry, I'm sure his grudge will wear off eventually.

Dragons do purr. They are temperamental and moody. Everlass tends to spring up in places they frequent. You must've noticed the way the everlass field in the Royal Wood has expanded? That wasn't just because of me. It started after your first visit at fourteen. That patch started as just a few plants. It grew into a whole field under our care.

Yes, Finley. You are a dragon. I wish I could've seen the color of your scales.

I lied about not knowing what you were. The magical gag would not allow me to tell you.

I also lied about something else. I felt I had to at the time, but that's no excuse. I am not a nice man. I told you that.

With your healing talents, your power level, and your dragon, you would've been entered into the court at eighteen. You would've taken commissions for healing and working the plants, learned to fight, and quickly risen in the ranks of nobles. Given you are also my true mate, yes, my father would have had no choice but to let a previously common woman without a dowry mate his son. He wouldn't have been able to pass up the heir we would've created.

You should know by now, however, that I wouldn't have cared about his approval. I would've mated you in a heartbeat, claimed you, and imprinted. "Princess" is not a nickname. It is your rightful station at my side. Though...yes...I was a bit condescending when I first used it. I'm not known for my politeness.

To break the curse on our kingdom, we would've had to claim each other (mate truly) and imprint. After reading all those books, I'm sure you know that to imprint, both parties need to be hopelessly in love with each other.

I am hopelessly in love with you, Finley. I have been for some time. No, I was not great at showing it, and I wish you were here to punish me for that. My love for you was the only reason I was able to keep from claiming you for so long. It was unbearable, but I knew it was necessary. For you.

From what I gather, my father just wanted me to marry a dragon noble of good standing and high power and reside on my throne. But the demon king, wanting to make the curse nearly impossible to break, added in true mates, claiming and imprinting. I wonder if, in a moment of clarity, my father added in the clause that the villages would age, but the castle residents would not, giving me virtually forever to find my true *mate.*

If the curse had not happened, I would not have found you, Finley. I would've been out of the kingdom with someone I didn't love. I would've missed knowing you. Missed fighting with you. Missed loving you and claiming you. The curse brought us together. And though it is hell, I'd endure it all over again for you. I'd wait forever to fall in love with you again. Gladly. Out of the ashes of this kingdom came a perfect love. I will cherish it always.

I will love you forever.

After your travels through the library, I suspect you knew some or most of the major points in this letter. I could see you piecing things together with each new book. I remember the look on your face when you realized my fate. I know that you are trying to help me right now, but I just want you to find your freedom and live the rest of your life in happiness. There is nothing here but that ruined throne Dolion spoke of.

Fly free, my little dragon. I hope to meet you in the next life.

Forever at your command,
Nyfain

P.S. When you do get to freedom, send some new books, would you? The library needs a refresh.

I smiled through my tears. Yes, I'd pieced most of it together. Though I could scarcely believe it, all the signs of us being true mates were there, like his delicious, comforting smell, the four-way bond, our animals' desperation for each other, and his dragon's primal breeding frenzy. I'd also read the signs of what I might be.

But hearing him say it…

Tears dripped down my face. My heart ached.

Part of me wished we could've imprinted and ended the curse. We'd been so close! But of course that would've been an opening for the demon king to march his troops in and finally take Nyfain out. It was essential that we didn't.

Still…I couldn't help feeling the longing.

I folded up the note and held it to my chest as I watched the dark shores of my new home draw nearer.

I would need to survive the next leg of my journey so I could get back to Nyfain and finish what we'd started.

THE END.

About the Author

K.F. Breene is a Wall Street Journal, USA Today, Washington Post, Amazon Most Sold Charts and #1 Kindle Store bestselling author of paranormal romance, urban fantasy and fantasy novels. With over four million books sold, when she's not penning stories about magic and what goes bump in the night, she's sipping wine and planning shenanigans. She lives in Northern California with her husband, two children, and out of work treadmill.

Sign up for her newsletter to hear about the latest news and receive free bonus content.

www.kfbreene.com

Made in the USA
Monee, IL
25 November 2022

18484546R00360